ROSARY WITHOUT BEADS

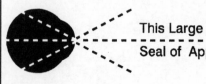

This Large Print Book carries the Seal of Approval of N.A.V.H.

ROSARY WITHOUT BEADS

DIANA HOLGUÍN-BALOGH

THORNDIKE PRESS
A part of Gale, a Cengage Company

Farmington Hills, Mich • San Francisco • New York • Waterville, Maine
Meriden, Conn • Mason, Ohio • Chicago

LIBRARY OF CONGRESS CIP DATA ON FILE.
CATALOGUING IN PUBLICATION FOR THIS BOOK
IS AVAILABLE FROM THE LIBRARY OF CONGRESS

ISBN-13: 978-1-4328-4477-6 (hardcover alk. paper)

Published in 2019 by arrangement with Diana Holguín-Balogh

Printed in Mexico
1 2 3 4 5 6 7 23 22 21 20 19

To Lorenza and Reyna —
Enjoy from your heavenly view.

ACKNOWLEDGMENTS

Northern Colorado Writers and Rocky Mountain Fiction Writers gave me valued camaraderie in those lonely times. Writing comrade Pat Stoltey pointed the way when the next step was not always clear. A special thanks to Summer Wood and her Taos Writing Conference Master Class for questioning, probing, and pushing me further into the story. A special recognition to Nancy Strong, who took the manuscript to her book club and test-marketed the subject matter, multicultural language, and interest. Nancy Strong, Kay Theodoratus, Marti Moraga, and Joy Wingersky beta read. And then there's Gordon Aalborg, editor extraordinaire, who believed and pointed the novel to its end with no-nonsense reprisals and kind praises. Lastly, but not the least diminished, a big embrace tightens around my husband, family, and other friends who unceasingly encouraged me.

CHAPTER ONE

Hondo Valley, Territorial New Mexico, 1877

My mother's things did not die with her. Her apron, splotched with bits of past meals, rested on the larder, unwashed. In the pocket, I found brittle mint leaves she had meant for a soup or tea or something. Even from their resting place, her leather-cracked shoes, crusted with mud from the last time she worked the garden, brought me pain. My father, Apá, expected me to wear them, but no, I would not.

Her rosary still hung on the bed frame and reminded me of the many nights I heard it clink ever so softly. My mother's pointer finger pressed against her thumb in a heart-shaped motion. She pulsed one bead, round and round with the slow steadiness of passing time. When she wasn't strong enough to hold a bead, her fingers still moved as if a grinding mill held an invisible kernel.

I ran the pad of my finger over the small crucifix. Nails through His hands and feet forced me to recall Mamá's suffering, which seemed no less than His. She had coughed a dribble of glistening red onto her chin and told me she felt too tired to go on. Her final days tormented me as I recalled our last words.

"No, no, you can get better." I held a glass to her lips, but she pursed and turned away.

In a hanging puff of air, Mamá forced the name of my sister, "Sinforosa."

"*Ya,* rest. Now's not the time to worry about anything. Get better." I wiped the slurry from her chin, rinsed the rag, and washed it over her cheeks.

She collapsed onto the bed. "The mother, Ambrosia, you now."

I told her not to talk and wiped her forehead again.

She lay against the brown pillow, pinkish with spittle and yesterday's sweat. Slitted, dark eyes drove panic into me. "Hear . . . hear me, now." She strained at every word. "Sisters don't love like mamás." She hacked a cough and ended with chesty gasps. "Sinforosa and Garita need you — mamá now. Bring Sinforosa home."

"*Sí,* Mamá, what you say. Yes, okay, now rest."

My father, Apá, with my young brother, Yginio, and my littlest sister, Margarita, stood silent in the room. After that, Mamá's time on this earth dwindled into weeks, then days. Her fingers, holding the rosary, stopped and opened up, like a dead bird's beak with nothing in its mouth. She quit asking for her lost prize — the beautiful one, my sister, Sinforosa. It was then I knew Mamá had fallen into a dark place where our prayers could not bring her back. We buried her in Lincoln up the way three weeks ago, or was it four, maybe four weeks ago — thereabouts.

That deathbed promise, like a sticker burr, wrangled into me. *Care — not like a sister, but like a mother.* Guilt mixed with grief — to make good or ignore her dying wish measured my love of her.

Today, I'd end it. Today, I swore, those sad memories would find their grave. I was going to bury it all and choke these wasting memories.

I hung my mamá's rosary back on the bedpost. Not the rosary, I could not bury the rosary.

Dull, morning beams threaded through the curtains of the bedroom. I opened the dusty shades for light enough to search for her things. Below the slatted bed sat her dusty shoes. I reached and tucked them under my arm. Her underwear, rolled up and wrinkled in a wooden box hid among two worn blouses and an old skirt. Her Sunday dress went with her. I held her ragged leftovers over my heart and grabbed the apron on my way out.

Behind our adobe, somewhat sheltered from the wind where no one frequents, I found a spot. Weeds, past their summer greenery, cleared easily, but the hard dirt would not give way. Chickens scratched in the distance, and a cowbell pierced the silence. Crisp fall air filled me. I jumped on the blade and broke ground, driving down my memories.

Hairpins and a tarnished looking-glass — I would bury what little bits Sinforosa left here, too. Five weeks, I'm sure it had been five weeks since I last saw Sinforosa. My mother's low moans forced me to tend to Mamá. That tending pushed Sinforosa's empty place at our table into tomorrow's longing. When my mother finally died, I collapsed. Just now I have the strength to think about Sinforosa. What happened for certain, I can't say. She could be a gagged slave in town. Jagged recollections, like gusts of wind, squinted my eyes, and Mamá's sleepless words, *like a mother,* echoed.

12

Dull thumps of stone on stone rattled me into today's present moment. Margarita, the baby of the family, shuffled close by. She hummed as she tossed palm-sized rocks into a tin bucket. Then she stopped, picked a few from her holdings, and flung them back onto a new place. We called her Garita. She waved. Her mind was not right, so the strange look on her face seemed just another thing for that day. She kept to her idle task as I did to my urgent one. The growing wind lifted the dirt I had loosened. The hole grew deeper.

Garita surprised me from behind. She dumped rocks into the spot I had just unearthed.

"No, Garita, I'm working here. *Ya,* quit that. Keep your stones and don't bring them here. Understand?"

Her lips quivered into a tightened smile, but I couldn't be bothered. She took that twisted frown with her as I bent over to get her useless stones out of my redemption hole. Then a rag dropped in.

"No nothing." She tossed a few rocks on top of the *nothing,* then flicked her wrist in a motion that meant good for nothing, trash, some kind of waste to be rid of.

I looked. For us, everything had some use. Leftovers were worked ten times over. We hog fed, ground, reworked, or composted remains. Our dogs and pigs gnawed corn-cobs and bones into dirt chips. Piñon and pecan shells moistened plants until their sturdiness dissolved. Eggshells mashed into a fine powder to cover face blotches. The most tattered threads made tie-braided rope. To bury Mamá's good things was a desperate act, but my sister had no such cause.

When the rag looked to be Garita's drawers, stained with a red smudge, with what I dreaded, I stopped and picked it up. A liver-colored mark wormed onto the white of her unders. No, couldn't be, but then what else would make such a mark? I looked again, wanting something else. But there it was; the blotch ended in dried, black edges, dark as my thoughts. I rubbed an ache from behind my brow.

She watched, yanked it from me and, between a dangle and a shove, shook it as if she had a right to throw it away, and I was to blame.

A dust devil picked up around us. *"Aquí está,"* the wind seemed to whisper. "Here it is." The breeze laughed up my sister's dress to show us the *it.* But the long pants of my brother, her version of pantaloons, hid the whites of her legs. I pushed her dress down

14

around her, and with my other hand held my own skirt.

"Is that what you want to tell me? Is that why you're dumping here?"

Garita nodded, smelled the rag, and put it up to my nose.

"Yes, Garita, I see it." I stepped back, hung my elbows in the cups of my palms, and pulled into myself. "Don't put it so close to my face. We'll go inside and fix it." I grabbed her hand, and left Mamá's little things and the half-dug hole. Like the vacuum in my heart, it would sit half-empty.

Fix it. How easy to say *fix it.* Make it all better. Impossible, nothing could change this.

"I *mala* — bad?" Tears flowed over her eyelids and tracked two streams down her dusty cheeks. She drew her drawers across her cheeks to wipe the wetness.

I stopped and hugged her. At least she wasn't gone like Sinforosa. At least she was here with me. "No, don't cry, Garita. You're not bad. It's just that this thing happens. This thing . . . like . . . never mind. Just come with me."

Her two-word tongue, *mala* — bad, *bueno* — good, doubled up and gave her a small try to be understood. Her mind was different. She saw white when it was black, or

15

she saw up instead of down. In this case, she didn't know if she should use Spanish or English, so she used both and thought she doubled the meaning. But it didn't help. Didn't sink any more smart into her broken thoughts. The blood mark should not carry shame, but this morning my little sister, like me, with my sadness, didn't know where to bury her feelings.

As I pulled her along, she nodded little headshakes, "I *muera* — die, Ambrosia. Mamá *muera* — die."

I shook my head. "No, *Mija,* this thing doesn't mean that."

She sensed a trick, a foul-up, a black sunrise. And it was all of that. Her mind had stopped short of reason long ago, but the rest of her, that's to say, her womanly passage, had not halted, and she could not figure what this meant. Nature's cruel joke — that's what it was, for her and me.

The cross of a burro with a horse or a goat with a sheep made creatures without off-springs. Those odd animals were future blanks, misfires, an end right there. That made more sense than what we were facing this day for my little sister. Garita was no more ready to care for another human than was a sterile mule. I took the drawers from her, adding up what this meant for both of

16

us. *Dios mío,* my God Almighty.

"Nothing you did, Garita. Understand me?"

"No nothing." She wiped her eyes.

This problem was mine alone. Three of us now lived with my father. I was the oldest. Sinforosa, the second in line, ran off. Yginio, only son, was younger than me and Sinforosa. He, lucky him, carried the Salazar name, which seemed responsibility enough. Slow Garita would never have any permanent responsibilities. Mamá was gone. My father, Apá, saw it coming, but he didn't help either. His eyes ricocheted off Garita's changing body, in that way when truth slaps us, words don't come, and worry just hangs there. Anyway, he was a man, and men do not speak of such things. No, my little sister's care fell on me and only me.

With Garita in tow, I pulled our house door open and slammed it behind us. November wind whistled through airy cracks in the doorframe. Thank the Lord, Apá and Yginio were on a flock run this morning.

The empty flour bag ripped without much of a pull. I shook white powder from the material and folded it into two pads. "Here, to catch the leak. Use this one today." I handed her the first rag. "*Esta noche,* after dinner tonight, we rinse it. See, then you use this other one. Understand?" I handed her the second, "until the first one dries." She nodded and took her business to the back bedroom.

I hustled to the barn and saddled Luz, our gentle, gray-lady mare. I mounted her and rushed back. My words filled the house. "Are you finished with that? Come. You and me. We're going to Lincoln."

Garita pulled herself up with the help of my boost and wrapped her legs around Luz's rump without any *what for* questions. If she'd asked, I would have told her, I intended to drag Sinforosa back home. Maybe my lost sister's reason for leaving had changed. If she was kept against her will, I'd find out. I needed her help, but more than that, I needed to keep my promise to Mamá. I was not going to sleep until Sinforosa was home, until my word to my mother rested with honor.

We made our way up the road. Luz's black mane flitted over her gray coat; her wide nostrils snorted, and her old legs plodded along. A babble greeted us as we neared the noisy Ruidoso River. We edged it and moved over the water. After we crossed, our skirts whipped over Luz's flanks, and the wind muffled us quiet. Garita leaned her forehead

18

into my back and held onto my waist like a corset. Glued like that, we headed east toward the Bonito River, a route Luz knew without any pull of her reins. But after the second mile, the old horse slowed down.

"Hey *ya, ándale,* Luz, go." I puckered and sounded air kisses. "Now, not tomorrow." She pumped her head and plodded as best as she could.

None too soon, before midday, we heard the Bonito's water murmur and saw two balanced boulders on this side of the river. Stacked like granite potato rocks, they marked our path north, upriver. As we made that turn, the wind stopped, and I eased into some relief.

"Cucuy," Garita said in a low whisper as if her quiet words might awaken a lurking force.

I pretended not to hear. *Cucuy,* an *Oowee* wild spirit, was believed to roam and haunt Hondo Valley. It shifted shapes. Could be a blood-sucking bat, a devil-human, an earth crawler, or whatever. Rumors told of a wind-spook that not only sucked people's blood, but the blood of whole cows, sheep, and mountain lions. Brittle carcasses, they said, had been found. In the minds of some people, *Oowee, El Cucuy,* drank itself full and left the rest to rot. The thing, whatever

19

it was, came with bad news, like our unwanted, red-curse calling.

"We trust the Holy Spirit, *Mija,* not those arroyo stories. Father Martinez told us just last Sunday to think of other things, remember? Think of birds, baby rabbits, and what Mamá wants for us, not *Cucuy.* Think of how we can get this horse moving faster."

"No nothing," Garita answered as she took ahold of my waist again.

What she said was what I feared. Nothing — Sinforosa might give us nothing. Maybe she was dead or maybe the forces that kept her were stronger than me.

The road beside the Bonito flattened, and what lay ahead rose above the distant horizon — buildings gathered together far in the distance. One big, white box with sharp wood corners put the little ones in its shadow. Tall as a mountain, it was the place of gringo gold, pay-ups, and takedowns called Murphy House Mercantile or as those hereabouts knew it — The House.

I had a good notion Sinforosa's change started right there at the mercantile. She worked for Mister Señor Murphy. One day went to two. I could see something had come over her. She'd clean her fingernails and look at the soot beneath mine. Then, her hair — she'd leave the house with it

20

combed back so that her golden waves pressed down. On her return, little strands fell across her forehead. The feathery wisps brought attention to her moss-green eyes, which none of the Salazares or any others in all of the Hondo Valley had. No sir, nobody sprang a color of that sort. Sinforosa's markings made people look twice like they double-gawked the six fingers on my cousin's left hand. Except they'd smile after taking her in and frown after him.

I remember I had asked her one day a while back while she sat beside me. "How is it?" I was scrubbing clothes on the river rocks. "Your new work with Señor Murphy, you like it?"

After a long pause, she said, "Easy, very easy." A half-smile lingered on her face like unsettling dust, shaken from an over-used rug. The words *very easy* came out with a slow nod. She flipped a blade of grass into the river and watched it float away.

My hands were worn raw from scrubbing, so I left Sinforosa by the river. Mamá's sickness had kept my mother indoors. She heard none of this, and someone needed to hang the clothes on the garden fence, so I did it.

But Mamá knew Sinforosa had convinced Apá three days of work in town instead of two helped us more. I know Mamá didn't like it. That was the first time my mother spoke to me about caring like a mother. But my ailing *madre* probably didn't notice those extra days changed Sinforosa. One Friday, her sass walk didn't come home. Then Mamá dropped hold of the rosary, and her eyes seemed to look in, not out.

Memories of Sinforosa and Mamá shifted into mind shadows. Straddled atop Luz, the fall day's noon sun warmed me. Against saddle leather, my upper thighs moistened. Then the weight of Garita's head dropped onto my center back. We were about a quarter mile this side of Lincoln.

"*Can-sa-da* — ti-erd." She nodded her head into my back with each pronouncement and repeated "c*an-sa-da* — ti-erd" again with head knocks.

"No, we have to keep going," I said.

Luz dropped a trail of green, moist splotches behind us — yesterday's meal. The horse seemed to feel Garita's upset.

Again, Garita head-banged me slower but much harder this time. "*Can — sa — da —* ti — erd.*"

I arched, but she leaned forward to reach my shoulder blades. "Hey, *ya,* stop it," I said.

She pounded her head knocks and repeated, "Stop — it — yes — here."

Our old horse knew this trail well and also knew we usually took a break at this gate. She nodded her bridle to our left toward the Salamanca home. It was Luz's way of saying *cansada*-tired, too, so I gave in.

When he saw us, Ramon Salamanca swelled up tall and waved from his front yard. As we trotted up closer, his thick black hair and dark eyes, set into a square jowly face, glowed in the sunlight. As a boy, Ramon had grown out for every inch he grew up. Everything about him was thick; his beltline, his neck, his forearms, and his fingers padded a good layer of undergrowth.

The Salamancas and we Salazares had been *compadres* for many years. His mamá and my apá, now without their mates, saw their future in Ramon and me, as husband and wife.

On a horse, Ramon's attachment to the ground disappeared. Suddenly his movements became light and quick. The animals buoyed him into a floating grace. Ramon bred horses, the bigger and faster, the better. He picked the sturdiest stallions for the healthiest mares, so this type of intended union, the partnering of him and me, wasn't new for him. I feared he'd ride me like he did his horses, so the idea sat blank.

23

When the men of the hills came to town, they used his services and tipped their hats to his big figure. If he wasn't blacksmithing in his barn, he was in his corral roping, trading, breaking, shoeing, saddling, stabling, or farriering horses. His wide shoulders and thick fingers lent him good help. But when his fingers weren't occupied with work, those same helpful pokers roamed through his hair, around and in his ears, over his large belly. With time the runaway hands went unnoticed.

We stopped.

Ramon came toward us, heavy. He helped Garita off Luz, and her grasp of him went too long and too tight for my liking. Yesterday, she was a girl and such a hug was alright, but today she was a woman. I tugged at her skirt when I saw him make like he needed a breath.

"*Hola,* welcome. Come in, come in. So good to see you. Where's your apá and Yginio?" He turned to me, arms spread for a full embrace.

My nose sunk into his raised armpit as he gave me a twice-long squeeze. His shirt smelled of lye over lingering sweat.

"*Sí,* Ramon, *hola.*" His man's strength felt good. But when I feared I smelled of dirty unders and road dust, I pushed back. His

24

hold on me wanted to go longer.

"Mamá has *menudo,*" he said. "Come in, eat and rest. Taste her chili stew."

"*Sí,* Ramon," Garita answered for me, "*gracias.*" She wrapped her small hand around his.

I didn't want *menudo* on this restless day. My stomach did not want tripe — more hot stomach. Doña Hurtencia would be one to rid her cow guts on us. I smiled, and Garita did the same as she stood beside Ramon. My *thank you* stuck in my throat.

Ramon's mamá, Doña Hurtencia, watched from the open door. Always fussing with something, she wrapped some loose hair strands back into her bun.

We hobbled Luz and walked toward the house.

"Come in, sit, rest, have some food and coffee," Doña Hurtencia said.

Her face had weathered many years, but her handsome features had held up fine. The gray in her thick hair glimmered like a string of silver lights. Her eyes sank into her face but seemed to make her eyelashes longer. Liver spots marked an unexpected natural rouge on her cheeks. And like undying wind that wears sandstone smooth, time was good to her.

"So good to see you, welcome, welcome."

Her open palm patted Garita's shoulder as my little sister let loose of Ramon and walked in.

The kitchen hung a delicious scent of red chili and oregano, which filled us with comfort. It was no surprise to see coffee-handed Father Martinez sitting at the table. His worn Bible, flat-brim hat, and his elbows marked his table space. He smiled his *"muy buenas"* greeting, leaned forward, and with dough-like hands raised his cup.

"Hola, Padre," I said as I walked into the room.

A pea-sized round with four tiny out-shoots marked his right cheek. The splotch was whiter than the rest of his face. When he spoke, jaw jitters moved the birthmark as if it wanted to jump a flight. Doña told me, Father Martinez told her, when his mother saw her baby's face stained with that little white dove, she knew he would be a man of the cloth. And that he was. Black-suited, except for a small white square under his neck, he was a well-fed man with saintly eyes. His eyebrows arched up to balance the curve of his smile.

Garita came alive in her run toward the table. She found an empty tree-stump chair and sat. I stood behind her. "I *mala* — bad," she said to everyone in the room, but we

26

knew it was intended for Father Martinez.

He nodded and smiled. "No, *Mija,* remember, what happens might be bad but not you."

Garita stared at the little white movement on his cheek as if the message came from there and not Father. She rubbed her own cheek and looked for some whitewash on her fingers.

Hondo Valley worshipers attended Father Martinez's services at the old, adobe San Patricio mission church. The rest of the week, Padre traveled from Capitan, to Ruidoso, to San Patricio, to Tinnie, or wherever. On his mule-back pilgrimage, he baptized infants, heard confessions, gave death rites, visited the sick, and replanted good standing with *Diosito.* I wondered if that was why he was here. The priest sipped, stirred, and stared at us.

"Good to see you, Father." I looked at the priest and then at Ramon. "We can't stay long. We have business in Lincoln." I tapped my sister on the shoulder, "One little bowl, *Mija, no mas.*"

My sister nodded and grabbed a spoon on the table. She thumped twice, stopped, licked its emptiness, and thumped it again four more times. She quit licking but repeated the beat.

"Business, what business, without your apá?" Ramon always looked for ways to take care of us. More than I wanted. His loose fingers rubbed the side of his face.

An ant crawled through table crumbs, and I brushed it off, away from Father.

Doña dipped a tin spoon into a large cast-iron pot, sitting on the stove. She swirled chili broth and brought up white chunks of honeycombed tripe, mixed with hominy. The top floated bits of onion and oregano as she served it into a bowl.

"Blood — *sangre*." Garita watched the red broth steam into her tin bowl. "Me."

I pressed her back as I leaned around her shoulder, so she could see the shut-up sign across my lips. "Shhh, here's your *menudo*. Just eat."

His holiness rested his cheek bird in the palm of his soft hand.

In a willow-vine cage in front of the main window, swallows sounded rare indoor chirps to accompany my sister's noise. Tap, tap — tap, tap, tap, tap.

Padre didn't stir in his wait for my reply.

Ramon squeezed what seemed to be sore-ness from his arms as he stared at me.

"From . . . from the Murphy Mercantile. Flour, we need flour," I finally said.

"Can you get flour without your father?"

Ramon ran fingers over his thick mustache, cut to the end of his lips with a slight downturn. "Do you have money?" The movement over his chin seemed to squeeze worry.

Father nodded yes-eyes at me.

Doña looked from my sister to me and back again.

Garita ate, stopped, and tapped her spoon.

I smiled a silent answer.

"You heard about Rumalda Espinosa, didn't you? The one who worked for *el* Señor Murphy," Ramon said. "She cleaned his house during the week."

Father crossed himself. "*Diosito, Santísimo,* very bad. God rest her soul."

"How's Sinforosa? Wasn't she cleaning Señor Murphy's house with poor Rumalda? Has she come home yet?" Doña asked.

My head turned from one to the other.

"*Amorosa,* Sinforosa." Garita dribbled broth over her chin and wiped it with her fingers.

"Yes, my sister will be home soon. She needed to earn a little money with Mister Señor Murphy," I said. "That's all. Soon, it will be soon."

They glanced at each other, a look that showed they knew I was lying. And I knew they knew. I might have to confess later.

But Sinforosa did leave to work for Señor Murphy, and yes, we did want her home soon, a half-truth. Everyone seemed to know where Sinfo was and what she was really doing but me.

"*Pronto* — soon," said Garita, nodding her head. "*Amorosa* Sinforosa."

"She was shot in her own home, plucking a chicken in front of her kitchen window — Rumalda Espinosa, I mean. Bad news when an innocent woman is killed like that." Ramon tucked his giant fingers into his armpits and held them hostage.

"Very bad, very bad." Father's face-bird jumped a jiggle as he shook his head.

"You have to be careful, Ambrosia. No time for no woman to be alone. When will your apá and Yginio be back? Do you want me to go with you, to town?" Ramon handed Garita his handkerchief. "Do you?"

Garita unfolded it and put it under her bowl.

Ramon guarded over Sinforosa. When she stumbled, he clutched her waist in a fright. He never boosted her up on the saddle without a smile as big as a harvest moon — before me, always. I knew he favored her, taken in like everyone else. She was the Salazar daughter he craved. As Apá would have it, I'd have to be the first promised, the first out the door, at least with permission, not how Sinforosa did it. No, if Ramon went with me, Sinforosa would feel a posse had come for her. No, I had to do this alone.

"Yes, very bad, *terrible.* No, I hadn't heard. Poor Rumalda was a friend to Mamá." I knocked knuckles on Garita's shoulder and gave her a hurry-up motion. "In two days, Apá and Yginio will be back. Don't worry, Ramon. They're running the west lands toward Nogal Canyon. Back on Wednesday. *Ya,* finish Garita. We have to get going."

"Do you want me to go with you?" Ramon asked again.

Garita scooped the last bite and wiped her mouth with her sleeve. I grabbed her hand and headed toward the door. "Gracias, Doña. Too kind of you. *Adios, Padre.* I'm okay, Ramon. Don't worry."

Ramon walked out and hugged me before I could un-hobble Luz. His thick, well-muscled arms felt solid and warm. We waved our goodbyes.

When we reached Lincoln, Luz's clomps rumbled the street silence. Those inside, squinted beside their drawn curtains like those who loved to look in on other people's business. Those outside stopped and watched. Men stared, noses up like they

31

were onto Garita's secret. Almighty *Diosito,* help us with this business.

We trotted past *Tunstall Wares, Ferrier Needs, and Whatnots Here,* a new mercantile on the right side of the street. A tall, well-hatted gringo stopped and smiled. I snapped the reins on Luz's rump as best as I could around Garita and *heyahed* loud enough to move us away. Past the Wortley Hotel, across the street, stood Señor Murphy's Mercantile House.

"Tehde *vive* — live." Garita pointed a lone finger toward the white building.

"No, Garita, don't point or wave." I kept my face forward and, without thinking, yanked back on the reins. Luz reared and stopped.

"No? Apá *sí* do it," Garita said.

"Hear me good. What did I say? No — Apá's a man and you are not. These *señores* might be mean, and this is not a fiesta. Don't smile over there or at any man — *nunca,* never." I clicked a go-ahead.

Luz snorted, jerked a nod, and stepped forward again.

"I seen her. *Mira* — look; there, *mira* — look." Garita's finger fixed itself again to the Murphy House Mercantile.

Tehde came out of the huge wooden door. Her movement grabbed ahold of us like a whirl of quiet. Her skirt flowed Christmas colors over buckskin boots laced with porcupine quills. A limp swayed her body in a slow, back-and-forth snatch. The triangle tip of her shawl broomed a tiny, dirt zigzag trail, only a person like me would notice. And her eyes, *caramba,* her eyes, sunk into her dark face like night-lights. They usually looked down, but when she gifted you a glance, dark gems flicked sparks back at you.

The Mercantile House, from where Tehde came, ruled the town. In the wilderness, wolves howled their dominion. Together, they circled and ate weaker animals. In the bunch, one wolf hound stood apart. The pack helped the leader pee-mark territory, chew up prey, and keep others afraid and timid. Same in this little town, Murphy, top wolf-man, pressed the little ones. Seen it myself with my own father. That place raised fear in me, but I had to start my search for Sinforosa there.

Tehde worked for Murphy. She heard Garita's voice, stopped, and turned.

"*Sí,* yes, *Mija,* that's Tehde. But she doesn't . . . she doesn't live there. Never mind. Just stay still and don't wave at anybody here today. Do how Mamá and Apá would want you to — like a *señorita.* Hear me? A lady?" I started to say, *like the*

33

lady you are now, but I didn't expect a goose egg out of a hummingbird.

"*Sí,* you see." Garita mixed words as she saw Tehde turn around. My little sister then tried to jump off Luz's rump. "Tehde," she wailed.

Stretching my weight in the opposite direction to hold her on I led Luz toward her.

Our Apache friend ambled in our direction. Two leather pouches hung from her neck. A long braid, twined with feathers, swung with her. Except for the crow's feet, fanning away from her eyes, her dark face ironed out smooth and gave no hint of her past winters. She carried a tall crooked mesquite root, smooth to the touch. She looked but did not smile at us. Her name was Tehde Crowdark, Black Flower in Apache. And many, but not us, stood away from her.

Garita left her effort to jump off, and I reined Luz up beside Tehde.

"You here, for what?" she said, without at least a *ya ta hey* — what they say for hello in Apache.

"I blood woman, Tehde." Garita could not be held longer and jumped down.

The Apache woman looked up at me, long and hard. Twinkling, coal eyes stared until my yes-nod gave her the truth.

"No talk here. Go to back. Many ears and eyes on street," Tehde said.

Garita took Tehde's free hand, and I led Luz on a path between the Murphy Mercantile and a small lodging next door called La Jewel Parlor. We stopped on a grass berm behind the two buildings.

"Hurt?" Tehde pointed to my little sister.

"No," She took her hand away from Tehde's grasp and waved her fingers. ". . . see." She reached for Tehde's hand again. "No *duele* — hurt."

Instead of taking Garita's hand, Tehde went for something in one of her pouches. Out came dark-red, almond-shaped leaves with gray veins. She rested her walking stick on the ground, picked up two, long, yellow blades of grass, and tied the dry leaves with a thin cross knot. "You take." She patted her own lower stomach. "For this little one, for later. Leaves only, boiled in water, not grass." She mumbled a few Apache words and handed me the delicate packet.

I dismounted and put the little medicine bale into my brassiere, relieved to have Tehde's stash. Wisdom another woman understood.

"For what, you here?" The Indian asked again.

35

"To bring Sinforosa home," I said.

Tehde pressed her lips. "She not at mercantile no more. Next door at ladies' place."

The Jewel Parlor — so Sinforosa had moved without any of us knowing. Worse than bad, she wasn't at the mercantile. She wasn't mopping floors and tending to Murphy House chores. I wondered if Señor Murphy sent her there or she went on her own or someone else pulled her over. What could she be doing? Nothing, nothing but bad. What would Mamá have said? If my mother wasn't already in the grave, this awful news would have landed her there.

Hopelessness and shame waved over me. *Care like a mother not like a sister.* The gut-punching idea of my sister whoring stared me right in the face. Here it was. I thought about going home, but I had to try. Mamá would want me to try.

"This one . . ." I raised my chin toward Garita, "has a new watch on her. You know, how she is now. Any old no-count could set his sights on her and do what he pleases. Can't do it by myself. Mamá wanted Sinfo home where she belongs, not here where . . ." My long pause gave Garita a jump-in.

"Sinforosa, *casa* — home," she said, louder than Tehde or I wanted. "I blood woman." She picked up her skirt, and before she could unlatch her blue-jean pantaloons, I grabbed her hand and put her skirt down.

"Remember, *calma*, Garita," I said. "A secret, nobody needs to know." I tightened her hand with force.

She tried to jerk it off.

Tehde shook her head. "She, that one like sand, called Sinforosa — no leave. Got crazies, man crazies, not good. Named Tun . . . uh . . . stall. Big *wampum*, white talk, like river water against flat rocks. Big much, she likes." Her last breath sunk into her, too many words for one day.

Like sand to Tehde meant of light skin. That was how my sister was known. Garita and I were the color of clay, the darker muck that holds the sand together but of less value. Afraid to ask what *crazies* and *wampum* meant, but it sounded like Indian talk for bad love sickness and big money.

"Never mind what she's got. Mamá didn't want her here. No place for her. Please, can you watch this one? She would have to wait outside alone. I can't take her in there."

Garita pulled my grip off and chased a mangy cat under a woodpile. Tehde pointed to her eye, then to Garita, twice, then jerked a side gimp after her.

I settled myself on Luz and trotted the twenty paces to the next building. A tree by the door gave me a tie branch for my horse. Outside, wood white, not dirt adobe, held a big glass window. On a second floor, small frames, for what I thought were little bedrooms, poked tiny lookouts. The drapes were fancier than Doña Hurtencia's, the best in all the Hondo Valley, no, the best in this whole territory. I could see why my sister might think these holdings were fine. The letter board outside read *Ladies Jewel Parlor House,* written with slants and back curves.

A huge door, with wood enough to build a pigpen, brought me to a cold stop. Beside the entry sat an Indian with a bony dog and an empty whiskey bottle. So drunk, he could not lift his head. When I knocked, he jerked awake and rolled his eyes to a tick pinched onto his dog's ear. He picked off the bloodsucker, twirled it between his fingers, and ate it like a midmorning snack.

I knocked again and wished my sister was the type to be happy with us, at home, doing her part to care for Apá and Garita. This was a sinful *Oowee* place of echo lies and ghost secrets. I knew that. And I knew it was somewhere I didn't want to be. Through the lace curtains, my eyes drew into the darkness. Black marble sunk in front of a stone fireplace, rich and warm, for nothing more than the soles of dirty shoes. A maroon chair sat close to the window, but no one claimed its soft cushions. Back to the front door, I knocked again.

"No knocking . . ." The Indian by the door said with closed eyes. "Just go-in place." He was smarter on these things than me.

And he was right. No one guarded the door. Behind a large curved bar, a whiskey server stood. Hanging over the bar edge, a few cowboys hovered over their burnt orange or red drinks, glassy eyed. A sweet vinegar hovered in the air and mixed with ladies' perfumery like Doña Hurtencia's bedroom, only heavier of honeysuckle. In the dark corners, men sat at tables, shuffling or holding cards, no concern for anything else.

"Shot right through her kitchen window," said one of the men at the bar. "Sent a bullet through the chicken and her. God Almighty, imagine how the plumage flew, enough to stuff a pillow." He laughed. "Bet the feathers splattered like a cow-turd target. Won't be serving Murphy none no more. Who'd do such a thing, when there's plenty of deer to shoot at and have meat to eat, sides?" He spoke to the barkeeper, but

39

the one behind the counter didn't pay him much mind. The blabbering cowboy leaned back and took another swig.

As if his hard look would get words out of my mouth, the bartender stared at me. But a bulky man stole my attention. He sat toward the front window, feeding a mouse bits of what looked like wheat seed. The varmint crawled onto his hand for the taking, stood on its haunches and sniffed the air for another mouthful. When the meaty man caught my eyes on him, he whisked the little vermin up and put it in his pocket.

I felt the server's burning stare on me and turned away from the mouse man. "*Por favor,* Señor, Sir, can you please tell me where I can find my sister, Sinforosa? Sinforosa Salazar, she is here?"

Those at the counter eyeballed me into discomfort. I had set myself into a living nightmare, and if I had half a donkey's sense, if my feet could move, I would have turned and run. But there I stood.

One man shook his head and chuckled into his drink.

"Hey, Charlie, what do you say?"

The voice bushwhacked me from behind before I could ask for my sister again. I jumped and turned.

This one stood smiling and had a spread

40

of straw-colored hair under a lopsided hat. His nose, small enough to balance his face, was sunburned, right nicely. His mouth hung open as if he liked what he saw. The least ugly among those here, he flashed eyes of blue, not quiet sky-blue, but more like raging heavens before a violent storm — piercing as a wolverine's stare. Those luring eyes held me like I was underwater, choking. I couldn't catch my breath, and at the same time, they made me want to sink in and wade among his thoughts.

His smile reeled me in. Then he winked. "Howdy do, ma'am? You're a right-mighty charming sight for this dark place."

Was he funning me or did he mean kindness? He seemed to be rounding up some notions, but he corralled them behind those fierce, friendly eyes. On another day, in another place, I might have smiled back.

None too soon, in what seemed like many long seconds, my mind yanked the reins from my heart. I was in La Jewel, an unholy, unsafe place. Nowhere to trust any cowpoking fool. I forced my feet to move aside.

He kept his watch on me but spoke to the bartender. "Set me up with a Monte table, will you, pard? After you take care of this lady, of course, who appears to have lost her sister."

The whiskey server pointed the cocksure, shimmering, blue-eyed man to a table with three other *hombres* in the back of the room.

I sounded a little cough. "Yes, I'm here to talk to my sister who is in this place. She is Sinforosa, Sinfo Salazar from near San Patricio, by the river."

"Oh yes, golden Foro, she's in the upstairs quarters, but don't know if I can let you go there. Does she know you're calling?" He leaned away from the bar, wiped his hands on his apron, and pushed his cowboy hat back.

"Yes, she should know I am calling her here." My voice squeaked. I coughed and gave the mouse man a second glance, then looked at and away from the strange, fierce man.

"Well, she's a busy lady, kept occupied by John Tunstall. He's paid for her keep, so she's not free to others." He stared at my skin, darker than sand. "A sister might be a different story. Have a turn up the stairs and knock on the first door to the left."

CHAPTER TWO

The door away from the men's drinking quarters pulled open with a hard jerk. The rumbling chatter of that romping room dimmed my echoing steps. Off to the side, double doors opened to a big kitchen. In the center, covered with a white cloth, stood a long wood table. From that room, the smell of roasted meat came over me even though I could not see food cooking. Slumped over a deep stand-bucket, a woman with buckskin boots and long dark braids clanked dishes.

Across the hallway, a doorway drew thin light toward a large bedroom. From an outside window, purple curtains filtered an incoming plum-colored glow just enough to reveal a mound of something big. It was a large woman, sleeping on a mattress for two and then some. Must be the room of an important person. I lightened my steps to keep her in her faraway state.

Along the corridor four pictures decorated the walls. In one, a woman sat, wide-legged on a red-velvet bench, waving a fan while blond, curly-haired cherubs fluttered around her ears. The floating baby angels whispered something that surprised her. Another picture framed a luring enchantress, dressed in a thin-threaded yellow dress with large white ruffles. Long dark hair rambled over her white skin as she leaned back without a care. These winged babies fingered her hair while she stroked them with a large red plume. She didn't show a bit of shame as her *chee chee* breasts and her snap-up garter were there for all to see. This lady looked back at me as if to say, "I have the goods, but I'm not giving them up." Unholy mix of such women with innocent angels. I strained to keep my eyes from the last two nasty scenes of the same loose layabouts.

The pictures and hall ended with an end door. When I opened it, a landing readied me for a short stairway climb. A smooth, waist-high railing ran up the wall. I held on, only to get the feel of it, for this was the first step-up I had ever taken. Felt like I was going to a sacred chamber.

As I reached the second floor, another corridor with doors spaced the same distance apart lay ahead. A dull laugh, like someone trying to fill an uncomfortable pause, came from one of the rooms. Then a knocking barked out, slow and steady, as if a rug was taking a beating against a creaky bed. I wished myself invisible, but my shoes announced my calling.

So this is what my sister chooses. This is what takes her away from us.

I tapped the first door on the left like the man said. No answer. I heard a bed-frame rasp against itself by what seemed an unweighted bounce. I knocked again louder than before. "Sinforosa, Sinfo, it's Ambrosia, your sister. Are you in there?"

An eye-level crack in the wooden door flashed a sliver of light through to me. Something knocked and soft padded feet came to the door. The tiny beam cut out. Someone stood, blocking the light on the other side, but did not turn the knob.

"*Pronto* . . . Sinfo, I need to see you," I whispered. The quiet in the hallway echoed every noise I made. The slightest feather, tumbling to the floor, could give those around here reason to listen.

No one answered. I rubbed the sweat off my fevered brow and waited.

Slowly, the door cracked opened for a single eye-view. Thank *Diosito* it was her,

Sinforosa. I wished I didn't have a door in front of me, so I could hug her.

She spoke first. "*Carajo,* Ambrosia." She held her voice down, and her eyes came at me flat and cold. Her burlap-colored hair screamed around her moss-green eyes. A mole above her red lips drew down like a heavy weight into a frown. "Jesus Christ, why you here?"

"Thank the same Jesus you're alive." I lowered my voice. "Mamá, she is gone from us. We will never see her again in this world."

Behind her on an unmade bed, a good-looking man, with a thick head of hair and light skin, sat. Through the opening, I saw his powerful, hazel eyes shoot toward us and then back to his business of filling a *J* smoker. The pipe, with a brown crisscross pattern for the cup, ended in a gold mouth-piece. His straight bearing held him like a *haciendero,* owner of it all, her and her bedroom, and half the town.

"I know about Mamá," Sinforosa said. "What else you here for?" Her voice soured the air.

The stench of it all curdled in my throat. I blinked my stare away from the man who must be John Tunstall. The one Tehde spoke about. "Listen, it's important."

"Important, what? The cow's dried up, or

46

the hens won't lay eggs? No, you listen." She tightened a lacy, see-through silk covering her bulged-up chest made so by a tight undergarment. "This is no place for you. Go back to the *rancho.*"

This was not the Sinfo I remembered. She looked like the ladies in the hallway pictures, except her eyes were of chocolate green not light blue.

"Think I want to be in this . . . this tick-eating, mouse-crawling, drinking place? Remember Garita? Remember her, your little sister?" If I could just find the right words, get her to see truth or unleash some little honor in her, we could go home. I tried to push the door open, but it met her stop. "Mamá's gone, you know that, okay, but you don't know our sister has started her flows."

"What? Are you crazy? What does that have to do with me?" Her cheeks steamed a rose color.

The man on the bed coughed. "What in the bloody name of Christ is it, Sinfo?" His language was English but not. Words came out mushed-up in an odd way like butter onto dry toast, which made it soggy.

"Never mind, John T. It's nothing." Her stone eyes turned to me again.

The door wouldn't budge.

"It *is* something, Sinfo," I said, louder than I wanted. "I need your help. Mamá didn't want you here. Garita can now have —"

"Sinfo, what we have coming this afternoon is but a few fleeting hours," the man said. A puff of his smoke lingered sweet tobacco around us. "I don't fancy frittering it away. Can you please give this lady some assistance, so we can have what's bloody left of today?"

What kind of man wanted blood left for today? Cow's blood or human blood? What next? Will he ride away on a two-headed lizard? This place made Garita seem normal — *Garita, Dios mío, Garita, my little sister, she's roaming the streets without me.* "*Ya,* Sinfo, please," I begged.

Sinfo started to close the door until I put my boot in the narrow see-through. I spoke through the door crack. "*Por favor,* stop this. We need you home. Garita needs our watch, both of us. God . . . God would want —"

She kicked my foot out of the opening and slammed the door. My palms pounded sore until I heard the click of a metal door latch and saw light through the door crack again. I gave it a good horse boot. "*Carajo,* open this up, Sinforosa."

"Go away." Her low but firm voice penetrated the door.

"Oh *sí,* yeah, I see, sinner. Did we even have the same mamá?" I kicked the door again.

"What's the problem here?" A voice bounced off the walls at me.

The large woman who had been sleeping in her bed was now awake and faced me. Her breasts hung like overgrown branches from an old tree trunk. A French roll twisted high off the top of her head and was held down with silver hairpins like nails into a beehive. When she spoke, the skin under her chin waved *adios* to every word out her mouth. Her beautiful rock-gray eyes, sunken into deep face holes, shocked me into silence.

"We can't have this screaming and pounding. This is a respectable business, a *quiet* business." Hands went to her hip and her bosom leaned out, unbridled. She rewrapped her cover-up. "Who gave you permission to be in these quarters? Out the front door is your best bet, Missy, and do it without a ruckus."

I kicked the door once more, headed back down the stairs, and thundered my steps on the wood floor to the drinking room. When I got to the bar, I saw none of the no-count men had moved. They all turned and stared.

Midway to the outside door, I felt an arm rope my waist.

"Hey, now, I like your wench kick-up. A wild banshee bitch, are you? Sure shooting, I can get that fire out of you." His sweaty hands soaked through to my skin. "Let's take a lie, right now, back up the stairs."

Bullet blank eyes and his tight grip pushed me back toward the hallway. The whiskered *bruto* had me.

I turned and pushed back, but it wasn't good enough to rid me of his tobacco and liquor stink.

He ruffled my hair. Crusted brown teeth, like the inside of a rusty enamel basin, showed themselves.

"*Ya pues,* get your hands off. Let me go," I screamed. "I'm going out of this place."

He widened his smile and tightened his squeeze.

I glanced at the bar and caught sight of a silver badge. The sheriff — Brady by name, an enforcer of the law stood, nodded, and turned back toward the bar.

"You're here for a reason, I reckon. Heated up, ain't you?" the man said.

I caught my breath, forced it out from the noose-hold he had on me, and again worked at unleashing his clutch. "Not here for this, *pendejo* fool. Get away." He came at me

50

like a rutting bull. I dug my fingers between his huge hands and my waist. A fleeting thought flashed — *What'd Garita do if I didn't get back to her?*

"Sinforosa," I screamed when the floor hit the back of my head. Slimy tobacco chew from a tipped spittoon seeped into my clothes. I wrestled to cover my legs. When I pushed myself up, I felt his boot sink into my chest.

"Like I said. I'm going to give you what you want." The greasy, fat man began to pull his shirt loose.

"Lady said, *no.* Don't you have ears? I believe I rightly heard her ask your hands be removed and your boot heels taken off her. And I best reckon you might ought oblige. She's not in this here place for your kind of rough doings."

From my fallen state under the man's foot, I saw the fierce-eyed man speak from the corner shadows. His smile was behind an iron peacemaker pointed in our direction. My savior didn't look at me and steadied his eyes straight ahead at the *bruto* man.

"Hate to end your day like this, partner, but there's plenty more willing skirts around who'll take your fill and your money . . . mighty much better than this unwilling

51

lady," the bright-eyed man said. With a smile, he looked down at me and nodded a short, up-jerk chin. His voice, from that dark corner and from such a young man, grumbled rock-hard. "Let her go, I said, or you'll be the one lying flat on the dirty floor."

"Holster it, Billy. His kill don't balance out for the bean-eater." Sheriff Brady, from his bar seat, huffed out deep, scratchy words — all badge and no heart. "And you, Brub, let her be. I ain't saying it twice."

The *bruto* man lifted his boot from my chest and jerked his head in a spit. "Greasy Mexican, get your shitty ass out of here."

The wet from his mouth caught the back of my head as I lifted off the floor.

Sheriff Brady turned away. With interest in nothing more than the shortest path out of this forsaken place, I took a fierce run out the door without a glance back. I mounted and rode Luz to the back of the Parlor House, but Garita or Tehde were not by the woodpile. I loped my horse back to the front and saw no sign of either of them. This was the last, worst thing I needed today.

CHAPTER THREE

Our Salazar adobe *ranchito* sat near San Patricio, a village close to the Ruidoso River in the Hondo Valley, east of the Sacramento Mountains. It flowed toward us from the range's tallest peak, Sierra Blanca. Shallow water gurgled above half-buried rocks, making its way between hanging willows, fat cottonwoods, salt cedars and weedy bunch grass. A sister river, the pretty Bonito, flowed in the same direction just east. The Mescalero Apache Indians in the nearby reservation called the two sister rivers Earth-Heart Veins.

We were picking wild spinach along the Ruidoso when it happened.

That day was twelve years earlier when autumn was changing to winter. When a tragedy robbed us of future happiness, took away a different Garita. The mishap stole what could have been and left us with an imperfect sister. And in changing her, changed us all. Soft breezes blew, and leaves of deep, roasted colors danced on the ground. Sinforosa and I twisted soft, willow branches into a spiky neck, twig legs, short arms, and long thin fingers — a stick dolly.

Garita wore high-top, white baby shoes and wool pants, much too heavy for the heat of the day. She squatted and pushed her little fingers in the riverbed sand, slow and then in fast scratches like little *bebés* do. She loved rocks even then and began to throw riverbed pebbles into the edge water. We were alongside her, not far from where Mamá gathered rich, dark spinach to boil with the *pinto* beans we left cooking. My mother moved beyond the curve in the river to the next patch and left us — me and Sinforosa — to care for Garita, who had just started to walk.

The start of it had something to do with our new toy doll, whose neck needed a head. I ran away for pine cones of different sizes. Sinforosa would pick one. I was the oldest, but she, the fair beauty, snatched everyone's favor, including mine. That's why I was the fetcher and she, the chooser.

"We can pull a few woody-petals off the pine cone for eyes. You know, the little nut holders. That's where her eyes will go," Sinforosa said. "Where Lupita can see out."

"*Sí,* uh huh . . ." I said without looking back. "We can paint each *ojo* black with burnt wood. Tomorrow morning, I'll get a charred stick before Mamá cleans the wood burner."

Long neck twigs around and through the pine cone would attach the head, complete with brown woody, fluff curls. I remember thinking Lupita was not a good name. Something like Pearl belonged with the curly queues, like a modern English lady. Miss Pearl, I wanted it to be Miss Pearl. I ran, one, maybe two, hills from where Sinforosa weaved and tied the willow branches.

On the way back, the dolly's name moved me without any other concern. I would try to change Sinforosa's mind. But I expected she'd droop her head and pout her lips until I gave in. I balanced my legs down the hill while my hands bobbled three cones. Sinfo would probably get the name she wanted.

When I came upon my sisters, loud screams within me left no air to make words. The vine branch doll bounced aside our little sister as Sinforosa tried to lift baby Garita out of the river. Our baby faced down, then up in the water. I grabbed Garita's other arm and together, we got her to the muddy bank.

A word finally screamed out of my

cramped throat, "Mamá."

She came flying.

Wild spinach, pine cones, and the willow branch doll floated, now worthless in the water. My mother's rapid strength grabbed Garita and put the limp baby facedown over her knees. Mamá beat Garita's back. The baby's limp mouth hung open.

"How could you take your eyes off your sister, Ambrosia?" Mamá screamed so loud the birds flew away, and the water gurgle disappeared.

Garita then spit water, and her eyes rolled back.

"A *bebé* can't take care of herself." Mamá lifted our Garita girl onto her side and rubbed until she coughed and showed a little color.

Stained with guilt, Sinforosa and I stood with no words to explain. Like an apple of a forbidden garden, I kicked a pine cone, which would never be a dolly head. We ran alongside Mamá as she carried the boneless baby back to the house.

Little Garita lay on Mamá's lap, silent, still. Her breath short and quick. My father's stare came later when he arrived from his sheep run. His black eyes made holes through my skin and grew bitter bile at the back of my tongue. I ran out, retching to relieve myself of my father's stare and my insides.

When I came back, my brother had his cruel questions. "You were playing, eh? Weren't you?"

Sinforosa and I shook our heads.

"Oh, *sí,*" Yginio said, "I know you two."

He was too little to be talking to us like that, but Apá did not stop what he himself wanted to say.

For an hour, Mamá cried, as she rocked, rubbed, and kissed the baby. Sinforosa and I stood beside her, sweaty with blame. We held each other's hand tight and waited for orders to help bring Garita back to full life. Many came. "Boil some water with wild tea. Get wet rags for her head. Bring the softer pillow." I ran fast and noticed I was the only one running. "*Pronto,* we need dry blankets to warm her." Finally my mother said, "Garita is pushing against me. *La Biblia,* bring Matthew, 14:2."

"Ma . . . Matthew, 14 . . ." My fingers moved down the page, seeking any line. "Juan El Baptista, he is risen from the dead; these pow . . . powers . . ." I skipped over unfamiliar words. "powers work in him."

"*Ya,* see, she's coming back from the dead. Holy Almighty *Diosito* has given us a lesson, Ambrosia," my Apá said.

I looked at Sinforosa. Her eyes went down to her feet and then out the window. She went to the bedroom and sat alone. She was not there when Garita's stronger puffs came out. Not there when I thanked God and promised not to abandon Garita or my mother again.

My parents were right. *Santo Dios* answered our supplications. Margarita, little Garita, lived and became a blessing and a burden. Since that day she has been a heavy ox yoke, my life's act of contrition — a mix of love and hate, work and worry. Father Martinez said I had been the special chosen one as if I had won something. Sinforosa didn't carry anything but her strut. The shameful load was mine, especially now that Mamá was gone.

Garita's rebirth in my frantic search for her this day in Lincoln arrested me. I didn't want to lose her again. The *bruto* man's stink clung as a smelly reminder: one second, one person, one wrong move can yank you a path downward. Salvation came with the blue-eyed man. Now, the hunt for my sister chewed up my insides. Sinforosa had shut me out with no aim to come home. One sister I could not keep; the other, I was her constant keeper. What else would happen this day? Ramon was right. I shouldn't be here alone in Lincoln. Now neither Garita nor Tehde were nowhere around.

Luz and I rode up the ways north, almost out of town, toward the tower we called the *Torreon* and back again. I looked behind the Jewel Parlor House once more. "Garita, Garita," I whispered under my breath. When there was nothing else to do but ride to the Salamancas' or home to see if she had gone there, I saw a large body in a tree behind the Murphy Mercantile.

Tehde stood below with Mister Señor Sir Lawrence Murphy, the Mercantile House owner, suited up with a small derby hat and heavy, dark-brown coat and pants. "Get down, off there, child," I heard the mister man say. "You're going to break a leg, and I'll not be responsible."

It was Garita.

Mister Murphy rubbed his neck as if tired of looking up, then looked down, leaned on his cane, and looked up again. His long lazy eyes didn't miss a thing, and I was sure he'd soon, if he didn't already, know Garita's secret. Slow but steady, he glanced at the branch above, at Tehde, and now at me on my ride up to them.

My little sister stood balanced on two weeping willow branches, one foot on each. Wearing Yginio's pants, under her dress, was not something I liked Garita to do, but I thanked her half-wit soul she had them on this day. A tiny red dot showed itself, and I prayed Mister Murphy had not noticed.

I jerked the reins and pulled my horse alongside Tehde. "You were watching her. How did she get up there?"

Tehde nodded, lifted her shoulders, and spoke to the ground. "Too bad to watch a she-cat like this one."

Garita looked down, smiled, and said, "Brocia." She rattled the leafless branch she held, "¿*Donde* — where Sinforosa?"

"Never mind with that. Get out of there like the mister says. This is not how to act. We go home now," I said.

"Are you hers?" Mister Murphy asked. "Her sister, I suppose."

When he took off his round bowl hat, I could see grease had darkened the inside rim. He whacked it on his pant legs and set a cloud of white specks around him. His half-smile made me feel undressed without a tree to hide behind. I didn't want him to look at Garita or me. Wanted to hide, hide Garita, hide myself, and hide our stuck-in-the-tree mess. His judging presence turned our little problem into *mucho mas* more than a sister in a tree.

"Yes, *Señor* Sir, this is my sister. Sorry

60

she took her playing up there."

He ignored me and took another snipe at Garita. "See, here, little lady. Quit this and listen to what your sister here says." He turned to me. "I'm fixin' to get a rope and lasso her down myself. Want that? Maybe you can climb up, tie her, and lower the girl down. Got to do something here. She's about to crack that branch and ruin my shade tree."

"No, please Mister Sir, if we throw a rope, we could knock her down. If I climbed up, we will have four broken legs." I looked up and tried to catch my sister's eyes. "Garita, not funny anymore. Find the way you went up and get down. Mister *Señor* here wants his tree back."

Tehde clacked two gutted peach seeds, tied onto two whip sticks. "Here's for you. Claw down like cat," she said.

The peach snappers didn't draw Garita's attention, and she ripped off small dried twigs and dropped them on us. Tehde brushed one branch snarl from her hair and clanked the peach nuts again.

Garita jumped up and down without a care. The branch arched toward the ground as each of us choked on our breath. "*Amorosa* Sinforosa," she said, straining the trunk that held the branch.

I thought I heard a crack. "*Ya,* enough, Garita, we mean it. Put yourself down and quit that jumping. Look, I'm going to ride Luz under the tree, so you get on her back. Hear me, *ya basta,* no more of this."

"What's wrong with this little one?" Mister Murphy asked.

People always thought of Garita as little even though she was almost thirteen. Her acts would always keep her small in the minds of others. Señor Murphy was no different. He put his hat back on and dusted his chest slowly, moving down to his lower belly with his fat hands. "Checking along on my place and saw this here Indian employee of mine chasing after this one. She's a right nice looker but sad on the thinking side, I must say."

Tehde handed me a couple of shelled pecans coated in sugar and pointed at Garita. "See, she wants."

When Garita saw the sweet treats, she squatted down and jumped a straddle-landing on Luz's back.

Luz snorted and steadied herself.

"*Ya, ya,* easy girl." I settled Luz who trusted me not to break her back. "Here, take ahold of me. We going home." I nodded to Tehde and Señor Murphy on my way to the main road out of town.

"Phew, stink throw-up," she said soon enough. Her head drew back away from me.

I had forgotten about the tobacco spit, soaked into my dress. "Never mind."

I flung the reins up and over Luz. We bolted by the mercantile, drove hard through town, hoofed by the Salamancas', and walked just enough to rest Luz. Garita endured the sour smell and clung so tight she had no peace to eat her pecans. After the right turn at the stacked potato rocks by the Bonito, we forced up a hard trot down to the Río Ruidoso. We crossed it and soon saw our house. Horse-girl Luz flared her nose and dropped white foam from the side of her mouth and seemed as anxious as I was to get us home.

When we opened our door, the *Cucuy* wind we left here had blown to another spot.

CHAPTER FOUR

Weeks after Sinforosa's door and the drunken man's boot went against me at the La Jewel, we searched for a missing ewe. The bruise on my chest had itched to greenish yellow and disappeared. But the wound my sister gave me inside my chest might not ever heal. That gash heaved a raw mix of anger and sorrow, which festered way below the skin and into my being.

Twin lambs of this absent ewe and I had now had learned the law of *never ever* — nothing never ever stayed the same. Time, like the hot flow of lava, never stopped, covered its path with a new surface, remolded what was there, and sucked matter away. If only scalding time could erase memories of the past. But it didn't. Back in the barn, the twin lambs felt the loss of their mother's nurturing milk. Things were changing for them and me. Mamá was gone, and Sinforosa would never come home.

Apá in a rare moment let us ride with him to find the ewe. Yginio herded home a flock, pastured toward Ruidoso in a temporary hold. Their corral had been a harvested cornfield that offered them something to chew on until the snow came. Then we would feast them on dried hay.

Garita rode behind me on Luz while Apá patrolled ahead of us with his keen eye. Brisk air cooled us in the shade, and in the sunlight, heat warmed our backs. A couple of crows rode the air above as if they, too, were searching for the ewe. The first snow of winter had not yet fallen in our valley, but it had dropped white lace on the much higher peaks of Sierra Blanca in the distant west. Soon, Yginio with his Winchester and Garita with her sling would look to bring home a Thanksgiving turkey.

"There's our old mother sheep. See fluff in the shadow of that salt cedar. Or what's left of her." Apá wrestled Noche's reins as the black stallion shied, jumpy. He tightened the leathers and jerked them in the direction of the gray-brown spot. Along the river by the fence, Garita and I followed him and watched.

"Only the hindquarters were taken. No animal eats the best parts and leaves the rest. That, what did it, didn't chew." As Apá scratched the back of his head, he waved the front *V*-rim curl of his greasy cowboy hat. A heavy, faded bush jacket closed him in over his horse.

Apá learned flock keeping from his father, and his father learned it from his father. He was a good shepherd who sacrificed his days breeding, fleecing, moving, and feeding his animals. The graveyard in Lincoln and a hill back behind our house rested those who came before. They, like their sheep, claimed land above and below ground. Our past slept there.

Yginio's voice above a chorus of bleating animals penetrated the span between us. My brother routed his way up the road. "Back around, *chi chi chi,* there, there, Campeon. Now *yup, yup* the other way, Gordo, other way, *yup, yup,* good boy." His calls painted my mind's eye of him and the flock. Our loyal collie, Gordo, would be swerving strays on the right while our sheepdog, Campeon, would be tending the left flank toward the holding pasture. Yginio would be center behind on our old mule, commanding it all.

My brother had his job, and we had ours. I walked Luz up a ways along the fence edge, looking for breaks or any other fallen sheep. The mystery of the neatly slaughtered ewe rolled around in my head.

Garita opened and shut her mouth as if she were biting a mutton leg. The words, *Oowee, Cucuy,* came out, part whisper and part moan. She, too, had done her own accounting.

Pine needles shushed air through thin blades above us. I pulled my jacket tighter around me. "The eater is no animal," I said. Apá couldn't help but know it, and one of us had to say it. I rubbed my chilled arms. Happenings since Mamá died uneased me. As in Psalms, we, here in Lincoln County, walked in the shadow of death. First Mamá, then Sinforosa, who was as good as dead, to us. And Rumalda, Mamá's friend, plucking a chicken, brought down for no good reason. A gunless woman, slaughtered like this little helpless ewe. I rode back toward Apá and stared at the innocent animal with its open jaw and dry, white tongue.

Apá paid me no mind, so I said no more.

He wiped his face with his arm sleeve, pulled a shovel tied to his saddle boot, and threw it on the ground.

Garita broke the silence. "*Oowee Cucuy* got good eat." Her reasoning for the kill was ignored as much as mine.

"Not so tight." I pushed my arms back and leaned forward to weaken her hold on me. But the horn pressed hard against my straddle bone, so I sat back again. "No more *Oowee Cucuy ya,* Garita."

"Yes, make up reasons, but each time we lose a sheep it's a big sacrifice," said my father. "You women will never know. It don't matter why, how, or who ate it." Apá bent over and creaked his saddle leather like his old bones were rasping against each other. He got off his horse and brushed flies from the dead animal.

A piece of driftwood, floating away as if it were in a lava flow of passing time, bobbled. Along white edges of rushing water, it bounced downstream and disappeared.

"Ambrosia," Apá called.

My life, like a stone in the muddy river bottom of the Ruidoso, slapped by the same water, the same labors day after day, sat. Strapped here like time had left me behind.

"Ambrosia, Ambrosia Salazar, you dreaming again? Wake up. Your eyes are locked up like rabbits before we shoot them. Got to dig a hole here deep enough to keep the coyotes from dragging this dead animal off." He pointed to a spot. "Get down and cut the ears while I dig the pit. Here, take this knife. Garita, you help her."

"Just the ears, what about the rest? The front legs might make a meal for the pigs." I pushed against Garita, so she would dismount.

His old eyes met mine. *"Por favor, Mija,* mind me, *ya.* Just do what I say."

I took the knife and brushed a starving green fly away from my face.

"Sheep ear *chicharrones,"* Garita said.

A delicacy for us, *chicharrones* were deep-fried pig skins. With just enough fat to crisp up the tough hide and just enough salt to season the rinds into a meaty treat, they made a pig slaughter well worth it. *Chicharrones* were nothing close to bloodless sheep ears. It was past noon, and Garita must have been getting hungry. With her simple focus on food, my little sister was making a sow crisp out of a dirty, waxy lamb's ear.

Apá stood and turned toward us. "Not for eat, Garita." He waved a finger at her. "These ears show Señor Murphy how many I lose. You hear me?" He pushed the spade and scooped out a big dirt clod. "The Murphy man can see for himself. Proved the kill." He stooped over the shovel again. "Not enough meat for a starving coyote. Leave it. We'll stick two dried branches, where it fell, so it will be easier for Mister to find it if he wants."

As Apá dug, Garita and I stood over the carcass. I grabbed the tip of one of the ears

69

and began moving the blade along the skull, thankful there was no blood splatter here. As I drew the blade, the blank sheep face jerked with the knife movement. Since the knife was duller than an unshod horse hoof, and the hide as tough as dried sinew, I had to force the blade over and over to sever the first ear. The furry thing stayed in my hand while the poor creature fell to the ground like an unfinished Indian scalping. Its eyes sunk in flat, and I wanted that black pitiful stare off me.

Garita stood on the dead sheep legs to steady my second cut. The push and pull jiggled its tongue until this one released easier than the first. Earless and legless, so much had been taken, it became a thingless creature. None too soon, Apá kicked it in the four foot grave, and I put the ears in my saddlebag.

We mounted, and Luz snapped familiar steps back to our rancho. The rock of her hips swayed us into a soothing calm.

"*Cansado* — tired, Apá? No Sinfo, no Mamá." Garita had her way of not only uncovering the stone but kicking it at you.

"Yes, tired," said Apá. "Ain't easy. Señor Murphy is waiting payment, and here's the third one lost this month. If I don't have enough to sell back, I will be short. And, we need some for ourselves. The ears prove the dead, and I'll tell him where they fell. Garita, leave the ears in the barn. For showing not for eating."

"Señor Mister sell ear *chicharrones,*" Garita stuck on the forbidden.

Hoots ricocheted against the quiet. Dried sheep's ears instead of delicious pork skins, but Garita's notion was not far from the truth. If there was a way to make more money, Señor Murphy wouldn't pass up boiling fur lobes in red-hot chili to make a fool think he was getting delicious pork skin *chicharrones.*

"What good are ears, anyway? Murphy can say we killed the sheep and used the meat ourselves and just gave him the ears? Or we let someone else get away with meat?" I came to a wide clearing in the trail, stopped, and looked at Apá for an answer.

As if she understood, Garita nodded her rosy chafed face toward our father, too.

My father shrunk into his loose coat. Times had changed sheep ranching. Like all in the Hondo Valley, he suffered with everyone else. He shook his head and kept his horse moving. "How Señor Murphy wants."

Four words was all I was going to get.

Ramon told me Mister Señor Murphy came to this valley as a Civil War soldier.

71

When it ended and the Mescalero Apaches had been rounded up and settled on the reservation, the Irish man stayed. And like stars no one can see til it gets dark, one day his big house just appeared and dark it got. Soon after, Murphy claimed most all open land, which before was free grazing.

My father thinks the sheep belong to us, but Mister Señor Murphy owns them. We run them, move them, breed and shear them, but the house grabs their share no matter how many we lose. Señor Murphy feasts on my father's hard work.

But we need the house mercantile. Murphy gets alfalfa, corn, and other goods from farmers who work his land. Apá pays Señor Murphy with spun and unspun sheep wool or gives him on-hoof or butchered mutton for our land use. We hear tell that Murphy, with his sidekick, Jimmy Dolan, sells our meat to Fort Stanton soldiers up the way or to the Mescalero Apache agent for the Indians. Our grain, flour, salt, cloth, tools, and those such things go into our count. The house doubles its take at both ends, and we, like orphans, get half a blanket for the cold winter. The next closest general store is Tularosa or Mesilla many miles southwest. Until the *Inglés,* John Tunstall, made his new store, *el* Mister Lawrence

Murphy was the only place to barter goods.

Garita, Apá, and I soon turned with the curve of the river and saw our house. Yginio with Gordo and Campeon had made their way before us. Yginio waved as we trotted up the road to our *ranchito.*

"Found sheeps, Ginio." Garita kicked Luz's flanks, so our mare would move faster.

"I've got the reins. Stop kicking," I said.

"What, Apá? Lose another one to coyotes?" Yginio asked.

"*Cucuy* with *diente* — teeths," Garita said.

Apá waved his pointer finger in a *no* motion to Garita and turned to my brother. "Don't know. A hungry animal would eat the whole thing."

"*Oowee.*" Garita pushed all her weight against me.

"No, Garita, you know that's not true. Get down." I took my foot off the stirrup, so she could step down.

She paid me no mind.

"Sheep ear *chicharrones* for Mescaleros," Garita said.

Tired of her force on me, I grabbed her hand to boost her down. I could breathe again.

Yginio was the only one to laugh.

"Garita, don't touch the ears. Apá *ya* told you," I said.

"The tracks around looked like a small man. Maybe, five feet with some inches." My father turned Noche to face Yginio and spoke.

Apá had not given me and Garita these details. Only Yginio, the other man of the family, deserved these particulars. A small man's tracks? Dolan and Riley, Mister Señor Murphy's helper men, were small. Would either of them take what could be our Salazar payment to save the pasture grass? Short height could be many men in this area — my apá, one of them.

"What kind of shoes, Apá?" I asked. "Cowboy, Indian moccasins, or buckaroos?" Hard-driving cowboys wore boots pinched at the toe, and those others, like Señor Murphy or John Tunstall, wore shoes spread wide in front. High-top buckaroos were for those who stayed out of mud manure. Indian buckskins would leave a smooth, sunken track.

"These were boots of someone who works animals," my father said. "What I saw was not fancy or smooth. Wasn't an Indian. And the deepness of the track makes me believe it was not a heavy man, maybe one hundred and fifty pounds like the size of a fat she-boar." Noche ruffled his wide nostrils as Apá dismounted. "But if they are against me because my sheeps have overgrazed the land or if they want to help Señor Murphy take more of what's left, that is reason for . . . reason for . . ."

I scared the chickens aside, left his unfinished sentence, and rode toward the barn. I knew the answer — *Nada,* my father would do nothing. Forces were bigger than him, and his young-man strength had withered long ago. Yginio had the energy but couldn't deal with Señor Murphy. And Garita and I were women, those expected to sit quiet, waiting, accepting. I stepped off Luz, unsaddled her, stalled her, hung the sheep's ears, and walked to our cooking pit between our adobe and the barn.

A top board covered a metal grating that supported a large cast-iron pot above glowing embers. This morning, I'd started wood inside the pit and let the flame die out to glowing wood cinders. Garita and I dropped the grate and two pans, one with mutton, potato, and green chili and the other with pinto beans. The heat cooked the food while we were gone. With an *S* hook, Garita and Apá lifted the pot handles from the dirt oven, and Yginio took Noche to the corral.

Our large wooden table sat in the middle of a main room. One glass window looked out to the road. The outside door opened a view to the barn; one small window brought light to the bedroom. A stone, gray fireplace against a far wall provided heating and some cooking on winter days. A bed cornered two walls where Apá and Yginio slept. It became a sitting space during the day. Opposite the fireplace, our stove stood. Dried corn and red chili *ristras* hung from the ceiling before shelves of blue-dotted enamel dishes, jars of herbs, canned vegetables or fruit, and cooking supplies. A door, behind the stove, opened to our bedroom with two slatted beds. Apá and Mamá had slept in one, but since Mamá's passing, Apá moved out with Yginio. Garita and I slept in our own beds but before morning, she'd find her way to mine.

I dropped wood into the iron stove and mixed tortilla dough and began rolling. With each push onto the *masa,* an uneasiness came over me. How could my tired father manage Señor Murphy? To need a cheater was like begging the Garden of Eden devil for scraps of much-needed food.

"Let me come with you, Apá. To Señor Murphy's. I can speak English better than anyone in this family." I set a stack of fresh hot tortillas on the table with the other food. "I met the mister man one day in town. He knows me."

"*Ya pues,* town? What were you doing in town?" Apá eyed me like he would a stray sheep.

"Begging Sinforosa to please come home," I said. "Something has gripped her soul — *Satanas?* Money? Señor Murphy? I don't know, *Cucuy?*" I knew it was Tunstall, but even though Sinforosa had slammed me away, I wasn't giving the real reason. I wasn't going to hurt Apá straight out.

"I *alludo* — help," Garita said. "Give ears for *chicharrones.*"

No one laughed.

"*Chicharrones,*" she giggled to herself as she jerked her shoulders up and down. Tortillas were within her reach. Looked like she was going to fold one into her own sheep ears. Instead, she dipped it into the hot pinto beans and into her mouth.

"I would go and take a ride to town, too," Apá said. "Bring Sinfo home, I mean, but there's no use." He shook his head, took off his hat, and hung it on a nail.

"Not me. I don't miss her," said Yginio. "Let her tramp herself and don't come to us with any problems."

"Not what Mamá wanted," I said. My promise to Mamá could be put to rest. I had done what I had said I would do. Not

77

my fault she holds on to her ungodly flesh tumble.

"Sinforosa," whispered Garita as she chewed on her tortilla.

I leaned closer to my father, away from Yginio and Garita. "Let me go with you Apá. I could help."

"*Mija,* you think it's easy. Running sheeps from cold hut to cold hut during the year is hard enough, but working with those house men is worse yet."

"Just crazy threats, Apá." Yginio took what was left of a tortilla and followed Garita's dip into the beans. "Don't give the house *nada,* no more. *El* Mister Señor Murphy shouldn't get the same money if we have less animals grazing."

"Think again. Mind me, everybody. Not easy. It's rough, even for a man. In no such way, could I let my daughters face Señor Murphy." Still shaking his head, he grabbed the last hot tortilla, dragged it in the chili, and gave it a good chew.

While my father's mouth was full, I saw an opportunity. "It's too much for you, Apá, and Mister Señor Murphy, well Señor Murphy, he —"

"He mean man — *La Biblia* says." Garita took my stage.

"Margarita, I'm talking here." Since she

had begun her monthly callings, she had become bolder than a starving badger. I pushed down hard on the tortilla *masa*.

Yginio couldn't keep his face from breaking into one of those smiles a sister doesn't find funny. He pointed to Garita and winked. "*Loca,* Ambrosia, that's what I'm going to start calling you, fool woman. You think you can talk to the king of thieves. Apá's right, women don't know sheeping. Not you, Garita, you're not *loca,* you just don't have no sense."

"Wha—"

My half-word cut short with a knock on the door.

CHAPTER FIVE

Tío Ruperto, the shorter, younger brother of my father who lived west toward Sierra Blanca, stood small at the door. Dusk light, behind him and another figure, darkened their forms as they stared in on us. The squirming man, my uncle held, squeezed between the frame and him. More and more rowdy drifters were coming to Lincoln County, and this looked like one of those night rustlers. The man with Tío tried to shake away, but my uncle's strong arm lassoed him in.

Once he was put in front of us, the stranger brushed his sleeves and crooked his narrow rim hat in a slant fashion. That tilt gave a silent message — meant he was not from these parts and had no care to be like us. Our rules were not his. Something about him egged me from the get-go. Where, in the few places I had frequented around here, had I'd seen such a spectacle? Everyone gawked at this new mister like he was Christ resurrected for his second coming. Yginio put his hand over his mouth to hide a smile for only himself. I had the same feeling, but I kept it off my face. This is one *something* from another world, I thought.

"*Mi Dios mío.*" Garita whispered words which amen-ed our stare on him.

He appeared bigger than he really was. Blushing, baby-like lips hung opened just a bit. Like weeds, blond hair fuzzed out his chin, a chin angled with strength. His thin body, below layers of clothing, fluffed around him. The scarf around his slight neck hung like a red and blue wattle and fattened up his throat. That and his raised chest gave him a banty rooster look. If he were a rooster, he'd be a fighter. His belt, made for someone much bigger, flapped out into what looked to be a shameless tongue gesture at us. Most big was his moon-slice smile, offering secrets from that other-world place he'd left.

Little things, an overlapped tooth, a large ring on his point finger, mud on his wrinkled boots and dirty pants might be ignored by the others but not me. What couldn't be ignored by anybody was his third leg, a *pistola*. The six-shooter hung like an extra tail on a rattlesnake.

"He look . . . he look . . ." said Garita.

Before she could finish, I gave her a *shush* sign along with wide eyes and a finger in a *no* motion, which then crossed my lips — full force. When I moved my attention from my sister to him again, it hit me. That blue I had seen only once in my life, soft and fierce mixed into something like a human version of a friendly wolverine.

No . . . couldn't be.

At first, his fire eyes didn't stick on anything. Here and there, near and yonder, those ponds of ice blue flashed. He glanced at the green chili, moved to the *refritos,* held seconds on Apá, zipped back over Tío, brushed a pleasant swipe across Garita, smiled shortly at my brother, and then settled on me. His eyes lingered up and down. They seared a hot branding iron through me, caused my out-breath to battle my in-breath, and they both lodged in my throat. That trance held our locked stare. Did I dream him? When a tortilla was about to burn, I shook my head and grabbed it off the hot stove. The cooking grill scalded my fingers. The heat off the griddle and the heat off the man raised sweat beads above my lips.

Apá coughed and the stranger's attention moved from me to my father. Tío Ruperto grabbed his arm and missed as the man jerked away, almost knocking over our ragged stool. In no time, my uncle clamped the stranger's shirt, as if our visitor had somewhere to run. Without the least shame, the newcomer stared again in my direction. My fingers shook on the rolling pin. I could feel his eyes on me.

A second *ahem* from my father took the man's eyes off me. Any minute the stranger was going to paste them again; I just knew it, so I un-griddled the last toasting tortilla, put it on the table, and moved toward the corner of the room. Never had the likes of any one man put such a churn in me.

Garita grabbed my skirt and followed. She giggled. "He a . . . a thing."

True. He was some sort of apparition thing, a resurrection from that dreaded day — here to haunt me. I put my arm around my little sister and hoped what happened at La Jewel would stay hidden. Surely he wasn't here to report to my family what had happened. "Let's just stay quiet here. Watch, don't talk," I said.

"Who is it you have?" My apá finally gave attention to the stand-up truth in the room. I breathed a sigh of relief.

"*Sí,* found this *pendejo* on the east side of the river, by the junction to Lincoln by

Señor Murphy's windmill tank. Sheep meat on his spit fire. I've been missing sheep, and I know you have lost more than me. Together I thought we could figure out what to do with this *cabrón* sheep eater."

The man jerked away from my tío. The words out of his mouth were something none of us expected.

"Hey, *qué va,* none makes me a lowdown *pendejo* fool, and I'm not a durn *cabrón,* no way, no how, either."

Hearing that deep, gruff voice pulled that ugly recall from where I'd hoped I could forget. The nasty at La Jewel happened so fast it was a blur. My mind couldn't reason particulars, but this cocky man had to be the one. Every passing moment as he shuffled his boots, eyed me, smiled, and spoke added bits and pieces of that nightmarish memory. Was he the one from the dark corner of the La Jewel Parlor?

"So you know what *pendejo* and *cabrón* mean? That don't make you an *inocente,*" Tío said.

Had to be. And he was more than the one. He was an outsider who could speak our valley Spanish — was he a sheep thief, too? A man who protects helpless women and takes on drunks and a sheriff man twice his size? A *gringo-Hispano*? Good or bad? What

84

was he doing here and what was he going to do next?

"Now wait a dang minute. Hear-tell my rendition. Don't be making me into no chuffy I ain't. Not a *pendejo*. No sir, no sheep poacher neither." He caressed his third leg iron as he spoke. The one he had pointed just weeks ago at the *bruto* man who booted me down on the floor.

"Pistola." Garita leaned toward my ear, smart enough to keep her voice down. "He *mata*-kill and take our ears to Mister Señor Sir."

"Garita, not funny." I gave her the *shush* sign again.

She was right, though. The *pistola* advantage, hanging from his hip, carried something bigger than a hornet stinger. How foolish of Tío Ruperto to bring him here. Any little cricket man with a loaded shooter, savior or not, could kill us. He caught me looking at his iron and took his hand off it.

"Yeah okay, I see you'all are good, and I see Ruperto here is a good *hombre*." He looked at my father and went on. "He's just out to catch a weasel in the sheep pen. I see that. Well, I tell you the truth. It ain't me."

"How we know this? You feasting on sheep. I know sheeps meat when I smell it." Tío tapped his chest when he said *I*.

"Right, alrighty, s*í, sí,* but see, this here, too. Standing in front of you'all, ain't I? I'm outnumbered, but don't be fooled, I got fire power enough to keep more than one man away. But no, I came to face you and tell you myself." He turned to my father. "You, too, *buen hombre,* a good man, I know."

When his gaze landed on me, his ferocious sky-blue eyes drove a piercing spike into me. I smiled until Apá's stare sent my head down. I smiled at the floor. It had to be the man at Lincoln's La Jewel. The one who stepped in when Sinforosa, Sheriff Brady, and all others let the *bruto* drunk put his big boot on me, fixin' to have his way.

My brother's face wasn't laughing anymore. Yginio seemed to have noticed my change and glared from me to this new man to me again.

"Yeah, *sí, bueno,* I see you got a big gun on you. And high-fallutin New Mexican talk, but hear me, whoever you are, you can't fancy out of this," Tío Ruperto said.

"No, Tío." Garita spoke, but it might as well have been to the hoot owls.

None of our men heard her, but the stranger man did. Heard, turned, and winked at my sister.

The batter of her eyelashes stirred the air. Always a game, always making the horse

86

gallop when it should lope.

I wanted to speak. Wanted to save him like he saved me, but salvation words would not come. I crossed my arms and stared hard at my little sister's free manner.

"Why did you have fresh sheep meat, eh? This day, we found one with back legs cut," Apá said.

We waited for his answer.

"I ain't killed no sheep. The warm, fallen meat set there, and I took it to good use — what the other left. Understand, see here, if you were in my boots with the ache in my bowel, you wouldn't have done less. I tell you, the dirty deed laid there before me. I just made the other sin less sinful. It was going to rot another day anyway. Like vultures, they're not hateful critters. They don't kill. They just clean up. You can't blame them. No, I ain't no thief. No *señor.*"

Yginio nodded until a strand of dark hair fell loose. He fingered it back away from his face.

Garita rested her chin in the palm of her hand and yes-jerked as if she knew he was telling the truth. My trembling arms tightened around her, but she broke free and stood her own ground.

Tío's rugged face softened as he took a step back and unfolded his arms.

"It . . . it . . . *mata* — kill for . . . to . . ."
Garita shook her head and began again.
"Other one *mata* — kill," she said.

"You're the only uncocked one here," he
said to Garita.

Her eyes danced and reminded me of the
way he looked at me the first time.

"What's your name, Angel?" he asked.

She lifted her shoulders, took the end of
her braid, and brushed it over her closed
eyes. Then she swiped the hair tip over her
lips. She was painting her face quiet. When
she drew everyone's attention, she widened
her eyes and said, "Gar . . . Garita."

"Margarita, Daisy in English, but most
call her Garita." I spoke until my father's
frown stopped me short.

"No, we don't explain nothing here about
names. We talking dead sheep," my father
said.

"No, now wait. This here's important, too.
I know Margarita is a daisy, and I know
Garita in Spanish is little bird claw. That
must be to grab hearts," the *gringo-Hispano*
said.

"No, like little rag." Yginio had to poke in
his two-bits. "That's what it means here,
too." He yapped like somebody gave him
the go-ahead. He was as shameless as my
sister.

"Okay, okay, I believe it if you say so," the man said. "Listen, Garita, there's times a rag is needed more than . . . more than let's say a rock or a flower or dancing shoes. Yes sir, who wants all that when a rag is needed?"

"Now this is about sheep killing not dancing shoes." My father squinted, and the edges of his lips tightened.

Everyone took a softer bearing except Apá. Yginio yanked a handkerchief, wiped the corner of his lips, and leaned back. Tío Ruperto sat down on the sofa bed, took out a pocket knife, and began cleaning his dirty nails. Garita stepped away from me and eased closer to our visitor. She smiled sweeter than before — a difference between drippy syrup or flowing honey.

"And you are who? And what you want?" asked Apá.

"I guess I have a name as doubled-up as Garita's. Name's William Bonney. Some call me Kid. Some say *Chivato*. Like *chiva* or *cabra*, you know, goat. Baby goat or kid, *chivito*, little goat, *chivato*, big-little goat. For short — Billy the Kid. Mind you, this Chivato can mightily knock cornbread out of any wrangling buster, mean or otherwise." His chest expanded and his thumbs threaded through the loops of his pants, and in a quick jerk, he yanked them up. The holster, strapped to his lean but well-muscled leg, stayed firm against him while his spurs roughed up a clatter with his every move. He looked at me, caught my eyes, and grinned.

My hair had been pulled loose that awful day. Tobacco spit had soiled my clothes, panic stretched the skin on my face. Doubtful he recognized me. He wouldn't be able to put me in that place that day.

"*Sí,* you come with a big story. How do I know to believe you? How I know you're not the one killing my animals? Know how many sheep I lost this month, Señor?" Apá said.

"One, that's all I know. Don't know 'bout none others. And I tell you, hear me with both unwaxed ears — what I cut off the hind leg was left by another. I just gave his kill a note of reason, *sabes,* like the buzzards do for an old fallen deer. Done dead already. Took care of some waste. Maybe another animal knocked it down and had to flee. How many times do I have to say it?"

"*Sí,* Apá," said Garita.

I didn't do anything to put an end to her little interruption and wished I had the courage of my lamebrained sister.

This Chivato winked at her and went on.

"Not that his poaching, whoever it was, carried out a good thing, mind you. Right sorry 'bout your loss, but I didn't start it."

"What you say Bonneh, Señor Bonneh, don't matter. Anyway, you the one with the hand in the *sopa,* and you the one who's gonna pay. That sheep meat is going to cost you three days' work here."

This Señor Bonneh glanced over at me. His eyes squeezed in a bit and his head moved with a very slight nod. In a room full of lookers I couldn't give anything back, yet an unleashed desire burned in me to meet his eyes head-on, to nod back, to smile, to say thank you. I coughed and wiped my moist face with my apron.

"That's a deal." He showed his teeth in a sly grin. "And then after, you and me, us two, will call this even-Steven right up to the end. Solid on the promise, then no more grief."

This William Bonney, Kid man, put out his hand, and my father shook it with much caution. It appeared my apá didn't know what to make of this Chivato's flashing eyes either.

"Howdy do, Señor, and your name?" The Kid man spoke to my apá.

"Salamon, I'm Salamon Salazar. I'm a herder in these lands."

91

"Salamon Salazar, *mucho gusto.* Has a ring to it, you know." The little-big goat man, *El Chivato,* pulled up his pants and put his weight on one foot, then shifted to the other. "Anybody call you Sal?"

"A few in this valley do."

"Mind if I'm one of those few?"

"*Es* okay, Señor Kit."

"Kid, it's kid. Never mind. Salamon, Sal, I ain't got a problem with that what you say. If I can chow down and bed in your barn, I'd be happy to earn my take of the mutton, little meat as it was. I have no cause to eat free."

My father turned to my uncle. "We say okay, Ruperto. Now, your work is done. You stay and eat with us, eh?"

Uncle scratched his head. Graying waves below his sombrero pressed onto his forehead. "*Gracias, muy* nice. I have my dinner waiting for me upriver. Good luck with this one, eh." He pointed to this Beely, the Kid man. Tío stepped out, and we soon heard his clicking tongue and loud *ehaw* as he moved his horse down the road.

I reheated the cold food. Pancho Gallo, our rooster, who thought us his featherless family, came in through a hole in the screen and jumped on the table. He, as bold as our visitor, flapped his wings and little feathers

92

fell in the *refritos*. Beely Chivato grabbed the rooster and handed him to Garita, who threw him out with a long toss. I stood next to Beely the Kid, smelled his outdoor, earth scent, and with shaking fingers, scooped fluff out of the beans with a fork. I felt his eyes on me but had no courage to set mine on his. I feared they would lock on me again, and others would notice.

Yginio dished a hot plate with spoonfuls of chili verde and beans and topped it with a warm tortilla for our barn lodger. He pointed the way to the outside, and this Beely man, this little-big Kid-goat, whoever he was, disappeared out the door. I was sure he hadn't recognized me.

We sat to eat, rattled plates, and filled our stomachs. I prayed that God bless our food, spare me from living my mother's life, and bring Sinforosa home where she belonged. The food, like a rainbow after a violent storm, quieted jitters in my stomach. I sat with my chin rested in the palm of my hand thinking of this day and about this Beely.

"Ambrosia . . . Ambrosia, those faraway eyes again," Apá said. "*Ya,* no time for that."

Garita came in with a bucket of water to heat on the cast-iron stove. "I *hago* — do dishes, Apá. Ambrosia dream for sheep ears."

"*Ya,* Garita, enough with the sheep ears. We tired of it. Here, put the bucket on this hot grill," I said.

She went on. "Tehde — *dice*-say . . ." She shoved her right fist into her left palm, then pulled her hands apart. "*Oowee* every-where."

I shook my head and put the dirty dishes into the wash bucket. Maybe the *Cucuy* mystery spirit *did* blow this Beely the Kid over here to me.

Tehde believed in the *Oowee,* and she read eagle feathers and prophesized. She said my mamá's death was one of my threes. She said, important things came that way. I thought of the Father, Son, and Holy Ghost, the trinity of faith. And the universe — sun, moon, and stars. That gave us years, seasons, and days. Tehde worshipped water, wind, and fire, each by itself powerful enough to create or destroy man. She had held up three fingers at my mamá's funeral. Said the first was Sinforosa's depart, the second, Mamá's death, and then she wiggled her third finger. She said it would replace them both with happy pain and said it was com-ing soon.

My life was changing. And, yes, like Garita said, *Oowee* wind sucked life dry. This kid man, Beely, saved me, took fallen sheep meat from my father's herd, and showed up here, drawing me to him. Did he save me to torment me?

A gust of wind banged the loose screen and interrupted my thoughts. I finished the dishes and went to bed.

CHAPTER SIX

Pancho Gallo, our flaming green and red rooster, sat on my window sill the next morning and flapped his wings. He fidgeted a nervous *ca-doodle*. Some things, regular happenings like sunup, a rooster's morning call, spring births, and winter fires gave comfort. They made God's blessings. With the goodness, also came the struggle — care of our animals, shelter, and our daily bread, what we squeaked out to stay alive. Weary morning thoughts of the night before kept me in bed. Surely, the little-big Kid-goat had not recognized me and had snuck away by now. My bones felt as round and full as the thick elm trunks I could see from my window. I sighed so deep it stirred Garita.

She moaned a snort between her pillow and her arm and rolled to face the wall with her knees up against her chest. Without a rustle, I got up and dressed quietly. Ashes and shiny brittle of yesterday's burnt wood needed to be swept from the stove. After I put a few sticks into the grate bottom, I snapped the sulfur light and set it afire.

Our coffee grounds sat in a tin on the larder shelf beside the cast-iron cooker. These grounds had to last a month, and if the precious chicory went before, we would have only wild tea for morning drinks. Yesterday's wet dregs would have to make another day. I set *refritos* on the side grate to simmer.

Apá and Yginio's corner bed in the main room across from the stove sat empty with blankets pulled over the lazy man's way. The men had gone northeast to pasture some of our flock on a neighbor's dry corn patch toward Lincoln. I crushed stale tortillas into my make-do skirt bowl. Mixed with crushed, dried corn from the coop house, this would breakfast the chickens. The morning's fall crisp breeze carried familiar manure odor from the animal pens. The droppings smelled good, and for me, the raw, natural dung connected yesterday to today, and today to tomorrow. Out from the ground, grass came for animals to eat. They ate and dropped digested plant nourishment for animals to eat again in the future. It was something God had arranged in perfect harmony.

97

The sun broke visible in the east sky, bringing flat streaks of orange rose, peach, and blue like a floating campfire on the horizon. A crow cawed in the distance, and Isabelle rang her clanker and mooed. I crossed through the pole corral to the *pollo* coop, and as my back held the door open, I knotted my *chal* around me and grabbed a handful of cornmeal. Pancho Gallo and his chicken wives knew what my up-skirt meant and clucked around me. I scattered their morning meal. They ate — a life of eat, lay eggs, and die — these hens, much like all the women in Lincoln.

Hobbled outside the barn, the Kid's short-legged pinto mustang stirred. So our lodger hadn't hightailed it out of here last night. That surprise was joined with a gruff cough from the barn. An airy lift pulsed through me.

"Like your flashy master, eh? You didn't make it inside yet? Tonight will be warmer." The nervous stallion harrumphed white air from his nose and bulged his dark watery eyes toward me. It was a beautiful animal. I rubbed his ears and stroked the side of his head.

If this Beely had caught a glimpse of my lifted skirt as I fed the chickens, it was my accident. For him, I'm sure, getting his eyes

98

full of what was put before him — just like the sheep meat he ate — was not his wrong-doing. He took only what fell in his path, made good use of another person's wrong, not his sin. Just as Eve, poor woman, suffered the pain of childbirth, not Adam, who also ate the apple. It was never Adam's sin. This Beely would say it was me who ignored the many barn holes which put me in front of his eyes — not his fault. Men — all a bunch of Adams, except maybe Ramon, maybe. I imagined Kid Beely's hungry, hot blues on my legs, and the thought, as much as I hated it, warmed my loins.

Wondered if he did look. Nothing no one needed to be punished for. Yes, there were a few hairs, but I had good, firm legs. Ramon loved Sinforosa, but I know he admired my strong back and my large, full breasts. My face was not that of my beautiful sister, but less than her was still good. I expect if the Kid man did partake, it was a pleasured reward, not a punishment. *Válgame Diosito* how did my mind take such a turn? Forgive my wild thoughts.

I made my way to the well for the day's water. The heavy bucket weighted my arms so much I stopped halfway to the house door.

Campeon's and Gordo's barks drifted in

from up the road. I rested long enough to see my father rounding the corner from the river to our adobe on his return from the nearby dried corn pasture. With no wave or hello or *buenos días,* he trotted his horse toward the barn. "*Ya,* Ambrosia, food now." He moved past me. "*Café* and breakfast ready?"

I trudged to the door with my full bucket.

Apá got down and banged the barn door. Ramon and Yginio followed behind in no rush to hobble their horses besides Beely's pinto.

"Time to get up, Señor Bonneh Beely," Apá shouted, with enough force to echo off the nearby mountains. "Come out." He banged on the wall again and walked to the house.

Garita appeared and tossed a few rotten tomatoes and corn ears to the pigs. "*No grita* — yell, Apá. Here, we *oye*-hear you."

I took eggs from the larder, warmed tortillas, and poured heated water in the coffee pot to reuse the wet leftovers. After two days of brew, the flow had little darkness, so I scooped them out and threw in new grounds. Today we needed it.

"That *gringito,*" my father began as he swigged his coffee. "Beely, Chivato Kid, goat boy, Señor William Bonneh — whoever he is. That Kid's going to give me a day's work, not half a day. Time for him to get up."

I cracked eggs into the frying bacon and glanced out. From the open door, I saw Beely shake his hat and crook it on his head as he walked to the house.

"Oh oh, Señor Beely, *zapato* — shoes . . ." Garita, who was still outside, announced plenty loud. "Walk this way and that." I glanced and saw she pointed to the north and south. "Break you in half."

From the doorway I could see what she fussed about. Señor Kid's wrong-footed boots pointed in opposite directions like drunk, backward bull horns.

Ramon came and stood beside me. "This Chivato has more *locuras* than the traveling circus." His eye glinted and his lips smiled to one side, a look saved for a fallen enemy or a tripped-up sheriff.

"Shush, Ramon. He speaks Spanish," I said. "You will be the shamed one, not him."

Dark thick eyebrows peaked high on Ramon's face. He didn't listen. His *at-you* not *with-you* grin wandered out, looking for more funny acts.

What happened next rolled in like a blue-sky lightning bolt. Within seconds the Kid's crosswise boots walked to Ramon, and before any of us could blink twice, his revolver pointed up at Ramon's face. He spoke for all of us to hear. "Think a man's mishap deserves a snicker? I see that look on your face, and I don't cotton to side sneers. Swear, I got the cure right here."

Ramon's brows collapsed from high to straight and narrow. The big Salamanca looked down onto the challenger and in one slow movement, eased the barrel away from his face.

The Kid leaned in and forced the gun again toward Ramon, this time at his neck. "Don't make me hurt you. Think it's okay to laugh at what's not meant to be?"

Chickens clucked and searched for food; a faraway skunk bird squawked; river gurgles whispered. We made not a rustle. I braced one arm with the other and felt the thunder of my heart. Ramon's upper lip twitched; his eyelids peeled back wide. Yginio's smile vanished, and Apá stepped outside, sniffed, and wiped his nose with the side of his pointer finger.

"No," Ramon said, "easy. Did I say it was funny? No cause to send bullets into anyone's head. *Cálmate, hombre.*"

"Me no neither," said Garita with a short laugh much like the bird call we had just heard.

The Beely man considered Apá and brushed his shirt sleeve. He inspected Garita and glanced back at Yginio. "Real good, cause I ain't got no desire to hurt nobody this morning." He stepped away from Ramon, twirled his *pistola,* blazing silver around his middle finger, and holstered it as smoothly as he pulled it out. In another quick second, he squared a seat on the well bench and righted his boots.

"*Sí,* good morning, Mister Señor Bonneh." Apá wiped his face with a brown handkerchief. "You won't need that shooting iron for the work we have here, *sabes,* you know, for your debt."

"Name's Bonney, not Bonehead. William Bonney. Come from Silver City, and I ain't no rustler. Told you, I aim to work off the sheep meat, and I will do just what I said. You'll see. A man would starve out there." He unbuckled his holster and hung it on his horse.

He faced my direction. A fly buzzed by me. I realized I still held the door open and shut it so fast it slammed a loud *cabang.* The eggs in the bacon grease took a slow fry. I left them and went back to my usual place at the door for another look.

Señor Bonney put his sights on Ramon and Yginio, whose open, frozen mouths hung long. The Kid turned a slight smile to Garita and a larger grin landed on me. Today, I found the strength to glance back, if only for a brief moment. Our eyes met, stuck, parted, and met again. His smile didn't have any sign of shame and neither did mine.

"Ahem, *bueno,* okay, you say you work, but I already fed you one sheep, one meal, and one night's bunk. How much more do I give before I get something back?" Apá eyed me with a frown.

"Now, I ain't no taker. I stand pat on that. At least no taker from those of meager means. Don't eat and run, either. I told you, going to work, and you won't be disappointed."

"Yes, *sí,* no disappoint," my father said.

I turned, stirring the beans, green chili, and eggs. I poured the coffee. As soon as the others came in, Pancho, the rooster, landed his perch on the doorframe. Garita, who was the last to reach the portal, harnessed his wings and gave him a good toss back to the chick coop. At the table, Ramon sat on the end with enough room to spread his huge legs. Apá and Yginio took one side, and Garita grabbed the space next to Beely.

I brushed away the same annoying fly and set out the morning tortillas, scrambled eggs, *refritos,* chili verde, and bacon. Our full table brought a meeting of thankfulness. Not only for food, but thanks the Beely man's gun didn't blow Ramon's face off.

The grub soothed us until Apá spoke.

"I think what you took . . . I think that's six days' work." The top of his white forehead, where his hat sheltered the sun, made Apá's brown face look half its size. His gray hair laid back onto his head, flat and oily. He took a drink of coffee, leaned back, and crossed his arms.

Ramon's slow stir of his dark brew kept his head down. It jerked up when Apá said six days.

"Wait a dang minute, Sal, you said three days, *no mas.* That's what you said, and that's what I agreed to, no adding more kernels to the ear after they've been chewed. No, *hombre,* I'm doing this to set the record straight and ain't got that kind of time. Got to find me a real job."

"*Sí,* yes, but now I have to feed you for the time you work, so I say at least *cinco,* five days. One sheep is *mucho dinero* for me."

Yginio smiled.

Ramon's lips tightened. He tapped his horse fingers on the table hard enough to make me nervous.

Beely looked at my father's leathery face, at Yginio, glanced over at Ramon, and settled on me a bit too long. He acted like a lost relative who belonged at our table. "Here's what I'll do, Sal, just because I know you're a good man."

Apá smiled.

"I'll give you a hand today and tomorrow . . ." He found my eyes among the others and shot me an unbridled gaze I hoped the others hadn't noticed. " 'Cause I can see you're in a hard place. But, I need to secure a job with money. After that, I cut and run. Then I'll come back again, later."

Beely's eyes bounced toward me like a flame that leaps in the air and catches fire somewhere else. "Check in and give you a hand every now and then, *sabes*? If you'll keep that corner in the barn for me, I'll be happy to fill it now and then."

Ramon stopped his finger thumping.

Apá, opposite the big Salamanca, claimed another kind of look. His eyebrows squeezed — like he was looking into the sun at high noon in a windstorm. Ramon did the same.

"Yes, sir, you'll see Señor Salazar, Sal. That bit of sheep meat you lost is going to be the best bargain you made this year. Where do you want me to start?" He glanced out the door at the dilapidated chicken coop, slanted outhouse, half-fallen pole corral, and airy barn walls. "Looks like this place could use another set of hands none too soon."

Billy was the first to leave the table.

Garita followed.

I began the dishes while the other men sat.

"Words are cheap," my apá said. "This Señor Bonney, wait to see what happens."

He meant a handshake don't mean a thing, worthless, until time shows what's real or what's just a finger fandango. My father always said the real judgment crouched in the bushes until the giving partner showed himself to be a gentleman *caballero* or a *desperado.* Could go either way. The important part was not the word square-up; it was the partner's deliverance of the promise. That was the test of his insides, test of his true worth. For that followed him wherever he went. And that was more valuable than a loyal horse. In Lincoln County, newcomers, drifters like Beely, with nothing more than *y'all'll see,* stood between the shadows of first light and twilight until the agreed-upon showed if the dealer was a *count-on* or a *no-count.*

I knew my father and was sure Apá

thought Beely to be one of those no-counts who'd run out on his promise, who'd gallop away in the dead of night or sneak away while my father's back was turned.

Everyone left the table and headed to their morning chores.

Beely stood outside with my father, and from my place in the kitchen I could hear him begin his debt. *"Es-coo-saw-doh."* He squinted as readily as he smiled. "*Es-coo-saw-doh,* what in living tarnation's that?"

"Escusado." My father gave the pronunciation we knew and finally pointed to the outhouse. "Not that one — stinks up too high, need hole for new one." He fluttered his hand over his nose. "Bad smell, *ooo mucho.*"

"*Escusado, escusado,* okay, you mean crap closet, dump hole, privy. Got me on that one there, Sal, sure did. I learned a new word, and it's a handy one at that, mighty kind of you. *Escusado.* Yeah, okay, I get it. A pit hollow, an *escusado* holding tank. Sure enough, *hombre.* I thought you'd come up with something good. No, sir, I ain't no stranger to that kind of need. Where's the pick and shovel?"

Beely looked at the tools laid out against the wobbly fence nearby. His face circled around, glancing for the audience — us

108

ladies. He smiled at Garita, who stood close by. He tipped his hat to me in my usual lookout, the kitchen doorway. He followed Apá, his new boss, to his payment job, carrying the tools.

"You work here while Ramon, my boy, and me take some of this flock to Sanchez's cornfield up the way to chow down on the stalks. We'll be back soon, not long. ¿Sí, understand? Got your needs, shovel there and the pick right there. Put the dig here, so it's not close to the house. ¿Eh?"

"Yes, Siree, Sal, that's all fine and dandy. I get it better than good. Going to put the old hutch here, right over a new hole. So a three by four by what? Five? Okay?"

"Sí, yes, good, muy bien." My father put up four fingers and pointed them to an imaginary line in the dirt for the length. With three fingers he moved his hand back and forth to mark width. His whole outstretched hand went down for how deep he wanted it. "Move the other over here, not now, later when you end." He slapped his palm midair to show a stop, turned, and winked at Ramon. After Beely's unkind take to Ramon's snicker about his shoes, I thought Apá risked an iron up his nose with that wink.

Ramon stood, plaster-faced. Yginio, it

seemed to me, held his lips from crack smiling. They soon mounted their horses and ordered Gordo and Campeon to drive the sheep on up the road. A white cloud of baaing drifted away from the house.

Their backs to us made me wonder why my father left us with this strange man unless he was sure this Chivato would take off right after their depart. Garita and I went to the barn for our work. With one eye out the barn door, Garita and I tied fleeces to make ready for Señor Murphy. Later, we would wash and spin a few piles for wool yarn. Wool thread balls took time, but Murphy was willing to pay five cents a spool. As usual Garita's attention found something else more interesting. A south slat with a big hole gave her a full view of our new helper.

Her eye stuck to the hole. On my turn, Beely was driving four wood stakes to square a rope line for the new *escusado* hole as if such a crap gathering needed good measure. With a face of a happy child, he whistled and dug. His chest popped out *duro* — strong, to use Garita's talk, and his hind loins, like a racehorse, filled the backside of his trousers. *Lead me not into temptation.*

Garita pushed me, took another snoop, stiffened, and drew in air. She held the top of her blouse. "Dead? Kid man hole."

"No, *Mija,* what? You think a dead person's going in there. No, this is a new place for our . . . for our . . . No other way to say it — *mierda.* Apá will put the old shit shack there and bury the filled-up pit."

"Dead — *mierda.* Go to Mamá?"

"Yes, dead crap." I kept my eye out the open knothole. Garita gave too much of the naked truth. "But no, it doesn't go with Mamá. God leaves it here. The old cesspool will stay, too. But this one he digs is without stink."

She giggled and clamped her fingers over her nose. *"Oowee,"* Garita's shrill struck high enough to be heard outside, so I palmed her mouth.

She would not be stopped and jerked my hand off. *"Zapato* — shoes." With feet and fingers pointed in opposite directions like devil horns, she snickered louder than a horse even though my hand was over her mouth. Soon, she sat and waved a small leather strap at her kitten.

Thank God she quieted down. With the better part of my mind on what was happening outside, I packed fleeces into bundles and watched my sister and her kitten.

Garita and Tigressa were miracles. At birth, the white kitten lay apart from the

111

others, helpless, without a cry. Like my sister, we took the little albino for dead. It was Garita who pulled a healthy kitty off and forced the mother's teat into Tigressa's mouth. Slowly, the kitten's little suckles pulled milk. It grew strong until she could fight for her space against her brothers and sisters.

Both saw every moment as an opening for new happiness. The mouser hopped up and chewed the brown leather strap. Garita giggled, her thick eyelashes opened like daisy petals in full sun. She and her pet suffered their own lameness, an incompleteness that wouldn't heal. The pink-eyed mouser could not hear, and Garita's mind saw things from a different lookout. Undone in one way and blessed in another. Both were gifted with eagle-eyed vision. The kitten for any movement and Garita's simple words for things others did not see.

I set aside five loosely-wired *bultos* of sheep wool. "Here, let that playing go, Garita. Come hold this, so I can tie it."

My life was not so simple, and I would never be happy like my little sister. I felt I was walking death. I worried about Apá without Amá, Sinforosa without us, me with Ramon. Since childhood, I looked to be Ramon's promised one even though I was not the one he wanted. He and Beely — one, I was expected to like, the other a liking unexpected. But Ramon's attention, like a faded dress that once made me happy, for the first time felt old and worn. Strange Beely didn't leave last night when he had a chance. We twisted baling wire around the fleece heaps until Garita tired. She went back to the barn hole.

"Move from there." I pushed her away for my own look.

Beely's back arched as he circled and landed the pick into the dirt. The bulges of his upper arms tightened his shirt in fierce mounds. He whistled as he worked. Under his slanted hat, beads of sweat rolled down his blond fuzzed cheeks like tiny streams through winter grass. His moves, always quick, darted two for one as he leaned the spade into the hard ground. The dirt had loosened inside the roped area, and a three by four section sunk down about a foot. His arms did not stop for rest and his back was strong for his size.

A strange desire grew in me. My insides felt light and moist heat seeped out of delicate spots. I wiped my brow, waved my underarms dry, and aired my legs with quick skirt fans. *Thy will be done, your will or my will?* I turned from my spy hole. The *bultos,* stacked inside the barn, needed to be loaded on the outside wagon. *Thy Shall Nots* went through my mind as I gathered what I could carry in one load.

At the door, I paused and caught my breath. Finally, sheer nerve forced my feet forward and outside the barn. With a bundle in each arm, I glanced in his direction.

He stopped his whistling and picking and showed that overlapped tooth. I heard a chuckle, a deep out-breath, and a long *uh huh.* When I turned again, he began to unbutton his shirt. It was November, not a summer day. Not freezing but bare skin this time or any time, sweet Virgin Mary, was as bad as pulling off chicken feathers to decorate the house for the winter while our fowl froze. It was not done.

I tried to put my eyes anywhere, on the cow, the goat, the sky, or the clothes on the line. But like Eve, my search for him could not resist a tiny peek. With a will of their own, my eyes took another quick look, a feasting. As he shoveled, muscles rippled below his skin like water over stones. He stopped and wiped his face with his bare arm and smiled. The wagon was not far but seemed miles away. With a thud, Beely threw the pickaxe aside. I heard no shoveling and felt a blue-eyed burn on my back.

Deliver me . . . I held my eyes toward the wagon and only the wagon. The fleece fell soft onto the buckboard. I gasped and took in air as if I was on top of Sierra Blanca. Hoped my lungs would not give out. One little look, just a quick peek before I made it back to the barn.

The shovel plunged without pause. My eyes went there. Hairless, like the Apaches, his chest swelled as he pushed on the heavy tool. Ribs streaked his middle in lean, curved lines. He glanced up and smiled. "Howdy do," he said without a bit of shame.

I turned, wordless, as skittery as a squirrel.

A dog barked. Apá — I looked again to the road. The Sanchez cornfield was not far away. He, Yginio, and Ramon would return soon and find the shirtless *escusado* digger.

It was a squawk bird, and it sounded twice more. *Thank you, Lord.*

I was on my second or maybe my third or fourth trip to unload fleeces, I couldn't tell which. I didn't know if I breathed out or in or if I headed into the house or back to the barn. He was the first man I'd seen under his clothes. *Forgive me, Almighty,* but I didn't have the strength to look away. Truth be told, I gaped like Garita. And Beely smiled and took his free liberties. No men

115

around here opened themselves in such a scandalous way — not how things were done here. Yet each move he made gave me the feeling the apple could be delicious.

He stopped. "Whooee, this dirt's harder than rock."

My shaky legs took me back to the barn. I leaned against the inside of the door and after a few heaves, caught my breath. Ramon would never strip his chest like that. We had grown up together, and I couldn't say how his chest was. I imagined black, hairy curls but never took a gander. If Ramon or Apá knew our visitor unclothed himself in this way, they'd run him off whether he paid his debt or not. Garita came back into the barn, said she was hungry, and went straight to the lookout.

"*Blanco* — white. Beely's belly," she said.

"Don't look any more, Garita. We are not to see men without their shirts."

"*Sí*, you *ver* — see." She pointed at me and the peephole.

"No, Apá would not want us to see . . . to see . . . Wait, what's that? Hear something?"

Horse clomps iced my lungs. A killing was in the making. I looked again and watched Beely button the top of his shirt. God spared us mercy and saved us from a slaughter.

116

Ramon, Yginio, and Apá turned the corner onto our dirt road and went inside the house without paying any mind to the shoveler, who was now three feet deep into the pit. He rigged a rope to climb down and out and another to yank up buckets from the bottom. He jumped down, filled buckets, jumped out, and hoisted them up for unloading. Garita and I went back to our baling and stayed away from the tempting barn holes.

Beely Chivato didn't stop but for a few bites of hard, dry tortillas and water. No long visits to the *escusado,* no rest. While the men sat inside, drank coffee, and discussed the day's happenings, the top of Beely's head disappeared into the hole. Once in a while, he climbed out with the stump rope, leaned down, and uploaded dirt.

I joined the others inside and began the noonday meal. As I worked, I imagined dust on his ever-present smile, dirt dots in the corners of his eyes, and his clothes throwing off a white cloud every time he moved.

"The little Spanish-speaking *gringito* is *ya* almost finished with one of his jobs. Good." My father took off his hat and waited for his meal.

"*Que desgracia,* Apá, why do you let anyone do such a thing? No one should be

117

digging an *escusado* for us. Why disgrace him and us with this hole dig for our . . . for our — *mierda*?" I set hot *refritos*, potatoes, and red chili on the table and the few tortillas I had rolled.

My father moved the beans and chili into his flour spoon. A dribble of red sauce streamed down the side of his mouth. He ate and didn't lift his head until he wiped his face with the palm of his hand, twice over.

"What will be next? Rake manure from the stables and the bottom of the chicken perch? That's *mierda*, too." I rolled a tortilla so hard and thin I couldn't lift it without leaving a hole in the middle.

"Why not? Digging is digging. He's almost finished anyway," Yginio said. "It don't matter what we're putting into the hole. That Kid Billy man owes us, and Apá decides how his sheep-take should be paid back."

"*Piensa* — think . . ." Garita began.

"Never mind, Garita. I'm not talking to you or Yginio. I'm talking to Apá. Look, the Kid man didn't say he didn't eat the meat. His aching stomach made him do it after coming from wherever he was."

"Silver City — in that area, through Mesilla he told me," Yginio said.

"*Ya vez.* See — he came from far, traveled many miles, and he didn't run scared. He let Tío Ruperto bring him like a roped-up Indian. Didn't fight or shoot. Looks like we're punishing him for his truth and hunger." I stacked the last tortilla on the pile and sat. "What if it was one of us who did not have food?"

"*Ya,* what shame, *Mija?* That *hombre* is the one who should be ashamed. Don't believe he wasn't the one who stole and killed one of our sheep. No sorry feelings for him. Don't deserve it. He owes me more than one day's work, and I'm going to get it from him. Crying women, worried about him and his hunger. Anyway what about that? Did anyone give him something to eat?"

"He said he was not going to stop. Garita gave him some of yesterday's tortillas." I mashed *refritos* and served them to my brother and father. "*Por favor,* can't he work on something respectful like fixing the holes in the barn or tightening the barb wire so the cow and goat don't get out? Or even the pigpen, but why you having him . . ."

"Hold your sorry feelings, Ambrosia, *ya.*" Ramon's mouth was not full enough to spare me his interrupting words. "Your apá said it already. That *gringito* took a sheep, slaughtered it with his own knife, and was cooking it right near the flock run. Hungry or not, it don't matter." If Ramon would have looked up, he would have met my scalding eyes.

"*Seguro, Mija,*" Apá said. "I need a new pit for the *escusado,* and *ya,* that's it. You and Yginio don't want to do it. The other one is full enough to smell up the whole valley, and I ain't got the time. Besides, I never like thinking about *mierda* when I'm eating, and tomorrow that easy talker and Yginio can repair some fences. You women take your sorry feelings and put them into your own work. Anyway, he's only here two days, not ten."

The men finished their meal. Ramon and Yginio took the loaded wagon of fleeces to Lincoln. My father stayed home and cut dried corn stalks for the pigs. This was not the father I knew. I believed Beely. My apá's hard line must be because of this business with Señor Murphy. Must be, he didn't trust anyone with white skin.

Garita and I washed the remaining fleeces and dried them on the fence.

Beely spent more time in the hole filling the buckets and showed himself only when he pulled and emptied them.

Yginio's return from Lincoln marked the need of another meal. In my glance out the window before cooking, I saw piles of dirt, no more ropes, and heard no noise. I shredded dried lamb jerky into a stew. The meat, squash, and zucchini would nourish him after his hard work.

We all sat for the evening meal. Silent, as if a quiet knot above our table had choked our thoughts. We ate. Garita was the first to speak.

"Dead *mierda* hole." She scooped food into a tortilla and stuffed it in her mouth. She chewed with her mouth open.

"Yes, looks like he done it in one day. *Mañana* we move the sitting bench." Apá hunched over his plate, paused a minute, and began eating again.

"*Bueno* — good, Apá," Garita said. "Beely?" She wrung a twine of hair through fingers not occupied with food.

"We'll see tomorrow. How he does? He could still leave cheap words behind him here tonight. Too much for him." My father stroked the side of his jaw, still doubting, I imagined, that Beely would pay all of his debt, and I was sure Apá was not going to make it easier on him.

"He deserves a hot meal, tonight," I said.

"*Sí*, yes, okay. Garita, fix him a hot plate and take it to him after supper." Apá motioned to Garita and didn't look my way.

121

After we finished our meal, my sister didn't wait long to gather food with two tortillas, not one. She stepped toward the door when I grabbed the tray board.

"I'll take it," I said.

"Both," said Garita.

"No, I can do it. This little tray doesn't take two people. You stay and start the dishes."

"*Mira* — look Beely's belly, too," she said.

"Garita, *ya* quiet, no such thing, crazy *locuras, shhh.*" I turned my back to her and walked out the door.

"You both go and see if he has enough blankets. Go *ya* without sorrys he don't deserve." Apá made sure I didn't go alone and waved us out the door.

"See, *sí,* huh?" Garita followed behind so close I could hear her breathe. She was too taken by this Kid man.

The barn door hung open, and we stood silent. Beely sat straddle-legged on a bale of hay in a corner away from his pinto. Bullets sat between his legs — baby irons born of his shooter. Flicking the chamber open, he spun it and held his eye to the moving pistol barrel. It twirled like a moth flutter until it stopped and again he eyeballed it close-up. With a small twig wrapped in a rag, he rubbed the inside canister. He yanked the rag loose and used it to clean the outside, as if the gun was a helpless being he kept alive. When he heard Garita sneeze, he jerked around and pointed his empty firearm at us.

We froze. "It's us. We bring some food," I whispered.

"Whoa boy, nothing in the wheel anyway, ladies, but *chihuahua,* you scared me acock. Million pardons, *señoritas.*" He picked up his iron and spun the wheel once more before setting it aside. "Just a reflex, I would never shake a cat stick at any woman, much less aim a firearm at beauties offering food. I'd rather eat a cow chip than haste either of you away."

Garita laughed and shook her head. "Beely, eat shit chip."

I tightened my brows at her. "Never mind that kind of language, Garita." I loosened my brows when I turned to Beely. "Apá sent us with this grub. He doesn't want you hungry or cold, and my father likes what you did today."

A dim dusk light streamed through the dark barn, and a lantern threw a faint beam onto his belongings. His horse blanket lay spread in the corner, and his saddle sat on the top edge for a type of pillow. After a river wash, his neck scarf and dirty shirt hung on the horse stall railing, limp and wet. He wore a different solid green shirt. Thoughts about the skin below his garment, the white underneath, blazed through me. "You have blankets, okay?"

"Oh yeah, I'm no stranger to cold. This lodging is better than I've had in a long time. But I'll take that extra if you don't mind, *mil gracias.* Add another layer of comfort, a bug in a rug."

Garita handed him the blanket.

"Much obliged." He put the extra on his horse blanket.

The tray went onto the sitting bale, now with space when he slung his legs to one side.

"If it gets too cold, just pull some of the raw fleece strands from those *bultos* and put it between the blankets. That is what we do sometimes."

Garita nodded.

"Tomorrow, just put it back in the *bulto.*" His sky-blue eyes skewered me until I forced a glance onto the sheep bundles and then at Garita, who had moved to the horse stall to search for her kitten.

My sister kneeled and didn't mind her skirt was halfway up her leg, enough to see long pants underneath.

"What's the name," he asked, "of the crit-ter?"

I hung a loose hair strand around my ear and answered, "Tigressa."

"Tigressa, now that's a name if ever I had a notion on how to call a cat. Dainty and vicious at the same time," he said.

I reached and pulled Garita's skirt down.

"What *day-in-tea* says?" Garita asked from her all-four position beside Luz's stall.

Her question was something I wanted to know, too.

He smiled.

I unlodged an air hiccup locked up in my throat with a cough. My fingers circled my neck.

"You okay? *Dainty* is nothing to get choked up about. *Dainty*, yeah Garita, it means fine-a-fied, fragile sweet, *delicada, elegante,* just the contrary to what people think when they see a barn cat. A swing between two mean-ings like lots of names."

He flamed those burning eyes onto me.

"Right, good idea with the fleece wool. But this here extra will do me just fine, *muy bien,* better than *bien.*"

Garita sneezed as she stood with Tigressa in her arms.

"Bless you," he said soon after the *achoo.* "Don't let the dust get up your nose there.

You ladies both got some air tickles." He spoke to Garita but stared in my direction.

"Come, Garita, let's get back. The dishes are waiting." I wrestled away from his silent hold of me.

"No, wait. I know Margarita or Garita's name. Also got Tigressa, Yginio, and Salamon. What's yours?" His stare shot blue fire arrows in me.

I looked down. "Ambrosia," I said, "Ambrosia Salazar."

"Ambrosia — knew it'd be something special. Like the nectar from flowers, ain't it? That which draws bees to the new blossoms or sweetness gathered for the gods, honey gifts for them. Is that the Ambrosia that was meant by your name?"

"The mother of my apá, her name. That's all I know. She died before I came to my family. Just a name from her."

"No, not just a name — a fine-a-fied name — as high-falutin' as they get. Your apá done good in keeping it for you. Makes you close to a goddess on my score. Like a queen. Like Tigressa, it has double meaning, soft and hard — delicate power."

I don't know how long his trance held me. The tips of my fingers trembled; my feet pushed a cow chip aside. My hand went to cover a dark spot on my cheek when words from outside broke his spell.

"Ambrosia." The house door hinge creaked open. "Apá's calling for you. The food on the dishes is getting hard. That's your work." Ramon's horse galloped away as my brother, Yginio, shouted. Soon my brother's footsteps sounded closer, and he walked into the barn.

"Hey, Yginio, thanks for calling. Pleasures me to have almost everyone in the family here in my dusty corner."

The Beely man stood and shook Yginio's hand. His easy words made him seem as if he belonged, as if he came to where he was always meant to be. As close as any good *amigo* and all he had to do was dig one *escusado* hole. He moseyed back toward the hay bale where his food sat, cold. His paint horse huffed air through his thick nose while Garita moved over to pet its soft muzzle.

"Yup, Billy, good, you have your food. Don't you want to eat it?" Yginio said. "Are these women keeping you?"

"No, not keeping me. I mean yeah, my food, yeah. But it's okay. It's a right nice gesture, *chihuahua.* Better-most vittles." He more than glanced in my direction. Yginio noticed, and my brother's stare brought a hot flush to my cheeks.

"*Mañana* we work together, eh?" Yginio

said. "Apá wants us up early, okay?"

Why did my brother have to be here? Break into our conversation? Bring his judging eyes?

"Right, okay, the *escusado's* done like your pa wanted, and I'm ready for my last day's job." He put his gun aside, shifted the plate onto his lap, and took up his fork. Garita with her kitten sat next to Beely's hay bale. I moved to the barn door. My breath pumped air into my blood and with each intake, my feet rode air off the ground. I leaned next to the barn door with no strength to say another word.

Bits of talk over, Garita left her kitten beside Beely, and she and Yginio walked out before me. I turned one last time. "You should not be eating with the animals. *Mañana,* you sit and eat with us inside."

"Well now, that'd be mighty good for my last night. Right nice but didn't expect no add-on's. This here's right nice enough. Never you worry. *Buenas noches,* good night, Ambrosia. And you, too, Garita and Yginio. Look forward to seeing you tomorrow."

The kitten jumped off the hay bale and rushed back to the stalls. Beely's last words hung out for each of us to receive in our own way.

CHAPTER SEVEN

Early the next day, Beely, Yginio, and Apá set out to bridge the old, wooden dump shack over the new empty hole. Beely carried his corner handily without a strain, which is more than I can say for Yginio and Apá. Corners and edges landed just so. I could tell Apá was pleased to have new space for our deposits, and Beely was pleased that he was pleased.

Apá then pointed me to the worst of what was left. The dreaded job was supposed to fall on Garita, too, but the barn swallowed her. When I complained with my eyes, Apá said no one who had dumped into the hole had a right to refuse the duty, so, by myself, shovel by shovel, bucket by bucket, I loaded dirt Beely had pulled from the new hole to cover the old one. Heard Garita giggle and knew she was looking out the barn hole with no notion to help.

Shit burdens were never a stranger, so I

kept quiet, hoping I would become invisible. A blind soul, guided only by their nose, could find the reeking cesspool I was assigned. Flies hovered over the purple streaks in buzzing droves. Thick stench waved insults over me, but I trudged on to finish before Beely took notice of what had befallen me. As I flung dry dirt over the wet goop, flies sprang in all directions. Drawn in, the waste feeders re-landed onto oily patches of the yellow soup mix. A slight relief came when I walked back to the dirt mound to refill my bucket.

Beely and Yginio were distracted with their own jobs. They faced the pasture fence away from me, minding the *how-to's* of their next chore from Apá. I heard my father tell them they were in their own charge while he left northwest, this side of Capitan, to fetch twenty more sheep for wintering.

The wretched cover-up job never got easier. A gag-swell strangled me, but any throw-up would call attention. So I worked as if this was for the good of all mankind. Only stop was when I realized one breath could not last a bucket dumping. The job required an old rag around my nose. I felt my lungs expanding and went on.

Beely and Yginio were digging post holes, driving down fence woods, resetting the holding, and re-nailing the barbed wire to the posts. Their work noise was far enough away only distant clamor came to me. From my vantage, I could see Beely was quick handed, but he had only two, so Yginio followed, lending him his slow hands.

Soon, I had to board up some support, so I could dump dirt in the middle. I dragged a small section of a discarded corral door and laid it down over the pit. With my full bucket, I teetered on the plank to toss the dirt. As I did, splashes of brown muck fell on my skirt.

Finally, my many trips mudded over the wet stink-pool, and as best as I could, like Apá directed, overlapped wooden poles, broken tree limbs, and rotten boards. Setting stones across the wet mess would keep any person or animal from sinking in. No one wanted to find themselves in *mierda* or having to haul out a shit-coated pig. It did nothing for the smell, but it was done, and in that job alone, my father had his money back from that lost sheep.

Instead of dirt, I pumped a load of water into the bucket, rinsed brown splats off my dress, refilled it, and carried it into the barn. There, I found Garita sleeping soundly in the hayloft and took this private moment to search for the men through the peephole.

They had begun a distance from the barn and were working their way closer to our barn. As they came in our direction, their talk came with them.

"Why can't I? Look. Those nail heads are at least a half-inch wide. See here. This bullet tip is smaller. It's not above our bend, I tell you. Easier than all that hammering. We just have to make mighty sure we're far enough away, so the steel head don't dig in too deep. Maybe just a quarter inch or so. Secure as a church bell in its tower. We can try out the force with a rock on top to see how far back it lands."

"In a pig's eye, no, I don't think so, Billy. Impossible, *hombre*." My brother laid heavy on the *eh* of *hombre* and shook his head.

Like many days, I washed dirty fleeces, readying them for spinning spools. I listened as if I had the ears of a cat. Even with an open barn door, the cold was less bothersome than not hearing the men, so I moved my work within earshot.

"Wrap the wire around the nails, tap them just a bit, stand back, and let me buzz 'em in. Betcha I can — no harder than picking tulips." Beely's voice rang higher in his excitement.

"No, too much fire power. It will make a tunnel right through," my brother said.

"Naysayer, you'll see. Set one in. I got it handled. Ante up and step back." Beely's big brag belted out.

Garita woke up, dipped a fleece, and watched bugs and dirt float up, so I left her with that and walked outside to drape a wet one over the fence. "Nah, just talk. Senseless as chicken chatter," I muttered under my breath.

"Go ahead. *Pronto,* put a fist-sized rock on top, just for a little practice and tell me where it lands." Beely settled in on a shooting stance, but I still thought he was fooling.

When I walked back in the barn, the first shot rang out. Shock forced Garita and me to the wall hole, facing south to get a view of things.

"Let me take a few steps back. I think that was just a tad too much. Try another rock," Beely said.

A second shot *kabinged* louder and clearer.

Garita wrapped her arms around her head. "*Duele* — hurt," she said.

"*Santa Maria, y Jesu Christo.* What in God's name are they doing?" A November rattlesnake or something came up on them. A bobcat? They couldn't be shooting rocks. I looked again.

"Leave the head out at least an inch and make sure the wire is wrapped tight around the nail. Shoo the goat over, and you step aside, too. Can you tie that animal up over there? Your pa didn't cotton to losing a sheep. He probably won't curry none to finding his goat down by a stray aim either."

I could see silver spin around Beely's middle finger. He stopped and took aim. "Good, alright. I can do it. Yeah, right there *hombre.* You'll see. Wanna put a wager on it?"

"What is wrong with Yginio that he's letting Beely shoot up a fence post? He's bad as that Chivato Kid — no, even worse," I said.

Garita squinted, took her peek, and nodded fast head jerks.

My eye strained out the knothole. *"Locos."*

"Malo — bad," said Garita. "Big shoot. Bad Beely boy."

"No, I ain't got money to put up," Yginio said. "But if you do it, I will give you a swig of some demon rum."

Garita took a deep breath and left her mouth wide open. *"Mucho muy malo —* bad."

Guns, the sight of them, and ear shattering sound kept us in the barn. Garita iron-clamped my arm with both hands.

"It's okay, Garita. We stay in here. Don't know where the *locos* might point that gun. You keep behind the door. Understand me? Right here in this barn."

I heard the word *money* and put my eye just out the door. A sliver of rough wood dug into my cheek. When I reached to pull it out, my hand shook it in further. Garita followed close behind me, and I motioned her back. With my hand over my face wound, I took another look from the portal and heard the word, *sister.*

"Whiskey, nah or *dinero* either? Who's talking about greenbacks?" said Beely. "How about . . . how about if I drive it in, you'll . . . you'll put a little lean on that sister of yours in my direction. *Sabes,* simple as cherry pie."

"Not Garita, right? But which one?" asked Yginio.

"What you mean, which one? How many you got?"

Looking for something to hide me, I jumped behind the door, pulled the wood sliver, and felt blood dripping down my cheek. Salt sweat mixed into the cut and stung like the dickens. I bent over to wipe my face with my skirt hem when Garita bumped me forward and nearly landed me on my face. "Get back. Too dangerous. Stay

135

here, right here, no *mas.*"

"*Tres.* And none of them good," said Yginio. "Two dark sisters and a light one."

"Three? I see Garita and, of course, Ambrosia. Sure enough they're the color of smooth brown gravy. Where you hiding the light-skinned one?"

Garita waved skittery fingers in the air. "He say me."

"*Ya,* Garita, don't talk," I said. Beely's words pulsed air, more ear-fetching than the gunshots.

"Number three is Sinforosa, but she don't live with us. Been gone for a spell, at the Jewel Parlor, downtown. Makes her own life there."

"Oh yeah, I seen that parlor, been in a time or two and know about the Jewels. Who don't? Nice enough place, but a Salazar sister there, that's a rare thought. Does she look like Ambrosia?"

I wondered if he remembered — me, the woman on the floor, under the mercy of a crazy man.

"*Ir* — go now," Garita said.

"No, not yet, wait." I held her back with my free hand.

"No, the opposite," said Yginio.

"Then she must be *ugggly.*"

"They are my sisters, and I don't see them

136

in that way, but most say Sinforosa, she's the most beautiful one. But she never wanted the life of a sheep herder's daughter."

"Don't say. Must be hard on Sal. A Salazar girl of the line. Well, I might call on a brother's help but never paid for a woman. Don't need to. Manage okay and have reserve in my pocket. But wouldn't mind seeing the goods."

They rattled about and laughed up their fool talk.

Then Beely spun his pistol another go-round. "Which sister? Now that's a good question. I ain't gonna answer. You figure it out."

Holding my hand over my wound, I came out of the barn and saw him stand, facing the fence, wide legged, with his pistol pointed at the post.

"*Muy malo* — bad," Garita screeched behind me.

I pushed her back into the barn, threatened her with a horse-whipping, and walked out just short of their view. No part of this I wanted, but Yginio wasn't going to stop, and somebody had to put an end to it. With stiff, hard steps, I moved forward, but a stampede of buffalo hooves couldn't take

Beely's stare off the wooden target in front of him.

Another shot rang out, and I saw Yginio's head bite down with a snap and straighten up. He jumped and ran to the railing, screaming *yeehahs* in full force.

Gunslinger Beely ballyhooed like he discovered gold. "Drove her in like grease lightning, *primo.* Just like I said, see there."

"No, it couldn't be," I whispered under my breath. They wouldn't be that *loco,* and Yginio is not this man's *primo.* Some cousin — bold, dangerous, and gun crazy.

Beely stepped aside. "Set the next one up. Hurry, I got the hot aim right here."

Yginio put the nail in with a tiny tap and strung the wire around the nail head. He stepped back. Beely sent his second bullet into the fence post victim.

Garita ran into the house and shut the door.

"Didn't think anyone could do it this way, Billy. Today, you are my *primo.* You did the impossible." Yginio ran to set up the third slat.

Within twenty feet of their blasting range, I came upon them while they paused, but I was too late.

Billy shot and missed.

"Yginio, *Dios mío,* has all your sense left

138

you? What are you doing?" My voice could be heard down the road and back.

Before my brother could answer, a faint mewl sounded in the line of fire. Not but about fifty feet away, a small puff of white fur, hardly visible in the dried brush, lay.

I looked and relooked. "What, what's there? Tigressa? Is it Tigressa?" My question slurred, muffled by my fingers, and my set-open mouth.

"Now let's not get flusterated. Hold your horses. She's just taken a little hitch." Beely ran as he yelled to me, without turning around, without his cooing Spanish.

Yginio kept pace with him.

It was clear the little ball was now a red blob on the ground.

I couldn't bring myself to go any closer and stopped in my tracks. "No, is she . . . is she dead?"

"Nope but wounded bad." He took his gun, and before I knew it, Beely fired one loud blast into the small lump. "Now she is. A merciful death. No cat could live boogered up like that. She'd prefer what I done gave her."

The push-pull inside me raged. Beely, who I thought was good — was good for nothing. My tight fists wrapped around my waist. "No, no, *Diosito Santos,*" a suffocated moan deep in my throat muffled out. I trusted Garita was not watching and did not see her cat slaughtered so without reason.

"See there." My voice echoed up and then some. "See there, Yginio, I blame you most. Now how you going to make Garita understand that your *primo* here killed her cat. Useless, shameful, and for what? For nothing. And you, Beely, your first debt barely paid, and now you have another owed to my sister."

Both men walked toward me in silence. Yginio moved to wrap his arms around me, but the little up-corners of his mouth made me push him away.

"It was just a cat," my brother said.

"You're as bad as this one, Yginio," I screamed.

"It ain't his doings, Ambrosia. I did it by myself. It's my fault, no one else's." Beely for the first time made some sense.

"Don't . . . don't say my name. I never ever want to hear it out of your mouth not now or ever."

"Now, Ambrosia . . ." Beely tried again.

"No, stop. I told you. I forbid you to say it and yes, you killed the sheep and now this little creature. Who knows what's going to be next? This is why I hate guns."

"Now, whoa . . . wait a dang minute. I don't take kindly to falsifying evidence of the past. No ma'am — didn't kill that sheep. Now you see the mouser here dropped in accidental damage. We ain't mean it to be like that. Seen other cats hereabouts that move away from noise. What's got this one so dumb?"

"Because . . ." I grabbed my blouse collar to wipe red water from my eyes and thorned-up cheek. "Because it does not hear. It's deaf."

"Okay, okay, not that this weren't a good one, but Salamon won't even notice, and I will face the dragon with Garita." Beely holstered his wretched pistol.

"That's right," Yginio said. "Ambrosia, get back in the barn to your work. This is our man's job."

"Wait now, Yginio. This here's a hard case. Even if we won't miss Tigressa, some others might," Beely said. "The fat's drizzling in the fire afore we lay the meat in. Let's stand up the fence with no more shenanigans. Okay, Ambro . . . I mean Ma'am Salazar."

He didn't finish the last word when a chorus cloud of sheep and barking dogs and horse hooves rose up the road. Apá and Ramon turned the corner with the last of this year's flock.

"You finish up here, Billy," said Yginio. "I'll bury Tigressa. Only a few post to go. Ambrosia, get back into the house and keep your mouth shut. Don't upset Apá and Garita with this."

CHAPTER EIGHT

Forks and knives clattered against tin plates. Our silent tongues, like wingless cicadas, moved food, not words. Beely sat next to his new *primo.* The gunslinger's head stayed down, moving white *papitas* over to the green chili and mixing it with brown beans and greasy bacon only to round it back to where it came. His eyes, like his shooter, had lost their flash and didn't search me out. Ramon, next to Apá, stirred his coffee four times til I'm sure its heat went cold. Garita, silent since Beely's first shot, appeared more deaf and dumb than usual.

Apá's eyes moved from Yginio, to Beely, to Garita, to his food, and back again. He looked at me and jerked two or three long nods. *"¿Que pasó?"* he asked, pointing to his own cheek.

I touched the red scratch on my face. Turned to roll another tortilla. *"Nada,"* I said, "a little splinter."

I knew he sensed something more than the smell of food hung in the air.

"*Ya* the fence, I see standing. The cow, it is good in the corral." He looked at Beely. "The cow — in a place where she can't get out."

"*Sí, Señor,* I gotcha the first time," Beely said. "It's all good, Sal." He re-circled his food.

"*¿No problemas?*" Apá asked.

"No, none at all. Just sink down posts, wire and nail them, and make sure they hold against the will of a dumb animal." Beely stared at his food. "Just like you wanted and just like you got."

"Yeah, simple, Señor Kid Billy," said Ramon, "why do you wear guns to fix a fence?" After his little snicker concerning Chivato's backward boots, Ramon, as huge as he was up against Beely, took a high-fallutin' risk. Nobody wanted to see Beely draw his equalizer again, and I know that included Ramon. He softened his question by raising his chin up and lowering his voice. "Think you need it?"

Beely held a straight-eyed stare right back at him. His spine stiffened, and he took a brown kerchief from his pocket and snapped it. "Keep black-eyed Susie handy, Ramon — always."

144

"Big shoot." Garita came to life after a long silence. "Boom-boom." Her words overlapped Beely's, but hers were lost in the man talk.

"Why is it your business?" Beely wiped his mouth.

My watch on Garita held until she understood the need for quiet. She dropped a fork and bent down to pick it up. Her stubborn message would not drop with the fork. "Big shoot," she screamed below the table, "big boom shoot." She sat up and tapped her fork like she wanted to say it again.

Apá was the only one who paid Garita any mind. His eyes shifted from her to the men.

"And what business do you have hereabouts anyway, Ramon?" Beely asked. "See you coming and going like a two-bit plow hand." He finally put a spoon of food in his mouth and took a long chew.

Ramon raised his bearing up tall and seemed to take on new courage — or blind ignorance — any which way a bystander wanted to see it. "What business? My business? Here or for *dinero*?"

"Either, one different from the other?" Beely sat back and tilted his hat more than a slant. He put his wipe rag to good use over his mouth and set it back in his pocket. Still did not look at me.

145

"Ramon has always helped —" Apá took it upon himself to answer until Ramon cut him off.

". . . help my *compadre*, Salamon, and his family. They are more than *amigos*." He gave me a locking-eye pause when he said *more*. "I work horses, mules, and burros. All things — shoes, saddles, breaking, forging, buying, selling, branding." He palmed his mustache, slow and steady as he stared back at the one called Kid goat Chivato.

"Horse to Ambrosia," said Garita.

I hushed her with my eyes, and Apá waved his point finger at her.

"That right?" Beely said. "Yeah, I get the picture, a smithy and then some. Where do you do the tending? Besides the time you're here."

"In Lincoln," said Ramon, "just outside, south, I have my work barn there."

"Oh, where I'm headed, tomorrow first light, meeting a friend at that locale. Got a little horse job myself, but none of what you do," Beely said.

"Apá, you can see the fence doesn't lagged to the barn here anymore. All done," Yginio said. "I can go with you, Billy, tomorrow, to Lincoln. Okay, Apá?"

My father stared at me, long and hard, and moved that same look to Beely.

146

Beely wiped the last of his plate clean with a piece of tortilla.

Yginio waited for Apá's answer. We all waited. My father turned to Garita, to me, and to Beely as if sniffing our body heat like an Indian tracker in search of a wounded animal. "No, Yginio, we need you here to see to these last sheep." He took a swig of light coffee. "*Bueno,* good, you two finished. Everything went good today, eh?"

Yginio and Beely nodded.

"Like I said, Salamon, easy as cake." Beely held his eyes right on my father.

His bewitchment had lost its hold on me, and my will was strong enough to pull my lips tight and break away from his blue-eyed trap if he'd looked. The picture in my mind of Beely with his gun pointed down on little deaf Tigressa boiled inside me. The thing happened. It was not a planned shoot. A cat killing is not something anyone would seek out. But guns, target games, sad happenings — all were Beely's specialty and seemed to follow him wherever he went.

My foot below the table tapped against its wooden leg.

Garita looked down to see where the ruckus was coming from and kicked me.

My father stared at us. His eyes scratched for something more, something between words — some wandering shift, a nervous pause, a stutter of trouble. He mixed potatoes and *refritos* onto his tortilla, sunk it into his mouth, and with unblinking eyes, tore another cut for a reload.

I imagined chancy acts excited Beely and lost lives, human or animal alike, no matter. Appeared this is how he liked it — hog-tied to danger, strung around a tree branch, hanging from a rock ledge — over an arroyo 500 feet deep — in a thunderstorm at night. And he would probably be one to use an old jute rope — burned in the middle. This Beely figures a way to stretch the gambling risk til he beats the doubtful word of impossible. And like Tigressa, I watched like a deaf fool and may find my own blasted end. I quit knocking the table leg and stood to clear it.

"Yes, this cake, easy." Apá scraped the last bit of food off his plate. "Got done what you said. Your sheep debt is *ya* over. You go tomorrow to your work, but you come back here for more work any time."

Ramon caught a piece of dry tortilla in his mouth and coughed so loud it brought a jump from Garita. She pounded his back. He spit into a dirty rag and set it aside. She kept knocking him. The big man was forced to motion a breathless stop. He shook his head and raised a palm as he called out a throaty *basta* to Garita.

None too soon, she halted.

Yginio nodded a look of pleasure.

I picked up the empty plates and set them in standing water without raising my eyes to anyone.

"Guess that means, Mister Señor Beely, you are an *hombre* with a true word. Something that doesn't always come . . . uh . . . come about to be." My father wrestled out his hesitant thought.

Yginio smiled.

"Call me Billy, Salamon. No misters, here. Or call me Chivato. That'll be good. Everything's okay. Mighty fine." For the first time that evening, Beely smiled at me, but it fell on half-shut lids.

Everyone migrated to their beds.

CHAPTER NINE

Many days after Beely left, Apá gathered things we had to sacrifice for the House Mercantile trip. A familiar, heavy air of doom had hung over breakfast, and that, not the food, had filled our stomachs. I watched as my father loaded bartering booty — two, one-pound squares of goat cheese, balls of spun yarn, spare jars of preserved green beans, and three dozen eggs. The twin orphaned lambs and two others would be sacrificed. A loss we might miss for our own meals.

The sheep ears, he had warned Garita not to touch, still hung in the barn. He coughed a dry hack. His fingers trembled as he moved the knife against the tattered cloth rope holding them from the rafters.

Go, be gone worthless remains. Pointer finger tightened a pull to small finger, I drew milk from Isabelle's teat. *Stupid ears,* a false promise hung in the dust of our barn.

Nothing but shriveled bait in a steel trap, set for my father to believe he had something coming back to him.

"Apá, I can go with you." From beside Isabelle's bulging udder, I squeezed long hard streams into a bucket and spoke around her. Yginio was off on his line camp run and never seemed to be around when my father tended to this kind of business. My poor old apá should not go alone. A silent weight hung over us. Everyone in our family hated these trips when payment was due, less Garita, who still after weeks, had not given up her search for Tigressa. She was at the Baca's, the next ranch over, looking for her beloved kitten.

The damned ears clicked against each other as Apá carried the gunny sack like precious cargo. I bore my eyes into him wherever he moved. He kept his head down as he tied the top of the sheep-ear sack, rattling their stiff jumble, until he found a place for them on the wagon beside the two dozen eggs embedded in a box of sand.

"*Ya que,* we have already had this talk. Told you then. Can handle this alone, better alone," he said. "Don't need you to speak with the mister man. Your mamá would not want you to go, and you know it."

"*Sí*, I know, but Mamá's not here anymore. Things have changed, and you need help."

"No, I don't need no help." He untied and retied the gunny sack.

Nothing could be heard but the milk hitting the side of the tin.

"When you can't haggle with Señor Mister, what happens then? Pasturing the sheep is different. Yginio knows that business. We all do the shearing." I slowed up the milking as I searched for just the right words. "But you are the only one who talks with Señor Murphy. A wise man looks down the road. Someone needs to see these dealings and learn how to give this for that or whatever you do, especially with those ears. I don't see what difference the ears make."

He hooked the cinch on Luz and put the pole shafts through leather loops hanging on her sides. His less than nimble hands checked the hold back. Our old horse rolled her huge eyes and nodded a chortle as she tapped her hoof. Apá grabbed the harness from a nearby nail and snugged it over Luz. "Yes, I have thought about it. I'm the father. When the time comes, Yginio will go with me."

Milk streams buffeted the sides of the bucket like whitewater rapids, nonstop.

Each flow stronger than the one before. I thought of how smart Sinforosa was for leaving and what she might be doing away from here.

He stopped, pulling a tiny pad of white crisp papers from his front shirt. He thumbed one out. With his other hand, he flipped the lid of a small red tin and tapped rich brown bits of tobacco into the paper fold. With the precision of a watchmaker, he rolled it, wet the ends with his tongue, and twisted them shut. The white roll hung out his mouth as he arranged Luz's bit and checked her head gear.

"Yginio's a man, Apá. Almost a full grown one, and he's strong for carrying, but you know and I know, he's quick to laugh or get mad." Isabelle worked her cud in long side chews as I moved to the other side, closer to my father. I patted her hindquarters, then rubbed her milk bag softly. "Maybe you haven't thought of other people who might surprise you. Maybe with bystanders around Señor Murphy can be shamed away from such a hard deal, take sheep ears for less rent, and lighten his wager. I can go and be learning."

He stopped and let the reins lay loose on our old horse's back. Flicked a match on his pant leg and lit the end of his smoke.

Blew a gray stream out the bottom of his lungs. His head moved up and down in that thinking way, and his fingers rubbed over the back of his head. A smoke circle drifted up in dusty blotches, sucked by an up-draft to barn rafters. "*Ay, Mija,* I said, *no,* and I say, *no,* now. Why can't you hear me? Never give me no peace, *nunca.* What you would see there is nothing but two men who think the other is taking more, and they're getting less. Always the same, and besides, we have a problem with Garita. If you go, she has to go. And if she goes, she has to be watched. But maybe you could go see Sinfo."

"Every day, with Garita, that happens, Apá. You know that. The problems, I mean, with Garita, are never new. I will watch her. Forget your worry. After I finish here and you tie up the lambs, I'll get her from wherever she is. Then we go, Apá, yes?"

He stared at me.

"Yes?" I asked again.

He didn't say *no.*

Apá knew his daughters, but not well enough to think I'd try to bring Sinforosa home again. I had other, many other reasons for going. I wanted to know more of a man's world, to see firsthand this Mister Señor Murphy who made my father miserable. Mamá's death had opened up my boundaries. Someone in this family needed to learn about what really went on. I didn't have brute strength, but I could mix words and come up with different ways to think if only I could find a man who would listen.

The clank of our buckboard, with goods loaded for Lincoln, rolled down the washboard trail like a Mexican gypsy wagon. Our tied-up animals, bleating behind us, held back, then let the rope tug them along. The few people we passed, nodded the familiar, *buen día,* as bags and boxes bounced and swayed on the buckboard, and the lambs filled the air with their haunting cries. The *día* was not *muy bien* for us today.

As always, I took the steering, and Garita sat between me and Apá. The winter morning colored our breath a foggy gray, and January iced the edges of the Ruidoso. To cross it, Garita had to get out, untie the lambs, and help Apá and Luz pull the wagon wheels slowly through the sandy, cold water bottom. Garita retied the lambs, jumped on, and dripped half-frozen mud onto the floorboards. We huddled in the early cold until the sun came out and warmed our backs. My sister pulled out her bola sling, took off her boots and socks, and put them on her lap to dry. She wrapped her feet with an extra gunny sack Apá brought.

As we rattled along, the Bonney Kid came to mind — kind and unkind thoughts. How could I forget he stopped drunken, mad hands from tearing into me? How could I not recall boozy stench breath and the cold ooze of tobacco spit into the back of my blouse? I had managed to push that day into a forgotten corner, but now the familiar road to Lincoln set new panic in me. Awful thoughts, La Jewel mind shadows, like floating ash out of a burning fire, drifted up. One thing was certain. Apá would never hear about that day. I prayed this trip would go better.

Garita waved her socks in the drying air. They came a little too close to my face, and I pushed them away.

Tehde's ramblings came to mind — threes — Mamá's death, Sinfo leaving, and something else? A third, some tortured joy. What? Sinfo comes home. I have longed for her return, but she, that sister, would surely bring her old misery. That's tortured joy. Or Garita is planted with a baby by some *bruto*. Babies are miracles of happiness but that one would be a sad burden, another mouth to feed. A painful happiness. No, please, Lord, do not let that be my next three.

Could it be Apá? He dies like Mamá. Yginio and I have to carry on with Señor Sir Murphy. That doesn't sound right, either. I'd bear Apá's death in the worst way even if losing his tight rein would bring new freedom, a small reward for such tremendous grief. Could the eagle feathers be mistaken? A misread? A third happening — some kind of happy misery. Prophesies, earth signs, maybe yes, maybe no, Tehde didn't venture anything beyond that.

The piggyback boulders by the Bonito River marked our turn to Lincoln. I pulled the reins left. The Bonito's riverbank came and went like a hide-and-seek game as we headed north. Today was calm, no *Oowee* wind stirred our hair. Not far from that point, a half-filled dirt tank set the lambs bleating for a drink, so we stopped. They bellyached for their mothers, and like us, they were headed to Murphy's slaughter.

Almost to Lincoln, close to the Salamancas', a wagon wheel came loose. Only two eggs, stored in the sand box, cracked in the upset, but the goat cheese spilled beyond recovery. Apá called on me to shore the wagon while he remounted the wheel. Garita, barefooted, gathered the green bean jars, which needed nothing but a wipe. When I mentioned to my father our

157

hands would have been missed, he didn't as much as nod his head.

The Salamanca house came into view, and I was ready for a stop. Garita shook her partly dried socks and put them and her shoes on. Soon, Doña came out to greet us. At the door, she held her upright standing like the Queen of Spain. As proud as she stood, Doña Hurtencia, too, had suffered. Ramon's father, Doña's first husband, broke his neck in a horse fall when Ramon was four. That first husband died soon after. She remarried an older Salamanca man who owned this fine house. One November, that unfortunate took his son, not his stepson, elk hunting close to the Sierra Blanca crest. A very rare, early, hundred-year snowstorm came down with little warning, and they never made it back. Some believed a mountain lion or grizzly took them until a blue, unmangled hand showed itself the next spring. An avalanche had choked them and their horses at ten thousand feet.

Much like a rock tolerates its fungus, Doña tolerated me. Often, she winced at her precious Ramon's unguarded affection. Sinforosa was never a choice for her or for Ramon. I was her only destiny for little Salamancas. She combed her usual hand reinforcing her bun and let us in. "*Buen día,* welcome. How did you manage that full wagon? Come in, please, everybody. Salamon, I have fresh coffee."

The smell of dark, rich brew and bacon grease spread its soothing aroma over us and made me realize I hadn't had breakfast.

"Ay gracias, sí," Apá said, "Ambrosia and Garita are with me here today. My boy told me Ramon was going with him to the west pastures by Ruidoso."

"Yes, Ramon left early this morning. I didn't know where." She looked at me, tight lipped, sliced sweet bread and offered one slice to Garita. My sister took two.

"Just one, Garita." My words bounced off the walls and left me facing Doña's half-scowl.

"Leave her, *ya.* It's okay," Doña said, but her face told me she thought otherwise.

I broke a small piece of my little sister's second sweet bun and looked to get another until Garita moved it beyond my reach. As anxious as I had been to arrive at the Salamancas', my short rest soon made me impatient to get to Lincoln.

"Did Sinforosa come home?" Doña would have to ask. "I woke up this morning thinking about her."

"No," Apá said, "she will be home soon, very soon. The girls might go today to bring

159

her back."

"*Preciosa* Sinforosa," said Garita with a mouthful of escaping crumbs.

Dry bread bits into the wrong pipe choked me to a heaving gag. Apá would consider me a girl until the day I died, shallow-brained as both my sisters. Garita pounded a rattle into my shoulder blades. With no speaking voice, I turned and held her hands from slapping me. Doña's glass of water helped. I nodded thanks and hoped Apá didn't think my nod was saying *yes* to his idea of seeing Sinforosa.

Doña refilled Apá's cup. "Ramon tells me she's keeping with the English man, the one from, where is it? Britannica or something like that, a very long ways away, across the ocean."

"No, I don't know nothing about that." Apá's head went down, and he stirred shame into his coffee.

"*Sí*, Salamon, you should know. I'm just telling you what we hear. This man, Tunstall, or something like that, has bought the Feliz Ranch. He's running cattle and horses and has the new mercantile in town. I've seen him ride by on that big, blind, white horse of his. First horse I've seen with little brown dots on its pink nose, mind you, like a freckled horse freak. This *Inglés* fit leath-

160

ers from a dog to the horse, to him on top. Leads it with the dog, so the horse feels how steep the ground is. *Raro,* such a thing for animals. Ramon helped him rig it, and my boy says once you understand his kind of English, he is a nice *Inglés.*" She glanced at me when she said *my boy.*

"No, I haven't heard nothing." Apá's head, a sunflower in winter, drooped.

Garita, a sunflower in spring, sat so alert she left the sweets. And I, like her, held off on asking Doña to tell us more.

"*Preciosa* Sinforosa," Garita couldn't help herself and shouted out more of the same, "*Hermosa* Sinforosa."

"Was she? Was she, Sinforosa, with him?" Words, I wished I could suck back into my throat, leaped out. With my mouth covered, I waited for the answer.

"One day I did see her on that horse, mind you — four of them, the dog, horse, *Inglés,* and Sinforosa. Didn't ever think our beautiful Sinforosa would chance such a contraption on an animal like that. I mean, she was laughing and holding Señor Tunstall and that dog and the horse were running, *Chihuahua,* fast, mind you, they were running. Can you imagine, galloping on a blind horse? Nobody would get me on a thing like that."

Not wanting to hear more, I dragged Garita and Apá out, and we were on our way.

In Lincoln, riding by Sheriff Brady's jail place, I saw him poke a tired lookout, turn, and go back to his big chair. Eyes from each window seemed to stick on us and slow our movement. From our commotion, they must have thought a traveling circus had come to town. Soon we saw the tallest building up the road, Murphy Mercantile. Our rumpus shook our trading goods and churned up the gravel in the bottom of my belly. Here was the half-hidden world we couldn't live without. We poor Salazares had to follow silent laws, hidden rules, misunderstood nods, and unexpected headshakes. Had to try to avoid covered potholes or the next waylay. Garita, the only calm face, sat with her elbows and braids over her knees.

"Now, Garita, no lifting your skirt, eating sheep ears, or waving to nobody here today, hear me? Be like Mamá would want you to be," I said.

She shoved her bola sling into her boot and nodded.

Asking Garita for a quiet-lady act was like asking a duck to plow a wheat field. I left it there, but she was not leaving my sight.

"When we get inside, take my hand." I

162

steered Luz closer to the store entry, down a ways from the house lodging door. "And don't let go," I said. "This man doesn't like people climbing his trees or touching his things."

Apá straightened his old greasy hat like he was readying himself for a bronc ride. "*Ya pues,* let's go," he said. We left our cart outside, lambs and all.

A little dangling bell jingled as we pulled the door open. The inside felt warm. In front of us, the likes of the Murphy Mercantile House spread out. This spectacle brought the word *mercantile* to life — for it was a true getting place. A wall of preserves, brought in from farms — red apples, peaches, apricots, plums, green beans, and the likes decorated three or four shelves. My eyes filled. The very few times I'd been in this place, I never knew where to look. Barrels with pecans, walnuts, purple prickly pears, flour, dried beans, sugar, and salt formed a line along a side wall. A smaller barrel half-filled with piñons rested there, too. Another row held treasures of soft deer skins, beaver furs, saddle leather, buffalo robes, blankets, colored cloth in rolls, and fleece wool, probably from our ranch. I held my stare there, wondering how a beaver could end up a hat. Then I noticed the men.

163

A young, jittery man leaned against a wood stand topped with a counter. He had little bulb ears, fairy-boot feet, thin lips, yet his words shrilled large as he tapped the edge of the counter. "Doesn't matter," he said. "They can't own the county or Fort Stanton or Santa Fe like we do. Catron's put a lean on the legislature to move J. B. Wilson out and put ours into the strong-fist office. Soon, his time's coming. Yes sir, Alex McSween done tied his noose. The slip-knot's wrapped, so the more he pulls, the tighter it gets."

Murphy nodded.

"He's suffering for air, and it ain't to be had." The mini-man went on. "Absconded with Emil's estate money, our partner's money, our money. We got him there, and McSween, with all the Chisums in New Mexico, is not going to clear himself on that score." He quickened his voice and shuffled his pint-sized boots.

Señor Murphy's seating gave the mister man a throne as he looked down at his slight partner.

I was trying to figure out what *absconded* meant.

Apá limped away from the main desk. We followed as the men's conversation yapped on behind us. This section held boxes of

164

horse shoes, nails, spurs, animal traps, and tin dishes. My father picked up a nail as if he were measuring its size. Garita started to pick up a flat tin until I stopped her.

The little hustler went on. "And Tunstall, the other one, well, that English royal blue blood just got on the wrong side. Thinks his easy Brit money can buy him an empire here. He doesn't know how we do it out West. His new store don't stand a chance."

"Yeah, but Tunstall's not a gun-gutless McSween." Señor Murphy gathered papers and put them in a pile on the corner of his station. "You know that, Jimmy, don't you?"

The one called Jimmy laughed like a screeching mouse in a fry pan. He earthquaked the window glass and made Garita put her hands over her ears.

Apá stayed by the metal holdings. Garita and I moved away from the shrill to a corner with hanging jerky, red chili *ristras,* and bundles of dried corn.

"No sheeps' ears," Garita whispered.

"Never mind. Soon enough he'll figure out how to sell them to some poor fool." I whispered it more to myself than Garita.

My sister tried to pull my hand off, but I tightened my grip and followed Apá closer to the men. Apá coughed. Took a knife from his pocket and began scraping the skin off a large callous on his palm. The men went on talking. My father scraped.

On a high desk, there sat a large jar of floating eggs, another of pickled cucumbers, and one of asparagus with red chilis. *El* Mister Señor Sir Murphy rested himself on a long-legged chair and leaned over his working papers on that same desk. The mix of rich aromas possessed me and made me wish I had three noses. Then a smell of vinegar that hung over the mister man came my way and made me wish I had no nose at all.

"Yeah, well, the Englishman is getting himself guns and crazy-gutted men," Jimmy Dolan, the dink of a man, said. "Dick Brewer is standing pat with McSween. And that wild-eyed William Kid never stops ass-sessing. He's joined up. With him comes Frank and George, the Coe cousins, Mc-Closkey, and Widenmann. They're half-cocked on a spring-loaded trigger and mean, they're mean-spirited, all of them."

I heard the word, *Kid,* and wondered how another person had come to town with the same name as Chivato. Must be someone else's last name, too.

"Good morning, Mister, Señor Murphy Sir," my apá trembled in a different voice from what we knew at home. He coughed again, put his knife away, took off his hat, and showed a blanched strip of forehead. He combed his hair back.

Señor Sir Murphy *al fin* noticed him. "Listen, Jimmy, keep me abreast. See you back at our place later."

His half-sized friend took short, fast steps to the door — so loud, if I hadn't seen him, I would have thought he was as gigantic as Ramon.

"Good day back to you, Salamon. I see you have some company. These yours?" His eyes squinted on Garita. The look told me he might be remembering her high-tree act. Today, her hair was braided, not ponytailed, and she stood held down by me. He smiled long and hard at her.

"*Sí*, yes, these are my girls," my father said in a low voice. "They bring help for me here today. Got my load outside and the lambs for your pay."

Apá's shoulders sunk. He blew air whizzes in a low, feeble whistle, something he would yell at Yginio for doing. A gentle sweeping caught my attention, and I noticed Tehde in one of the holding rows, pushing a broom slowly. She didn't look up.

Garita pointed and smiled. *"La India amiga,"* she whispered.

"Okay, that's five on the hoof you owe me.

I'll check the ledger to see if you have any outstandings, and we'll square up. What else you got?" He scratched a dark mole on the side of his head, below his ear.

"Yes, remember I delivered four fleece *bultos,* extra, last month." Apá said.

"That should be in my ledger." He opened a hard-covered book with green squares across and down the page. It was filled with figures and writing.

"*Ya,* okay, I got some four jars of green beans, to trade for coffee and flour and maybe pinto beans. Oh yes, got eggs, too, almost two dozen to give in the barter. Our goat cheese fell into the dirt, too bad to serve anyone." My father folded his knife and put it in his pocket.

"Stop sweeping here. Get on that back row where the dust is piled up." He tapped his pencil and turned back to us. "My Lord, you'd think these Indians would see dirt. They live in it, so I guess they don't have an inkling." Murphy straightened his sitting bones back onto the high chair, a king on his mercantile throne. "Well, let's get the trading items."

Tehde turned and went the other way.

Señor Mister and Apá went outside, and we went toward Tehde, who worked the back of the store beside the barrels.

"Keep tongue." The Mescalera rested her head on her hands, which clung to the broom handle. "Know about chicken-pluck lady? This one, he want quiet. I not talk."

"*Sí pues,* Tehde, okay. Don't make a show for nothing." I pulled Garita with me back to the counter to wait for Apá. Many minutes passed.

"No, that's not what I bargained for, Salamon, I said five yearlings." Señor Murphy spoke with power.

"*Sí,* I know, Señor, but this month has been very bad for me, losing too many sheep. I have the ears to prove it." My apá twisted his lips into a weak smile.

"Heard you. That's what you said before, and I can see the dried evidence, but I have my expenses, too. Have upkeeps, rent, and employees to pay. Like this here Indian, she claims eighty cents a week and out of my heart's kindness, I send her home with items close to spoilage. Can't flex on my agreement with you, no sir." He waved a couple of gnats from his greasy face and a flush of red beneath his cheeks came into view.

Apá followed behind him with our box of eggs. "Ambrosia, go for the green beans and bring them."

I figured Apá didn't want us to hear him

quarrel. As we walked out, another couple of men walked in, shuffling their noisy spurs. I grabbed four jars of green beans, and Garita took the other three. When we stepped back into the mercantile, we heard Apá's timid voice.

"I have a hard time, too, Señor Murphy Sir. With fewer sheep eating, your fields don't get grazed as much."

"How does your loss affect me, Sal? I rented you the pasture, and your pay is five sheep a month, not four. It's not my plan to change our deal because of your bad luck. If I did that, I'd not make a cent. My take doesn't change — even if you lose half the flock. A deal's a deal." His sharp-edged voice broke the ice air around him.

"Sí, Señor, but please, what about the five sheep, dead gone with nothing coming back to me?" Apá's words muffled out as if he had dirt in his mouth. "What about them lost sheep?"

"What about them?" Señor Murphy tapped a pencil with his fat fingers, then spread an open palm on the countertop. His riches surrounded him. So little for him to give a few *pesitos* and so much for my apá to give more sheep — my father begged for a thimble of water from Mister Señor Murphy's cascading waterfall.

170

"*Por favor,* Señor Murphy Sir, since I got less animals, I got less to shear for money, less to sell to others, less to buy goods at your store. You, Señor, have less pasture grazed. When one animal falls, it takes *mucho* other things. It's a big . . . big *perdida. Perdida*-lost, yes, you see what I'm saying, don't you? The loss, I mean, it gets bigger and bigger, please, Señor Sir. What do I get? Twenty-five cents for each one sheep meat I bring for you, count that with my rent pay I owe you, too. It don't give me enough to feed my other animals or my family."

When Garita and I moved to the counter with the green beans, I could see the tips of my apá's fingers quiver.

Señor Murphy's hands were as solid as rocks. "It's hard times on you and hard times for me. See here, I wish I could help you, *amigo.* It's an economic fall, one that leads to another, just like you say. But because you have less sheep, you have less fleece, which is again your problem. I offer you what price I offer other sheep ranchers. Apart from my five animals you owe me for pasturing, I pay twenty-five cents for on-hoof sheep and fifteen cents for bundled fleeces. That's it. I can't give more. And see here, I'm the only one buying them from you."

Garita and I stood away, quiet. The fullness of this place, the power of riches, closed in on me and appeared to have the same heaviness on my sister. We stepped closer to the counter, holding the jars. I stood lock-jawed even though I wanted to jump in and defend Apá. Yginio was right. I was crazy for thinking I could talk to *el* mister man Murphy about such things. I looked for Tehde. She held her face down, sweeping and limping behind the broom as if it were moving itself.

"No, Señor Sir Murphy, Tunstall is offering thirty cents for each fleece *bulto*. I just want to give you a chance since we have been doing business many years. Please, you just think, *por favor.*"

We set our preserves on the counter, and I pulled Garita away toward the door but not in time to avoid hearing *el* Señor Sir's next words.

"I have thought about it, Salamon Salazar, and I will not pay a penny more. Got my own problems, just lost ten thousand dollars of an estate I had coming. It's gone with the cheat lawyer I got rid of. Never mind, you can't reckon the value of it. If John Tunstall gives you that price, take your fleeces there, but you will not rotate your sheep in and out of my pastures, *sabes*?

And the door here will be closed to you. Although you might consider a back-fill for the money you lost on those ewes. That gal of yours, the one who . . . who was in the tree."

When he said *tree,* I stopped and let Garita go out the door ahead of me.

Praise *Diosito.* My apá spoke in a voice with more thunder here.

"In a tree? I don't know who you are talking about, which tree?" With his new voice, Apá straightened his hat and folded his arms.

"Well, one of yours who talks little. Whose care is taken up by that other one of yours in the Salazar family."

"Margarita? You mean Garita? And Ambrosia? Yes, they are these daughters. But she was never in no tree. What she got to do here?" my apá asked.

"Never mind about the dad-gum tree. What I'm getting at is you letting her tend to my lodge, cleaning and maybe some cooking. She could help this Mescalera I got now."

The men lowered their voices, but I walked back between the rows of merchandise goods and leaned in for their whispers. Tehde looked at me and shook her head in a way both of us understood.

"That would add some income to your account. Not a lot, but enough to help your bad times."

Mister man's skin, wet with oil, bounced off light. "Think about it. One less mouth you'd have to feed every day and a little more money for food and such. If she does a good day's work, I can add a few items to her take-home on Friday. Could be a good move on your part."

I fisted my hands and could have found my voice, but Garita was starting to walk toward the Jewel Parlor. I ran out to catch her.

My father's answer, garbled and low, took refuge away from my ears.

CHAPTER TEN

Early February could bring late snow or rain. Today, both fell. Bruised clouds shrunk the valley and covered our little rancho like a widow's black *mantilla*. Light snow dusted us last night and now an ice rain fell. Insects and animals disappeared in sheltered hiding. When I walked out the door, I smelled soggy animal hides, and the chickens were nowhere to be seen. Budding leaf swells, draped with heavy wetness, shivered on the branches. Sierra Blanca's western peaks had disappeared in the horizon, and I wondered about the roof over Yginio and Apá as they ran the west sheep camp.

The men left yesterday when the sun promised good weather, and they would not be back until later today. With them gone, cooking was not a demand, but regular labors still fell on us. A better truth, on me, for I did them. Shielding my face from angry rain, I sloshed mud as it sucked my feet down. Garita slept while I planned puddle-jump steps to the coop. When I opened the door, I saw hens, hovered in their nesting boxes like old ladies on a church bench.

"*Pio, pio, pollos,* smarter than Pancho Gallo, eh? He's roosting on the window sill, wet as a hen." I smiled at the thought. "He doesn't know enough to get out of a storm. You girls take your vittles dry in here today."

I dropped wheat seeds and dried cobs, but the chickens didn't take to it. Eggs will come soon enough later. Through my drenched eye and a wet curtain of rain, I saw a man and horse. Steam lifted and circled off the horse's sweaty rump as the animal nodded, ruffling a loud *uhuh huh huh.* The man opened our barn door and pulled the paint mustang in. I jumped back into the coop and peeked out. Apache? Beely's beautiful mustang?

After many moments, I forced my feet toward the barn and cracked open the door. Wet leather and moist alfalfa drifted a sweet earthy scent toward me. The horse turned its blazed face and rolled its large dark eyes. Half of one eye, circled in black, gave Apache what looked like a wink. Beely stood shaking his horse blanket where he had made his bed on his last spell with us.

"*Hola,* Beely, *milagro,* we have not seen you in many days." Ice rain beat the barn roof, heavy and rushed. I felt small against thunderous power. Its pounding closed us into a hidden privacy like huddled rabbits inside a safe burrow.

"Well if it ain't the one and only prettiest *señorita* of this here Hondo Valley come making sun on this miserable day. Mighty good hello, *muy buenos días,* Ambrosia, happy to hear you're still speaking to me. See you ain't got your back up anymore. Am I right?"

"Why? Why not speak to you?"

"From what I remember it was a case about a Tigressa, a little furry cat." His nose glistened from its rain wash.

"Yes, Garita looked and looked for miles around. She called for Tigressa until her voice went hoarse. She cried many, many nights. That cat was part of her. *Al fin,* I had to tell her it must be gone to the heavens with Mamá. These days she knows more about these kinds of leavings."

"That's one of the reasons I'm here, Ambrosia. I can call you Ambrosia now, can't I?"

"*Sí,* okay, Beely."

"Want to make it good for sweet Margarita. Take a look in my saddlebag."

I shook the wet off my clothes, pulled my soaked *chal* around me, and walked to the bag slung on a nail. The wind blew through the side boards, and the rain beat faster, harder drops as if *El Cucuy* was shaking the universe. From out of the saddlebag, two little eyes, green like silver peas, stared up at me.

"It's a piebald. Black and white markings that give it a coon cat pattern. Right nice mouser. As sweet a looker as the other one. Well, maybe not that sweet, but pretty sweet, ain't it? Never seen one with bandit circles around the eyes like that."

"Where did you find such a creature?" I asked.

"My boss, John Tunstall, had a pack of new ones in his barn. I snatched what I thought had the most extreme markings, one different, to suit Garita. It's a little she-devil when she's not held up in a horse bag. You'll see. Think she'll like it? As Garita says, *gusto* — like it."

Here stood this very strange man, half *Hispano,* with a tender side. One who uses the same pistol to stop a laugh, kill a kitten, or halt the violation of a weak woman. Lucky for me the storm muffled my heartbeats, for they were banging harder than the water drops. "Garita, she will be happy. She likes anything with a shell or fur or wings."

He shuffled his feet in that quick nervous way. "How about you? Will this little kitten take away my bad score?" A flicker in his eyes like a waxed thread through a flaming needle drew me in, melted me.

Wind, rain, and hail drowned his words. I took steps closer to hear him and met lingering eyes. He was a *desperado,* no matter how sparkly his face, how wide his smile, or how well he spoke my language. *Madre mía, Mamá,* although you are gone, you know I'm smothered in days of the same. And here is Beely — air for a choked woman. A wanting in me, like sap from bark, seeped into my heart's desire.

"Score? Away? What do you mean?" I said.

A drip fell onto his hat, curved up around the brim, and flowed off the side, wetting his left shoulder. He moved away from the leak toward me.

"Never mind, score. I was hoping both you women, how do you say it? *¿Me perdónan?* You know, pardon, ease off your soreness. Rein in that mad sentiment. You against me." He moved his rough finger into a *no* movement, pointed at himself, and then at me. "Come on, Ambrosia. I seen you last time I was here. I could tell. *Madisimo* at me."

Madisimo, a crossbred word like Beely, something Garita would invent — a mixed language for a mixed man. The edges of my mouth changed from one who suffers to one given a gift. "Mad, no, I'm not *madisimo* like you say, Señor Beely. Garita does not know you shot her Tigressa." I balanced one arm on the other and rested my chin into the palm of my hand, shielding my smile. "I'm afraid, you know, scared." My single black braid fell to one side over my breast like a plaited horse tail over the largeness of its side rump.

"What? Frightened of the wind? The ice rain? Scared of me? Not me. Lordy not me."

Another person might hide a front overlapped tooth, but Beely flashed it like a winning card, so much so, that's what it became, an ace of hearts that took the match over a king or a jack. He stood with the tips of his fingers in his front pockets, staring. Apache's large, black horse eyes turned to his master, and the animal seemed to shoot him a wink.

"Not rain — guns, Señor Beely, I never like gunning," I said.

"Not a señor to you, Ambrosia, it's Beely, I mean Bill . . . Billy."

I took a closer step, as if hearing made for better understanding. "Apá, my brother, or

Ramon, they have no guns always strapped on them. If they go hunting, then they have a rifle, but it is rested away on the wall in its keep — not on their bodies. Your irons give me a big scare. Yes, I'm afraid of what they do, even to poor things, horses, kittens, children, or women who have done nothing to no one, have no sins, *inocentes.* Salazar rifles are used to hunt food, not to settle anger or make one man pay the price of a joke, a smile, his color, a lost gamble or drunken doings. You use bullets instead of words or fists, which bring blood but not the end of a life."

"What do you live for, Ambrosia?"

"Live, what do you mean? I do live for many things, Garita and Apá. Most for God."

"No, I mean, that what brings you happiness? An inside jubilation that helps you sleep at night and wakes you up in the morning. *¿Sabes?*"

"I never think of such things." My forefinger stroked a heart shape movement on the pad of my thumb in repeat madness as if my hand prayed a rosary without beads.

"I can see why you might feel thataway about guns, given you never had to face a biggity bully, holding you down for a wimp joke or a mean, fire-watered lunkhead nailing your back to the wall. Those kind deserve a stop with no sorrow. On the other matter, a deer or hog killing never calls for anyone to knit an animal shroud, no funeral there. And the meat is needed for you to survive, sure enough. Believe me, I know that kind of need but ask that you see my point. This is how I see this here iron strapped to my leg. It keeps me happy with myself, safe to sleep at night, and wakes me in the morning — a much needed item to keep living."

His boot spurs rang a dull clink above the storm. "In this world, where some's got them and not all the someones are good ones, I need mine. I depend on it like a necessity, a life preserver. And if I have one in my keep, it's going to fire faster and send bullets straighter than the rest. *¿Sabes?* Without an iron, as I see it, me or any man is nothing more than a powerless lamb. No good shaking the good book or a twig stick at an angry bear. And, rightly more so, Ambrosia, that mad bear won't hesitate if it sees you down on your knees praying." These words were loud and nervous, but he ended with low soothing Spanish. *"Es una necesidad."* And added a smile no gun-fighter should ever possess. "Life happiness — my gun."

I stood without words. My dress dried away from me, and I could feel my face relax.

" 'Sides, I have a job now, Ambrosia. A good paying one, with a good man. John Tunstall, the Englishman, you know of him, right?"

"Yes, I know of *el* Señor Tunstall." I knew of him too well.

"Bit of an ill *ignorante* to the ways of the West, but a handsome Belvidere all the same and a big ranch augur to boot. *Chihuahua,* he's the finest I've ever crossed. He's going to change Lincoln County in a good way. Yes sir, right and steady. You'll see. Speaks to me a heap better than any I've ever met. My name means something to him and even though you hate the guns, to John Tunstall, that's what he respects most about my talents." The ice rain softened to something like the rattling of dry leaves.

"But here's what I'm thinking, Ambrosia. It will take some time, but I aim to work hard and lay a little money aside to get some territory here. Raise some cattle, maybe I won't need to be heeled with this canister none, anymore. If others can realize a peaceful life, why can't I?"

He took off his hat and set it aside. His

face, washed fresh, looked whiter. He took off his leg iron, looking at me as if he understood my reason for no guns. Shuffling his boots, he hung his *pistola* on a nearby nail. Still a bit soaked, his shirt hugged his lean chest and solid arms.

The kitten mewled, a soft patient sound. Apache, his paint horse, moved its head up and down in a *ruh haha* answer. The mustang seemed to sense the little squeaker's need for attention. Beely picked the soft bundle from the saddlebag and came so close our arms touched. Its nose poked down into Beely's arm, leaving two ear points. After a moment of down-headedness, it lifted its bright eyes.

How it must feel in Beely's hold? A floating *ah* grew inside me, and I realized this was the closest I had ever been to Beely with no one around. So close I could see thin hairs on his chin and the outline of his lips. The nearness caused a need in me to back up, but my feet rooted firm. The smell of campfire smoke, sweat, damp leather, and pine — what a man who rides the wilderness has about him, claimed Beely. Body heat from his presence surrounded me, warmed me. His up-twist smile showed he knew the unbridled fit he arose in me. He moved yet closer and cradled the kitten up to my rapidly pulsing bosom.

"Are you going to name it Tigressa like the other one? Nah, maybe better to have its own calling. A new start so the circumstances of the other don't come to mind. How about *Vida* or Blossom or Spring or something that means life's new start?"

I felt clouds lift me. I couldn't do more than nod my head. A small drop of either rain or body dew trickled down my back. I forced a smile from strained, stiffened lips.

They soon softened with the press of Beely's mouth against them, rushed and clumsy at first. Before I knew what he was doing, or better said, because I knew what he was doing, I stood unable to move. In a frozen state, like in a dream when something must be done but nothing but panic fills the paralyzed body, I didn't know what to do. But in this dream, I did; I yielded. No will of mine resisted him. *Diosito,* have mercy. I sank; I gave into his body embrace — soared like a leaf against a fierce wind. I kissed him back and pressed against him. He dropped the kitten and wrapped his arms around me with the force of a man in need. His mouth moved in surprising open and closed thrusts. Lightly his tongue flicked against my lips between hard kisses. Then urgent, lightning hands snaked under my skirt.

My mind shifted to what was happening outside and rushing thoughts inside. "Ambrosia," he whispered. His palm against my thigh came with a deep pleasure moan. My mamá's words of caution woke me. *A woman's body, Ambrosia, is sacred, given only to her husband. Virgin de Guadalupe be your witness.* I pushed him away and ran out the barn to get Garita.

In my run out of the barn, a force between happy and terror mixed inside me. Angels and demons fought. I didn't want Beely's kiss to wash off, yet staying with him, pressing our bodies together, was a dance with the devil — a devil I desired. Cold raindrops fell on my face, but I didn't feel them apart from my tears. Fire blazed so hot inside me, rain steamed off my skin.

Beely's caress let loose hidden want. He opened a hunger, and his touch, onto my virgin skin with a thousand yearnings for him, starved for something to live for. A vile — a naked nastiness, a dirty, cruel torment, it was. Temptation tested my strength, bucked against a desire for purity. I failed and craved his flesh like forbidden water, poisoned food, and wicked air. I wanted more of what was outlawed. Lord guide me; only you can do it. I can't.

As I made steps to the housedoor, strange

clods lifted in an unusual drift. Clumps, big and little ones, bounced in the water. When I stepped on a mushy one, a foul reek came up out of what I thought was mud. Top rocks and the boards I had placed months ago were floating over the cesspool. Heavy rain filled it and drifted *mierda* out. Stench invaded our yard and mixed with the manure of our corral animals.

My shoes, deep in the filthy, putrid water, soaked up the stink and coated me. This is my life — sunk in shit. I jumped onto the door step and stomped my feet in the watery mess. I shook myself away from my memory of the kiss in the barn, to now — to where I was, who I was, and my responsibilities. I wiped my face with my skirt and went in.

"Garita, come to the barn. Something for you." I hid my distress and wiped foulness off my shoes. I had just sailed a dreamy universe and landed back in hell.

"*Ojo* red." She pointed to her eye and then to mine.

I shook my head. "*Nada*, it's nothing."

"No-no," she said, "here, *seca* — dry." She pointed to herself and her chair.

I wanted her to do just that, stay here and give me another few minutes alone with Beely. I thought about turning, rushing back to the barn — a chance that might never come again.

"Listen, *Mija,* you want to see something good, don't you? A new animal."

"*Lluvia* — rain, no." Garita was spinning fleece into string yarn, something that calmed her when she couldn't go outside. She was good at it, much better than I could do. The wheel spun whispers.

"Mister Beely — he's here." I sat next to her and brought the motion of the spinning wheel to a stop.

"Beely, *camisa* — shirt," she said, "no big shoot?"

"Yes, that one." I took her hand and pulled her up.

She dropped the wool thread and together we jumped the brown, bumpy balls of digested, past meals to the large wood door. When we opened it, Ramon and Yginio stood beside Beely as he held the squirming kitten. Green crystal kitten eyes with long black slivers shot back at Garita and me from Chivato's strong arms.

"Señor Beely," my little sister said, *"gatita — kitten."*

Minutes ago this audience would have found Beely wrapped around me. Thank our Lord *Diosito,* I forced a halt to our barn romp — the only one good thing about our stop.

Ramon banged his voice out above the rain. "What you see, Garita, is a cowboy who thinks we need more cats around here. There's so many already we can't count them. But, this one here . . ." he pointed at Beely, "thinks we need more." Ramon grabbed his hat, shook the rain off, and put it back again. He rubbed water off his wet white shirt where dark nipples showed through.

Beely stared at Ramon but there was no anger there — yet. He smiled and nodded. All of us knew Beely could change as fast as a wildfire on a dry prairie. Ramon had put himself into a storm where nobody knew where the next spark might catch. I wanted them to know Beely had brought the kitten for Garita and wanted Ramon to keep quiet. Wanted to say Beely was doing something good, but I held back.

Beely looked at Garita. "This isn't just any little creep mouse. Look, Garita, it has coon markings. See black with white rings around the eyes. I think it's half coon. Take a good gander. Its ears have white edges, and the tail has little white rings. Just barely but you can see them."

She stood next to Beely, holding her hands

off the kitten. I knew she wanted to grab it, and I was glad she knew better.

"Ain't it the dangest? Sorry my cussing." He looked at me. "If its eyes were black 'stead of green, I'd swear its pappy was a night coon." Beely stroked its head and grabbed its fluffy neck and held its smallness in midair.

"I *mira* — look-see, yes?" she asked.

Garita took it from Beely and stroked it. The kitten sunk its head under Garita's arm. "*Gracias,* Señor Beely."

"You, darling, are right welcomed. Both of you, real special little things. See here. This coon marking means it has a pure soul, like you. A Margarita daisy of a fine creature. Can't get much better." His eyes drove into me, hard as a nail into an oak tree.

"Don't tell me, Señorito Bonney, you rode all the way out here to bring this . . . this what you say, very fine, raccoon cat for Garita. She has so many *gatos* around here there's no food for all of them." Ramon waved his large hairy finger in a *no motion.*

"Hey, this cat will catch mice for its keep. Anyway, it's not a wasted trip, Ramon." Yginio took two steps toward his *primo.* "Billy has friends here, and Apá said he could visit any time." With an alfalfa blade in his mouth, he nodded toward Beely. "Hey *hombre,* how you liking your new job with big boss, Tunstall?"

"Yup, yup, huckleberry above a persimmon, I'd say right up and above snuff — can't say I've had better than this one. And fell into it like it was supposed to happen. *No hay ningun mal que por bien no venga.* That's the saying, ain't it? A bad thing can turn good real fast. Like what's happened to me. Makes me happy enough to ignore someone's call of a kettle black for tending to a young lady." He glared at Ramon, smiled, leaned over to Garita, and stroked the kitten's head. "One who lost her deaf cat, a time or two ago."

I stood by the door and willed Beely's attention away from me, but he roamed here. And his smile made the others look.

Ramon eyed me, coughed, turned his head, and scratched the back of his neck — the thing he did when he didn't know what to say. Then he spit a yellow tobacco chew, which landed on his boot. It glowed on the polished leather. The ruin would be blamed on Beely, I was sure. Ramon coughed again. "You've done your good deed here, Señorito. Shouldn't you hurry yourself back to your new work? You wouldn't want to keep John Tunstall from having what he wants you to do."

I tried to bring my lungs air. "Come, Garita, bring your kitten." I spoke in half-breaths. "The rain isn't so bad now. We can walk back to the house." I didn't want to watch what was going to fume up here. And maybe my leaving would take an audience away from two men — one a toro bull and the other a fox — and might help them go their separate ways.

"Billy, stay for lunch. We have food enough," Yginio said.

I could hear the conversation at my back. Heard Beely's last words.

"Right nice, Yginio, *gracias* but take a rain check on it. I see, the rain's spilled its full barrel now. Hung the drench off myself and delivered this offering to Garita. Cash in on that offer some dry day real soon. Rest assured I'll be back."

I watched Beely double-slap his reins on Apache out onto the muddy, washed-out road toward Tunstall's Feliz Ranch. Garita built a bed for her kitty, named Mapache, raccoon in Spanish. The name began with what sounded like *mal,* which meant bad or sickness, but this little thing, I was certain, was good, only good.

CHAPTER ELEVEN

Wind blew most every day in February of 1878. Those twenty-eight days stretched into what seemed an endless monthly existence. A tick, measured by a metal arm on an old face clock sitting on a shelf, beat time eternal. I tended to its winding, and in February of 1878, I cranked it morning and midday. Didn't help. Didn't rush time along. Results of this thing called time could be seen on Apá's wrinkled face, but otherwise its invisible force had no color, taste, or weight. All I could feel was a burden of nothingness. And since Beely's soft lips had pressed against mine, had teased and invited me to him, passage of time ticked me a new meaning. My mind wanted to say two weeks ago it happened, but my heart said six. And sometimes it felt like yesterday we had rubbed against one another. I willed the wretched timekeeper to tick counter movements. That is to say, go backward to that day in the barn and stop, so I could live the rest of my life in those few moments, over and over. But, time had its own will and moved painfully forward. The sun came up and went down, tick, tick, tick. Memory of Beely's wet, musk scent, his friendly smile, and loving charm lingered without promise of another embrace. Time was no friend of mine.

February's sun seeped in and stirred thoughts of his hand on my upper leg, arousing unclaimed urges. Instead of relief for an ended day, night brought regret another day was coming. Mornings dimmed in dreariness as if sunbeams broke through layers of thick ice, as if the moon had homesteaded the sky, tick tick. I read and reread Job's story. He lost his children, his woman, money, and shelter, yet his faith in *Diosito* held strong. In his suffering, he found reward. I wore Mamá's rosary beads thin with endless Hail Marys and Our Fathers. When her rosary wasn't in my hand, I prayed on empty fingers.

Beely's question, "What do you live for?" haunted me. Did I have a what, a who, a why to live for? I was Job. I wanted to believe if I did my duties, always with a giving heart, I would someday find happiness. God tested the faithless, the weak, like me.

Would He call Beely a sinner, someone who lived for each day, lent himself a happy life, looked to save the weak, or made his own justice without *shoulds*? I raked animal manure, yanked milk from cow udders, pulled feathers from dead birds, fleeced sheep, grew and cooked food. I lived for work. I survived but lived for nothing. Then there was Ramon. The last time we laughed together seemed in another life. He was a good, solid man, but that path seemed like a worn trail, too much like my mother's life.

On the eighteenth of that February, Garita carried in six black crows she had knocked down. She set them on the table, settled onto the table bench, and smiled. I knew she was good with her rocks and sling, but I said nothing. My misery swallowed any kindness for others. Together, with wild spinach, the crows would make a stew. I clamped their spindly legs, set their limp bodies down, and cut each neck, one by one, to get their dead eyes off me.

Lunchtime brought Apá. He sat, pulled a paper, and filled it with loose bits of his precious tobacco. This was one little luxury he gave himself. He knew I did not like it, so he hid his thin roll underneath the table, but the smoke, unharnessed, still drifted up around me.

I waved a table rag over my work area to clear the *cigarillo* smell from my cooking pots.

My father snuffed what remained of his smoke and hid it in his shirt pocket.

Soon after, Yginio came in, slammed the door, and sat across from my father. He straightened up and without warning banged his fist onto the table.

We jumped.

"Jimmy Dolan and Sheriff Brady's gang killed John Tunstall — for no reason — crazy sons-of-bitches. Everyone in Lincoln is talking about it." Yginio made his hand into a pistol and jerked it like he took a shot at Garita. "*Así, cabrones,* boom boom."

I expected her to scold Yginio for cussing, but instead, she frowned and moved to the other side of the table.

"Billy says they're making a group of those who worked for Tunstall, and they're going to give Jimmy Dolan and Sheriff Brady some of the same. Be a posse of . . . of . . . how you say it, Ambrosia? Those who take care of weak ones, you know."

The sound of Beely's name stopped me from cutting the last bird leg. "Vigilantes," I said as I chopped the joint and dropped the bird into boiling water with the others.

Apá nodded like someone at a funeral who

196

wants to keep his insides from showing.

"Yes, that's it, vigilantes, but this here group is going to call themselves Regulators. See, the name means they're going to enforce or regulate law because, Billy says, Lincoln County's so-called defenders don't do it." Yginio took the claw of one of the bird legs to clean the dirt from under his fingernails. The crow legs sprawled in front of him like a pile of dried twigs.

Garita took two of them and walked their claws across the table as if they were still alive.

"Quit that, both of you. Garita, you know better," I said.

No sound but the rhythmic tap of my rolling pin against the table filled the room.

"Lord, bless our souls," broke the silence. I wrapped my dough-caked hands around my quivering stomach and realized the utterance had come from me. Tunstall — Sinforosa's lover, the good man from Britannica, a new future for all of us, killed. Sinfo left us for him and now she has lost twice over, but I'll be an old mule skinner before I go back there and ask her to come home again. I motioned the sign of the cross, spooned the hot birds from the boiling water, plucked their feathers, and began to pull small bits of meat from their naked bones.

"*Cuidado, Mijo,* careful," Apá said. "This Chivato Kid Beely and them others you speak of, they don't care for no one. They shoot, and you could be caught in between. We know Señor Murphy *ya* has had his way in this valley for years, and no one's going to make him change. His partner, Jimmy Dolan, is small, but he's mean, and they have the best of the *brutos.* Stay away from this fight. Ain't no winners."

"How did they do it?" I asked.

Yginio looked surprised I was even listening. "There were four of them together with Señor Tunstall. That guy named Widenmann, Dick Brewer, a rider named Middleton, and Billy. Right there, *tu sabes,* just ten miles this side of Lincoln where the trail goes down to the Río Ruidoso and then comes back up."

"I know that place," Apá said.

"They split up when Widenmann and Brewer went after a covey of turkeys. Middleton and Billy stayed back and saw the house posse going straight for Tunstall. The *Inglés* was by himself. Billy took cover. Middleton tried to get Tunstall to go with them, but he stood his ground. Señor Tunstall knew he had done no wrong. So,

Middleton joined Billy behind a hill. Jimmy Dolan's gang with known slingers and Sheriff Brady caught up to Tunstall. The *Inglés* was going to talk reason with them." Yginio wiped the sweat from his brow and upper lip.

"After they shot him, they killed his horse. They stole Tunstall's livestock, pigs, and everything from his Río Feliz Ranch. Said his goods were something called a court attachment, whatever that means, for the lawyer, McSween's debt. The *Inglés* had nothing to do with McSween's business. It ain't over. Billy says the house men are going to meet their maker." My brother shook his head hard and low, like a brahma bull ready to charge.

"Válgame, Dios," I said, *"hombres locos."*

"*Malo* — bad," Garita followed my disgust with her own croak, "*mucho muy malo* — bad."

Apá put his finger to his lips to silence us. "Yginio, *Mijo,* this is not our fight. Don't be a fool. *Sí,* we all liked *el* Señor Tunstall. He, from what I saw, treated people good without high . . . high almightiness."

I stood silent, hoping Beely hadn't gone badger crazy. He knew justice, and no risky danger stopped his notion of right. Tunstall opened a door for him and earned Beely's loyal friendship. Maybe because of his small size, maybe a bully *bruto* once wrestled him down, maybe his mamá taught him his idea of right. Who knows where he got it? Like he had said the day we were alone, he knew what he lived for and who he lived for. Standing by, while others beat an underdog, would never happen while the Kid was around. I knew that.

Yginio beat a fork against the table and tapped his foot in nervous jitters. The hard surfaces took the whipping for what he felt inside. "Yeah, Billy said Señor Tunstall was the only man who gave him a chance." My brother looked as miserable as me.

"Yginio, *ya,* we sorry, but mind me, we don't need to get into nobody's fight. We have our own troubles enough with Señor Murphy," Apá said. "He keeps high prices for less pastureland. No matter how many animals we lose, he won't give more for my stock. Now he wants the employ of more of us." Apá looked at Garita.

"*Christo* saves us, Apá." Garita never without an answer.

"You right, *Mijita.* The Lord is our Savior, but now set the *papitas* on the table," I said.

I fried the little pieces of bird meat with wild spinach and the white onions I had canned last fall. The smell filled the room, and Garita put the tin plates on the table.

"This ain't new, Apá, Señor Murphy's never been fair with you or anybody. And he will always take enough to keep us poor and begging," Yginio said. "That won't change. Don't you want to see something different in Lincoln? And who is it? Who does he want from this family? He already has —"

The door banged as Ramon closed it behind him. "*Buenos días,* smells like I got here in time." His large eyes roamed the room and landed on me.

"Come in, Ramon, yes, we're here talking of poor, dead Señor Tunstall," Apá said.

"Very sad; he was a good man." Ramon spread his bigness into our small kitchen. The fireplace and stove heat warmed us. He leaned back into his chair and forced others to shrink their spaces. "*Pobre Inglés,* Jimmy Dolan and his gang shot him up bad. His face tore against the brush when they carried him horseback to Lincoln. What I saw go by was a blood ball of meat, like vultures had pecked him into red rags." He played with the bird legs until I picked them up and threw them into the pig slop bucket.

Ramon went on. "They brought what was left of him to Señor McSween's house, laid him on the table, and cleaned him up, best

201

as they could. I stayed outside with others, but I could hear the little *gringito* Kid, that one who was here the other day. He stomped the floor and raised a noisy ruckus."

I dropped the tin cups I was carrying to the table. Ramon jerked a look at me and went on.

" 'Yeah,' the *gringito* said, 'Let's get 'em. I swear on this day we'll make their wives widows. They gonna pay.' Or something like that. He's small, but his voice cracked loud like he had lost his own mother. I thought he might cry, but no, he just yelled and yelled. He got the others stirred up, and they started their cussing, too."

Garita said, "Mamá gone — *fué.*" She looked at me, shrugged her shoulders, and nodded her head in long movements. I nodded back.

Ramon ignored her. "Then the little Chivato drew his six-shooter. *Carajo,* he opened his cartridge and whirled it. All fired up, he pointed his *pistola* toward Sheriff Brady's office. Looked like he could start shooting anybody, anyhow, right then. You know the sheriff was with the killing pack, eh?"

We all nodded.

"The Chivato Kid was locked up for having a JT horse, you know, the *Inglés'* brand.

Tunstall paid Billy a jail visit about his stolen horse, then turned around and gave him a job," Yginio said.

"Shoot," Garita said. "Big Beely shoot." I walked behind, put my hand on her shoulder, and pressed her into silence.

"Yeah, I know. Billy told everyone," Ramon said. "Oh *sí,* the Chivato claimed some Mescaleros traded the horse for brew. In the son-of-a-gun's words, 'Those skins put me in dutch with the true owner.' " Ramon nodded his version of his truth like it was better than ours. "*Tu sabes,* he always blames someone else."

"Ramon, you don't know. Maybe the Indians did steal the horse, not him." I lifted my hand off Garita and started rolling again.

Garita moved beyond my reach, then wiped her shoulder where my hand touched her.

Apá took the half-burned cigarette, stored in his front shirt pocket, and relit it. The tip smoked, then glowed bright red.

"That's right, Ramon," Yginio said. "The *Inglés* respected him, so why can't you?"

My lips couldn't smile but my insides did. Yginio was growing up. Beely had told me this same story. Tunstall not only gave him the horse, but gave him a handshake pardon and hired him to cowpoke. I imagined Beely's rage was hotter than a branding iron onto his stomach, heating him into crazy, blind vengeance.

Ramon went on. "Anyway, at that moment, Dick Brewer, you know Dick Brewer, right?"

"Yes," said Apá. "He's a good, honest man. He's not one to make a hell for nothing."

"Apá, not hell — heaven." Garita made a *no no* sign with her finger.

"*Sí,* Garita, okay, I meant the other," Apá said.

"Mamá *en cielo* — heaven. Blue where Mamá is," Garita said.

Ramon smiled. "Let me finish, Garita. Dick Brewer said he would lead the Regulators against Murphy."

"I already told them," Yginio said.

I remember one day Dick Brewer rode by, tall and straight on his horse. His strong square jaw reminded me of what a *conquistador,* if they were Anglos, might look like. His chin kept its position high and quarter-sized curls rolled up in his shirt collar. His handsomeness of rare making rode west and I rode east. Our faces met. My eyes fought to resist feasting on him.

Now Señor Brewer brings new reason to this man-against-man nonsense. Without

Señor Tunstall's general store, our position weakened. The poor would get poorer if we had to deal only with Señor Murphy. I set the tortillas and food on the table and everyone served themselves.

"To me, it sounds like a war. Yginio and you, too, Ramon, better we stay out of this." Apá sucked air through his thin roll, tipped it out on the table, and put the tiny stub back in his pocket. He began eating.

Ramon nodded. "I know, Salamon, I don't want no part either." He looked at me and held me in his stare until I broke my attention from him. He fiddled with some food on his plate, something I hated anyone to do. I let it go unnoticed; I didn't want his calling lights on me again.

"We should help Billy's Regulators," my brother said.

"Yginio, didn't you just hear me? You see it's a fight between coyotes and wolves. Dead people can't change anything. How many ways do I have to say it? We need you here, alive. Both got guns, and they all are going to kill each other," Apá said.

"Regulators need to win, Apá. You know how bad Señor Murphy is. You know better than anyone he's a cheater. He will forever keep us poor *Mejicanos,* helpless and hungry. Tired of it. I think we should help Billy."

"No, *Mijo,* hear me good. We stay out of this," my father said.

"Your Apá is right, Yginio. Everyone should keep away. I told Sinforosa the same thing." Ramon's voice pitched high and louder than before.

"¿Sinforosa?" Garita said. "¿*Mi* Sinfo?"

Ramon looked my way, and this time my eyes could not resist his. I stared back, waiting to hear Sinforosa's business. She has lost the *Inglés,* her white keeper. Me and Sinfo, orphaned lovers, charmed by *gringos* new to this area, except now, her waiting was over.

Apá whispered, "Sinforosa, you sure?"

Ramon had the telling stage and wouldn't stop. "Yes, she was at the *Inglés'* funeral. Never seen her like that before. So thin she could hardly stand. Lupe, the daughter of Rumalda Espinosa, the woman shot in her Lincoln home, held her up, the daughter not the mother. Sinforosa kept saying, '*Cabrón* murderers. He didn't deserve this. He wanted a peaceful life here.' It was bad, real bad. I asked her if I could bring her home, but she was howling too loud to hear. They dragged her away."

I imagined Ramon following and pulling at her, begging the way I'd seen him do so many times before. "Never mind, we don't care," I said.

"I *quiero* — want," said Garita.

"No, Garita, we don't need to hear anything," I said.

"*Sí,* I do want," she said, "anything and nothing."

"Does it matter? She forgot her family. Wouldn't come home. Didn't show up at Mamá's funeral. She didn't mourn for her like the rest of us."

"Sinforosa *preciosa.*" Garita whispered and put a stare on me, which pinned the others' eyes on me, too.

"Who's stupid enough to care?" I gave her quick head and finger shakes.

"She was in between the two," Ramon said. "She works for Señor Murphy and Tunstall. Murphy shouldn't punish her, but he might. Everyone saw her and Billy Chivato talking."

The two names in the same sentence slapped me as hard as the loud tap on the door. We all looked to see Señor Lawrence Murphy, standing with his hat in hand. What else?

CHAPTER TWELVE

I stared, not with curiosity but with fright. *El Cucuy* demon spirit brought him here for some curse — had to be. Out of place in our worn, beat-up doorway, he was a lost traveler in search of his castle — a fattened rat gawking at a nest of skinny mice. The news of John Tunstall's murder had just wrenched my nerves, and now the center of his killing stood right here. Like an avalanche after a deadly snowstorm, this Señor Lawrence Murphy fell on us. My urge was to bolt the door, but I couldn't move and couldn't be ill-mannered to the señor sir.

Mister man didn't appear as big as he was behind his counter or beside his willow tree. The skin on his face twitched looser and fleshier than I remembered. Dark crescents drooped to the middle of his nose. His fallen eyes roamed over our poor house as he glanced down at our wild spinach, crow stew, and then back again at Apá.

"Came to see about the matter we discussed at your last delivery. Have you come to any decisions?" He brushed dust off his black suit coat and fingered a loose thread on his pocket, worn open at the bottom. A handkerchief hung out that same pocket, and his thumb shook as he moved his cane from one hand to the other. His flat eyes perched like sad birds who wanted to fly out into our place.

He pulled out the handkerchief, blew his nose, and looked at Garita. Turned and looked at Apá, and back again at my sister. Out of his rich mercantile, he appeared timid, like a fox who plays dead. Apart from Apá and Garita, the rest of us were invisible to him.

"He for you, Apá." My sister pointed from one man to the other and went about the business of moving a hair strand between her thumb and pointer.

"*Ya,* okay, Garita." My father held his brown-stained cigarette stub. Ashes hung loosely and fell onto his plate. He squashed what was left of his rollie. "*Por favor,* Señor Murphy, we go outside."

Apá's smoke butt sat, and I wondered why he hadn't saved those few bits of inhalers. Usually he took the last greenish-brown crumbs and re-rolled them with fresh tobacco. Yginio, Ramon, and my eyes met and bounced off each other. What was this mister man after?

More whisper talk outside.

"Not yet, Señor, no time . . ." It was my father's voice. "Ya, too quick."

"No, what about two days a week?" Murphy said. "Reduced northwest pasture rent . . . Good deal . . ."

"Pantalon Gallegos is going with the house men." Ramon boomed over Apá and Señor Murphy's voices.

"*Ya*, Ramon, *basta*, enough, no more. We're all tired of hearing about the crazies in Lincoln. Who did what to the other? More killings. Why is Mister Señor Murphy at our rancho?" I picked up Apá's plate and scraped his leftover *cigarillo* into the pig slop bucket. "He has no business at this hour here with Apá unless he's going to give us back sheep ears and money."

"Sheep ears," said Garita. *"Chicharrones."* Her words drifted up and out the window.

"Yginio, do you know about this?" I wrapped the tortillas in a rag for tomorrow.

"I knew something about some little thing, but I don't think Apá will . . . will . . ." Yginio's muscles tightened, and he looked at Ramon.

"Will what? Doesn't this man have enough

of us?" My brother's face told me he knew more. I turned to the other one in the room. "Ramon, do you know?"

"No, I don't know nothing about nothing." Ramon's fingers tapped the sides of his arms like they were their own boss.

"I can't say because he probably won't do it," my brother added.

"*Por favor,* what in *Santa Maria's* Holy name does that mean?" I began collecting tins off the table.

The door slammed on my last word, and Apá came and sat shut tighter than a steel trap.

I went about my business but couldn't let go. "What Apá? What's a good deal? You know that man's wicked, and a good deal turns out to be only good for him. Might as well sell your soul to Judas."

His silence screamed he had done just that.

CHAPTER THIRTEEN

After the *Inglés,* Tunstall's, murder, I spun wool and prayed the wild, senseless fighting would tamed down and be over. March dirt storms blew like a New Mexico *Cucuy* witch had gone mad. Meant something horrible was coming, but we didn't hear of more killings. I craved the heat of summer when life was a little easier. My father and Yginio worked the flock from sheep line camp to sheep line camp. Sometimes together and sometimes with Ramon's help and sometimes each by himself.

A month later in April a rare invitation came about. Apá asked Garita to go with him and Yginio that morning. They would bring one quarter of our flock, so they would not overgraze the northeast pasture. Garita took her sling and promised quail for dinner. I didn't protest. A quiet home welcomed me.

After the horrids of March, this spring day

came with perfect breezes, so I opened a window. I pulled and twisted raw wool onto spooling balls. This Lincoln County War was our own Civil War where neighbor fought neighbor. Father Martinez said that war ended slavery, but this war had no such purpose. *Inocentes,* like Dick Brewer and many others, had been pulled in. For what? Rich men stayed rich, and slaves were still slaves.

El Señor Brewer had suffered cheat dealings with the house, too. Brewer paid money to Señor Murphy for land he later learned Murphy didn't own. So his money went into a trick hole, and Dick Brewer couldn't get the money back, didn't own the property, didn't want to repay the real owner, and didn't want to lose the land. *Pobre* Brewer found himself in a bear trap with iron claws from four directions. He led the Regulator fight. Many others had their problems, and we had ours. Spinning relaxed me from my nervous war worries.

As I finished one spool and started another, little clomps sounded and caused me to lift an ear. Floorboards creaked as I went to the open window for a look, but the caller had already passed. The barn door's rusty hinges whined. Fever chills grew and skipped down my back. Throat muscles swelled my windpipe closed. *Válgame Dios,* could it be?

I broke a strand of wool thread. When I brought one string over the other to catch the two ends together, it slipped. The room suddenly got musty and airless, yet the window was open. I gasped, swallowed hard, and coughed to clear my throat. The yarn broke again. I put the spool down and spread my hands over my dress to dry the wetness of my palms. The moisture seeped into the material and darkened patches on my skirt. My innards knotted into a stomach pain as I tried to shake the material dry. Yet, I felt chilled.

As I closed the window, two wide, dark eyes stared back. My face, off the glass, was raw, unkept, frightful. Whisker-like hair stuck out of my single black braid, hanging over the bulging buttons of my blouse. I wet my fingers and moved loose strands back into my braid. I pinched my cheeks red and moistened my generous lips. I scraped fingernails over my teeth. Still no one opened the house door.

Outside, the sun's brightness made me shut my eyes and raise my palm for shade. With no recollection of the exact time, I knew it was late morning. Yginio? Maybe Yginio had come back before he was due.

Or Ramon — could he be unloading something here? I kept my pace toward the barn.

Nobody came out. Isabelle and our old mule left their salt lick and stared at me. The chickens scratched the dirt around the yard, and one dropped a green pool of what looked like pea juice beside my foot. *Enough of that.* I stepped around the goopy slime. The April breeze swayed a small branch just recently covered with tiny spring leaves beside the barn. No sounds of human voices. I crept closer and listened again for some conversation. I swung open the door.

Beely stood with his back to me.

He had unsaddled Apache and brushed his flanks in long strokes. His horse blanket covered his corner of the barn beside the haystack just as before. My nose filled with the air of a hard-driven animal, horse manure, fresh hay, old wood, and new leather. As if he had backside vision and knew it was me who opened the door, he didn't turn. I let the creaky hinge close the wood door against my back until it fell quiet onto its frame. He didn't turn around. I stepped in. Mapache, our coon cat, would not let me come unnoticed. She wandered up, curved herself around my leg, and purred. I knelt down, and stroked her soft fur.

"*Hola,* Señor Beely Chivato. I see your fast pinto remembers this place."

He turned and smiled, the one I remembered so well. "You know ole Apache boy here, he tries to turn this direction every time we pass. Thought I'd make him lucky today. Mind if I give him a little rest."

"From what Ramon tells me, Señor, he needs it. You have been riding him hard all over from Seven Springs to Blazer's Mill to Lincoln, to Fort Stan —"

"Good to put my eyes on you, Ambrosia, or is it Señorita Salazar? Course not, that'd be like me calling Mapache here Missy Lion from the house of barn dwellers. And if that tale you're getting is from chickabiddy, Ramon Salamanca, the smithy with one eye out the window but no gumption for fortifying any one side, well . . ."

I stood up. "Ramon doesn't run with wild, rough men — *locos* in one group and *tontos* in the other. He stays put, safe, *gracias a Dios.*"

"Yeah, safe, *muy seguro,* and when it's over and done with, he'll come out and enjoy the freedoms we *locos* have brought to town. Look, let's tame the bronc words, okay? Didn't come here to fuss, but think about it, an upstanding innocent John Tunstall was brought down and all his belong-

216

ings, horses, cattle, house goods, and mercantile wares, strung out for anyone's keep. His body dealt with as if it weren't worth but a kick of cow pile. Ain't right. Some lick spittle while we others push rightly back. It's a bad box, *muy mal,* but long as you take the kicking, the other devil will gladly oblige and slam the boot further into your hurt spot. No sir, *ya basta* with thieves in high places, something's got to stop. Even the Bible says an eye for an —"

I cut him short. "Don't tell me about *La Biblia,* Beely. Explain your justice using God's words — no. Enough." I had forgotten the deep blue of his eyes and his nervous shuffle-steps. Inside me, an agitation could not be calmed.

"Look, Ambrosia, it ain't stopping. We just done jimmied another bull two days ago. The devil's beehive has just been cut open, and they ain't flying back into the nest. That's it. Gone past stopping."

"Jimmy with a bull? *Un toro?* What do you mean?"

"Sheriff Brady, the crooked badge murderer. You remember him. He was ready to let that rotten beef bag violate you in front of a bunch of low-life scoundrels. Thought that horn-dog's life was better than yours. When Yginio said your sister worked at La

Jewel, it didn't take me too long to put the two ends together. Took me awhile, but the memory of that day finally came to me."

So he did know.

"Lower than ant spit, Brady was in Jimmy Dolan's so-called posse, enforcing the law. And he watched or lent a hand in killing Tunstall. Just like he sat, bystanding, not protecting, you that day. That's who we're talking about here. We bedded him down. Got his forever sleep two days ago. The ante's been upped, and I reckon a bloody —"

"Sheriff Brady? *Santa Madre.* Sheriff Brady?" I made the sign of the cross. "Already, Señor Tunstall and those three *hombres,* dead just lately. Now Sheriff Brady? Who else is it going to be?"

"It's four of them now who worked Tunstall's crucifixion. But counting the fallen enemy makes it a vengeance, and it ain't that. It's justice, Regulator style."

"You next, Beely. Stop, got to stop with this, *ya,* no more. Talk to Apá. You can come back here and work your stay until you find another good paying job. Get some sense before it's too late."

"Wasn't one iron who took him down, wasn't just me, no way. The whole lot of Regulators fired like Jimmy Dolan's devil tribe did to Tunstall. Stop? That's what I'm trying to tell you, Ambrosia. There's no stopping. Yginio can clarify that for you."

I looked at the ceiling and crossed my arms. My head went down. I stared at light penetrating the cracks in the walls for there was nowhere else to put my eyes. My heart beat against my insides, thunder in a cave. Beely's mustang blew air out his snout and shook its head. Then snapped his right foot against the dirt and little specks floated up into those same beams.

"Who's next to die?" I said. "Have you thought of that? My brother? Murphy? Dick Brewer? Me? You?"

I felt a warm arm around me in a firm yet soft hold.

"You know he's wrong," Beely said.

My knees shook. I pushed back and sat on a bale of hay. "Everyone is wrong."

"No." He took my arm and lifted me back up. "I mean, Yginio's wrong. Sinforosa is not the most beautiful, you are."

"No, you're wrong. She is." He was so close I could feel his breath on my cheek.

"What do you mean, no? Now, now — maybe some like their coffee light and watered down. But I like mine dark, strong, and punch hot." He tightened his hold. "Look, Ambrosia, this man war ain't in your calculation. Like you say, men's *loco* doings. Yes, I could die, but you got to understand — not ramming back is another kind of loss, another kind of depart. Which'd you have? A gone-away for an old man who'd taken daily lickings, beat down so far he had no place to lay his shame? Someone who never reared back? What kind of life and death would that be?"

I thought of my father.

"Or going down hard in a fit of fire, fighting for your own decent respect and the respect for those you care about. Only thing that gives me an iron-branding ache is leaving this earth without knowing and without feeling your touch."

He took the hair around my face, twirled it in his fingers, and pushed it back. His eyes seared into me. He moved my braid from front to back. Pulled my numb body closer and pressed his fullness onto mine and kissed my neck. With sudden quickness, he lifted me, twisted us around, and together we fell on his blanket. Our lips met, and I felt tiny flicker flames over me in unexpected places. I didn't resist. He roamed his hands, fast, desperate, calling on my starved skin to enjoy his touch. Soon the buttons of my blouse came undone. He unhitched my brassiere. Fire kisses grew to blazing waves of moist heat. He lifted himself up, smiled, and took off his shirt. His skin to my skin joined, steamed together in our body oils.

"Beely, *no sé.* I don't know what to do."

My naked breasts enjoyed the air, but I covered them with my hands. Beely pulled them away. "Look at you, pure Ambrosia. A virgin beauty, more than words can say." Beely's cheeks brushed back and forth against my breasts, stirring a wicked want. He moistened my brown peaks with his lips. For a short moment, I feared milk would come out.

"Hold my back and feel me where you'd like. It's not wrong," he said.

My hands smoothed over his tight, back muscles I admired on his work day here. Breath stole my words. An animal drive stampeded deep within me and wanted all of him. "Yginio or Apá will come." My voice came from another place, from another woman, not from the one with Beely. That woman did not want to stop.

Beely ripped off all his coverings and his white skin crouched over me bold and brave. "Yginio is keeping Salamon and Garita at Ramon's," he said between short breaths. "My *compadre* opened the gate and is holding the watch. Relax, don't think about them."

He kissed me again and raised my skirt, took down my unders. I breathed in his being. He separated my legs as if he were unyoking a calf and let his swell brush against my hot, damp, giving body. His sacred spot pressed against mine.

"We fit just right. Nice. No need for more." He blew the words softly into my ears.

An entry, like the first blade into a deer gut, opened me with a sting. Smoothed out. Then each gentle thrust, like kindling made to grow hot flames into a wildfire, stoked me. My heart beat glorified, lifted me off this earth. "Beely, my sacred God . . ."

"Shhh, no more prayers. This blessing is what your God has given us. Ain't no sin. Can't be wrong." His whispers did not stop his movements. "Meant to make you a whole woman and me a man with a supreme joy before I die."

Together we made one and moved to each other's rhythms.

His deep scream startled me, a wild shout reached the roof timbers and beyond. Tears streamed down his face, tears no other person in this world would see. I wiped them. Beely fell on me, weak, and as I looked up, I saw Mapache, our cat, watching us from the loft.

We rested. My head fit into the crook of his neck. His breast heaved and welcomed mine. I breathed in his out-breath and had enough nerve to wrap my leg over him.

Our precious moments over, we fumbled for our clothes.

A red stain had seeped into the jute cross joints of his horse blanket. The red blotch was shaped like a ragged sun. I went to wipe it, but Beely held my hand back.

"I'll never forget this, Ambrosia. You're something deep in me now."

He dressed me and kissed me again. We gave one another full body holds, without resistance. Our tightness held a natural hankering of a woman for a man. My old life, a dull glass reflection, blurred, was of the past.

Out the barn door he galloped, hard — toward a place from which he might never return.

With each bounce on Apache, his crotch touched my given blood, the stain we made together on his horse blanket.

CHAPTER FOURTEEN

Otro lado de felicidad es barbaridad. Saying goes, "The other side of happiness is wretchedness," and it was for me. I had been a starving bird who, for a fleeting two hours, gorged on dry grain. Now the feast in my bowel swelled wet. Buried me in a sinkhole so deep I wondered who I was. Alone, I wept the loss of the other innocent Ambrosia, and at the same time yearned for Beely's touch. My third life event hit me — joyful sorrow, which Tehde had predicted. I was sure of it, and I wanted more. His touch thrilled me, yet it came with a price — loss of him and loss of myself — tortured pleasure. I worried about bearing a fatherless child, on top of my responsibility for Garita, Apá, and Yginio. I worried about bringing our family shame, as bad or worse than Sinforosa.

Chatter from Apá and Yginio broke me from my contrition. As they turned onto the road to our rancho, I ran without stop, for I did not see Garita. I thought she would be clomping along on foot as she sometimes does, but she was not there. I stopped.

So often, I hated Garita's clinging need, tired of worrying about what she might do or where she had disappeared. Now God punished me for my sinful lust, for giving myself so freely to Beely. My pleasure and this pain were attached.

"Apá, this is worse than all the crazy *locuras* of Lincoln County War put together. Senseless killing and you leave a simple girl right in the dead center of danger." The *bruto* man's sweaty hands around me at the La Jewel House came to my mind, *Greasy Mexican get your shitty ass out of here.* "Hear me, Apá, *por favor,* Garita is not yours to rent out, especially to Señor Murphy. Remember what happened to Sinforosa? Yes, it started first with a one day and then three, then she never came back. Is that where you left Garita? Is that what you want?"

His silence answered my question.

"*Caramba,* my little sister is not one of your sheep. She is still a baby girl, your daughter, *tu hijita,* a blessing. Who knows what Señor Mister will do? Cheat you like always. And now you don't even have sheep ears to prove anything. How could you do

225

such a thing?"

"She's happy." He slumped his shoulders over the table with his head in the palm of his right hand. "Happy with a good Mescalera, and Sinforosa is close by. There to do work, and we can have a little *dinerito* and cheaper pasture rent and free things from his mercantile. Don't worry, *Mija.* He won't hurt her."

"*Jesu Christo* help us — Sinforosa? You think she's in good hands with Murphy and *puta* Sinforosa? You remember what happened to Rumalda Espinosa? She worked for the mister man and was found dead in her kitchen. She was just plucking a chicken. We never found out who shot her, but we know she worked for Murphy."

"*Oye,* listen to me. Don't talk about your sister like that," he said. "At least Señor Murphy is no gunslinger."

"No, he doesn't carry a gun, but his little partner, Jimmy Dolan, does. And Rumalda, I heard, the poor lady spoke too much about what was happening in his Mercantile House. That's why she caught the bullet, so strange how she died. That's probably why he wants Garita and Tehde — neither one has a voice, at least not one anybody listens to. True, Apá. You know it. And you know what kind of lady Sinfo is. What she used to do with John Tunstall, and now with who? With whoever pays? She is one of those nasty ladies, and she never took care of Garita or cared for any of us. Your favorite *hijita,* still, I know she is. Look, Apá, we can find another way. If you want to save money, why don't you quit smoking and get Yginio another job. He could work for Murphy and make extra."

"Señor Mister don't want Yginio. He wants Margarita." Apá rubbed his eyebrows and followed that rub over the back of his head.

"I'm going right now, and I'm bringing her back." I started to the door with enough will to ride to Lincoln that very minute.

As I was heading out, Yginio walked in. Like plucking a runaway chick from the henhouse, he grabbed my arm and pushed me back to the table. "Sit." His tight face, like he had grown twelve point buck antlers overnight, pierced horns into me. "Look, I don't like it neither, but Apá is the father in this place, and these decisions are his."

"Oh yes, *gran* señor you are. You haven't taken care of Garita — ever. Why don't you get extra work? You're gone all the time with Regulator *locuras.* And our apá has told you not to do it. You can break those rules, but you expect me to mind this one. It's been me with Garita with no help from anyone, and I say, *no.*" I remembered Beely's words — how he stands up for what he believes and how he holds his ground with *brutos.*

"*Calma, Mija.* I told Señor Murphy, I would go tomorrow morning to check on her. If she wants to come back, I will bring her," Apá said.

"You will bring her back even if she says *yes* to staying, Apá. You know Garita. She can say *no* to us but not to other people. That's why it's crazy for her to be there without us. Anyone can do what they want with her, any way they want. She'll become like Sinforosa." I rubbed Mamá's rosary I had taken to carrying in my pocket. *Diosito, forgive me for my sins.* "No, it's not okay, and I will not rest until she comes back. Will not clean house. Will not cook. Will not feed the animals or milk the cow." I slammed my hand on the table as I imagined Garita sitting on Señor Murphy's lap, scared, and trying to please him.

The next day Apá left at first light. I busied myself with any kind of work to stop my worry. The sensual pleasure of Beely today did not bring me joy. Those feelings did not mix with the loss of Garita. I prayed two rosaries, washed sheets, cleaned the coop, swept the kitchen floor, and promised

Diosito if he gave me this one, I would never be with Beely again, never ever give myself to him.

Before noon, I heard horse hooves. I dropped my rag mop and pressed an urgent run outside, shielding the sun from my eyes. Luz trotted an up-down rhythm with Apá on top, riding her bounce — solo. As if nothing were new, he rode past me without a glance. I didn't wait for him to go into the house and followed after him into the barn.

"Before you start yelling, hear me. Margarita is happy. She takes very well to the house store, and she's working with the Indian woman called Tehde. They go together everywhere. She is not anywhere near La Jewel." He patted Luz and gave her a flick of hay.

My chest sunk into the hollow of my stomach like a rock. "No, Apá, you said she would be back today. Why isn't she with you?"

"Listen to me. She would not come," he said. "You know her. She's a *bruta*, stronger than you or me. I would have to hog-tie her and throw her onto Luz. Doña Hurtencia and Ramon have cleared a corner in their place, and she's going to sleep there at night. *Calma, Mija,* they have given me their word to watch and care for her. And she

229

can walk to the mercantile in the morning to do her labors next to this Tehde. Margarita's a woman now. She's grown, and you don't have to watch her so much anymore. Leave your worry. *Ya,* let matters be. We can use the extra."

The shock of it all turned to rabid anger. "No, Apá, no, she does not have the mind of a woman. If Mamá were alive, she would fight you on this. You know it. She would never leave our *inocente* alone in Lincoln. I'm bringing her back by force if I have to. I tried with Sinfo, but it was useless. That's Sinfo. But Garita's different; she's not in charge of herself, and she can be forced to come with me. It's the money you want, huh? The little extra and for what? You will sacrifice her for that little bit. How many times do I need to say it? Make the other man in this house work. He can go to Lincoln and get a job with Señor Wortley at the hotel. Or with Chisum running cattle or whatever."

"*Ya pues,* they have never wanted him, and I need his help." He spit what looked to be chew out the side of his mouth. "Yginio has the energy for sheeping I don't have. Besides, salt, flour, beans, and coffee are not extra. It's no little thing." He turned and started to unbridle Luz.

"No, don't unsaddle her, Apá. I'm going right now. Garita is coming home *ahora,* today, — now." I hopped on Luz and dug full boots into her. "Let's go, Luz, we can't leave such things to *hombres locos.*"

I'm sure Apá watched me leave a trail of dust from our rancho to the Río Ruidoso crossing where I rode out of his sight. The double rocks on the Bonito River bounced into view. Luz sensed an urgent calling, caught a vicious second wind, and pushed through the flat land. After the Salamancas', toward Lincoln, I reined her in and praised her. Like an enemy gate, the moment I saw the House Mercantile with La Jewel Parlor next to it, the solid-ice strength in me melted and drained hot fear into my bones. I had come this far. I had no other choice.

Rather than clamoring full-bore on the paving stones, I dismounted close to the house and noted the main street held an unusual quiet, a hanging dread, a calm before a lynching. Nothing could be heard but Luz's footfalls. Window curtains were drawn, doors were closed, fence gates locked, Sheriff Brady's post abandoned, and no one was to be seen anywhere. An *Oowee* breeze blew a tumbleweed across my path. A lonely dog barked. A door slammed, but when I looked, no one was there. Seemed I

231

was not the only one with water bones.

After posting Luz on the outdoor railing, I went to the mercantile door. A sign outside read, *Closed.* The distance to Mister Señor's lodging portal was not far. The lace curtains for the main window had a dark layer, which looked to be a blanket covering. A lush honeysuckle vine beside the door refreshed the air around me, and I wondered if I'd ever have such a scented luxury again. I banged softy, then more loud. The tap reverberated in what seemed an echo valley. It repelled off the darkening night and bounced against the street silence. I knocked again — no answer.

Back to the horse post, I patted Luz and wiped the sweat from the sides of her head and the nape of her neck. She nuzzled her *you're welcome* head against me. The thought of going to the Jewel Parlor to look for Garita sickened me. I considered going back to the Salamancas' for Ramon's help, but he'd put a man-face on my search, bring more attention, and make it worse. If I couldn't find Garita, I'd have to go home. Maybe this was too much for me. With no other choice, I walked back and banged again. It creaked opened. Tehde faced me and behind her stood Garita.

"Brocia," my sister screamed, and the

sound of my name from her lips ripped a sheath of joy in me. She pushed Tehde aside and hugged me. A band of feathers hung around her forehead, down not up. They ruffled around her face. One day away from the *rancho,* and she had become a Mescalera Apache. Her hair smelled of dust, but she was alive, unmolested, and still happy.

"I'm here to take you home, *Mija.*" Her arms around me felt warm and tight.

She reared back and stared.

I could see she needed more convincing. "*Casa* — home, you with me. Mapache misses you. Apá and Yginio miss you. I miss you." I doubted my words alone would get her to come. If Garita got into a stubborn streak, I would have to trick her or outright force her. Apá was right. She was much stronger than both of us.

"Too long you not come to this place," said Tehde. "Yesterday, I want to see you. This one don't work for nothing. Want to play every time. Want to go out with cat or shoot squirrels with sling rocks. Sweep little, cook nothing. The mister like her for his laugh."

"Is he here?" I asked. "The mister man?" For once Garita's mind-stop brought good.

"He upstairs in the quiet room with little Jimmy. Shadow spirits in street. Only big pistol men and brave dogs walk roads, no women. Can feel hate of ghost bear. Many fall. Boss man, he grow red rash and jerks too much. His worry, heavier than thick winter snow." Her arms froze to her sides.

"Terrible, awful," I said. This made me certain Garita needed to be home. "What about those on the other side, The Regulators?"

"Those called Regulators, they kill three others on Pecos river up-way. Now dead." Tehde pushed and pulled one hand against the other. "Right hand shoot left hand of same body. Each lose. Things worser." She jerked her hands loose and wiggled her fingers. "Left hand grow more fingers, and it hunt right hand." She shoved her left fist into the palm of her right hand, stopped, and caught her breath. "Very much danger to leave now. Those others you say Regulators, they killed silver-star man. Sheriff-friend of mister man gone now. The little one, Jimmy Dolan, he nervous with too many squirrel shakes. Big pow-wow — them two. Make troubled plans."

Our quiet Tehde had been rattled into a rattler. This war was stirring something in all of us.

"What else?" I asked.

"Sinforosa, that sand one, worser sick.

More bad than Indian earth or white man have heal-cure. Give two drinks at night but her eyes floating downriver."

"Sinfo made her choice. What about this one?" I jerked my chin in Garita's direction. "Do you think I can get her back home?"

"Not want yesterday but today, yes. Town fighting too bad. The mister say we stay in. Think now this one Garita ready to take leave."

I looked at Garita. "Here or *casa* — home?"

She stared at me and then at Tehde. "No, no *casa* — home." Shook her head. "Tehde." She let go of me and hugged her Indian friend. "No *ir* — go home."

Her stubborn will didn't surprise me. "Tehde, you want the reservation where it is safe, right?" I nodded until she joined my head movement. "Will Señor Murphy give you leave?" I reached my hand out for my little sister. So many times, I pushed Garita away, now she was pushing me away like Sinforosa had done.

Garita wouldn't let go of Tehde's hand and left me standing, hand in the air.

"*Ya pues,* okay, we will all go. Garita might leave with you. She can't stay if you're not here."

Garita nodded.

"Okay, both of you, pack your takeaways. We'll ride to San Patricio. There, you can sleep tonight, Tehde, and can go the rest of the way *mañana*. Easier for Garita to say goodbye to you from there."

The sun was just starting to go down, so we would have to travel at night. I waited on the street with Luz for what seemed hours. She snorted and swung her head toward me as I rubbed my palm on her softness. "Catch your rest, girl. You're the sister who never turns away, Luz." She uplifted her nose under my arm, and her horsey smell soothed me.

A light went on inside the Murphy House and a dark figure of a man walked by a lit window. Tehde has good sense. If anyone could make a getaway she could. That Mescalera and the mister seem to have an understanding. The light went off. I trusted she was right about his look in other directions. I turned again to old girl Luz and heard a door slam behind me. I jumped. Two were coming at me — one limped like a jackknife and the other clomped like a tired mule.

"The three of us can't ride Luz. One of you is going to have to walk. Who is it going to be?"

They both nodded, each with that strange headdress around their faces, feathers fluttering, their eyes pointed at me.

"*Pronto,* it's getting late. Who is it going to be?" I asked again.

They stared at me and then looked at each other. Garita mounted the saddle and boosted Tehde up.

"*Sí,* okay." Afraid they'd take off without me, I took the reins and walked Luz down the road. It was a small sacrifice to get Garita out of there. With each step, I wondered how the heck we were going to make it all the way to San Patricio at night like this. I prayed with my finger rosary.

When we reached the Salamancas', I saw no light. Our pace was slower than slow. It would take all of two days to get home, so I stopped. I tapped the door and brought Ramon and Doña out of the darkness of their warm home.

"What is it?" Doña spoke first. "Ramon was just getting ready to go for Garita. We didn't know what happened. She didn't come, and her bed is ready there in the corner." Her words were not unkind, but I felt a scold.

Ramon stood in a white undershirt, ringed with a circle of brown around the neck. Little black hairs curled out. Beside Doña, his huge figure and warm face gave me familiar comfort. He fiddled with his chest hair. "What are you doing, in this dangerous place at night? *Santo Dios,* there's a war going on. Who's that with you?" He soon lost that kind face.

"Tehde, our Mescalera friend." I rubbed the small of my back.

Doña clutched her night robe, then moved her grasp onto her son's elbow.

"I know there's a war, Ramon. I wouldn't be here if I didn't have to. Don't worry. We're on our way back to the *rancho,* but three of us on old Luz will kill her for sure, and we will hardly get there walking like this."

"Come in. Everyone come in. You will have to spend the night, Ambrosia." Ramon spoke, but Doña's eyes, after she saw Garita and Tehde's face feathers, were not so inviting.

"No, Ramon, we never wanted to bother you. *Gracias* but Tehde needs to make it to the reservation, and Apá will be worried. I have to get Garita home tonight." Garlic, chili, and fresh tortillas — food of love and family, seeped out.

"Ay que bueno," Doña said, "I was so worried about your little sister. First you lose Sinforosa and now Gar . . ."

"Ramon . . ." I didn't want to hear Doña talk. "One of your horses could help us. Tehde could ride it? I know she's good for it. She can bring it back when she comes to work next time."

"With all the gunning, who knows when that will be?" Doña shook her head and tightened her grip on Ramon. "If that Indian takes it to the reservation, we'll never see it again. *Tu sabes* how they are."

"Please, Ramon, *por favor.*" I squared my eyes right into his.

Garita waved her head feathers in a furious nod while Tehde stood, head down, not one feather fluttered.

"*Favor,* please, Ramoncito." My sister, for all she lacked, could always get more than any others.

"Okay, but not to the reservation. Only to your place. Then you and your apá and Yginio can figure it out."

Under the light of an oil lamp, Tehde and Garita rode Luz, and I walked with Ramon up the road to his smithy stalls. His large but agile hands lassoed a light-footed, young sorrel stallion. As he brought the horse into the stall, it huffed and raised his hind legs. The animal didn't seem tame enough to ride, but we had no choice. Ramon patted him until he settled, then topped him with a blanket and an old saddle. He cinched him and re-cinched him as if he knew this *bruto* needed tightening down.

Watching Ramon work his large gentleness on the fidgety horse brought to mind how kind he was to this beast and to us. It boiled up a memory — in the arroyo behind the church, his lips on mine when I was twelve. He had asked permission and kissed me stiff-lipped. I grew impatient and drew away. Neither of us knew what to do. How long ago? Not long enough to forget.

He worked the bridle over the sorrel's ears and under its chin. I remembered he taught me horses. We rode plenty of miles in our past. This night, his mother didn't want him to help us, yet he did. When he finished, he gave me, not Tehde, the reins, just as he favored Sinforosa before me. Not soon enough, we put our backs to the Salamancas and to the war.

In her mount, Tehde's horse rode ahead of us until the Mescalera reined him in like slicing a dull knife through hard tack. He reared back, bucked, stepped five or six paces, and took off fast again. She fisted her boss position for miles, and still that sorrel thrusted his jumpy giddy-up on her when she relaxed the leathers.

We were three women in the night, during

240

a war, traveling through a danger field on an old nag and a wild stallion. I felt Garita's arms tighten around me and heard crickets chirp with our steady clomps. It was our old mare's second ride to Lincoln today, and now loaded with both me and Garita, she did her best to keep up. Garita could have ridden with Tehde, but after almost losing my second sister, I kept her with me. Besides, two on the chancy bucking stallion might send him into a revolt.

An owl *who-whoed.* Then again.

"Oowee." Garita breathed in a quick gasp and held her face feathers tight against my back.

Long known in these parts the owl predator announced a passing, a killing, a death. Its song knew who was going to expire next. The prophesy bird's song mocked us because we didn't know. Only one who didn't believe its power was Father Martinez. He said it was only a bird looking for a mate. But this night, darkness, wind, weary bones, moon shadows, and that sound spooked me. Partnered with a *Cucuy* spirit, the bird and the wind could hover dread on us. It was best to move on fast.

Tehde's horse, two or three lengths ahead, set down fading steps. She stopped and spoke faint words. "We, okay."

I pushed Luz up to her hoofing trailblazer, so I could ride with her calm strength.

Wind blew whiny air through the pine trees, and in the distance a pack of coyotes celebrated a kill.

Garita tightened her grip on me even more.

"We're okay." I tried to give my voice something of what Tehde had. "These are only animals, and they do this every night. We're just not around to hear it." I neared Luz to Tehde's sorrel. "Men, not animals, are the ones we need to have an eye and ear for."

Tehde again broke the chilled air. "The deer those dogs kill keep us safe. *Onishta,* thank sacrifice. Coyotes eat them not us."

The heaviness of night sky bore down. I wiggled three fingers before my eyes, and I could not see them. Blackness pressed ailments, worries, and a heavy spirit down on me. Under clear skies, fears rested on my shoulders, not over my whole body like this smothering night blanket. Since Mamá's death, darkness choked me. I rubbed some warmth into my arms.

Having made this trip so many times, I knew dips in the road, the slanted pine tree, the washed-out draw, an old gated fence to Apá's rent pasture, and the curves of the

Bonito. In the darkness, these landmarks were erased and without them, the distance seemed longer and at times, I sensed we could be walking off a cliff. In the distance, I barely made out two humping boulders caught in a mating freeze and gave a sigh of thankfulness. We had reached our southwest turn toward Río Ruidoso.

My short-lived relief was interrupted by shots. Tehde mustered her young horse behind the large double rocks, and I followed. We huddled together — silent, breathless.

"Left-hand fire but right-hand no shoot back." Tehde's horse reared up, much too nervous for my liking, but she tightened him down. "Sound come upriver," she said.

"Yes, back toward Lincoln." I thought of Beely and prayed that slug wasn't planted in his head.

"Malos," Garita whispered against the sound of gurgling water, *"mucho muy malos."*

We waited until no repeat came, and it was Tehde who made the first move out of our hiding. Again, her horse's feet hardly touched ground. Tehde gave him full rein. I imagined her feathers and braids flying away from her face. She vanished.

Garita and I plodded along behind in the

dark as best as we could. Three miles down the road, we found the Mescalera beside the dirt tank. She must have given that beast some Indian medicine, for the young stallion stood calmly beside her, well-watered and in an obedient horse place.

"You okay? Did you slow that bangtail down?" I said as we dismounted.

"He know this squaw got hold back," she said softly. Her faintness never ever meant weakness. She was the cricket in the mountain lion's ear. A small chirp, but with time, the little insect's chirps would make, chirp, chirp, the lion, chirp, crazy and bring him to his knees. Garita and I, and now the young stallion, knew her quiet power.

Luz took her fill and Garita rested. We remounted and soon fell into a horse rhythm. Each beside the other in an even pace, we swayed on top of our steeds, and a slight sliver of a moon gave us dim light.

"Tell me about the face feathers, what do they mean?" I asked Tehde.

"Protect," said Garita.

"Let Tehde tell me." Her low voice beside us in the dark night was as valued as Father Martinez's Sunday sermons.

"My eyes see all around like the owl, and my ears double-hear. Smeller go a good faraway, and this Tehde feel others' spirit energy. I watch like a she lion who know bush medicine and season's ancient stories."

The wind picked up lightly. Garita's warmth on my back soothed my aching spine.

"Protect," Garita leaned her head in and whispered, "from *Oowee El Cucuy.*"

"The feathers give you all that." I thought of Beely and his pistol, his *protect.*

"Yes, this one — me, Tehde Crowdark — wear eagle feathers. Birds run in air, feet ride the sky, fast away. Wing power for me. This little one, too, need protect."

Her story brought us to the Ruidoso, and the view of our *casita* with its little lights beckoning us forward like calling stars. After trudging in the dark those hours with fears of the unknown, gasps at every sound — a sense of regret filled me. I was sorry our togetherness had ended, and now I faced Apá and Yginio — a different dread.

The men were standing at the door when we made our tired way around the house and into the barn. They kept watch but did not come out to greet us. Their easy muscle to unsaddle Luz and Ramon's nervous hoofer didn't come to us either. No matter, I took down the saddles with Tehde's help, unbridled the gear, and stalled the horses. I was relieved to have Garita home at any cost. This one time, I forced my hand. I could not stand silent and risk another sister gone.

"I walk from here," Tehde said.

"No *amiga,* too far and too late this night." I thought about her limping on the side of the road in the dark for many more miles.

"Yes can. Go now to reserve ground. Safe there." She hung her feathers downward.

"I know the eagle feathers give you protection, but it doesn't give you food. Come in and eat and rest. That was what we said, remember? And you can sleep here." I pointed to the corner where Beely bedded and pushed the thought of him away. "Please, *por favor.*"

Garita took her hand, and we walked into the house. When Yginio saw us with Tehde, he walked out. Apá stayed sitting at the table.

I wooded and fired up the grate on our cast-iron stove. Without words, we cut vegetables and Tehde added buffalo jerky Señor Murphy had given her. Even Garita kept her double talk to herself.

Apá sat and watched us from the sofa bed.

Tortillas on the grill and this safe place gave me a silent embrace. Three women in the kitchen filled the homestead with warmth, not from only food and burning wood, but from our woman success.

"Come, Apá, sit, eat with us." I waved him over. I had never crossed him before and did not have any force in me to stay angry now.

He sat motionless many minutes. He coughed, took off his hat, rose slowly, and took the empty seat next to Garita. For the first time ever, I saw him give Garita a quick pat. She smiled but didn't lean into him. Salazares had struggles enough, not standing together would make them worse.

"Everything's okay, Apá. With Garita home. And Tehde's eating and sleeping with us tonight. She has the place in the barn," I said.

Apá nodded and ate the stew quietly.

Yginio came in and whittled a tree branch into what looked like a snake. We finished our meal, and Garita took Tehde with blankets to the barn. That night I told Garita I loved her and missed her and needed her more than Mister Señor Murphy. She said she *sabe* — knew. I hugged her until she pushed me away.

With a lantern, I went out into the barn to check *La India.* Her corner sat empty.

I said two rosaries and thanked *La Virgin de Guadalupe* for giving me strength, and for Tehde to make it home safe, and for Beely, too.

CHAPTER FIFTEEN

Sheriff Brady was shot April 1, 1878, and the fighting didn't stop there. One killing begat another and that kill brought two more. On April 4th, *un señor* called Andrew Buckshot Roberts, a man in the house gang, fought off the force of ten Regulators at Blazer's Mill, where the U.S. Indian agent was housed. Tehde's reservation was not so safe after all. *Solo* in his standoff, Buckshot Roberts ran into Dr. Blazer's place and found his big fifty buffalo gun. With it, he spewed black powder like he was taking down prairie dogs.

Before Roberts took his last breath, Dick Brewer was one of the dead dogs. My insides cried to think of Dick Brewer's perfect face torn apart with that giant barrel. As I heard each word of the Blazer's Mill shootout, I waited for Beely's name as one of the fallen. Ramon said George Coe lost a forefinger, and adobe walls had enough lead to lay one section of the Santa Fe rail line.

Any circling *Oowee* wind was enough to jitter men into pulling their guns out all the ready. Moving rags or tumbleweeds in a dust devil became targets if there was enough dust to make them out to be a short man. Fear hung over Lincoln and the Hondo Valley. Beely didn't die in this one — yet. Like old lady gossip, stories trapped us in suspense as Yginio or Ramon spun details of the next showdown, shootout, or lowdown doings. War did not stop.

I ached for Beely. One morning I found bloodstains on my unders and experienced a feeling between relief and disappointment. A baby was something I did not need at this time. Every day I told myself I should have forced my body away, kept myself whole. But that same many times and more, I went back over each tender touch, luscious smell, his smile, thunder of his legs on me and mine open to him — the danger, the regret, the urge. Beely didn't belong to anyone, and even if he was not mine, I, *sí, seguro,* was his.

No how, no way any of my foul pleasure made sense. Even if I had the strength that day to say no, I'd still suffer. Joyful emptiness filled me like a bucket with holes. I tried best as I could to keep going. I made *masa* for tortillas and shaped the dough into little rounds. I caressed each and thought of how I would apply a soothing grasp on Beely if ever I had another chance.

Months went by and one hot July day I made tortillas same as usual. I worked the dry sticky ingredients with flour until the dough rounded up. I had not patted but four *masa* balls when hard galloping sounded. A trail of dust blazed brown over the side path outside. No riders. I called for Garita, who was supposed to be out hanging clothes. Before I could step out, Yginio's face appeared in the opening and leaning into him was Beely. Their faces dripped dampness and held *desperado* eyes, each as bad as the other. Garita came in behind them. My cheeks burned as hot as the warming grate.

"Quick, Ambrosia, boil some water. *Compadre* Bonney took a bullet. Now, help him, *pronto,*" my brother barked.

Bonney was a name I'd forgotten. But who, how, why, when questions didn't come out. This must be more punishment from Holy Almighty I knew was coming. I dropped the dough, took the griddle off, left the *masa,* and ran out with a bucket to pull water. When I came back, Yginio had yanked Beely's boot, cut his pant leg, and held a bloody rag below his legs to catch a red stream. Too much for the cloth, his blood ran off in a slow, but constant dribble. The blood spot I left on Beely's blanket came to mind. Shook the thought and began cutting long rags from a sheet, new enough for more use but old enough for this cause. No time to think about barn love or usable sheets. Half-serious, half-amused, Beely rested himself on his elbow and put eyes on me that spoke a secret only he and I knew. I didn't look away.

Garita, who usually loves new experiences, stood with her back to the wall, her face white and her mouth open.

"What? How do we do this?" My shriek shook any calmness I might have. I had birthed calves, scraped and pumiced horse wounds, washed blood saliva from Mamá's consumptive mouth, tied broken bones, but never this. "*¿Como?*" I looked to Yginio and then to Beely. His smiled carried wrinkled pain and fell back, and my brother didn't reply.

"Quick, okay, we can do it. *Pronto* let's get started," I said. "We don't want to lose him."

Yginio grabbed what was left of the sheet and ripped long strips with his teeth. "Hey, *compadre,* you alive, ain't you? Only a few of us made it," Yginio said. "Leave this one in, eh partner? Too deep. Heals by itself with the iron in. We'll just clean it up and wrap it. Ambrosia, pumice the hole, and we'll wrap it."

"No, no *compa.*" Beely shook his head mightily for a wounded man. "Not carrying around this slug. Rather have a deep scar. Get it out," said Beely. "Heard tell of men who left some in, and it pained them every time they moved. Out, ow, ouch, I want it out. What forsaken luck came at me today? Dang it." He wrapped his hands above his leg wound.

Then he sat up and rubbed around the bullet hole. "Ambrosia, get the sharpest and longest knife you got. Does Salamon have whiskey? Oh, Mother Mercy, hurt, hurt, hurt go away." He stopped and took in a deep breath. "Never take the stuff but give it to me and dig the God-dang slug out." He squeezed his eyes shut, and when he opened them, they fixed on me. "Sorry, Ambrosia, I got to cuss it out. Don't judge me responsible for anything I say here."

"I have a knife, but Yginio doesn't have any liquor," I said.

Yginio took a little piece of Beely's torn Levi pants and rolled it. As he twisted it, blood seeped out over the floor. "Put it in your mouth and bear down on it. Help with the pain. Ambrosia, is the water boiling?" Yginio raised his voice to the ceiling.

"Yes, almost, *ya,* okay? Garita, get Apá's pliers. I got the knife." I wiped the beaded wetness from my forehead.

"Mercy me, is it far in? Get a spoon or fork to move the meat back and push it from the bottom up. Son of God, put out the pain, beh geezers." He rocked back and forth holding his laid-up leg. "Ride it. Come on. Get on the bull and run him ragged," he said to himself, but I felt he was yelling at me.

Like water spiked up from hot grease, drops of sweat raised up and dripped down Beely's face. The memory of our time when a different wet sprung on our skin rose within me. His body screamed a fire of pleasure, not pain. His face had the same rich emotion in an explosion of peaked joy.

I didn't see my brother leave, and now he stood with a slender bottle of amber drink. Garita and I both turned to him.

"Here, *compadre,* take this." Yginio handed Beely a full whiskey bottle. "It will help."

"Ginio, *malo* — bad," Garita whispered

as if the soothing whiskey was not a blessing.

"It's okay, Garita," said Yginio. "*Está bien,* it's gut warmer from the back of the chicken pen. Don't tell Apá."

"Yginio's right, Garita. Keep this to yourself." For once, my brother did something good. "The water is ready and the pliers and spoon and knife are cured. Beely, take a good swig, and we start. Yginio, tie his leg down. He can't move it while I'm digging. Garita, tighten up his arms. I see the bulge." I pushed down where the bullet was lodged.

"Jesus Christ, God damn, Ambrosia, holy mercy, I thought you was going to wait," Beely screamed.

"I touched a little bit, *no mas,* to know where it is. It hurts only at first then you'll see it loses the pain. There, *ya,* nothing on top, so I know how it has to come up. *Valiente,* Beely, stay *valiente.*"

"Ay, ay, ay," he stopped to catch his breath. "Caught it on a big killing day. Things happened there, ladies, I'm glad you didn't see." The drink moved his mouth in short sentences with lots of breaths in between. "Don't want that kind of memory for you ever."

His liquored lips chattered. "Some eleven

black soldiers, no less than twenty-four infantry, ay oh, in full soldier dress." He paused. "Aimed not a pistol or a rifle or a buffalo gun, but what'd they say it was, Yginio?"

"A how . . . how . . . something." Yginio held Beely's leg and nodded as his *amigo* spoke.

"Witzer, yeah, a howitzer. Was a cannon barrel made not for shooting but for spraying bullets like a waterfall barrel. Oh, oh, oh, it's getting better. Ache's dulling out. Yeah, well . . ." He took a long swallow, draining half of what was left in the bottle. "This howitzer was aimed at McSween's front door. He is . . . was the house and Jimmy Dolan's enemy, and he was Tunstall's good lawyer friend. The house *gangers* were fixed on taking McSween."

Garita held the bottle as our patient leaned back and let the golden brew sink in.

"People in the home, McSween defenders, absquatulated behind whatever bushes, outhouses, fence planks they could find. Coward turncoats. Some with blankets over their heads. But Yginio and I stayed steady. Right, partner? We'd never put a rag over our heads. No sir. Go ahead, Ambrosia, I'm read . . . read . . . ready."

I waited for the whiskey to flow down before I pushed the wound open with two spoons. He screamed off the bed. Garita put the bloody, rolled rag into his mouth, and he bit down between screams and moans.

"Garita, clamp him down," I said, "with more force. You know how to do that."

She pulled his arms back over his head, and Yginio held his legs tight. Like a trapped animal, he fought them.

Soon the rag fell out. "Sweet Jesus, Savior bring down the saving. Okay, give me a jolt of the anesthesia and take the hot branding iron to me again. I got a hold on it."

Garita let go of his arms and put the rag roll back into his mouth. He bit down and passed out. I worked fast. Once the base of the bullet glowed silver in the bloody skin, I prodded it near the surface. With another hard push, it popped out like a slimy birth calf. Garita took Beely's loose arms and shook him. She wet the bloody pants rag in cool water, squeezed it, and rubbed his face. His eyes opened, less wolverine and more puppy.

"Holy criminy, mercy me, out? Did you get it?" He brought his head up and collapsed back onto the bed. "Bless you, Ambrosia."

"Over, Beely, it's over. Garita, get me the creosote. That little flat jar with the green juice. And bring the Aloe Vera moss water. *Sí,* that one." I filled the wound with the poultice. The strips of sheets turned red as I circled them tight around his leg. I didn't stop until they stayed white.

"Praise the Lord, his father, and the other one," Beely said. "It wasn't bad now that I'm looking back on it. Yginio, give me another gulp of the lightning, would you? Ole deuce devil can wait a spell longer for me. The Savior has spared me and has blessed me more life pleasures." He looked at me, and I stretched the sheet gauze over his wound so tight he jerked.

"There now, Ambrosia, take it easy." Hazy blues smiled at me. "Never mean to sound short. What you did, I'm greatly indebted. All of you alls."

"*¿Que mas,* Beely?" Garita asked.

"*Ya no,* too much, Garita, let Beely rest." I sat for the first time.

With eyes slitted almost shut, he went on.

"Nah, not too much for angel Garita. Dolly doll, let's see. Where did I leave off? Yeah, okay. The whole government tribe aimed at Susan McSween's home, and she, that being Susan McSween, called out to her Lord. She said, 'God, are we in a no-man's-land or in the United States of America?' "

"Say-so?" Garita laughed — not a leg-digging, down-in-the-mouth kind of laugh, but a happy-go-lucky howl.

"Yeah, the general in charge of the soldiers, name of Dud . . . Dudley, stood behind his men. His big loader made him a giant grizzly, facing a pack of field mice — horrible, trapped innocents looking out the windows. Women, children, and men, even Preacher Ealy pleaded for reason. Preacher said, 'God can move mountains, but can he fight the U.S. Army?' "

With legs spread, Garita hung her hands in the folds of her skirt and let her braids fall down over her lap.

I motioned for her to sit up as I wiped Beely's bloody face with a clean strip of sheet. "Beely, stop. You don't need to tell us any more. Rest," I said.

Yginio sat at the table and sharpened his knife with a gray whetstone.

"This ain't no blusteration, Ambrosia, I'm telling you how it happened. Alex McSween wrote a note to the colonel — a scribbled thing on a torn piece of paper. I seen it. He scribed, 'Why are soldiers surrounding my house?' "

Garita moved to him and caressed his

damp hair.

I shook my head and gestured for her to move away.

"It was the missus and me who walked out with that note. Colonel Dudley did not move not one step beyond his first posture. I seen . . . oh, oh." Beely moved his leg to one side. "Old Dudley hump his craw to take the note from Susan. He floated boozy breath and had been hitting the Kansas sheep dip long before he came with his troops. Worse, much worse than I am now."

Garita did not take her hand off Beely's sweaty forehead. "Beely? Big shoot?" Then she took his hand into hers and held it.

"I know, Garita. It's coming. Let me get this part in. The old codger said, 'I have no desire to parley any correspondence; if you so desire to blow up your own lodging, I do not object.' Or some fool thing or another like that. Imagine him a protector."

I held my jaw firm, corralling my smile. Thoughts of his stroking hands took me away. If I had a charm to make Yginio and Garita disappear, I'd have used it.

"Then Susan McSween came back at the colonel. 'Do you have barrel fever? Can you see straight out those bug-juiced eyes? This, Sir, where you have your cannon pointed, is my home. I am not the enemy of the U.S.

260

government. If it pleases your remote rational mind, Sir, I'm a citizen and tax-paying owner of the armor you're intending to use on us.' Oh, Susan tore his big *ahem* apart. She's a feisty woman. That one is."

I reached to move my sister's hand out of Beely's grip.

She pulled it away and put it on his arm.

"*Amigo,* enough talk," Yginio said, "I can finish the story." He put the knife and whetstone back in his pocket.

"No, I'm a get . . . getting to the best part." He rubbed his leg before he began again. "Then I told the old Colonel Dudley, 'what she says is the truth. You're out of your line in this here approach. You best take your battalion back to Fort Stanton.' Thought the uppity military officer could take it better from a man." With his arm, unoccupied with Garita's hand, he wiped his temple. "Almost finished." He winced and went on. "Dudley then says, 'I will not correspond with you or this snivel of a slinger.' Called me that. Well then, I put my hands on my holster and said, 'Snivel, huh? Want to see inside of my sniveler?' "

Finally, Beely's head leaned back onto the pillow, tinted pink from his blood. "Yginio, you finish. I'm tired." He closed his eyes. "Ambrosia's right. I need to rest."

We looked at Yginio.

"Women and children ran next door to Señor Tunstall's abandoned store. The soldiers threw fire straw into the house. First the back kitchen caught, then it spread all over. Even McSween's wife's piano went up. Beely and I took a run from that *infierno,* and in that run Beely took a slug." Yginio nodded his glory. His smirk said it all. He was proud of his bout with death.

"Did the whole place burn?" I asked.

"Guess so, it was still going when we ran." My brother sat back with his feet laid out in front of him and his arms crossed.

"Bad, mean, *malos,*" Garita said, *"mucho, muy malos."*

Yginio went on. "Alexander McSween got shot when he walked out with a white flag. I think he's dead. We had nowhere else to go, so we came here."

Yginio was the first to jump at the sound of footfalls.

When the door opened, Garita and I took a leap.

Apá stood in the frame with Ramon behind him.

Chapter Sixteen

My father was pale as the day Mamá died. Heavy arms pulled his shoulders down. He stood like a fading shadow of himself. He eyed the room, starting with Beely's laid-up leg, glared at Yginio, then shook his head at the red stains on my dress. I looked for a hiding place, but the best I could do was bend down and mop blood from the floor with a soaked rag. We could not hide our doings, and the wet cloth hardly picked up more blood. My hanging head helped only in that I didn't have to look at Apá.

Garita kneeled beside me with her wrinkled *protect* band. She pulled it from I don't know where. It hung a few mangled eagle feathers over her face as she moved her bloody rag beside me.

Heavy, the air smelled blood heavy as if we had gutted a fatted calf and two pigs in our kitchen. Yginio stayed sitting, braced his arms, ready for a backhand, I guess.

Ramon shot bullet eyes at me when I lifted my face, and he held them on me and only me.

"What is this? *Eh, que pasa?*" Apá's angry voice, like we expected, turned us inward.

"Salamon, I can explain," said Beely. He sat up on his elbows with skin so white it matched the sheets.

"Big . . . big . . ." Garita began, stopped, and stuttered more useless words through her wrinkled headdress. "Un big *tiro* — shoot."

"Talking makes it worse," I whispered close to her ear. "*Cállate ya,* quiet, Garita."

Head down, she straightened her face feathers.

Yginio spoke. "Apá, we took a slug out of our *amigo*'s leg."

My brother did not say he was with Beely, and I was glad for his little forgetfulness.

"A slug, a bullet you mean? Why did this man need you to do that? I told you, Yginio, to stay out of this." My father's finger pointed right at my bother and waved an angry curse.

"Salamon, *amigo,* let me explain. You said I was welcomed any time in your homestead. You meant it, didn't you? Don't, please don't blame your children for doing a kind thing."

Ramon stood with his arms folded, *macho*-like. "I know why he came here. He's on the run from the brawl in Lincoln. We saw flames and smoke from the northwest pasture. All hell's broke loose there. I bet you were in some fight you had to turn your back on."

"No, it wasn't like that." Beely's bearing on his elbows weakened, and he fell against the sheets.

"These people never needed an *amigo* like you." Ramon's deep voice rattled my spine. "*Cabrón* trouble — you are. Yginio, you were there, too, weren't you? That's why you couldn't help your father with the pasturing today."

Yginio pinched his eyes and shook his head.

"Now wait. Let me finish, Ramon." Beely braced himself back up. "And Salamon, listen, *por favor.* This looks bad but who we helped, what we stood for, what we done was right." He sucked in air like he had come up from under water.

"Seen enough. Don't need to hear more." Apá flung his hat on the table and sat.

Yginio leaned back and cracked his knuckles.

Beely wiped the wetness from his brow and brushed light fingers over his wound.

I stood up and braced my body with my stiff arms against the chair back. Garita, beside me, grabbed my hand, and we sat down on the bed.

"Women, children, and poor McSweens — unfortunates who done nothing wrong suffered today much more than I did," said Beely. "Just like they done to our decent man, Tunstall, they did to others. Flames lapped all around us. We was lucky to get Reverend Ealy and the children to a safe place. Soldiers were supposed to take care of them. What kind — ?"

"Ya basta," Ramon said, "had enough. Do you have ears? Didn't you hear what Salamon said? Talk, talk, talk, I'm sick of it."

Like a grizzly on the scent of a blood trail from an animal's fatal wound, Ramon went for helpless, weak Beely.

"Keep your words. This family has more important cares than the Lincoln County War." Ramon glared at me. *"El* Mister Murphy's horse needed shoeing and he came by yesterday." He wiped what looked to be a tear from his eye. "Sinforosa is suffering worse than Susan McSween in her fire." He turned to Beely. "That's who this family needs to help, not Susan McSween or you."

"Sinforosa." Apá whispered her name,

nodded, then shook his head many times. Black smudges like soot hung below puffy eyes, the color of blood-mixed coffee. "Señor Murphy told Ramon, she, our Sinfo, is very, very sick."

"¿*Tiro* — shoot?" Garita asked. "Fire?"

"No, *Mija,* neither," Ramon said. "She's gone into a bad state, too deep for anyone to pull her out. She's taking this war inside herself, *pobre.* Killing and shooting has hurt Señor Murphy's Jewel place, and he would like for her to come here." Ramon, glistening eyes and slumped shoulders, put his hands on his wide hips to fake strength.

"That's it, ain't it? You say I don't belong here, but you're Murphy's calling boy," Beely said.

"What do you know about Señor Murphy and me? He's my neighbor who gives me business, *no mas.* Catron from Santa Fe has leaned his mercantile, and he's suffering, too. This war is killing all of us. *Pinche cabrón,* why do I tell you anything? This is not your house. You bring trouble where there was none. These people had peace and never needed to be fighting Murphy."

"Who cares about crooked Lawrence Murphy? He can't be worse off than what he brung on the McSweens. Yeah, we know whose camp you're in, Mr. Lickspittle. How does rich, fat man's spit taste, good? Wish it'd infect you. He was a big part in starting this war, and you know it." He braced his back with his elbows as much as he could and pulled himself up.

Ramon leaped at Beely and pushed him off the bed. Beely struggled, then lifted up onto the table, balancing on his good leg. If he'd had his pistol, Ramon would have lost his head.

Apá screamed, "Stop this now. We have plenty enough troubles. Ramon, you too, *ya, basta.*"

Yginio, next to Beely, leaped up and stood wide-eyed.

I could not keep silent. "Oh yeah, Ramon. You see he's injured. *Sí,* fight a man who's down. Yes, that makes you real good."

"It's alright, Ambrosia. Fight my own battles." Beely glared at Ramon. "That's twice I've graced you, *hombre.* Not many more hoedowns left before your hog killing time."

Ramon waved a fist at Beely and stomped outside. "Salamon, let me know what else I can do to help Sinforosa. Whatever you want."

From inside, we heard Ramon *yeehaw* a hard gallop up the road.

Beely's hobbled-up leg did little to help

him get to his barn corner. He rested on Yginio and hopped on the good one. Garita and I scooped up horse manure to give him cleaner air, added new hay to his corner, and even though it was July, we brought more blankets. When our eyes met, it became something closer to oneness, a breeze instead of a storm.

Apá was in bed when we went back into the grand room. Beaten as he was, he didn't have enough fight to put an injured man out when his children felt otherwise. His snoreless corner told me he was awake. Worse still, his children helping a Regulator whipped a backlash deep enough to keep him from sleeping not only tonight but many nights. He didn't want any part of the Lincoln County War and expected that from us.

The next morning at breakfast my *pobre* Apá said he quit his smokes, his last little pleasure. He was trying to save money. I had gone to Murphy's House alone to bring Garita, and that had shamed his position as the ruling father. I wanted to put my arm around him but knew his *machismo* wouldn't take kindly to it. Murphy's bartering conditions would not change, but it looked to me Sinforosa's sinking illness was what crushed my father most. I guess, he, like me, had wished she would some day return. *Ya pues,* everyone tried to act as if he was still our father of the past.

Chapter Seventeen

That next day, Sinforosa's trouble took us to Lincoln. Apá, still angry at Yginio, told him it would be better if he didn't show his Regulator face in Lincoln. I'm sure he feared someone from the house might just take him out for pure pleasure.

"*Sí*, Apá, whatever you say, Apá," my brother said during breakfast.

Deep down, I bet Yginio was glad to be with our injured Kid Beely instead of bringing Sinfo home. I wished it was me instead of him staying.

I giddied up Luz. We three, Apá, Garita, and I, sat arm to arm on the bench of the buckboard, like sad birds on a short branch. Seats, hard against our sitting bones, bounced us back to the forbidden town. A swarm of swallows covered a scrub oak and sang a chorus of gladness as we headed out. Summer was here, but I felt glum and unsunny.

Knowing our old lady mare would never bolt, I loosened her reins, and she hoofed across the Ruidoso and up the road to the Bonito. At the double rocks, we turned left and headed north toward *la casa grande,* less than eight miles from there to Lincoln. Far to the west, the beautiful Sacramentos showed off her dark purple peaks, crowned by its Sierra Blanca. Crisp air filled us. The sun grew warmer, and Garita finally moved from my cramped side, so I could stretch my right arm. Apá sat on the end, quiet. He tapped his fingers on his knee, then let his arms fall between his legs like a little swallow who had lost its wings. Luz moved steadily, each step a hollow thud toward dread.

The memory of Sinforosa, like the familiar turns in the road, came to me. We were, once, two girls, praying, picking wild spinach, carrying fleeces for Apá, and sharing dreams. Her love for Tunstall, who died just about five months ago, became her end. My begging for her return got slammed shut — locked for good. I prayed for forgiveness and wondered where in that past did her heart leave us?

When I cared, she felt none. When Garita called, I went, but Garita still loved her more. When I worked, she sat. When I prayed at night, she dreamed of other places. Sinforosa left me with Garita's charge, the one who thinks she can play with snakes and eat the moon. Her name, Sin-fo-rosa, sins for *rosas.* But roses soon turn brown, shrivel, hang down, and fade. This is where we had come now.

Whitetail deer hid in the brush alongside the Bonito. A doe, skittish with worry, flicked her tail and stayed close to a shy, wide-eyed fawn. Reminded me of my mother's favorite song, I'd heard her sing as she worked. A sad song about deer who took shelter in high ground. Their fear kept them in the mountaintops, safe, but they needed lowland water. So they jittered down, never in the light of day, never alone — always at night in the safety of a herd as if in the arms of a lover. The gentle creatures possessed my mother's kindness. How she would have suffered for lovely Sinforosa. Her death spared her this pain. Thoughts of Beely and Ramon, Garita, and Apá came and went. We were the nervous deer, heading into a Godless land, a cruel place where good was bad and bad was good.

At night tiny steps — *"Y de noche poco poquito . . ."* I sang of fear, danger, living water — love protectors. I thought of Beely and his injured leg.

Garita moved fake whisper words with me in song. I put my arm around her and smiled. For once I didn't silence her, but Apá did. He put his fingers to his lip and shook his head. I gave her a hug, more for myself than for her.

The deer, after taking their morning drink, sprang their white, heart-shaped butts into the bushes.

"Sinforosa, *hermosa. Amorosa La Rosa,*" Garita sang as we neared Lincoln.

Sinforosa, malosa, I thought. *Sins for rosas.*

In the distance this side of Lincoln, we could see the outlying homes and one of them was the Salamancas'. Unlike many other of our *adobe casitas,* theirs was not of mud bricks but of wood. The boards, worn-down gray like animal bones left in the sun, had seen better days. Usually in the summer, Doña tended her garden, or many times she stepped out and waved us in, but this day her house sat silent.

"Stop it," Garita said. "*Ver* — see Doña."

I snapped the reins and *yeehawed* Luz forward, for she knew this place and slowed up, hoping for a rest, too.

Windows faced the road, and I thought I saw Ramon in the front glass, but I did not want to glance in that direction. Nobody came out. Ramon probably banged the table when he told his mother about our aid to Beely. No matter.

Apá and Garita stared harder at the Salamanca place than I had wanted. For years, they refuged us. Ramon had been a solid rock in a windy river, a soothing future, one who shared my past. Doña guarded him. That would never change.

"Sí, Ambrosia, *para* — stop. Apá say so, yes," Garita said again.

I shook my head.

"Why *no*? Garita wants to stop." My father sliced an open left hand in midair and motioned a turn.

I whipped the leathers when we wheeled beside their gate. "No, Garita, we will not stop. We got to see Sinforosa." Today, I had only enough goodwill to face Sinforosa. Ramon and Doña's probing would wring me drier than a dirt tank in late July, and today I had the reins.

While taking a short rest stop, Apá, with a stiff, sunken chin, moved to the rear of the buckboard. I giddied up Luz and kept our rattle north. The wheels felt my father's back load and rubbed, true to how I felt, *clunk-sunk, clunk-sunk, clunk-sunk.*

There, in the distance, up the way, above the others, the huge House Mercantile laid its claim. Just east of the building, dim streaks, like torn witch fleeces, hung. Gray fog draped over the main street, and as we got closer, the smell of burned cinders filled our lungs. The odor did not resemble campfire smoke or gun smoke. It reeked of other things — cloth, leather, carpet, wall hangings, paper — not of natural material — and the mix carried a stink of human flesh.

"*Mal* stink," Garita said.

Apá jumped off the back and onto the steering bench with us. A white ash, like powder flakes of morning dew, covered everything, the bushes, trees, and road. Apá handed a dirty handkerchief to Garita; she put it over her nose, and then waved it around her face. I didn't rush Luz's steps, and we squeaked our slow molasses ride up through town.

When we reached the center, a circular line of smoke drifted around and away from what was left of the McSweens' home. It looked like Satan had gone mad and brought his *infierno* to earth, burning help-less angels. McSween was Tunstall's friend, the lawyer, who crossed Murphy. From what Ramon said, he was a good man, too. He never carried a gun.

What sounded most loud was the ringing

in my ears for lack of noise. The quiet like a death camp raised hot-ice bumps on my arms. I rubbed them. No one, nowhere, not a soul around to break the quiet, just like the last time I came looking for Garita. A bony dog crossed the street, and an eerie breeze blew the fire smell toward us.

I shuddered and pulled my light *chal* over my shoulders.

To the right, we neared what was left of a once beautiful home. Hot smoldering spots cradled embers, and when the wind gusted up over them, they blistered a red glow. A few wood poles, which were once solid boards outlining the foundation corners, poked up from the ground. Now they were upward black tips. Susan McSween's beautiful piano collapsed in a silent heap. Charred wood legs and white ivory rectangles lay in dark powder with glass chips from a broken front window. Nearby, the shoe of a small child and a blackened baby bib huddled together. Silverware lay scattered in the dirt. Susan McSween's fine white dishes, now broken shards, dotted the ground. Her lace curtain sashes curled around the floor like shriveled snakes. Looked like the end of time.

I wiped a tear, and Garita put her arm around me. Decent people laughed, prayed, sang songs, ate, dreamed, and loved each other in this place. Once many felt safe there. When I closed my eyes, I could see the preacher scrambling women and children to safety. Yginio and Beely running away. Alexander McSween walking out with a white flag and getting shot. Susan, his wife, screaming.

We lumbered by Sheriff Brady's old place. Empty.

Next door the beaten-up remains of the Tunstall's Mercantile sat abandoned. A wooden plaque read *Tunstall Wares, Ferrier Needs, and Whatnots Here.* Underneath, a bench with a broken leg folded under, collapsed below a low-shuttered window. Make-do cross boards were nailed over a bashed door. I could see through the slants. Inside a few wares and whatnots were scattered about like someone knocked their way in and took their share of what belonged to another. Soundless, the store's dark insides looked to be a tomb cave. A crow cawed overhead in the distance.

Luz nodded her way in the direction of La Jewel House. A mealy mouse man, a lawman's back, a greasy man's sour breath, a tipped spittoon came back to me. I took a deep breath and refreshed my courage. A burnt rag blew across Luz's path, and she reared. It was nothing but small trouble, so I *tlicked tlicked* her forward. Soon she stepped echoes off the lonely road like clopping pebbles into a tin bucket.

Solid, it stood, the winning gladiator, the winning rooster cock. The Murphy House chilled me. The door still hung the *Closed* sign. An Apache Indian woman swept the sidewalk outside. She was not Tehde. I didn't recognize her, and thought she must be Garita's replacement. She looked up and down quickly. Garita waved, but the Indian woman kept sweeping.

"Amiga, India," she said as we passed, "Ohwa."

"Garita," Apá said. "Down, put your head and hands down. Be still. You never know if one side or the other will think we're on one side or the other."

Moments went by.

"Feel it, Ambrosia?" He rubbed the hollows of his eyes, ran his hand down his face, and smoothed the curved edges of his jaw bone. "Man's black insides, *rabia*? Very bad? All around us here. Nobody knows which way to turn."

"Fear, I feel fear, Apá . . ." I kept my eyes forward. "My own."

"*Malo* — bad. But we not, Apá." Garita handled something in her pocket, and I

279

figured it was her *protect* feather band.

"Garita, *sí,* it's bad," I said. "You're right but don't say it so loud."

"I talk too," she said. Her crossed arms spoke for her.

Of late, and for sure since her monthly callings, she sassed more than Apá and I needed.

La Jewel Parlor, just north of the huge mercantile, hid itself in the quiet like the rest of town. One side of the front placard had come unhinged, so the sign hung lopsided — neglected glory of another time. The noisy place I had visited the day I tried to bring Sinforosa home was long gone. Heavy hearted, we rode to the front, got out, and walked to the large door. Garita took my hand. Apá knocked.

The curtains I had admired so on my first visit were still beautiful. I wondered what else hadn't changed. A large lady pulled the drapes aside, glanced out, and was gone. The fine threads were loomed thin enough we could see through to the inside. She moved from the window to the front entrance. The door opened just slightly as if we were there to do harm.

"Yes," she said, "how can I help you?"

"*Hola,* yes, hello," said Apá. "I'm Salamon, Salamon Salazar from up the ways near San Patricio." Crackly little voice, of what was left of my father, squeaked out, thin and weak and was so low I thought the lady could hardly hear him.

Loose hair sprung off her head, and fingernails, redder than a sugar beet boil, reined in her runaway bun. This woman was the one who found me at Sinforosa's door, and I prayed she would not remember me from that day. My good sense kept me quiet.

"I . . . uh, . . . I am the apá for Sinforosa Salazar. She is in this place somewhere, my daughter. We, these other girls and me, want to see her," Apá said.

I wanted to take over and speak with force, but that would make him all the more helpless.

"Oh, yes, these days I just never know who'd be coming to this place, especially on a Sunday. Howdy do, please come around the back to the northwest entry. That would be the best way to Foro's quarters. It's the door into a stairway to our salons. Just go in there and right up the risers. Her place is the first one on the left." She closed the door.

"Foro?" Garita asked.

"That's her. The same for Sinforosa," Apá said. "Like you. We say Garita for Margarita,

281

same, Brocia for Ambrosia. We say Sinfo and they say Foro. *Ya,* remember, *Mija,* head down and no talking loud."

Shades of our old Apá were coming to life. We stepped around back of the parlor. I knew exactly where Sinfo's room was, but for Apá's peace, kept my know-how to myself.

The large madam seemed the only thing alive in all of Lincoln besides a sick-looking Calico cat with one eye. A dried socket crept deep into its head, creviced into a dull, mossy eye-hole that glazed a whitish tint. Its throaty howl shook the air — hollow and deep, as if from a mourning mother. The scraggly being followed us and pressed itself between my legs.

"Tuerta," Garita said.

I distanced myself from the furry follower. *"¿Tuerta?* A good name — one-eyed. How do you know this thing?" Then I remember the cat she chased the day we were here for Sinfo. This must be the one that took her up the mister's tree.

"Señor Murphy's," Garita said. "His belong."

I rushed side steps around the cat as we continued our walk. "That day you worked here?"

"Sí." Garita reached down to pick it up.

"No, leave it." I pulled her in the direction of the back door.

Apá pointed his finger toward her and waved a *no.* He took off his greasy cowboy hat, and his head, without it, shrunk him into his clothes. His string-bottom jeans brushed the dirt, and his mud-caked boots rested on well-worn heels. I wondered if the purple lady saw our tatteredness.

Two doors faced the back. We peeked in the first one and saw a kitchen sink with a stack of dirty glasses, plates, and an icebox. A stalk of celery, an onion, two knives, and a plucked, white chicken sprawled on a counter. This room joined the front parlor by a narrow hallway. The other outside door, I knew to be at the end of the hallway, was much more worn. Curls of dried white paint like brittle wasp wings covered it. We, who weren't allowed the front door, stopped here.

"*Aquí,* this is where the *mujer* said to go in." A familiar feeling of shameful weariness, fear for what we'd find, came over me.

Apá nodded, and Garita made the same head gesture. The old cat kept its pace with us, one green eye and the other the color of a dull cedar berry. It begged for a touch. I moved it away with my foot.

Apá's first knock tapped weakly. His

second thudded louder, and I was sure if anyone was sleeping inside, they could hear. No answer. The cat meowed a long cry like a hurt baby. We waited a stretch, and the old mangy Calico drew itself against my legs again.

"*Oowee,* shhh *ya,* go away," I said to the *Cucuy*-possessed animal. "Apá you don't have to knock, just open it."

Garita moved the cat away with her leg. "Tuertita, *ya,* go."

Apá tried the knob, but the door appeared locked. He turned it with more force. It creaked worse than our barn door on its rusty hinges, but it opened. Apá went in first. We followed, tightening the door close behind to keep the cat out.

"*Hola,* there a soul in here?" My father said. "Anybody?"

"Remember, the lady told us we had to go up these stairs." I pointed up.

The railing ran long and smooth against our palms. Garita rubbed it like she was shucking corn. She couldn't get enough of the feel. We stepped up the planks, rising into another world, a den of disappointed dreams.

When we reached the second landing, a cough sounded from one of the back bedrooms. We moved into a long dark hallway with closed doors. A clink of metal and the sound of heavy boots landed someone off rusty bed springs and onto the floor. A deep voice, coming from the other side of the lodging, mumbled something about towels and sheets.

Apá kept going forward without any idea of where or how far to go.

"She said the first door on the left, this one." I led him back toward Sinfo's room.

"Smell stinky legs." Garita wanted to say more in her louder than a mouse voice until Apá turned and tightened his eyes on her.

"Shhh," Garita said and put her own finger to her own lips.

Another cough sounded from Sinfo's place. The door's thickness muffled a dry hack of phlegm lodged in someone's throat. We heard a person say, "spit." This brought back memories of my mother's suffering and the white dotted blue tin I had used to gather her droppings.

As if pushing a heavy coffin gate, Apá creaked the door open. In his tracks, Garita and I followed. Clothes hung on driven nails along the walls, and the odor of damp old clothes soaked in mint and alcohol hung rotten and tangy in the air. Even though evening was still to come, the room was dark. On the bed, a woman, curled in at the

285

elbows and knees, lay collapsed. Another with long braids leaned over her.

The one on the bed was light-skinned. When the caretaker moved, we could see the sick person was Sinforosa, and the tenderer was Tehde. Our *amiga* held a shallow tin filled with yellowish foam. She cut a string of spittle from my sister's mouth to the receptacle. Sinfo's once-fair face held a rosy tint as she heaved a wet hacking. Strange to be so close, after not seeing her for such a long spell. Like watching our favorite white bread mold and crumble before us. An urge to look but not look held me.

When Garita whispered "Sinfo," our lost sister set dreary, moss-green eyes on us. She held a glow as if from behind a thin-threaded curtain. The sun is no less spectacular at dusk than midday. That was Sinforosa. Her beauty, so deep, the wretched illness could not steal all of her radiance.

When she recognized me, her eyes shied away.

"Sinfo, we *ven* — come," Garita said.

The same redness on her face colored her hands. When I looked again, I could see she was swollen. Sinforosa fell back onto her bed.

"How bad?" Apá asked. "How long?" He

looked at Tehde.

Tehde lifted her shoulders slow and let them fall fast. She shook her head without a word.

Garita ran to Sinforosa and began stroking her hair. On the nearby dresser, a wet cloth hung over a jar, and she wiped Sinfo until her pale face turned away.

"Very sick. *¿Hay un doctor?*" Apá asked.

Tehde took the cloth from Garita and tended to Sinforosa without looking at my father. "One medicine man smoked out yesterday in fire. Fort Stanton one, but this Sinforosa say too much sick to go, and they no come here."

Sinforosa coughed a short bark.

"Boss lady give dead-bone pill but now say, 'no more.' Too much to pay. Indian earth medicine I got, but this one say, 'no more.'" Tehde cut her hand across her neck and ended with a waving forefinger to tell us her patient would not take what she offered. "Much sorry. This one turned sick when a Tuh un stall go away, dead gone."

Sinfo lifted her head off the bed. "Keep your words. None of you. *¿Ya por qué?* Why? I'm no good for this world." She stopped to catch her breath. "The other place can't be . . . be worse than . . ."

"No." Garita waved her pointer finger at

287

Sinfo. "Mamá no want you. Ambrosia say that."

"Eating?" Apá asked. "Eating?" he repeated as he motioned his fingers to his mouth.

Tehde shook her head.

A knock sounded at the door.

"*Ni sopa?* Soup?" Apá said. Hat in hand, his sweaty, brown calloused fingers curled the rim of his hat tighter than tight.

Before Tehde could answer, we turned to see the purple lady, leaning into the doorway.

"I see you found your daughter, very well. Been getting her through with laudanum and this here Indian, but poor dear, she can't sleep, coughs all the time, won't eat, and her stomach can't take the drugs anymore. Fear she has the Cupid's Disease — that's what it looks like to me. Make sure you wash your hands. She doesn't have the strength to move, and 'sides, we don't know where to move her."

Looked like the big lady thought she would catch my sister's infection, so she stayed her distance in the doorway.

The lower rim of Sinforosa's eyes filled, but it didn't appear to be tears. I couldn't imagine her ever crying.

Apá put his hat back on, shoved his hands

in his pockets, and threw his shoulders forward. "What we to do?"

"Well, her illness is not well placed here, and I know Mr. Lawrence Murphy would like you to take her home. Is that possible?" She wiped her hands with a white handkerchief and slipped it into her dress top.

"Away. Out of here. Leave me alone. Die without your *cabrón* eyes. Worse with you watching. Go, *con el favor de Dios,* go." Sinforosa heaved a shallow breath.

Her moan sent the *patrona* lady out, and I was glad to see her gone. She closed the room tight behind her to keep despair trapped with us. And it stayed. The room got smaller, hotter, and smellier.

"Sinforosa, *Mija,*" my father said, "we take you to the *rancho*. We have the flat board and blankets. *Por favor,* please come. There, Ambrosia and Garita care for you. Help you get better." He rubbed what looked to be a bad tooth throb in his jaw and his eyes swelled.

"No, no, Apá." She moved to turn her head but didn't have the strength. A whispered *no,* flat and soft, muffled out again. "How many . . ." a very long silence passed, *"cuantas?"* She took a breath. "Times . . ." She shut her eyes. "Do I have to take my leave of you?" True tears, real and wet, rolled. Garita fell over her and held her so tight I feared Sinforosa could not breathe.

I stood against the wall. My hair tangled on a nail. I unhooked it and moved toward window light. A fly, struggling in the lace curtain, buzzed loud enough to get my attention. Then something else caught my eye. A gold piece glinted on the dresser. It sparkled brighter than the eyes of a mountain lion caught in campfire light. The starburst glowed out of place with common hairpins, a dirty white ribbon, a wet rag, and a big red bottle of Dr. T's Liver and Blood Syrup. Captivating, the glow was a circle of ice glass, couldn't be diamonds, around a yellow stone, toasted hard like burnt butter. Light trembled off it. The most beautiful jewel, the only jewel, I had ever seen.

Sinfo stopped and gathered her voice.

"Apá," she pointed with her chin, "drawer." She paused for what seemed many minutes. "Green bills for you. Coins for Garita."

The stained sheet fell back with her. Her half-closed eyes ignored me same as always. Then they opened, moss acorns, floating in toasted cream. They landed on the ring, the golden burn on her dressing table. "Take it, Brosia," she said.

Forgiveness, given to my sister who didn't deserve it, tormented my soul, pointed its finger at me. Clutched me, but I didn't have mercy to give. Regret wasn't forgiveness. I knew holding it back would fester into a crooked smile or gloomy eyes. Put a nastiness around me others could smell. Would make me into something I didn't want to be. I knew all that and knew temptation, my own secret. I had drunk from the same cup of trembling, tasted a man's skin on mine, given in to lust. But mine was giving, hers, of taking. The fly found a hole and flew to the thick white bubbles in the bed pan.

Tehde wiped Sinforosa's face as Apá wasted no time finding the purse. Garita clamped around Sinforosa's neck. I unloosened Garita's grip, but she held onto the bed frame. Metal bed legs scraped the floor, sounding like an eagle in its fall from the sky, wounded and dying.

"*Ya, mi* Garita, *Mija, vete* — go with Apá." Sinforosa gave Garita a parting.

Garita is strong. I tried to wrench her off Sinfo's bed with no success. Apá and Tehde joined, and we broke her hold. Sinforosa, clutching tight to wet sheets, suffered the most in this battle. As we dragged Garita out, Tehde murmured prayers, rattled beads, and brushed eagle feathers across my sister's sand-colored face behind us.

The cat sat waiting, matted porcupine spikes from its furry back. I managed side steps around him. Its good eye planted on me like a cyclops. As if the creature knew what just happened inside and could feel my shame, it stared, silent. I should have forced Sinforosa to come with us. I should have hugged her, stayed with her.

Garita stopped. Tears in the corners of her eyes, she wanted to run back. "Apá, no," Garita said. "Sinfo sick." Her face was as long as the day we explained she could not go with Mamá. Hair sprang out, and her lips, like lines on an uncracked walnut, clamped shut. She crossed her arms and would not take another step.

"*No, Mija, por favor.* Sinfo wants us to go." Apá opened the purse. In his palm, he jingled two coins. He offered them to her. "We will kill her if we force her with us."

"Apá, no good." Garita shook her head and pushed his hand away.

I brushed her hair back. "*Ya, Mija,* I know it's hard to leave her to Señor Murphy. She made money for him. Now she gets back what . . ."

"*Ya,* Ambrosia, stop." My father jingled the coins and again offered them to Garita.

"No, he *malo* — bad." Garita glanced over what was in his hand.

"Apá's right, Garita. Listen. Sinforosa wants this, and we leave her and take you home." I took the coins and put them in her hand.

"No, Sinfo *mala* — sick, and mister bad." Garita put the two bits in her pocket.

"We leave now." I forced her to take steps. "A new day comes tomorrow." She dragged her feet, jingling the coins.

My golden ring bribe sat behind on Sinforosa's dressing table. A queen's charm, my one chance for precious luxury. What would I say to Doña Hurtencia, to Yginio, to Ramon? "Oh, *sí,* this treasure is from Sinforosa, my *puta* sister." It was nothing more than a bribe to take away my unforgiving bitterness — just a ring.

The mangy cat walked with us around the building to our wagon. When we skirted the Murphy Mercantile, I saw a round, black shadow inside the window. The king man expected us to take Sinforosa. Apá was right. Dragging her out in her condition would kill her faster. Impossible. Now the big mister could watch his sad makings.

An *Oowee* dust devil picked up and circled the ash remains of the McSween place around our buckboard like it wanted us to feel more misery. Little bits of char dust embedded the edges of our eyes and inside our ears. I tied my *reboso* around my head. Garita put Apá's kerchief over her mouth.

The Salamanca home, hushed with Ramon's anger or my guilt for helping Beely, wasn't one of my desired stops. I snapped Luz's reins to a full trot. Enough of this forsaken town for this day. Didn't need more talk. Apá and Garita didn't ask to stop.

In our route, a black robe straddled the sides of a good-size mule headed in our direction.

Apá undid two buttonholes and shoved the purse from Sinfo into his loose shirt.

We knew this figure well. Father Martinez, with his flat black hat, trotted toward us. I'm sure his high trots rushed him to the Salamancas'.

"*Buen día,* Salamon." Father Martinez's jowls caged his face-dove motionless until he said, "Girls." In that, the holy mark nodded in our direction.

"*Padre.*" Garita rattled her coins as she spoke. "Dinero, Sinfo, *mío* — mine."

Apá motioned me to stop her.

I grabbed her hands and settled them on her lap.

Father Martinez, distracted by his travels,

paid no mind. "Lincoln town is burning. I can see smoke from here and heard it is still dangerous, but I want to see Sinforosa and others. I thought you might be bringing her home." His restless mule wanted to keep going, and Father pulled back on his reins.

"Our *Dios* Almighty knows we tried, Father." Apá put his arms over his hidden waist treasure. "We wanted her to come, *tu sabes,* to the rancho, but she would not do it. Hauling her out would kill her for sure, sooner than later. *Sí, por favor,* please visit her and pray. And we will keep praying. Next time, when you come with your sacraments, I will give you a lamb."

"Unmerciful hearts, shameful, wayward, hateful acts, these are not men of God. Very sad, many are suffering. *Protestantes,* too. I will stop by the Jewel, and if she permits me, I will, yes, *seguro,* pray with Sinforosa and receive her confession. Seems just yesterday she made her first Holy Communion. They call it the Killing Day." He signed the cross toward us. *"Ya,* be on your way with our Lord Savior, *Vayan con Dios."*

We parted. He, toward smoky dark, and the three of us toward light.

When we neared our turn west, the smoke lifted. In that direction, Sierra Blanca came into view, and in the smoke-free air, my lungs inhaled and cleared like a wind tunnel. A blessing from our Lord God *Diosito* showed itself in a July shower. We welcomed the rain on our skin. Wet creosote bushes released an earth smell like holy air. Whenever that flavor filled me, I thought of birds singing and rabbits dancing. We needed happiness after seeing Sinforosa, and if it was only a savory smell, it would be celebrated.

Garita's sorrow held up until a covey of quail crossed the road. We stopped. Apá brought two down with his rock sling. Garita followed and got herself one, too. As we turned toward San Patricio, I *whoa-ed* Luz a bit to rest her a spell.

Apá sat forlorn, hands around his quail bag, like a poor ole miner whose life claim had just got jumped. He kept opening the bag to make sure the two quail were still inside as if they were going to find life and fly away. He and I knew he had something better stashed in his shirt, more valuable than dead birds. Maybe that's what made him nervous.

I thought of Beely most of the way back, but my memory of him was not of joy. The long sadness in my life weighed down the short happy moments with him. He was but a little bubble of joy in a river of rapid, whitewater heartbreaks — those little times could not change my long days, bearing our sin alone.

Thoughts of Ramon came. Since I'd known him, he was there to do anything for my family. Was Beely false hope, just as Tunstall was for Sinfo? In this short separation from Beely, in realizing Ramon's worth, in seeing the result of killing and burning, and most of all, in witnessing Sinforosa's choice to give up everything for love, I began to doubt this Anglo-*Hispano* man. When I left San Patricio, I lamented leaving Beely. Now I dreaded seeing him.

The gold ring must have been a gift from the rich Englishman. No one else in these parts had the slightest dream about owning such a gem. A love token for her cream legs around him. Just a ring, it was just a ring.

I kept Luz at a high-hoof pace, and when we crossed Río Ruidoso, near our rancho, we saw Beely and Yginio up on the barn repairing holes.

"Beely, good, *ya* okay." Garita flipped her coins from one palm to the other.

"They plugging holes. The *gringito* never stops. *Nunca* never." Apá came alive and looked like he forgot he hated the Chivato.

He and Yginio had heated pine sap over a campfire in an empty tin and were spreading the hot glue over the holes and nailing flattened coffee tins over them. As we neared, the odor of pine made a rich difference to the lingering smoke of Lincoln.

"Buena idea," said Apá.

Yginio and his primo Beely didn't look up and kept settling the metal to the dry rotted holes. The thrill of seeing Beely, a mix of hot and cold, boiled ice in me. I drove the buckboard into the barn, and Apá tended to the horse and carrier. When Garita and I went in, we saw someone had wooded and fired the stove and put a pot of beans on the top grill. The smell filled the kitchen. "When does any man do that?" I said below my breath.

"Beely *tiro* — shoot," said Garita.

"Be the only way Yginio'd do it — with a gun to his head," I said.

Garita laughed until I realized we were joking about guns and killing.

"Cállate ya, stop talking like that," I said.

Garita didn't quit laughing, and I was happy she had forgotten about *la pobre* Sinforosa in her dying bed.

"Boil the quail, pull the feathers, and add the meat to the beans, Garita." I served out a bowl of flour, landed a scoop of bacon grease, added salt and soda ash, and mixed it with water until the tortilla *masa* was smooth. My sister ran outside to pull more water, and I took to rolling. Somewhere else a man is afraid of what's behind the corner; a woman is now a widow without a home, and a sister is shrinking away, but today here in this little poor homestead we have food, at least for this moment.

The door slammed, and Beely limped in. A wet circle of blood, on the white sheet strips around his leg, painted his wound. No more than a little jerk to his step showed his past pain. He took off his hat, set it before him on the table, and stared, that sharp-arrow kind of way, viper onto a bird — like this was his table, house, and food — his woman. He twirled an alfalfa reed in his mouth. "See what we partners did, Ambrosia? Got some vittles in the pot. We're not as good with the spoons as you, but we . . ."

Garita came in, set the pan with water on the grill, and ran out. I tended the fire below.

"*Sí, está bien.* Yes, good, Beely." I felt my jaw tighten.

"And my leg, wrapped real tight, feels braced up. *No problema.* Thought you'd be pleased. No more than a little hitch in my giddy-up. What you did," he said. "I will never forget." His eyes were of his body, but seemed they had a heart of their own and lungs of their own, which threw off an irresistible spirit. Soon his no-care-in-the-world smile sprung up on his face.

"*Sí, está bien.* Yes, good." I rolled one ball of *masa* and put the round on the hot griddle. I didn't look up.

"Are you up in the back 'cause I aired my lungs the other day? Ambrosia, you got to know a man's mouth in times of pain might spout out an ill word or two."

He stopped, and, for once, the glimmer of teeth didn't appear. "Or what? What is it? Sore cause we waylaid Ramon yesterday. Straightened him out and sent him down the road. He's rope-tied to old man Murphy's hind end. Is that it? I'll be — gosh almighty — he's nothing but a turd puppet." He took the alfalfa out of his mouth and tapped it on the table.

Garita banged the door, followed by Yginio, before I could answer. Garita spooned the quail from the boiling water and began pulling off the feathers.

Yginio sat next to him, also with a hay twig in his mouth. "*¿Y* Sinforosa?" he said. "Thought you were hauling her home. *¿Que pasó?*"

Garita looked up from her quail butchering, "*Mucho muy mala* — sick. With Tehde.

300

Dinero to us." She tossed quail bits into the beans.

"Tehde?" Yginio asked. "*La India* Apache who hides her face with feathers, that one?"

"Tehde," I said, "the Mescalera. A very good person." I kept my eyes down.

"*Sí,*" Garita nodded.

I set the quail *refritos,* tortillas, lamb green chili, and potatoes on the table, and it was quiet when Apá came in. The enamel tin plates and cups soon got filled. Yginio and Beely sat on one side, and I sat between Apá and Garita on the other bench. Forks scraped against the serving tins.

"What's in with the beans and wild spinach?"

It would be Beely who'd break the silence. Always — he never tired of talk. He tried to lasso my eyes, but I kept my head down.

"*Codorniz,*" Apá said. "Those little head feather birds who run together. Yes, tortilla, please, pass it this way."

"That's wild quail you taste," Yginio said. "Gives it meat, some little thread for a man to chew. Like it?"

"Sure do, right much, *muy bueno.* Adds a punch to the lentils." He scooped a bit of brown, white, and green into his tortilla scoop and filled his mouth. A dribble made a trail down the side of his chin. He swiped

301

it with a table rag. "How about the town trip? Go okay?" His head turned toward me.

A long silence drew out my empty desire for words. Sinforosa and her suffering came to mind. I stared at my plate as if the beans had put a trance on me.

"Dirt *negro* — black," said Garita.

"Muy triste," Apá added, "the smoldering fire set off yesterday. Very sad, there's no one nowhere in the streets. Be good if the ones with guns are hiding, too."

"*Gato* — cat," said Garita, "*ojo* — eye." She pointed one finger to her right eye and then to me. "Ambrosia."

"That right? A one-eyed stray took a freeze when he caught a glimpse of her, eh? I bet it did. Can't say I blame the critter." Beely looked at me. "Saw a beauty."

His stare wrestled with my push away. I felt his eyes but did not look up. I picked up my plate and began the grate fire to boil dishwater. The rest in the room held their eyes on me. Sinfo was dying. Ramon raged. Beely tightened his lips and walked out to his barn corner. I washed the dishes alone.

First morning light came with three soft, horse commands outside my window. The tongue clicks moved a horse from a walk to a breaking gallop. Apache's familiar footfalls trampled over my sad awakening. Beely, in my mind's eye, fanned his reins astride my blood on his horse blanket, leaving me. I didn't know when I'd see him again. Garita stirred. She curled up against me so close I smelled her sour morning breath, and neither of us had space to turn. Trapped between the wall and her, I lay cramped, burdened by endless, tortured thoughts. Resting on the elm tree outside my window, the morning doves murmured, *coo, coo roo, gone from you.* Their cry was meant for me.

Garita raised her lids sleepily. "Sinfo got her wants." She wiped my eyes with the sheet.

I didn't realize tears streamed down my face. "*Sí, Mija,* you're right. Let's get breakfast."

A dark tomb of nevermore engulfed me. The once-new spirit I enjoyed, if only for a day or two, vanished, gone with Beely. True happiness drifted up like smoke into the heavens. Isabelle and the goats' teats swelled with milk, the chickens and pigs expected grain and food scraps, sheep needed fleecing, wool needed spinning, the men wanted their hot meals, and Garita clung to me always. Was that what I lived for? My heart beat lifeless again; my bones ached and my muscles sagged weak at the end of the day.

CHAPTER EIGHTEEN

Beely showed no sign of himself, and Yginio said he had found some paid labor at Seven Rivers up a ways east. His leg wasn't giving him any trouble, and he had been cow poking and playing fireside Monte. One hearsay rumor whispered he had gone to Texas. I imagined he had been doing his best to earn his keep, although the thought of him laughing and enjoying his life without me added a new self-torment.

When I went to the *río* for fine sand to mix with soda ash to clean my teeth, a reflection of a poor, tired *señorita* looked back at me. Hair, like pine needles, stuck out of my braid, and my brows made new wrinkles between them. My tired mother stared at me from the clear water — I was becoming her. She had a constant, nervous motion. Until her death, when not working, her point finger drew a heart over her thumb from sad worry. My own fingers stirred in that same way more and more each day. The movement grew with Beely's absence.

Stop it. The motion soothed and irritated me as I walked back to the house. *You are not Mamá and not Sinforosa.* I whipped myself and shook my hand, but before I reached the door, my finger, with a will of its own, drew the little heart again on my thumb.

To escape, I worked harder. Kept my hands occupied in other ways, so thoughts of Beely would wear down and leave me. One day's struggle folded into the next. I made myself into an obedient woman, one who didn't question, one who would satisfy Doña, please Apá, and earn back Ramon. With no earthly place to turn, each night I called on *Dios* Almighty for mercy. Prayer and work, more prayer and more work.

One fall day, months later of that same year, a knock arrested me into expectation. *Beely, he's come.* Apá and Yginio fixed the west fences, and Garita was in the root cellar gathering sweet potatoes with board in hand to rid us of the mice there. Alone in the kitchen, I was on the verge of making a sweet potato pie, a rare feasting for us. My fingers combed hair back off my face. When

I walked to the door, I saw Ramon. The black of his hair glistened against the white starch of his shirt. His eyes spoke angry echoes of our loving past.

"*Hola*, Ambrosia, good to see you." His polite words under the cover of his stiff jaw came out lies.

I turned my arched brows to my labor.

"In? Can come in, *bueno*, okay?" His white, straight teeth, such a contrast to Beely's front crooked one reflected brilliant light. A memory of our first holy communion flashed. My white dress and his dress pants play-acted what we believed was our future. At six years of age, Father Martinez had paired us, for he and destiny knew our lives would be connected.

I pushed away that long-ago memory.

"The door's open and you know it has always been, Ramon. I wonder why you don't have Señor Murphy in your shadow."

"He's a good *hombre* even though you never have believed it." His bigness took over the room.

Isabelle eyes. He gave me a look like our cow, Isabelle, when her udders swelled, aching to be milked. Those same eyes soothed me after Mamá's passing. Somewhere, somehow, something changed. He had the same soft calling, but what had changed were my answering eyes. They snarled back. "Yes, Mister Señor Murphy, *buen hombre* — a rear-end kick with a smile. *Sí,* what you say, Ramon. Good man for you, maybe."

"He does good things for people, especially *pobres,* like Tehde and others. He goes to our church, doesn't carry a gun, pointing it at people like some I've seen."

I wielded a knife over a few hard potatoes I was peeling. The knife landed on the table. My hands flew to my hips. "What did you come here for? To tell me something I don't know already?"

"Señor Murphy sent me. He is very sick and will move to his other house in Carrizozo. They say he won't live long and will let go of the mercantile."

"Oh, he's suffering like others. *Ya pues,* he better figure out answers to give the Lord when he dies. And you — his messenger, again, always, *eh*? That's not new."

A long silence followed. His soulful eyes paused me enough to hear myself. My raw and angry voice came from a bitter woman. I twisted my lips into something that might look like a pressed smile. "Okay, you here for him. What else?"

"It's about sister Sinforosa, your sister, I mean. Murphy saw to it that she stay in her own bed. Remember, he didn't make you bring her home or tell Tehde to take her to the reservation." His slumped shoulders began to heave like a rumbling avalanche. "Some never see what good he does. You have to say it's true. He didn't abandon her." Big pole fingers rubbed over water-filled eyes.

"Oh *sí* Ramon, and he didn't use Sinforosa to make money? That's true, too, *eh*? He got more than he gave."

Ramon loved Sinforosa more than his own mother. My sister was an untouchable charm, like a yellow, purple monarch breezing in on winged glory and floating away. He eyed her every movements. Me, I was his duty, Sinfo his deep desire. I worked the knife over the potatoes in rapid quick jerks. "Not interested in anything Señor Murphy has to say. Heard plenty of nothing already."

"Not what he says, it's what I say about your sister." He brushed a big ole horsefly from his wet cow face. It buzzed away and circled back. In one motion, he shooed the pest and wiped a thickening moisture on his cheek.

"Which one? The man tried to get his hands on both. Thank the Lord, I forced myself down that road and brought Garita back. With Sinfo, it didn't work. The one he ended up with is rotting away."

"No, not rotting. Sinfo's gone. Died this morning. *Ya no está*. That's what I'm here to . . . to tell you."

My legs buckled and I fell onto something below me, a bench, a stump chair, the floor. I don't know what. Strength to keep my head up weakened. I leaned over and dug my nails into my elbows. "No. God have mercy." I sat there, folded over, dazed. Time paced and circled around me like a mountain lion sizing up its kill. It wrung my innards and clawed my heart.

Ramon's hand on my back caused me to jerk up and move away from him.

He spoke softly. "You say Señor Murphy is bad, but he paid for the box and the diggers and the plot by your mamá's grave. He wants to know if you want any of her clothes — and if you want to see . . ." He sniffed his last words. "To see her buried?"

"Tell him to burn them like he did the McSween's place since he knows how to do that so well." I wiped my eyes.

"Ambrosia," he paused and stared. "*¿Que te pasa?* You've changed." A corner of his lips twitched and put his mustache into a jittery motion. He rubbed his fingers over the nervous ripple and down his chin. He took a step back and crossed his arms.

"No, Ramon. Everything around here has changed." I wanted to say, the path of circumstances, not him or me, had changed, but Garita clomped in and dropped a handful of sweet potatoes on the table.

"*Sí,* everything has changed, *cierto,* but still, anyway, I can't understand you. When will Salamon be back? I'll talk to him — thought you would want to go to her funeral," Ramon said.

"Apá gone — *fué,*" Garita mumbled, "too far gone."

"Why, Ramon?" I folded my arms and noticed a slight tremble in them. "Garita, please, *Mija,* will you go get more from the cellar. This is not enough."

"*¿Por qué* — why?" She plopped down and stacked her arms on the table.

"Because I need them, that's why." I pointed to the door.

"*Por qué* — why-why?" Garita looked at Ramon.

"I'm asking the whys here. Get the potatoes like I said — now." I put my sternest eyes on her.

She sighed and slammed the door on her way out.

"What do you mean why? Because she was your sister." When he said sister, his voice cracked, and he coughed a cover-up.

"She forgot us, Ramon. Brought Mamá suffering and never cared for Garita or me. No less Apá. With Yginio, the ax cut both ways and neither side cared. *¿Por qué*, Ramon? I ask you, why do I want to go? And why, *Dios Santos*, would I want her *cantina* dresses?"

"Can't you forgive the past? She did what she did and *ya*. It's over, *mujer*." He stood on one leg while his thick thumbs tried to make their way through his belt loops.

"Stop calling me that!"

"What? Calling you what?" His boots shuffled grumbles on the wood floor. Shifting his weight to his other leg, he leaned forward with his shoulders.

"*Mujer*, that's what!" A flash pulsed hot into my temples.

"Isn't that what you are? A woman?" He asked.

"Yes, but when you say it like that, it sounds like a . . . like a fenced-in animal."

"Good God, Ambrosia, anyway we're not talking about you. We're talking about Sinforosa. Besides, it's *ya*, over. You can't hate a dead person. She did what she did and that thing has ended or should be ended." Ramon unhung his thumbs, curled his large hand into a fist, and seemed he wanted to bang it into something.

"And the rest of us, we don't go down the pleasure road, like she did. We wait, work, and sacrifice. Do without . . ." I stopped and fanned my face. A welled-up tear found itself under my fingers as fast as it appeared. "Without . . ."

"Without what? Look, Ambrosia, all of us suffer. I'm sorry you are in this way. Señor Murphy, he just wants to know if you and Garita want her dresses."

"No, keep the fancy dresses. Where will we wear them? To milk cows? He can give them to the other *puta* Jewel ladies."

"*Bueno, bueno,* okay, Ambrosia. The funeral is tomorrow at one o'clock if you and anyone, Salamon, Garita, or Yginio want to go. Big shame if no one shows up."

He left. I sat and cried. We had just seen Sinforosa three months earlier. Life, sickness, death drained me ragged.

Before the sun rose above the east where the sky meets the dirt of our little earth, we hitched the buckboard and bounced down the road. Apá made all of us go even though Yginio and I spoke against a false show. He was still our apá, and we had to mind his word. Like a damp, white shroud, clouds hung low over the valley. Stout needle pines mixed with brown, gold, and red of changing, delicate leafy oaks, elms, and aspens. In my high collar, once white blouse, long skirt, and boots, I set my finest dark-blue wool *reboso* over my shoulders and cross-tied a knot at the waist. By the looks of the clouds, for the day's sorrow and with the road dust, the shawl would give me some cover over the bulging stress of the tattered blouse buttons.

La Garita wore the same as she wore to Mamá's funeral. A blouse with thin stripes of sunflower yellow and a full, brown skirt with a yellow sash belt. Her worn, wool coat, two sizes too small, would have to do. Only she could wear such brightness to a burial, carrying special exception as one who did not know better and did not deserve that any heaviness rest on her innocence. She clambered her high-top boots onto the open buckboard and sat spread-legged with her sling in her hand and rocks in her pockets as always.

On the wooden seats, Garita and Apá jerked over the potholes under the pull of our faithful Luz. Beside the wagon, Yginio held back his fast trotter, Noche. Trying to keep up with Yginio, after wheeling the Río Ruidoso, I drove our hauler faster than usual. Our back ends hardly touched the hard wood bench, before they took another bounce and fall again.

Midair, Apá reached over and tapped my shoulder, something he rarely did. "*Calma, Mija,* a hurried rush won't take pain away." His flat rear end hit the bench, wood on bone. He winced before he put in something else to slow me down. "Don't make our suffering less or rush our sorrow."

His words were for somebody else. The sooner this October day made its end, the better for all of us. When we upset what looked like the same family of quail in the same place, neither Apá nor Yginio moved to snag any. Garita swung a cramped aim from the wagon, missed, and stayed put.

Not far ahead, coming our way, Frank and George Coe headed west toward us and *howdy-dooed* their hats. Yginio stopped and talked with them until I left him behind, turned our riding board north at the double rocks, and lost sight of them. The Coes ran with the Regulators. Apá's already narrow eyes tightened. This, to me, meant he hated his *mijo* with those gang friends. Yginio's lag forced my father to take off his hat and wipe his pale forehead as he looked behind for my brother. He moved his tongue against the inside of his cheek so that it bulged and looked like it wanted out of his mouth. Strange, but I blamed it on the smokes he had given up.

Fanning his reins, Yginio caught us full gallop, and my father tamed his tongue.

We drove fast on the road straight up north, left the Salamanca place behind with no stop, and reached Lincoln about noon, maybe a little past. About three months had gone by since the fire. Someone had cleared most of the household belongings, bulk chairs, charred sofa, scorched wash basins, and bed braces. Señor Wortley, from the front of his hotel, gave Apá a sad half-nod and my father motioned back. The Torreon Tower marked our turn up the slope to the graveyard, so I pulled one rein in and loosened the other while I snapped them both on the curve.

As we turned in, we saw Father Martinez, waiting with his head down and his black robe flowing in the breeze. He stood at the south end close to Mamá's place, away from the road. Salazares, our people, for many years landed in this corner spot, where tumbleweeds filled the spaces between crosses, slanted and crippled in their claims.

One little wooden cross read Niño Salazar, Marzo, 1854. Just that, there was no first name. That was our baby, born dead. Another was for Julian, my oldest brother who fell off a wild stallion years ago, knocked himself into eternal life, and lay close to our lost *niño*. Mamá, bless her soul, between her long, lost baby boy and her oldest son, had found friendly earth. Now Sinforosa had her space near her. I wondered if Sinfo would have wanted to be buried by her *Inglés* further in town and not with her family. For us, this space was as good as any, for in this decision, she had no say to complain.

Graves, crosses, signs of death opened a grieving wound inside me, more for Mamá than for Sinforosa. There it was, a fresh mound of dirt, my sister's resting place. Her coffin sat, waiting to be lowered. Never had I seen one of light wood, oak, walnut, or something fine, unusual like Sinfo. A marble stone bore chiseled letters — Miss Sinforosa Salazar, March 13, 1859, to October 15, 1878, *One, who will be missed*. Señor Murphy showed his goodwill or his guilty conscience. At least, he didn't punish my sister for loving Tunstall. The men, Murphy's laborers, were pulling up the last buckets of dirt, and others were taking down the rope that marked the top corners of the grave.

My sister would have found the day's weather pleasing. In that bright, fall day, our pitiful group of gatherers huddled together, six people besides us. Lupe, daughter of the murdered Rumaldita, shivered beside the large *Patrona*. Lupe's skinny bones hung one of Sinforosas's fancy dresses like a stick scarecrow, and her lipstick glowed an oversized red, better placed on a ripe summer tomato.

The grand Madame, dressed in purple, of course, took up two places around the casket. She twirled without stop a glowing apricot-colored stone with white diamonds like stars shimmering around a gold planet. It appeared to weigh her hand down and made her ordinary finger into a monumental charm. The jewel, a token from Tunstall for my sister, found its way to a lucky observer. Some, like me, weren't intended to bear its glory. I trashed my thoughts, but its spectacular glint called to me, reminded me of Sinfo's lost dream and my lost dream.

To the side, Tehde stepped her ritual parting, mumbling and dropping dust and what looked to be herbs. Her chants added an earthy incantation, a guttural, rhythmic plea for mercy, Indian style. Sinforosa could use all the help she could get from this side. Ramon stood tall, and, without fail, his mamá clutched him. Doña Hurtencia drove stalking cat eyes into me, a mamá protecting her son. Things between the Salamancas and Salazares were changing. Father

Martinez held open his Bible, ready to guide the parting soul to the other side. I looked at this group of people. Hardly none in this funeral party would be with the others had it not been for Sinforosa's death.

"Sinfo with Mamá," Garita declared as if it were something to celebrate. As much as she hovered, mourned, and resisted leaving sick Sinforosa, on this day, without a visible, hurting body, Garita didn't suffer any. She was the happiest one here. What was hidden in a pretty, polished box was not of any concern to her. Mamá with Sinforosa might be the thing comforting her most. For my little sister, Mamá, wherever she went, would now have company, would now have cherished Sinfo. What we, here on this earth, couldn't have. Garita understood two together was better than one alone.

"Sí, Mija." Ramon put his free arm around her.

Garita twirled her yellow sash and pressed her head into his broad chest.

When Ramon noted my collapsed brows, he drew himself back. I reached for Garita's hand. That grave hole looked like something she would jump into. I tightened my grip. She was not roaming this cemetery today.

Yginio pulled his shirt sleeves, fidgeted with his buckle, and glanced toward town like he had left something there. All others occupied had not taken notice. But I did, and I watched him as he mounted and walked Noche away as if the animal wore cotton horse shoes.

In his sanctified pronouncements, Father's face liberated its holy dove stamp toward us. *"In nomine Patris, et Filii, et Spiritus Sancti. A . . . Amen."* He sprinkled holy water around the grave in quick shakes, dotting the dry dirt and lifting an odor of wet earth around us. Sinforosa must have given a confession of regret and contrition before she took her last breath, for she was receiving the final Catholic sacrament — claimed her salvation to Him, a much-needed holy parting.

"Through the sacred mysteries of our redemption, may Almighty God release you from all punishments in this life and in the life to come." Father's voice rang solemn but strong.

"Auk'ojo akoya, Ick' an a ceya, Ick' an a ceya, Ick' an a ceya, Auk' ojo akoya." One slow foot with one quiet voicing, Tehde mixed with Father's prayer.

Garita unstrapped my fingers and aimed for Tehde. "Sinfo *ir* — go with Mamá," she said again. "Me with *amiga* Tehde." She was ready to step-dance to Tehde's sacred chant.

"Not you, you stay here with me." My clutch on her brought red to my fingertips.

"May he open to you the gates of heavenly paradise and welcome you to everlasting joy."

Those in this world said, "Amen."

We watched the beautiful coffin sink into the earth. Braced by ropes, Señor Murphy's hires eased the box into her narrow resting place. Down, down into a suffocating hole, alone, it was hard to imagine our beautiful Sinforosa was more gone than when she was absent from us. The permanence of death, the end of the end, for she left me in many different ways before this. One thin man's brace-hold slipped. Sinforosa's way of yanking herself down. The casket hit the bottom, the ropes went limp, and the men drew them up. The jolt drew me to the moment at hand. Everyone stood mute.

Apá's tongue moved inside his mouth again; the loose worm was trying to dig its way out. He scanned the crowd, and I figured it was for Yginio.

Garita pulled off my hand.

Doña turned into Ramon's chest, and one of his stares came in my direction. Without his mother's hot scald on me, I met his dark eyes head-on until the thought of my naked skin on Beely forced my look away. Instead

320

of my pointing finger, my middle finger took over the beadless prayer on my swollen thumb. I shook it quiet.

Father Martinez cleared his throat and broke the standoff. His jowls, as well as the tiny white imprint on his face, quickened a dance with his next sentence. "Ahem, *por favor,* would anyone who knew her like a sister . . . Would they like to say a few things about Sinforosa?"

I stared at the birthmark.

Ramon glanced my way, and I looked at my father. Apá looked down.

"*Preciosa* Sinforosa." Garita, always with words others could not find, smiled. "*Ir —* go to Mamá."

I rested my forehead onto my fingertips and prayed this gathering would end.

Ramon nodded up to the sky, and his mother wiped streams of tears.

Tehde mumbled her own Indian chant so low no one heard what we couldn't understand anyway. She shook dried rose petals, pine needles, and John Tunstall's *J* smoker into the deep hole.

"Yes, she was a child of God. Now with peace," the priest said. "*El Gran Señor* gives and takes away." He struggled to find words for a woman of late he hardly knew.

Like a lost light seeking a stopping place,

Father Martinez's eyes fell on me. Everyone put me in their beam, and I imagined Sinforosa was waiting and looking up at me, too.

The purple-clad lady sneezed and pulled a handkerchief from her dress sleeve. She wiped her mouth, not her eyes.

"She was my sister," I said. *"Mi hermana."* Their stare sent heat waves into me. For a moment, I wished I was the one in the coffin. A tightness pinched me. My own hand, milking as hard as I'd wrung Isabella's teat on a cold morning, attacked my finger, the one absent a golden ring.

Tehde nodded like she understood.

A tear rolled down a deep wrinkle on Apá's face.

Garita said, "Me — *yo,* too."

Apá covered our lack of honor by filling his hand with dirt and throwing it in on her casket. Ramon and his mother did the same. The *Patrona* lady did not dirty her ringed finger, turned, and wobbled as fast as her heavy legs would carry her to her buggy, followed by Lupe Espinosa. The men took to throwing the dirt into the hole fast. It was then I realized Señor Murphy's money was present, but he was not. Too sick to make it or too ashamed to face us.

Ramon's mother invited us to their home.

"Thank you, very nice, but, *tu sabes*, it's a long way, and we have so much work at home." I glanced at Ramon. Without Sinforosa, his yearning for what could not be, his lost wish would die with Sinforosa.

"Work can wait, especially on a day of mourning. Stop, and I give you sweet bread for Garita." Doña Hurtencia's tight mouth forced out strained words. She took Ramon's hand and the saddle horn to lift herself onto her horse.

Doña Hurtencia would not forget it if we didn't stop, but that kind of worry for me was over.

Apá nodded his "*Sí,* yes, okay."

We loaded our buckboard and drove the metal, squeaky wheels down into Lincoln. As we plodded through the main street, we saw Noche.

"*Malo,*" Apá said. "Yginio don't have no respect for nobody. I didn't raise him to be this way."

Yginio waved us over to the Wortley Hotel. When I didn't dash a turn, my brother tore off his hat and flicked it at us in a serious *come-here* motion. In his shadow were two men.

"Ginio. Stop — *para.*" Garita tried to pull the reins from me in the direction of my brother.

"No, we not going to stop, *adelante,* Ambrosia." Apá grabbed Garita's arm and pulled her toward him away from me. He signaled to keep moving with a flutter of his hands. "Go."

My brother called out again, louder as if we had not seen him, "*Aquí, ya,* hear me over here. Stop."

My apá's hands would not let up on his *go-forward* motion.

Not anxious for the ride back, I turned the buckboard. "*Un segundito,* Apá, just one second."

"Brocia *para* — stop." Garita reached for Apá's hand and forced it down.

The flatbed wheels skidded dust as Luz drew a fast left to the side of the street. With the rig turned, Yginio in full view stepped away from Beely and another who stood next to him. My heart dropped to the floorboards.

"Well, if it don't beat all. Salazares together in one local in town," Beely said as he showed us that beautiful, crooked tooth.

"No Sinfo, now with Mamá," Garita said.

"I heard," he said. "My heart feels your sorrow. Anything I can do, tell me. Just say the word and you got it." He looked at me.

My sore eyes fell on the man who had rope-tied my being, done what he wanted

324

— who brought me sleepless nights and tortured days — who had robbed me of my all — who gave me a welcome-back smile as if none of that mattered.

"See here, Ambrosia." He slapped his old wound. "My leg's good as new, and I ain't got that lead in there weighing me down." He pointed at me and winked. Our secret flashed between us in that quick pass. I was certain we both thought it.

He gave Garita a dark caramel wrapped in shiny paper.

"*Bueno* — good, Beely." She snatched her bribe in two seconds. "*Gracias.*"

Beely started his nervous shuffle. "Wish I had more to give you. That one was hard to come by, but I've been saving it for you, Angel. You're so welcome. Say, hit some good times. Fighting packs are calling a truce. Even little Jimmy Dolan, Murphy's sidekick, has raised a white flag, and things are settling down. Yes, sir, and better yet, the governor has offered what he calls amnesty for all Regulators and House men back in the day of the Lincoln County War. I'm hoping to stake my claim on it and get a reprieve."

"Governor, *el governador,*" said Apá "of all of this New Mexico territory?"

"Yes, the biggity, biggest toad in the pond.

325

That one. The gent he is, he will recall my warrant. I'm here from up north to clear my name, and I have a fashioned idea. *Diosito* be with me." His eyes met mine. "I reckon I'm on a side turn and fixin' to get me some land. Mighty good, be like others, why not me?"

"*¿Cuanto?*" Apá said.

"A few acres," Beely said.

"*¿No cuanto* time you been here waiting?"

"I'm here of my own volition, like they say, looking to see who it is I talk to. I want something official, so it doesn't hoof up again."

"Sinfo with Mamá." Garita didn't chew but rolled the candy on her tongue to make the taste last.

"I know, Darling, don't fret about it none. How's your coon cat, *Mapache?*"

"Yes," Garita said.

"Ambrosia, *ya, vamonos.* Go." Apá said. "Yginio, see you home. No coming in the dark. I need you to run the sheep *mañana.*" Apá straightened his cowboy hat over his eyes and crossed his arms tight.

As I pulled back and snapped the leathers, our old mare moved away. I looked at Beely. I didn't want to leave, but there was nothing left for me to do. Goodbyes did not come out of either one of us, didn't have to.

Though we parted, Beely would not leave my thoughts, no goodbye there. Lot's wife looked back at Sodom and became a pillar of salt. Now, I understood her need for one more glance. Beely's eyes watched my back, and like Lot's wife, I could not stop my head from turning. Again, our eyes caught one another. He smiled like the first day he came in our house. He waved, and my heart beat a fierce Mescalero war drum, so loud Luz stepped to it. When we made our way past Ramon's Smithy barn and came onto the Salamancas', my limp bones wanted off the hard seat.

"Stop *aquí.*" As if he possessed the guides, Apá signaled with his hands.

"Why, Apá? You said we're in a hurry. We can't stop." I didn't tighten back on Luz.

"You stopped before when I asked you not to. Now I want you to stop, so stop. Don't be disrespectful. Doña offered food. *Ya pues,* Mamá raised you better." Apá had suffered so much I couldn't add my wayward wants to his losses.

Against my will that pushed home, I turned into the Salamancas'. We knocked on the door, and Ramon's bigness filled the door. He looked only at me, and I realized the dark pitch of his sharp eyes. My eyes moved from his white shirt to the bits of

327

brown leather laid into his black boots.

"*Pasen, pasen,* very good you came," Ramon said.

A welcomed stop, Hurtencia Salamanca kept as good a place as her son's dollars allowed. They, unlike us, had cloth furniture not of wood. Always the table held sweet goods of some kind, and they never had a dry coffee pot as we did. Swallow chirps and gurgles from her birds along with an aroma of fresh-baked sweet bread filled the home.

Garita ran to the cages and put her hand through the vine-branch shell. Gray flutters and chirps of panic swarmed to the other side.

Ramon pulled a soft, fine chair in front of Apá and brushed it off with a rag, "Sit, sit, *por favor.*" He looked around for another seater.

Ramon hauled a tree-stump chair toward me. I walked to the window and looked out, hoping to see Beely riding by.

Doña Hurtencia set a tin coffee kettle on the table and took out bread buns sprinkled with sugar, something we never had in our kitchen. "*Comen, ya,* eat," she said as she poured a cup of coffee for Apá. Garita ran to the table, sat on the tree round Ramon had offered me, and took a roll of special *pan dulce.* Sprinkles of white dots around her lips hung a sweet coating. She licked it in long wet strokes.

After a long deep breath, Apá took a sip of his coffee. "*Ay ya yay,* our Sinforosa will now have the peace she didn't have here." A long pause silenced the room. "And looks like town is settled, too, *gracias a Dios,*" said Apá. "The fighting men are tired, *al fin.*"

"*Sí,* the House–Regulator war's over, but *tu sabes,* some drifter can come and raise trouble hell again. Those who want wild, they come here and make it whether we like it or not. *Pobre,* Susan McSween is still fighting Colonel Dudley, who let his soldiers burn her home and kill her husband. She has hired that one-armed Chapman lawyer. The ones in Santa Fe want it all stopped." Ramon, with one beautiful boot across his knee, spoke.

He hadn't told us anything we didn't know already.

"That's *el politico.* The head man governor is going to let those who were in the war go," said Doña Hurtencia. "*Ese,* Bonney boy is walking the streets like he's the new sheriff."

"That's what they say. Those in Santa Fe just want it over. Put it behind them." Apá took a long drink of coffee and for the first time in weeks, looked relaxed.

"Some have left the state. But those who have their land here like the Coe cousins of Ruidoso, they are here to stay," Ramon said.

"*Sí*, they passed us on the way here and looks like they quieted down. Everybody wants the fighting to be over." My father took a long gulp of coffee.

"El Chivato, Chivito goat boy, whatever it is, *ese* William Bonney's back in the street like he did nothing. Wish he'd go somewhere else." Doña Hurtencia poured Apá more coffee and crossed her arms like a fortune teller giving precious secrets. She wanted us to make sure we got the point on Beely.

I left the window and stood behind Apá. I nudged him from behind, so he had to balance his coffee cup. It spilled.

"Yeah, that little squirrel-spider Chivato. Talk, talk, talk, but he don't say nothing." Ramon picked up the same rag and wiped hot coffee off my father's pants. He lifted his eyes to mine, but I wouldn't give them back.

"Apá, Yginio just passed. He's on his way home." I pushed my hand against his back again.

"*Sí*, okay, very nice. *Muchas gracias*, my daughter has things to do at home, I guess."

Apá put his cup on the table.

"*Ya,* here, take." Doña sliced a small section of *pan dulce* and wrapped the sweet bread in the same rag Ramon had used to clean off the table. "For Garita, for later."

Hurtencia hugged each of us on our way out. Her wrap around me seemed less strained.

Ramon followed behind and shook Apá's hand and then gave a hug to Garita. He reached for me and brought me to him. I pushed against his shoulders, then released my stiffness. He felt muscle-hard and smelled wash-clean. He whispered, "Soon, we'll see you. Good that you came to Sinfo's funeral. Remember, hate never takes away sadness."

I nodded and pushed away.

Garita grabbed my hand on her way to the buckboard.

We headed toward San Patricio. Ramon's words and his eyes put me back into regrets about Beely. Ramon forced his hug and did it like he deserved me. He would never lift my skirt or put an ungentlemanly hand on me. Our ways were not of the flesh but of tradition and sacrifice and yes, respect. I knew my father saw him as my husband. But Beely's sinful hand on me, his unleashed touch on soft moist places, I wanted.

Luz knew the road and led herself to the familiar dirt tank stop. Cool dribbles ran down her snout as she breathed tiny sprays out her blow holes. She drank well. Garita cheated little bites of her *pan dulce* until nothing was left but a few specks of sugar on her chin. We never caught up to Yginio, and as we pulled into the barn, we could see Noche, unsaddled, and chewing on alfalfa. Apá took it upon himself to rest Noche. Sinforosa was gone, really gone. I fell into a state of wait and want.

Seeing Beely, even for seconds after Sinforosa's funeral, eased me some. I no longer held my eyes shut tight in the mornings, hoping I wouldn't wake up. He was alive and not far away. Our secret lurked in the shadows of my thoughts and held me hostage. Couldn't sum up whether not knowing where he was or knowing he was so close pained me more.

That evening I lay in my bed and wondered if we really made love or if in my loneliness, my mind had twisted a bent version of that day in the barn. The next day, I waited for Yginio to give any news of Señor Bonney, my Chivato, but this detail was not part of our talk. Apá did not care to hear any more about the damn *condenado* Regulators, so I got nothing from their conversations. Garita didn't know enough to ask, and I would never give Yginio or Ramon any reason to raise their brows. I kept my stay.

CHAPTER NINETEEN

Eight months passed. Lawrence Murphy had died the same month as Sinforosa, but we didn't hear about it until four months later in February of the next year, 1879. I wasn't going to miss him. Heard tell, Tehde found work across the street at the Wortley Hotel. Other men bought some of Señor Mister's property. Lincoln was no longer a hell-town. Last time I saw Beely he was staking his claim on a reprieve from Santa Fe. How does a slinger who rode with killers later get a paper to say otherwise? Sheriff Brady and Shotgun Roberts can't be brought back from the dead. And on the house side, Jimmy Dolan and his sidekicks — what about their misdeeds? Tunstall and Dick Brewer were gone with no one paying the price. Susan McSween wouldn't get the governor to erase her memories, rebuild her home, and resurrect her husband. Ramon said *pobre* Susan was still fighting her cause against the U.S. government and Colonel Dudley.

We, in San Patricio, too, hit hard times with the changes — had to get along some way. People did their own barter exchanges in the town plaza on Wednesdays and Sundays. Apá and Yginio were the only ones allowed to go. Grazing rent went down a few coppers but not enough to make much difference. It was June. Garita grew as tall as me, and her favorite cat, Mapache, had given light to many new families, but none of the little ones took her coon markings. She named one male, who looked most like its mother, Beellito.

In my yearning for Beely, I looked for ways to get out of the house, put my mind at ease. I foraged the land often. South where the terrain was drier, a spikey low bush offered a tea for good digestion. Wild mint, asparagus, and garlic sprouted close to the river. Up a ways, we collected a wild spinach, which went well with beans. In deep summer on much higher ground, tiny wild strawberries could be found. On horseback, I might go to Nogal Canyon to pick black walnuts from unclaimed, native trees, but those nuts required hard knocking for very little. Another treat was a type of forest gum. Large sappy balls seeped out of ponderosa bark. Some might think it was useless, but boiled down, it made for a good glue after it hardened. Or grinded with dried figs, the sticky clump made into a cud chew. I hunted and gathered delicacies away from our rancho and released Beely thoughts, the one who might be close by but not here.

One of my favorite earth bounty was *piñones*. Those little brown seeds looked like rabbit droppings to the unknown eye. A cross between a new potato and a toasted pecan, piñons gave us a luscious, easy treat. Every seven years, sharp-needle trees gave abundant nut loads. Not all were on the same harvest roundabout, so most years those pines gave little here and there. The pearl bits stored well through the cold, and on many evenings, sitting by the fireplace with a large cast-iron pan hanging on the S hook, they toasted just past ivory to light brown. They sent a rich pine scent into our grand room. Cracking toasted nut meats, our mouths were better spent breaking and chewing than talking. In the fall we had picked piñons nearby.

I took my sister from her play, and we walked across a fallen log over the river and up miles from our house north to search unpicked piñons or pine-tree gum. The air was just short of cool in the shade and very hot in the sun. Trying to forget Beely made me remember I wanted to forget, and there came the memory again. I walked, trying to erase Kid-man memories in the chase for nut and sap booty.

Soon we found a tree hole filled with a squirrel's stash of piñones.

"We're headed in the right direction," I shouted to my sister who came running. When I reached in for a handful, Garita held my hand.

"No, them *necesita* — need," she said.

She was right. So, with patience, we walked further into the hills for the brown nuts not yet claimed by other animals. Close by, we pulled sticky, cheat-chew from a large trunk and socked it away.

Carrizo, mesquite, and yellow-green Bermuda grass covered the first part of our lowland walk, but soon hills and evergreens sprung up. Garita found a tree seeping bark and collected the gooey blob. So far our bag flopped almost empty.

About midway, we stopped, brought out *burritos* and apples, and ate in the cool crisp air. I offered Garita water from a jute canteen and wondered if Beely was still in Lincoln. For all I knew, the governor decided to lock him up instead of untrap him.

We walked further toward the higher mountains where aspen buds were beginning to bulge in their branches.

We reached the edge of our staked claim into a pine-filled ravine. There we saw the precious nuts. The slanted terrain did not make our work easy. Our backs hunched over a small gathering space. As we kneeled, skirt material pulled us down. Without the skirt, our knees rubbed raw against the pine needles. And when those nuts were picked, we had to lift ourselves and crawl under the branches like a duck to find a new space. Thin, long, dried pine needles pricked into our skirts or pierced our skin. What sacrifice we paid for these little nut meats, almost as bad as the pain we give for a man.

Garita left the back-breaking work to chase a group of cottontails with her sling. I knew she would not last long at this hard work, but if she got a rabbit, it would taste good tonight. She ran to a nearby hill.

The quiet took my mind to a calm place. I moved to flatter land. Piñons dotted the ground around me, and these were the largest I had seen in years. Breezes blew air through the pine trees and made a high shush through their needles like whistling blades. The smell of earth in its glory filled me. A crow praised its view from overhead.

I looked for Garita but saw no sign of her. I didn't think about her again until a branch snapped.

"Garita, not so far. *Ya,* is that you?" She would not walk with such a light step, and I wondered what could crack a branch — a bear? A mountain lion? A sound of leather snapped onto metal and creaked — a man? The *uh huh-huh* of a horse startled me enough to move my head around as two horsemen came toward me.

"Who is it?" I asked with enough force to cover my fear. Garita's last route, was it east or south? I reached for a tree branch to lift off my sore, tired knees.

"Amigos, don't fret none. We're *amigos."*

The voice engulfed me, slow and hurried at the same time. I dropped the nuts in my hand and made my way out from under the tree to face them. *"¿Quien es?"*

"Yginio said you might be up here, where these forgotten, unselfish pines are," the voice said.

Oncoming light blinded me.

"Looks like you found an overlooked treasure," the man spoke as he kept coming at me.

I still doubted the familiar voice. *"¿Quien es?"* I said again. Blood rushed up from my numb legs and dizzied my head. In the blaze of light, their bodies waved. I tried to step away from the beam, but it would not let me hide, and it darkened their figures against the bright sun.

"And see by the bulge in the bag you been here quite a spell." He would not stop talking.

It couldn't be. I tossed my thick braids off my heaving chest. Then I saw Apache and that smile. "Beely, is that you?" The other rider was not Yginio.

"*Sí, Dios mío,* it is you, Beely," I said. "*Que milagro.*"

"Yes, me and my friend, Tom O'Folliard. We came by your place and saw Yginio for a spell. We're headed north, Fort Sumner way. This is the opposite direction of our route, but I wanted to come by and say *hasta luego.* Don't believe in *adios.* A man never knows when he's going to re-route his steps. Hoping to see you before I head out, being you doctored my leg and such. And Garita? You're not here by your lonesome, I know," Beely said.

"Garita went in that direction, I think. She was after a family of rabbits." My voice rang high, and he must know the nerve fright he struck in me. I braced my knees from their shake and stiffened myself up straight.

"Hey, what do you say, Tom? Think you

could ride up to that yonder ridge and see what terrain we're up against on the trail? Look for her sister-gal — a lovely dolly, but not a timid and quiet thing. You saw her the other day in town, remember? Move slow and don't give her any fright. She's not skittish, but she won't remember setting eyes on you. If you see her, tell her you know Ambrosia. No, tell her you're the *amigo* of Billy who brung her Mapache, her kitten. She knows me by Beely. Not fast, mind you, go real slow. Keep from frightening her. Bring her back. But let her take her sweet time."

"When she chases rabbits, she does not think about how far she goes," I said as my fingers roughed over my lips.

"See there. Let her have her long hankering. Yeah, good plan. Tom, if you never see her, take a smoke or something. I'll give a pistol shot when it's time to head on back. Thanks, pard."

The Tom friend trotted through the low bushes and pine grove I had pointed for Garita's hunt. His horse moved onto the side where there was less brush to stop him. Two hawks hovered alongside each other above in the distance. The pine trees sang thin air whispers. I did not have give-go words, but none were needed. I looked long at Beely.

He dismounted and let the reins fall. Put his wounded but healed leg up on a log, and he, too, stared hard, holding tight to my eyes, so much, I could not look away. He blew air out his slightly opened mouth. "Whew, it's been a while. You're a sight for these here sore eyes, Ambrosia. Eyes red from the lack of you. How do you say that in Spanish — *ojos rojos*?"

"Not none of those. We never have that saying." Two pine needles stuck in my dress, and I pulled them out. "Just say, *me felicíto verte*. Happy to see you." I moved the bag of piñons by the tree trunk. It didn't need to be put there, but my nervous hands went without thinking. "Are you a free man now without penalties? Did the governor give you unharnessed roam?"

"Well, free is a matter of interpretation, depending on how you believe it should be. I've not ever been without my roam. I mean, not free. When you saw me last in Lincoln, I chose that arrangement to clear my name, but they kept a close watch on me and made sure I was staying put. Then burro-brain Billy Campbell and Jessie Evans with Jimmy Dolan in hand went and stirred things up again. Swear liquor goes into their throats and funnels into their gun barrels. The

342

drunken louses downright murdered Susan McSween's counsel, poor ole, one-armed Chapman. Yginio and I saw it firsthand." He moved to shade himself.

"My own deal with the governor changed a bit. Wallace bargained for my grand jury testimony. The top dog made use of what I saw to get his verdict against those lunkheads, Campbell, Evans, and Dolan, I mean. Myself, I done made good on this end of the deal and was waiting for chief man Wallace's pardon — some proof in a written script from him. This case has been keeping me occupied because the governor was taking his sweet time and then some. I couldn't hightail it about and was under what they called a house arrest. They fed and tendered me well enough. Thought about you in that spell. Felt your closeness and wanted to come visit but none in charge would have taken kindly to it, so I planted my wait." His spurs muffled a dusty rasp against dirt, and I noticed his gun belt was unlatched.

"Done got tired of waiting on him. Plum tired. Tom and me, we took our own freedom. I could become an old man there. Got the notion to head north. Going to find myself a way to get some payment John Chisum owes me, and then I'll keep heading north." He crouched down, picked up a thin twig, and put it in his mouth.

"¿*Como?* Beely? How? If he's the governor and brings his arrest after you, what do you do then?"

"You know. I think they've forgotten about me. They want to put all this Lincoln War behind." He pulled off his revolver belt and hung it on his saddle horn. "Governor never showed in weeks, and I ain't letting my life rot up on his slow clock." He spit out tiny wood pieces and stepped closer to me. "I owe it to myself, and I owe lots to you, Ambrosia. You save me from a gimped-up leg."

"Okay, *nada.* Nothing to me." I stepped away. So long, I had waited, so long, with such misery. For it to begin again, scared me. I was just starting to work out my life without him in my future.

He took my hand.

"Yes, and I'm not talking just about digging that slug out of my leg." I felt his grip. He pulled me closer. I smelled his well-worn shirt, a faint linger of wood smoke, a solid outdoor man's smell. He let go of my sweaty fingers and put his hands around my face.

"You're the most grace lady I ever seen. Ambrosia, sweet nectar from god flowers. Just like your name says."

"No, Beely." I tried to move away and turn my head.

With a soft rush, he forced me back to his eyes.

"Garita and your friend," I said. "They are not far. This is no place . . ."

"Forget them. They're yonder away, but seconds are flying, Ambrosia, and we, you and me, well let's just say we have less than any time at all."

A wet heat seared that tender place I promised never to give him again. Sierra Blanca's peak was lost in the trees, and I couldn't remember if I was here to pick *piñones,* glue, or strawberries or where Garita had gone. The past Ambrosia free-floated away. And in that vacuum, another flew into my body. My own breath choked me. I was sinking into unwanted desire again, but I couldn't push him back. God save me from myself.

"Hankered a lot for you, and it's been those sober, mind-drunks that's been keeping me going all this time. Well worth it." He paused here reeling in my being. "God, you're beautiful."

"No, Garita and your friend," I said.

"Never you worry. The plan's in our favor."

He leaned into my neck, kissed it, and

stared again with those deep, blue eyes.

"I never wanted anything you didn't want to give me. Never wanted you to feel like a wrong move was taken or put upon you. An illegal touch been gotten off you, one you didn't want or a sin placed on you, Ambrosia. You deserve better. You know that, don't you? I do want you to know this. I don't jump on bed springs for just anybody. I mean . . . The chance comes so few times, like a sun eclipse or a seven-year piñon harvest. It's a long time to wait and shameful to waste that lucky feeling that comes very rarely. And maybe never will come again."

Apache stood behind me. Beely rubbed against me to reach his horse blanket, untied it, and let it fall. He turned, and I felt Apache at my back, solid in his horse stand, familiar in his animal smell. The mustang's large dark eyes, against his white face blaze, rolled at me. He harrumphed and tapped his foot.

The man, whose gone-away had squeezed my soul, had rendered me aimless, and at this moment the same man pulled me and rubbed my sore back. The soothing pressure of his touch ended, and we fell onto pine needles. He lifted me onto the blanket and straddled me. His long hair fell down from his forehead and over his shirt collar. Soft lips came down onto mine. That touch sparked a pent-up yearning, and if God chose to strike me with lightning, chose to punish me for the pleasure of Beely, let it be as my body urge could not be stopped. Bring the Lord's wrath, for I couldn't end the joy of these few minutes of *Gloria,* a craved ecstasy.

My back felt a chill, and I realized I no longer had the covering of my blouse. My hands caressed Beely under his loosened shirt, then found flesh below his waist and his rear mounds pushed against me. He lifted my skirt and lowered my drawers to fresh air as he had done before, but this time I helped him. His skin onto mine was finer than clouds warmed of fire.

What I thought was a pine cone caught between us, was Beely, upright and ready. What at first felt a weapon became a satisfier, softly and slowly. With urgency, it brought hip movements, given to him. We held onto our pleasure until his burst of fullness lit our merry makers. We filled the heavens with moans and yelps, like animals who after many winters had found mates, got their inner desires satisfied, found love.

"*Alla* — there," my sister's voice broke our union.

I heard branches break and Garita's shout again. She was leading Tom Folliard toward us. I gathered my unders. Beely jumped up faster than a cat and tended to his britches. I tended to my unders and walked into the woods in the other direction, snapping my brassiere and buttoning my blouse. I returned to see Beely sitting on the blanket, picking piñons as Garita stepped up to him.

"Beely, *hola, piñones.*" She had two dead rabbits tied onto her rope sling, balanced over her shoulders. Her hair flopped in all directions and a dry weed hung onto one of those strands.

"*Seguro,* yes ma'am, Dolly Doll. I'm gathering these for you," Beely said.

She brushed her hair out of her face and wiped her nose with the back of her hand.

"Whoa, see you got your own kill right there. You're pretty darn good with that rock lance. Don't want you to take my eye out in a fit of *loco* madness."

She laughed and sat beside him on the blanket and began picking.

Beely's friend stayed back a ways and didn't come forward until Beely gave him a nod.

"Thought you were going to wait til I gave my shot?" Beely said.

"Know what you said, but this one doesn't

keep slow. Her legs don't have it. She traipsed over boulders and under trees. I had all I could to keep up with her, and I was on a horse."

"¿Beely, *ven* — come *casa*?" Garita said.

"Sure wish I could, Darling. But we're headed the other way, north. But you know what? I know . . ." He looked at me as I sat across from them, and I, too, began tossing nuts into the bag. "I'll be back. Maybe sooner than you want."

He and his friend sat around the trees and helped fill the flour sack. Like shy birds our eyes flitted in and out of each other's vision, each time stoking my happiness.

"Take," Garita said when there was no more room to put another nut.

They didn't have a way to carry nuts until Tom pulled out two dirty socks. One had a hole, so he tied it up short. He and Garita filled them while Beely led me away.

"Listen, Ambrosia, did I hurt you? Never ever want to cause you any . . . any . . . anything short of better than good — the best pleasure. *Tu sabes,* never any pain, *no dolor.*" He stroked my arm, and I tried to remember that feeling later.

His Spanish was like honey onto toast, cream into coffee — when Beely put his Hispanic words on me, the sounds caressed the air, and I lost sight of his loose ways.

"God, I wish things were different. Hate for our dalliance to end like this." He walked toward Apache.

"*¿Dali dali . . . dale . . .* give?" I asked.

"No, never mind. Just hate we didn't have time to give tender thoughts to each other. More than just . . . well anyway, *tu sabes?*"

"*¿Cuando,* Beely? Back when?" I asked.

"I'm away til my face here doesn't land me in the Crowbar Hotel, Ambrosia. God, I love to say your name — Ambrosia. No inkling on when that'll be. You give me something special, and I won't forget it. Makes a man's heart want to settle down, live without no worry, have our pleasure within what's guarded, like a church or something. Trust you know what I'm trying to say here. I had something with you lots of sorry cowboys never get. Want to see you again, some day, *pronto,* some way."

His last words raised me up and knocked me down. Tender it was, but it was also clear in any language he was going, and I might not see or have him for many, many months, maybe years, or maybe never again.

He draped his piñon-filled sock across his saddle horn. The rattly bag moved with each horse step away from me. Tonight, when he sat around his campfire and ate those piñons, would their roasted bits remind him of our love pleasure? Would he remember how he got them, remember this day? Garita and I watched until we no longer saw their backs.

The return path to our adobe appeared much further than our walk away. The long haul dulled my steps. Again, I began another stay of penance.

Dread of an unwanted baby was over one month later. God's punishment would not come in that form. Instead, I bled into myself in a different way, not with child, but of a deep throbbing as if monthly blood was seeping from my heart, not my womb. No word from Beely. I was sure he had gone on from Fort Sumner to Texas or Mexico or met a *Cucuy* death alone in the wilderness.

CHAPTER TWENTY

In the long stretch after that, Isabelle parted twin calves. Apá said the extra animals replaced two ewes and a lamb lost to coyotes. Pancho Gallo, the rooster, got old, lost his feisty punch, and made us a good meal. Apá searched the neighbors for a new young cock. Gordo, the oldest of our dogs, died after giving us many years of loyal service. Foxes raided our coop as many as twelve times and made off with more chickens than we could count. We needed that new rooster to breed more chicks and a new dog to guard them at night. The last time I felt Beely was the day we loved each other by the piñon trees long ago. As hard as it was, life went on.

One day rolled itself into the next, like a snake swallowing its own head. Never satisfied, the viper's hunger engorged on all of what was too familiar. Loneliness swallowed me in the same way. The weather went from warm, to cold, to warm again. Each starving day ate the next one. No other choice but to let my insides feed on themselves. One year and a few months had passed, and it seemed like two lifetimes.

Any new voice, horse hooves, or rusty door hinges stiffened me. A figure riding up the road, a spark of light up the mountain, a passing wagon chanced a surprise visit from Beely. A mix of dread and hope took me to the window, but it was never him.

When I heard slow heavy clomps, I knew it was Father Martinez. His black robe skirted over the mule's hind end as he came for his three-month confessions and for his mutton. Each of us met with him behind our outhouse, back to back, so we didn't have to face his saintly birdie mark with our sins.

Like yelling to the mountains, he began loud and clear, always in the same manner. "In the name of the Father, Son, and Holy Spirit, Amen. May the Lord be in your heart and give you help and wisdom to confess in truth." He added *"In nomine Patri, et Filii, et Spiritus Sancti, Amen"* so we would feel we had entered the holy, sanctified world of God. The fresh air opened my inner torment, and Father Martinez in his holy service stood as an authority for my redemption.

His voice comforted me. I thought about the calming white birdie on his face and answered. "Lord you know all things. Bless me Father for I have sinned. It has been three months since my last confession." I paused and shooed a fly from my nose. The privy door scraped open and slammed shut, hard enough to upset my purge.

Both Father Martinez and I knew to pause and wait for the person to leave me my time without their ears. "*Diosito* has time eternal," I heard him say. We waited. I smoothed the dust from my skirt and tapped a rock away with my foot. The second slam broke the long pause. Moments went by as steps eased into faint, then into nothing. Standing behind the outhouse, I couldn't see the person, but it sounded like Yginio's boots. With plenty enough time for him to be out of our earshot, Father ended his *ehem* with, "*Ya,* keep going, Ambrosia. It's okay."

I blew out a lung full of air. "*Sí, ya pues,* I have not been patient with my little sister or Apá or sometimes Yginio. Ramon Salamanca's goodwill doesn't bring me goodwill. It brings me — a face of scowl. I have not forgotten, I mean, forgiven Sinforosa for living, loving, I mean leaving. Many nights I wish I could run away with someone not of this family. I know that's not good, but I feel it." I leaned my head against the *escusado* and grasped my hands in humble penitence across my chest.

"These things do not make you a bad person, *Mija,* child of God. Remember *Diosito* loves you, and I know you will do the right thing. You want to be good and must not suffer. Pray. Prayer will help. None of these people have hurt you deliberately. They are struggling themselves."

I imagined the dance of his skin bird if he was headshaking.

Didn't end there. He went on. "Forgiveness is very hard, but as you release anger, your soul opens to kindness. The urge to run away just shows how desperate you feel. Trust me, with time it will diminish. For your penance say ten Our Fathers and fifteen *Santa Marias.* A daily rosary will help, too. Anything else?"

"Well there may be some other little thing. No, never mind, not big enough to bring to my holy Lord. No matter."

"*Por favor,* don't hold back," His deep voice raised an up-speak at the end of the sentence and seemed to have the same time eternal he spoke about earlier. "Remember your vow. The Lord gives you wisdom to confess, so release your heart. Give this burden away to Him who can comfort."

A pause grew long between us. I wondered if we had enough coffee for tomorrow and what I would cook for lunch. I wished someone else would come and use the privy — but the door hung silent.

"Urges pull me, Father." I began so low I could hardly hear myself.

A long stretch of my timidness kept him waiting.

"Go on, *Mija.*" He said it quick, rushed, as if excited to get more.

"I fight against a power. Some kind of thing that rises in me for . . . for . . . I don't know what for, but the grab, the pull on me is like a claw strung from my heart to . . . to down there. It's a mix of bad and good. I mean, it doesn't feel like a sin. No, not bad in that way, but I need help and pray my wants are the same as God's." The edge of my sin, not the true center, was offered.

"That's what troubling you, isn't it?" He was as relieved as I, it was over and in the open.

"Yes, my holy Father." Another shameful lie from me.

"*Ay Mija, Jesu Cristo* made you in his glory. Blessed you with a healthy, strong body, one which will one day bear children.

These feeling are normal and in time, in time they will be given a blessed path forward. Instead of yearning for what God hasn't yet given, put those feelings into what is true now. Help others, your sister and your father. Trust that your reward is coming. Both things, Ambrosia, your body desires and your impatience are of the same root. *Sí,* Ambrosia, put yourself into your work. Yes, give it to the Lord. For your penance, pray with your heart and soul fifteen Our Fathers and thirty *Santa Marias.* He will help you. You will see."

With that, Father and I turned, faced each other, and he touched the sign of the cross over my forehead. "God, the Father of mercies, through the death and resurrection of His Son, *Jesu Cristo,* He has settled the world and sent *Espirtus Sanctos* for the forgiveness of sins. May God give you pardon and peace. In His name, I absolve you, Ambrosia Salazar, from your sins, Father, *Jesu Christo,* and Holy Ghost."

I said, "Amen."

Father Martinez heard Apá and Garita's confessions and spent twice as much time with Yginio. Soon, Father swung his mule down the road with a dead sheep tied to the back of his old mule. We ate rabbit for the rest of the month.

■ ■ ■ ■

Time moved like a slow landslide. December of 1880 brought us to dead winter. Snow fell and I spun fleece close to the warm fireplace. Horse hooves sounded of an animal carrying a heavy load, so much so its shoes scraped the dirt before each step. That noise, outside the kitchen door, began a mental avalanche. "*¿Quien es?* No, couldn't be." I half-stepped my way to the door, opened it, and saw Ramon. He had come often to our place, but if I was indoors, he stayed outside with my father and brother. At mealtime he hushed his usual boom into a quiet chewing and swallowing and left early. If I went outside while he was here, he stared from a distance. This day, he showed up and drove his large bay — two large rumps swung together into the barn. The bay's large air holes shot puffs of gray smoke this December day, three days after Christmas. My father was checking the sheep for winter fleas, known to make them sick.

Apá brought each animal in, scraped fur around the ears, gave them a once-over, and took them back either for dipping or a separate pasture-pen. Garita, Tío Ruperto, and Yginio helped him. I left my spinning, buttoned my worn, winter coat, and put on my working gloves. When I walked into the barn, the *holas* were over, and Ramon turned his deer eyes at me.

He said it as soon as I was close enough to the noisy group to hear, "Yes, sir, *al fin,* they caught the *cabrón* Chivato." His eyes shifted to more of a bobcat.

Beely's name, suddenly in our presence, shocked me. One short sentence, carrying some small thread of information like a drop of water on the dry desert floor of the Tularosa Basin. It gave me little relief. My heart froze. I sucked in my bottom lip and bit down until Ramon looked.

"Beely, big shoot," Garita yelled. Her nose was bright red, and she shook snow off her shoulders.

"*¿Quien?*" said my father. So much time had passed, looked like Apá had forgotten the once familiar name, but Yginio, Garita, and I had not. My brother and I looked at each other. This gossip was why Ramon paid us a visit. In this cold weather, he must have been desperate to give us the latest lowdown, especially if it was bad news for me. I drew closer, and my trembling hands began helping with the sheep.

"That Billy Bonney, *tu sabes,* the Chivato

Kid who stirred things up here during the Lincoln County War." Ramon looked at Apá until his last word. Then his glance landed on me.

"Oh *sí,*" said Tío, "that one, I remember the Kid-man. Since he left, it's been quiet here."

"What do you mean, Ramon?" Yginio was holding an unhappy animal on its hind legs while Tío Ruperto managed to inspect it and scrape the fur around the ears.

Garita and I gathered what fell and took it to a smoke pit for later burning. Roping, dragging, tangling and untangling animals, and runs to the holding pens cut my time for much-needed word on Beely.

"This new sheriff, the one those in Santa Fe wanted for Lincoln — *un gringo* named Pat Gar . . . Pat Garott." Ramon stretched up tall and expanded his chest. "Something like that. *Un Juan Largo* — tall, whew, that man is taller than tall. See his straight-up bones coming from miles away. Six four and then some, I'd say. His wife, Apolinaria, is from Fort Sumner. Anyway, *este* Garrett. That's it, Garrett, he was on a hunt for the Kid since he took charge. You know, for the Chivato."

"*Sí, sí,* I remember him," said Tío Ruperto.

Ramon nodded and smiled like he had a toad in his pocket tickling his merry maker. "Garrett followed his snow tracks to Stinking Springs, just north of Fort Sumner."

"Oh *sí,* I heard about this new sheriff. They say he's tough as he is tall." Tío Ruperto broke from the flea check, leaned back, and propped his leg against a wall. He searched for a leftover smoke, found it in his front pocket, and flamed its tip. He spit a loose bit of tobacco and pulled a long draw.

I forced an unhappy sheep to a holding pen and ran back as fast as I could.

"Who did you hear this from?" Yginio asked.

Ramon got more excited as he went on. "In town, just happened a few days ago. Everyone's talking about it. Saturino Baca came by with a rowdy stallion he wanted gelded. He told me. They followed the snow tracks straight to the runaways. They shot Charlie Bowdre there; *tu sabes,* he used to live close by here in Ruidoso and then moved north. Dead and gone, *ya,* just like that, with a bullet to his head. Wish it had been the other one, the Chivato."

"¿Beely *muerto* — dead?" Garita shook her head.

"No *Mija,* too bad, eh?" said Ramon.

361

Garita still shook her head.

"Ramon, *cállate,* stop that. You might like to see people killed but don't put those ideas onto Garita." *Alive, he's still alive.*

Apá crunched his lips and smoothed them out with his fingers as he shook his head.

"Go on, Ramon. What happened? Did they wound Billy or anything?" Yginio asked.

"No, not even a graze. That Kid has more luck than a weasel," Ramon said.

"Happy no?" Nobody answered or paid attention to Garita. She was still shaking her head.

"He's been arrested, shackled, and taken by train to Santa Fe. He's there now, trying to get the governor to pardon him like he tried before. Ha, after all he did. The Kid's going to rot there, and lots of people, including me, are glad."

"*El gobernador* said he would give him the pardon," Yginio said. "That one governor, what's his name? Wallace. Yeah, Wallace made him a promise. Billy gave him details in court on the Chapman murder, you know, Susan McSween's lawyer. Kid made good on his side, but the governor didn't come through. Then he offered $500 for Beely's head. Justice, that ain't justice."

"Justice comes only from the one holding

the gun, *Mijo.* Never matters if he has a badge or not." Tío Ruperto blew smoke up the rafters and a crack in the ceiling boards sucked it into the cold.

"Pat Garrett's going to get the well-earned $500 reward, too. They claim the Kid will stand trial in Mesilla for the Sheriff Brady kill." Ramon forced his little finger into his ear and dug around for sticky goop. He wiped what came out on his pants.

My pulse settled into half instead of quarter beats. Even when it looked impossible, Beely always found a way out. He could do it again.

"Brady's kill? What? How do they know it was Billy's bullet? Lots of people emptied their barrels that day." Even in this cold, Yginio's forehead, wet from his nerves, wrinkled up moist. He appeared to be as worried as me.

Garita left her place, and Tío slacked away from the job at hand. Wind blew roof tins loose and whistled between cold metal.

To have my ear in on this outlaw news kept me working. I forced sheep clear of fleas to the outside range or infected ones to the inside pen for dipping. I'd roped another and dragged it to Apá who seemed to be the only one still working. I came back as fast as I could to pick up useless bits of fur off the ground or another sheep for delivery.

"*Sí*, Yginio, you know he's the one," Ramon said. "He pointed his gun at the sheriff's office the day of John Tunstall's funeral. Said he was bedding him down. How do you know it wasn't his shot? And they're getting him for Shotgun Roberts's death, too. The one right here on the Apache reservation by Blazer's Mill."

"Same thing, Ramon. Seven or eight Regulators were firing. Why only one man takes the blame?" Yginio left the spot checking and stood against a nearby beam beside Tío Ruperto.

"Someone pays." Apá led the last shaggy sheep out and put in his verdict. "And that one here is Chivato, the Kid goat."

"Someone's got to suffer, and they have him, so let it be him." Tío, nodded and piggybacked Apá's accounting from his lean-back stance.

"Beely no pay," Garita said.

I nodded and looked at Apá.

Apá looked at Ramon, and Ramon squinted his eyes long and hard in my direction.

Yginio shook his head and pulled the sheep up onto its hind legs. Scraped the coat so hard, fast and close, I thought he'd bloody the poor animal.

Ramon stood and watched without lending any little hand. He rattled on. "Why? I know why. They say, Mescalero Reservation is federal. And Buckshot Roberts fought as a North soldier in the Civil War. That's why Chivato's ass is strung up." Ramon put his pointing finger in the air, then drove it down into the palm of his meaty hand.

Garita giggled, "*Culo* — ass."

"Going to burn his hind end. Sorry, *mujeres*." Ramon looked to see where I was.

I was on my way out and not standing close but Garita was, and she answered. "No burn."

She mouthed my thoughts. The lassos were re-hung, and sheep munched on winter hay. Tío went home. Ramon mounted his horse and left without eating. I didn't invite him to stay. My future with him blurred like the writing on the little fallen crosses in the graveyard.

CHAPTER TWENTY-ONE

On April 3, 1881, four months later, Beely
came to give his say-so in Mesilla Court.
That was Doña Ana County. The town was
very far west of us, beyond Sierra Blanca,
down into the desert. This was where these
matters are given an ear. Word got out faster
than a crow flying northeast from that
court-telling place to us here in San Patricio. Yginio said, in Mesilla, the listening
judge gave his word on these doings. Was
what Beely had done an innocent mistake?
Was he protecting himself from the sheriff?
With many guns blazing, who could say
which one hit the mark? Did he deserve to
be locked-up? Or death? For Beely it came
down to the last thing he had to offer — his
life. Depending on whether he was giving it
or someone was taking it, he would hang.

Ramon, always sassy with Chivato news,
told my father and Yginio that the law guns
in charge drove alongside our *ranchito* on

their way from Mesilla to Lincoln with Beely. That journey must have rolled by on one of my many tormented nights. I had no recall of any long caravan passing, but I do remember dreaming Beely was chained and put into a fire. He screamed. I ran with a bucket of water, but Apá held me from going to him. Ramon came and put chains on me. Beely screaming stirred a heat sweat in me, so bad, I woke with a wet pillow and soaked sheets. He was now in jail, across from the Wortley Hotel, the place where the House Mercantile had once been.

My Beely lived snapping with joy and quick to anger against what he thought was wrong. That mindful head of his saved me at the Jewel Parlor and took vengeance on Tunstall's murderers. He wanted to be taken down fighting for justice, moving, not limp on a noose. In a push-back, in a shoot-out, with his belly dragging the dirt, galloping through the bush, firing bullets, charging those against him — that was how he wanted to go.

Now his leaving would be in another person's hands, and the act would not be a brave passing but a choking defeat. If he left this earth with his wrists tied, his soul would be locked up in a curse of weakness, no honor in our memory of him. I suffered knowing his wants and seeing what appeared to be his last snare-hold. Didn't seem he could cut loose from this was one by talking, money, or a weapon. His ill-forsaken, future depart sat festering within me.

Apá and Garita drove up the valley with goat milk to sell to the Sanchez family west of us. I washed the morning dishes and gathered tortilla scraps and dried meal for the chickens. Threw the feeding out the front door as they clucked outside, same as any day. Isabelle rattled her cowbell and called me for her milking. From the pasture corral, I harnessed and yanked her and the goat toward the barn. The goat gave little, so I pulled its nervous bleeting back to the pole pen for the day. Isabelle was different. I softened her bag and with a lean in, squeezed her long teats. She gave me more than a dribble, and soon milk streamed onto the tin sides with a hard flow.

Yginio drove the hauler into the barn to load bundled fleeces for a delivery to the Tularosa Mercantile the next day. "Heard you rolling around your bed last night like a thunder cloud. You okay?" He stood against the buckboard with his arms folded, nodding his head. "Then your thunder cloud let down rain, not just a sprinkle but a hard shower. It wasn't Garita. It was you. Kept me from getting back to sleep. It's him, ain't it?"

"Him who?" We both knew who the *him* was. I jerked poor Isabelle so hard she turned and mooed.

"You know, *him* — Billy. The one they have in the Lincoln jail. I saw him looking out from the window, his face all bruised. That *cabrón* Bob Olinger pistol-whipped him more than half the trip from Mesilla. Wore him out bad. Has chains around his hands and feet like he's a rabid bobcat. It's April, not that warm, and he doesn't have blankets." He shook his head. "Not good, don't look good."

I wrapped my fingers around the second set of teats, letting milk fly. Apá and Garita or Ramon didn't know I pushed my feelings into a cold, lonely place, one where nothing mattered. My brother, of course in a different way, suffered with me. I sensed his misery, and he felt mine.

"*Ay*, Yginio, you know how he wanted his life to be. This is not it — roped and beat up. All that's left is for us to pray he doesn't suffer too much more before . . . before they . . ." I couldn't finish.

"I talked to him from the street. Half-dead but half for Billy is not the same as for other

369

men. He's going to try an *out.* I know it. I know him."

"How, Yginio? Too many have died already. *No mas* — and not you. Don't you think of jail-breaking him, no sir, not for one minute. Apá has suffered enough."

"Ambrosia, Beely . . . I mean Billy says watching from the shadows ain't justice. It just makes things worse. *Tu sabes,* he fought on the side of good men, Tunstall, Brewer, and the McSweens. Put himself in danger, stood up and told the truth about the Chapman murder, and the governor never paid him, never held up his end of the deal. Others were shooting, too. His was not the only gun firing."

"I know, Yginio, you said it many times. But nothing matters. They have to string somebody up, and they're going to kill him in a way he never wanted, without honor, a noose around his neck like a fallen saint who stood for right, but the real right never happened, never came here. There's nothing anybody can do." My last words quivered brittle defeat.

Yginio pushed his hat back off his forehead and took a deep breath before he spoke. "I've got to help him."

"No, Yginio, no, please, *por favor.* You will find yourself in his same locked cage. As much as I don't want this for Beely, I can't stand thinking of my brother beside him on that hanging tree." I moved to the other side of the cow.

He followed me with steel eyes and his mouth locked shut.

"*Dios mío,* for God Almighty, for Apá, for my sake and Garita, for the honor of our mamá, don't do it," I said.

He turned and began beating his fist against a timber beam.

"*Ya,* Yginio, stop, listen. I know it's hard, but we — you and me — didn't put Beely there. We have to go on." I set the milk can beside Isabelle and put my heavy head in the palms of my hands.

A person without food has will enough within themselves to search for something to eat. Another can fall in deep water, desperately swim to the surface for air. They strive to take another breath. But to be without hope — a person's insides give up, and they become a walking death. This was me. My brother and I were two false dreamers, clinging to a miracle, an impossible outcome.

I stood and walked Isabelle back to her stall.

"I can't watch him hang. Have to get him a gun," Yginio said, alfalfa in his mouth chewed to threads.

"Gun? Did you hear me? Do you want to kill Apá? How do you have a gun anyway, you crazy? In the shed with the whiskey? What else you have back there? *Dios mío,* Yginio, you're as bad as . . . no you're worse than the mouse who spits at a lion." But something in me rejoiced, and I halted my steps.

"Ambrosia, he never deserved to be taken and sacrificed like this. Especially since others ran and pulled triggers beside him. This Pat Garrett, he don't know the people of these mountains — those of us who are not from the government. Dolan, Wallace, Garrett — they should be the ones in chains, cold, and beaten."

"Please think, look. First let's talk to someone in town who knows how they're going to do it and when. Someone who's there but not there."

My brother stood more of a man than I had ever known. But he didn't think ahead and a trigger-happy revenge might get him killed.

"Who?" he asked.

With milk can in hand, a drawn-out pause took my shuffling feet toward the barn door.

I turned and faced Yginio. "Tehde — that woman can get into places no others can —

part cat and part fox — an Indian woman, a black, Apache flower with magic eyes. She can do much more than any man, even you."

CHAPTER TWENTY-TWO

Yginio changed my life from wait and want to think and act. Yet, my brother and I had no plan, only prayer and a pistol. God would not approve of violence or a hatched idea that put those less sinful than me into danger, but He taught redemption. In the end, like Sinforosa, I would ask for pardon. While I had *Diosito's* ear, I'd make a plea for Beely, Yginio, and Tehde. *Do not blame others for what I started.* My prayer felt undeserving, but I couldn't be in any worse grace than where I had sunk.

We collected barter, so my brother would have to make more trips to town to meet and talk with Tehde. Each day we gathered together as I milked the cow. Yginio and I planned the impossible. I found a purpose, more than jerking milk from swollen teats or slopping pigs, and for the first time in months I slept most of the night. With little power, we had to look for a way to cheat the cheaters, to surprise wide-eyed watchmen, and to unprison the prisoner. I prayed not for forgiveness, but also for His help to sin again.

"I don't think she can do it." Yginio stood with his back to me as he loaded a few fleeces. "I think this is something for a man, *un hombre con confianza.* Someone as brave as Billy, not a woman, an Indian woman no less." He looked at Garita, playing with a kitten in the corner of the barn, and spoke low.

"What do you mean? Tehde has confidence; she doesn't fear anything." I remembered her protect, her flying spirit, and how she broke that young feisty stallion. "Think of a little beetle who crawls in dark corners. People see but don't see her. They think if they touch her, they'll get her curse, so the fools stay away. They don't know her gift. She has the power of a *curandera* witch, an *encantadora,* and *milagro* maker. Did she take the pistol?"

"Yeah, she shook eagle feathers around it. Mumbled some words I never heard before and stood staring at me. Then she put those darker than dark eyes on me and said, 'Devil spirit weak. Earth heaven more wise.' What's that supposed to mean? Heaven and earth's got nothing to do with what we want. We need to get Billy someone who fires hell in front and behind him."

"So she did take it?" I asked.

"Are you listening? I just told you. She took it by the trigger, waved some feathers, and dropped it in her bag like it was an evil disease. I told her we didn't want her to use it — only get it to Billy. She said, 'Beads, roots, spirit callings more better than big shoot.' *Loca,* you know, she's buck crazy."

"That's okay. We don't have anybody else, and we don't know her way won't work. Give her time. She knows things, many things. Maybe she can work a spell, and we won't have any more killings."

"Oh *sí,* Ambrosia, you're as bad as her. This ain't for women *locuras.* We don't have no time for crazy spirts. Won't work, I tell you. *Chihuahua,* we're just wasting time."

We heard a giggle.

"Buck *loca* — crazy."

We both turned. Garita was building a haystack castle for her cats.

"Right, Garita," I said, "No nothing here."

"No nothing," she said.

Yginio brought his voice to a whisper. "Those two guard men, Jim Bell and Bob Olinger, mean ape men, haven't taken their eyes off Billy. He's dragging chains all night and day, in his sleep and when he eats. No rest. Only time anyone can see Billy is when they take him to the *escusado* for a leak. And they carry their guns. See, they, all of them, don't know nothing but killing. They're just hoping Billy will make one move, and they're going to fill him with lead. I know he'd like that better than a big crowd watching him choke his last breath."

Moving to the other side of Isabelle, I kept my voice from Garita. Yginio followed. "Did Tehde say she would do anything else?" I asked.

"Said she'd watch and wait and only move if a chance showed itself. She never looks at me, so I can't tell all of what she says and if she's listening or not. Then she mumbled some words I didn't get. It's not Spanish or English, and it doesn't sound like Apache. I think she said she'd gather what she called earth gifts, beast callings, and spirit finders to prepare the path for Billy." Yginio kicked dirt aside.

CHAPTER TWENTY-THREE

Late April of 1881, after breakfast, after the chickens were fed, and after Isabelle was taken to pasture, the morning was like any other. This one brought light spring breezes, and the trees' new buds sparked relief that God's promise for better weather was coming. But then a great clatter of chains sounded like a rail car had gone loose and dragged up a track, steel on steel to our house. Yginio ran up to the rider, and I could see him jump with excitement though I could not hear exact words. The man straddled a rifle across his chest, but he was too thin to be Beely.

Not yet down the road, Apá and Garita's jaws opened heavy like cast-iron doors. They had been holding sheep corralled for transport off to the side. When the rider motioned toward the barn and ran his horse closer to the window, I saw it *was* Beely. My God, his tongue had sucked in his cheeks, raising the bones on his face out. His tight, cut-and-run jaw unveiled a desperate man, not the happy-go-lucky one I remembered. The pan, in my loose grasp, dropped to the floor.

Tehde, bless your Mescalera soul. You found a way. I signed the Lord's cross over my face and folded my arms around my waist. When I bent over to pick up the pan, I realized I had no hands to grab it, and my legs could not move. With feeble strength I kicked the pan aside, unstuck my feet, and ran to the door.

Apá and Garita took their leave away from the pasture and ran into the barn, too. Then I noticed another horse clomping up the road to our place. Ramon, his figure could not be mistaken, was whipping and kicking his horse as fast as Beely.

"Santa Maria, Jesus, y Dios mío," I said. We needed the Savior Himself this minute to perform a miracle. My nerves, like stiff barb wire, paralyzed my body, yet I had to move, had to move, now. I rushed out the kitchen door with no idea about what I was going to do. Did Ramon need to be stopped? Was Beely in danger? Should I rescue Garita? Should we refuse help and send Beely on his way? Was Yginio in trouble? Would the tall sheriff come soon?

Beely had one ankle wrapped with an iron, and the other ankle iron dragged a chain like a bedeviled snake tail. What was once attached, counter-whipped in the opposite direction of his walk. Dirty, ragged hair hung over his eyes, and when he looked up at me, there came a weak version of his twisted smile. Thank *Diosito,* his tight lock-up had not turned him sour beyond hope. Yginio and I circled him while Apá and Garita stood in the corner of the barn, staring.

"*Pronto,* fast, hide. Ramon is coming up the road." A dying-eagle shriek came from me. "*Ay ya yay,* Apá go talk to him, so he doesn't come in the barn."

"*Ya, go* fast, Apá," Yginio said.

"No, I don't get into these crazy doings. Why should I lie? Ramon knows this is his house, and he can go where he wants." Apá with hands in his pockets stood firm.

"It's okay, Ambrosia," Beely said. "Let him come in. He saw me pass his place and was one of the few who followed. Big as he is, I lost him, but he had a notion where I was headed. We could use his help to take these leggings off. Can't ride like this."

"He's not going to help," Yginio said. "He's a Murphy man."

"No, but he won't hurt or arrest us either."

380

I knew Ramon could hurt Beely, but he would do anything to keep this family from trouble.

The door creaked open, and we all laid eyes on him. Ramon's swelled stomach, thick arms, and legs cut half the light of the door opening, and we sunk into the barn darkness. Wide Salamanca eyes wandered fast over all of us. *"¿Que pasa?"* he said.

"Ramon, *ya pues, hombre.*" Apá had it in him to come up with some calming voice. "We here with a little *problema.*" He rubbed the back of his head, blinked his eyes, and started that thing with his tongue.

"Right, Ramon, *un problemita,* but it's bigger than little." Beely moved his legs in a side step that dragged the chain and took Ramon's attention to the leg iron.

A post, meant to shore up the barn ceiling, held Garita as she hugged it. Then she made me her holding post, tighter than a pecan's shell to its inner nut. I loosened her grip from my waist and held her hand.

"You left Lincoln strung with dead deputies, people screaming, and blood running down the main street, Chivato *cabrón.* You thought you had problems before, now there's a target on your heart until it stops beating. Glorious day that will be. Those poor dead were cut down doing their job.

381

And now you bring your mess here to *Los Salazares.* These people have nothing to do with you."

Beely steered his eyes onto mine. I wanted him to see me but didn't want him to see me. I wondered if what Ramon said was true. Somehow I thought Tedhe would make him a clear and free path without hitches, without death — and yet if he didn't look at me, I would be incomplete.

"I agree. *Salazares* are good people, the best who've walked this earth. Hearts of kindness and minds of justice makes their total." Beely set down his rifle.

"Talk, talk, talk, hearts, minds." Ramon spit an oversized drool next to Yginio's boot. "*Sí pinche cabrón,* then why did you come here?"

"Problems are as big as any no-count makes them," Beely said. "Why don't you stop the talk and help get these irons off me. And I will be on my way, out of your worry — on the road, taking my trouble with me and not hurting anyone here."

Ramon knew where the hammer and heavy chisel hung. "Put your *pendejo* sit-down there and get your chained leg on this wood bench. Let's get what's holding you off. Yginio, put a strong arm on this *cabrón's* leg, and I will work the iron." He swung

382

and near missed Beely's boot.

Garita jumped and put her forehead into my shoulder. Ramon might whack his foot off just to see if Beely could ride without it. His next hit dented the iron ring attached to the chain.

"Just get the drag off. I will deal with the ankle wrap later," Beely said. "Can't ride with the chain hanging."

Ramon took another swing and twisted one chain link, close to the iron ankle.

"How did you get the pistol?" Yginio asked.

"When I made my way to the comfort house, I started seeing strange things. A bat I had never noticed clung tight in the corner."

Ramon took a bang.

"Then a dead lizard beside the *chee* hole, sleeping. Another time, I saw eagle feathers pinned to the wide side, the one where a person sits and faces. Seemed like someone was giving me clues. So when a lump sat, wrapped in an old rag, I found my hallelujah. My go-for-broke." He smiled and winked at me.

The strength of Ramon's blacksmith arm dented half through the chain link.

"I didn't want to hurt Jim Bell. The Man upstairs knows it. But the youngster wouldn't drop his weapon like I said, and I didn't have time to coddle a negotiation. Olinger, the other, Bobby Boy, didn't well up any kindness in me from the get-go. I let him drop easy, like someone would a grizzly coming at him. He'd been whipping my bad side for weeks all the way from Mesilla. Ramon's right. I took him down in the street, and this time it was my *solo* gun spraying. No blaming nobody else."

Ramon stopped to catch his breath.

"*¿Adonde* — where?" Garita asked.

"*¿Adonde?* There in Lincoln's where I was at."

She shook her head. "*¿Adonde vas* — go?"

"*Mejico,* Señor Bonney. You speak the Spanish language and with that you can make a good life down there. No bother like here where they hunt you." Apá's voice brought reason, and his notion would take Beely far away from us. I was sure that's what he and Ramon wanted.

Beely looked at me. "Yeah, good plan. But I'm going to backtrack first. Got some folks north I reckon to see. Then I will head this way and . . ." He looked at me so long, the others turned, too. "Hack me a *rumbo* south to Mexico."

Beely's boots protected his skin from the sharp chisel. Ramon took a final hard swing and snapped the iron link to the metal wrap. Free from the anchors, Beely lost no time getting on his horse.

"Wait, Beely, let me give you food," I said.

Garita and I ran to the kitchen and wrapped bean *refritos,* papitas, and chili in three tortillas. I wrote a little fast note in my best letters, "*Aquí,* here for you."

He was outside the kitchen door, sawed his horse back onto its haunches, and reached out for the food. I felt his fingertips. Garita's cries and the sound of his horse hooves, galloping away, pulled me to where I was, here again without him. I wiped a wetness from my face and was glad Ramon, Apá, and Yginio had stayed in the barn not to see me.

CHAPTER TWENTY-FOUR

"*Pobre* Ambrosia," I heard my father whisper in low tones every time I neared him. Was it the way my expression skittered into the corners anytime Ramon or Apá looked at me? Or the flesh to red to black below my eyes? Maybe because my face stretched down, long and heavy. Or could it have been the false struggle to feed myself or great effort to keep my fingernail from boring a little heart onto my thumb. These things must have brought their suspicions. They thought the downward spin came about because of Beely's last trouble. Yes, that was one drop of a full bucket — one sin to carry, among others that loomed onto a heavy load. Anything about Beely, they said, reasoned into no good for me.

Garita knew something drained me, and she helped wash and hang clothes some days instead of running away. But her innocence couldn't figure out what burdened me, and in a moment she'd forget and wouldn't care. Apá held me in his watch a long time and moved his chin from side to side in a way I imagined a mother bird does when her little one won't fly or eat. Yginio, as Beely's *primo*-partner, had his suspicions, also. He'd fix his watchful eyes on me with as close an understanding as he'd ever have for his sister.

Ramon, as always, came to our place often to help Apá. His wounded expression wavered around me, and I felt it land on top of my head. It was the top because my head would always be down. And when I looked up, he'd be there. Alone in the kitchen together, his huge presence would hum one of the songs Father Martinez taught us before Sunday mass. Grace Amazing or some old Mexican *ranchera* about love and forgiveness — mine or his, I didn't know which. He'd tap his thick fingers on the table, waiting for me to smile, look at him, or say some little thing. I would not. He'd walk out and try again the next time he came. No one but Garita ever mentioned Beely's name, and when that happened, no foolish soul would pay any mind.

Happenings changed a little, the day Apá stood in the shadow of the river's weeping willow tree, by my washing rock. My redraw knuckles ached as I moved fabric over the rough granite. Strange to see him where he never ever had been before. Summer heat and the water bugs walked the tops of still puddles.

"*Mija,* we worry for you." Apá's wood-stiff jaw, garbled words. "We lost Sinforosa, and I don't want you, *Mija,* to get sick."

His low voice scratched an imagined claw down my back. "No worry, Apá. Just tired, *no mas.*" I rubbed dirty socks, rinsed, and rubbed again.

"Worry, yes, something very heavy is pulling at you. Garita, she needs watching, but you must think about yourself. Make your own life." He took a closer step to my washing spot and flipped a twig into the water. "*Tu sabes,* your own family — daughters and sons. Garita can go with you."

"Go? Where do you think I'm going, Apá? I'm here with you." The stop gave me cause to squeeze and throw washed clothes into the holding bucket.

"But, *Mija,* you are not happy here — no longer like before. Yginio and I, we'll be alright. We can learn to care for ourselves."

"*¿Cómo,* Apá? How? What do you say?" I could not imagine them cooking and cleaning the house. Head down, I worked dirt out of sock bottoms.

He was not finished and began again. "Ramon . . ."

"What about Ramon?" I asked.

"Ambrosia, *por favor,* let me have my say." He squatted, tried to catch my eyes, and played with tall, Bermuda grass in front of him. "Ramon is a good man. The same as us here and likes everyone in our family. Knows how close you are to Garita and is willing to take her."

"Take her where, Apá?" I wanted to say, *to the Murphy House like you tried before,* but I had too much respect for him.

"Wait. Let me tell you. Ramon has asked if he can call on you to be his wife. And he knows Garita will also be in his care. Look, you're losing weight, *Mija.*"

The *eeeee* sound in *Mija* went on long — desperate.

"Life's hard for you. This marriage could be something good. We can slaughter a lamb and a *chiva* and have a big fiesta with music and *tamales.* We can invite the whole valley and celebrate a new day. Think about it. Don't say nothing. Just think. Ramon is strong, a fine provider and Catholic, a good Catholic, man of God who we all like. He has a work without guns. He has . . ."

"Ya, Apá, *basta,* I have heard you. *Ya,* no more, *por favor."* I dropped the heavy, wet

socks and stared, not at him but at the drifting river.

"Okay, I go milk *la vaca.* You don't need to do it this time."

That day ended and many more. Apá never again spoke out loud of his plans for me. A road with two paths drew a fork before me. One, a dry desert with nothing but Ramon and barrenness. The other, a trip to Mexico, with Beely, through land with hungry bobcats at every turn. If I worked, my father would leave me alone. So I labored just as Father Martinez advised and kept my head down.

So the day Ramon stood before me didn't give me any surprise. To me, he was like fried chicken livers left over from yesterday's meal, food waiting its serving. I chopped green chili as he let himself in. With that distraction, I slipped and cut my finger. But my expectation did not prepare me for what came with him — Father Martinez. I never before had missed the heavy-footed thuds of Padre's mule and wondered how that noise got by me — until I noticed Father was riding a horse, a fine chestnut gelding with easy, light-footed steps.

"New *caballo,* Father?" I pressed my cut finger between my teeth and tasted blood.

Father Martinez flashed quick eyes to

Ramon. He wiped the palm of his hand over his forehead and the back of his neck.

I squeezed the skin around my wound. "Is the new horse borrowed?" A tiny drop of red fell onto my skirt.

Neither man answered.

Ramon laid a sadness meant for widows and orphans on me. His eyes attached not to my face but to my heart. I looked for something to wrap my cut.

"Finger . . ." I pointed it at them. "Need to fix it, *perdon.*" I turned to walk away.

Ramon, in his gentle, giant way, pulled a clean handkerchief and yanked my arm toward him. His smell of clean brought memories of us as children. He, a young boy, always after us — Sinforosa, me, and Garita. He never tired of looking for ways to help. The tight wrap around my finger felt good and made me wish all wounds could be patched so easily.

"*Ya,* good, *gracias,* Ramon." I pushed away toward my work. Father Martinez sat, and my apá walked in. Six eyes stared.

"*¿Ya, que?*" I tried to roll tortillas but the handkerchief knot would not roll over the pin. "What's so important?" I asked.

"*Nada,* we just want you to be alright, now and later," Ramon said.

"What your eyes say is not what comes

from your mouth. Something more here. Father Martinez, you tell me. *Por favor,* you know the truth."

My apá, silent, dug dirt from his thumb nails.

Padre father spoke. "I'm here only to give Ramon a . . . a . . ."

The door slammed and Garita came into the room. "I *mala* — bad, *Padre, mucho muy mala* — bad."

Apá jumped and took her out to the barn.

Father took a hot tortilla from the stack on the table and bit off a mouthful — enough to keep himself quiet.

Ramon spoke. "I see a sadness you didn't have before."

"What do you know of what I had before, Ramon? Sticking in where you don't know anything. Nothing has happened. Maybe that's the problem." Wounded finger and I glared at him. To Father I softened my tight eyes.

"See, you never talked that way before," Ramon said. "So *brusca,* so sad, closed down with a rock over your heart. So full of hate. Why?" He shook his head and speared those dark eyes into me. "Not the same Ambrosia we all know."

"Yes, *Mija,* and God knows rage is hate and hate leads to sin," Father Martinez said.

"You two don't know . . . know of . . . never mind." I stirred the pot of *refritos.*

"Yes, Ambrosia, it does matter. You know all my life you have mattered. You are important. You and all in your family. You sink and, *tu sabes,* many others go with you."

"I'm not sinking Ramon. I don't need you or anyone . . ." Hardness iced me, but I had enough sense to offer three words of the old Ambrosia, "To save me."

"*Bueno, bueno* but just in case . . ."

Ramon liked the idea of saving me.

"No, no case here." My trembling fingers became fists.

Father Martinez left his eating and began earning his gift horse. His hand went to the wooden cross around his neck, rubbing fingertips along its sharp edges. "Ambrosia, you have a good, God loving man here who cares . . ."

"Brosia *Buena* — good, everything." Garita, who had slipped back in spoke from the corner. She walked to Ramon, took his arm, and wrapped it around her waist. "I eat now."

For once, glad to have my sister's demands on me, my attention went to the stove. "I'm finished with the chili. You, too, Garita, *eh?* Do your part. Father, will you stay and have some food? *Ya pronto,* Garita, set the plates and put these hot pots on the table."

Ramon gave my sister a hug. "Here, Garita, I'll help you." He never took his eyes off me.

Father stayed. Apá and Yginio came in and sat. No one spoke anymore of the mating promise.

CHAPTER TWENTY-FIVE

A cicada or *chicharra* — or some call the summer insects nothing but little buzzers. They creep up from the ground every seven years. Larvae stick onto a tree, fence, or anywhere it lands. A change happens. Another form breaks out, wingy, wet, and gooey. Its other life is left behind. Wings spread out from its keeping, become stiff enough to fly, and the new version takes off. Goes away for a joy ride. Following the buzzes, she finds a mate and merry mates much to her happiness. The she-cicada drops her eggs and creates baby slugs like what she once was. Then she dies. The next group spends the next seven years underground, half-blind in the dark, hardly living, waiting for the few days they can see light, make love, drop eggs, and die.

I longed for Beely, dreamed he would tap on my window one night, and I would jump on his Apache, and we would ride all night until we reached a low, warm plain. He would unroll his blanket just as he did below the piñon tree, and the cool breezes would blow over our wet, naked bodies. This would be the beginning of our lives. Mexico would be our home, and we would have many children.

I was the cicada, and I was in the dark dirt, waiting, but I didn't know what I was waiting for. Work plowed me through long days, hoping Beely would come soon and pleasure me.

Milk streams squirted light against milk tin as Yginio led his horse into the barn, dismounted, uncinched Luz, and dropped the saddle onto a nearby stump. He undid her bridle, pulled it off, and hung it on the nearby nail. Nothing about his big movements were different except from the corner of my eye, I saw his head shake. Moved my stool to the other side of Isabelle to get a better look. It had been a long time since we spoke together in the barn. The cow's udder had not been softened and was cold as hard *masa*. I stopped and kneaded her again.

He turned in my direction. Lately no one, except Garita, spoke more than necessities to me. And I expected silence from him, too. Yet Yginio was different since we saved

Beely. His down-headedness told me he was bothered, too. He loosened a flick of hay from the bale and fed it to the horse. He drew up its hoof and inspected its shoe, tapping for any loose pebbles or dirt.

I milked.

"You forgot the horse blanket. *Qué pasa, hermano,* something on your mind? Why you so nervous?"

Raised brows gave up his surprise. "Maybe *nada,* but I rode into town today. Ramon wanted me to see his new pony. He . . ."

"Another one he can give to Father Martinez to shame my unhappiness? Never mind, a new pony? Is that what gets you squirrel-headed?"

"No, it ain't."

"Then, what?"

"After I saw the pony, I rode into town and saw Tehde. She sits outside the sheriff's office, and she said she heard *Juan Largo* talking. You know the sheriff. His brother-in-law is married to a Celsa Gutierrez. They live in Fort Sumner. Garrett's wife, Apolinaria, told Garrett that her brother don't know what to do because Celsa is familiar onto Billy."

"*Ya, pues,* that's it? What got you riled up? Dirty gossip? Garita, Tehde, someone called Celsa, the sheriff's sister-in-law, his

397

wife — everybody loves Beely." I missed the bucket and shot the milk stream onto the dirt.

"Gossip, you say? What it means is, the sheriff knows where Billy's hiding," Yginio said.

"We both know Beely. He will be there only a little while before he comes back this way to Mexico. That's what he said. He will move soon. He's not dumb. They haven't caught him so far."

"Wait, there's more. Apolinaria, Garrett's wife, it's her brother who says Billy is there and is close not only to his wife but to Pablo Maxwell. You know, the rich *haciendero* who owns old Fort Sumner. Anyway, Garrett is fixing to see if this is just talk. He's moving to hunt him there very soon."

I let go of the teats and turned to Yginio. "Rumors, just rumors. *Tu sabes.* We heard the other day, Beely was seen in Mexico. And before that, it was Texas to join the Rangers. Then some said he was rustling in White Oaks. All talk, worse than old ladies." A heat swelled my throat and moved down to the pit of my stomach. Isabelle mooed for the force I tightened around her. So hard, the milk would not come out. I stopped and patted her.

"Maybe, but someone who isn't part of

the sheriff-hunt, might should get a word to Billy. If he's there, warn him." He pulled the horse blanket off Noche and set it on a stump.

"Yginio, how do we know what's true? Loose tales, gossip, nothing but talk, one lie after another — one speaks, then the second one says what he thought he heard and after that, another one whispers something worse than the first."

"But Tehde don't lie. She helped us and Billy last time," Yginio said.

"It's not Tehde. *Sí,* I put faith in her, too. Yes, she helped us many times with Sinforosa and Garita when she was left with Señor Murphy and with Beely. Not her." I swatted a pesky fly from the side of my mouth. "The others in this story chain, them others — Garrett's wife, her brother, then the brother's wife, Pablo Maxwell, just too many. Not Tehde, she speaks very few words but what comes out is always true."

"So see there. I have to go, got to see if Billy's there and warn him. He has to get out of that place."

"How many days' drive is it?" The question might come from one with hope, one who was asking because a saving journey might be possible — not from my defeated voice, the real me.

"Two, depending on the weather, but it's not winter now. It's July, and Ramon can lend me a good, strong horse."

I finished the milking and turned to face him. "If you go, I want to go, too."

Chapter Twenty-Six

Apá sat and snaked his tongue along the inside of his cheek, bulging one side of his face. The hollow of his eyes sank into his head. I put a *café* in front of him, hoping he would use his mouth in other ways. His lips pressed, tightening loose skin around the cup rim for a sip. He shook his head as Yginio spoke. The Lord's Fifth Commandment, Honor *El Apá,* stifled my urge to squeeze his mouth and shake his head into a *yes* movement.

"I can take Noche. He's strong and will make the trip easy. Ramon will lend us one of his young horses for Ambrosia and maybe Garita if we decide to take her. Ramon don't care how we use them. He won't ask."

"No — I say no, *absolutamente no. Nunca,* never," my father said.

"But Apá," I moaned as low and gentle as I could.

"No." His tongue now lashed instead of snaked.

"Apá, just a few days, that's all." Yginio spoke. "If he's not there, I will just eat, water the horses, turn around, and come back. Not much more than when we run our longest flock drive. Apá, you liked Beely. He is young and deserves to live. We can help him." Yginio lifted his head and gave me a look with his pleading eyes like he wanted me to say something.

"Papacito . . ." I began as best as I could. "My brother and I —"

"No, did you hear me? I said, no. We helped him too much already." Apá turned and stared at me. He had never heard me call him sweet *Papacito* before. "*Este, este* Chivato, he *ya* made his choice. Your place is here at home, not after him."

Yginio and I sat across the table, and Garita stood behind me and played with my hair.

"Big shoot," Garita said. "Ginio."

I grabbed my braid, turned, and put my finger to her lips.

"I should go, too, Apá." For the first time in months my shoulders pulled up from the frame of my body. "Yes, me too. Two people are better than one. Garita can stay here with you. She knows what needs to done in this place. She can do it if she has to."

"*Fuerte* — strong, Apá, *haga* — do," she said.

My father shook his head and spoke with force. *"Están locos.* Yginio, how can you put these ideas in Ambrosia's head? You suppose to protect her. Many, many months back, this Chivato came here and fought with others. He didn't just stab empty air. He killed people. I said to all of you, 'Don't get in this fight.' You heard me, Yginio. Now you come with this *locura."*

"Apá, we could have gone, just sneaked out at night, but we wouldn't want you to worry more. We want your *Vaya con Dios,* want you . . . want your blessing." My brother's voice echoed deep in the room, half boy, half man. After those powerful words, he grunted a feeble cough and said, "We want you to be with us like a father who cares for his son and daughter."

I finished for Yginio. "Apá, remember when you came to me the other day and spoke about my go-away, my future, about your plans for me. If you will let me, I will think about your words. When I come back, I will very much think about what you want. *Tu sabes,* about Ramon."

CHAPTER TWENTY-SEVEN

The parting of the Red Sea was a tiny miracle in comparison to our settlement with Apá. A few days — his blessed permission was for a few sacrificing days. That and lots of doubt, but we took it. Garita would stay, and when I returned, Ramon's offer would be my most important business. My secret plan was to find and leave with Beely to Mexico and maybe never return. Sinforosa had done it, so why couldn't I? Endless talking, thoughts of riding to Fort Sumner, lent me no good rest. Bed sheets covered me like hot coals. When I took them off, the cool air chilled the wet on my body. No position settled my worry.

"I go, Garita, *con Dios* y Yginio *mañana.*" Not knowing what Garita had understood about yesterday evening's conversation, I made use of restless, wakeful hours with soft whispers.

She could not sleep either and tears

streamed down her face. I back-wiped them with my palms.

"To Mamá *y* Sinfo?" she said.

"No, *Mija,* back, soon. Four days. Do you know four days? Let me see how many is four with your fingers."

She lifted three, and I pulled up one more. "See, not like Mamá or Sinfo. I'll be back, and we make dolls with willow branches and pine cones." That was too much for her, but she nodded.

She had her bola sling wrapped around her shoulders. She undid it. "You take," she said. The strap folded in the same fashion for me as for her, leaving the rock cup piece at my waist.

"See, yes, *sí.*" She patted it and reached below our bed for a bag of round stones. Mangled with them was the *protect* headband. Good thing the feathers stayed in the box. "*Lleva* — take."

"No, Garita, there's no danger, *Mija.* I won't need it. Back *pronto,*" I said.

"*Lleva* — take, yes." She tied the pull string through the last button hole of my shirt, patted it, and forced my hands over the little bag.

"Okay, Garita. I take. Now we both go to sleep."

■ ■ ■ ■

We left just as the morning light brightened the dirt hem of the sky. Soon within the first few miles, we heard the familiar rolling of the Bonito River. Water gurgled goodbye waves streaming southeast. But this time it was me who was leaving, too, and I was going northeast. Giddy-up clicks and a couple of easy leather snaps gave our fresh horses the go-ahead into higher than normal, white water wetting their knees in their prance across.

Everything was different. Dawn waved a specialness over me. Distant untrod trails waited for us, hidden in the horizon. Green leaves burst a glistening bright I hadn't noticed before. Quick young hooves jumped like they had landed on fire. A brother, I knew little, led me. Garita, Apá, Ramon, and hard-to-hold innocence lay behind. The wait was over. It would be me going to Beely.

Ramon had loaned Yginio a copper-silver roan with a jet-black tail and mane. In the evening or on a cloudy day, she looked copper, but when her hide caught light, she glinted like a penny polished with quicksilver. A magnificent beauty I called Esperanza, hope, for the little I had on that day — hope for Beely and me, hope for what we were going to find or not find.

The gate to my San Patricio world closed. Beside the granite boulders, instead of turning left, we crossed *el río* Bonito. We drove the horses away from the Capitan Mountains, bypassing Lincoln. I imagined those sleepers comfortable in their beds. Each stride at first unsettled me. Guilt sucked in with each heaving breath — guilt for riding away from my chickens, away from my cooking chores, and away from Isabelle's full udder. That feeling rode with me for several miles. What would Mamá have said? Will Doña Hurtencia talk up a big, bad story? How will *pobre* Garita and Apá do? They had done nothing to deserve my absence. Will Father Martinez double my penance when I confess weakness of virtue, the choice to leave my duties? Ramon, kind Ramon — what will he do when he finds out?

Young Esperanza stepped even with Noche. She was a top-bred horse as if for the Queen of Spain, head high and dancing hooves of Andalucía not the Hondo Valley. In her prissy gait, she was also sturdy. My legs hugged onto my new friend. Together we made one. I stroked her soft neck and patted her a *thank you.*

Ramon, the winner or loser? If he had asked any questions, Yginio answered in his own way — for now it didn't matter. His visit to Apá in the next couple of days would give him the details about where my brother and I had gone. The tall sniffing sheriff and saving Beely were more important than anything else. But then again, thoughts of Ramon rose from somewhere within me. My getaway soothed buried anger and made room to see a loving, forgiving man. He was a long slow waltz, and Beely, that man, was a fast shuffling fandango.

When Yginio and I rode side by side, he told me his reasoning. Seemed his young mind had gained some smarts when I hadn't noticed. But he was in charge, so I listened. We would move away from the Capitans and make our line as straight as we could to Fort Sumner. The trip would take two days, and he expected the horses could lope some forty miles at a stretch. Then we needed to walk and measure when we could push them again. In the long run, slowdowns were needed and hard galloping would do nobody any good. He'd tell me when. Along the way, dirt stock tanks and natural rain *tinakas* would water up the horses. Our canvas bags would keep them comfortable during dry times, and he had dry oats to feed them. At dusk, when we could no longer see our path, we'd make camp, and start the second leg early the next day. Late, on that second day, the lights of Fort Sumner would welcome us. My heart took a bronc leap when he said Fort Sumner.

Before midday we crossed Blackwater Draw, and the horses drank down a good gulp. Yginio said this would be the last natural water from the long Capitan down streams. After twelve noon, when we needed a bite to eat, we hit Rabbit Ears dirt tank. The stop was not long. Before my sit bones rested fully, we saddled up and pushed northeast again.

"*Mañana,* we'll hit the Río Pecos and its water spread," he said.

I accustomed myself to Esperanza's sway, which was longer and faster than our old Luz. The young lady, horse-queen trotted on without complaints. Soon, nothing but flat, low prairie brush lay before us, and we walked the tired-out horses for a while.

"How many times have you traveled this path?"

"Only twice, and one of them was with Billy."

"Beely? *¿Cuando?*"

"One time I met him when I was tending sheep without Gordo and Campeon in the northeast pasture. After the Blazer's Mill shootout, he wanted what he called a vanishing spell. That's how he put it. He was on his way to Sumner. Without the worry of the dogs, I went with him."

"You left the sheep? Don't tell Apá." Seeing this side of my brother made me realize how house chores and shoulder rubs at mealtime did little to help me know him. Our feelings for Beely did the most to bring us together, and here we were again.

"Why not, the sheep had all they needed, and I knew I'd get back for that reason. Kid Billy showed me watering holes, Seven Springs Road, and the west curves of the Pecos. Riding the river's switchbacks loses much-needed time, but if we set our horse noses straight and not *follow* the banks, we'll be fine. That way we won't have water problems either."

"Is Fort Sumner town like Lincoln?" I asked.

"*Chihuahua,* no. That locale is not pine trees like our valley, but it ain't bad. Very different, though. You'll see. The old army lodging used to house the keepers of the Apaches and Navajos at Bosque Redondo close by. The Maxwells bought the fort

410

when the government let the Indians go and didn't need it anymore. Billy said after the old man, Señor Lucien Maxwell, died, his son, Pedro, now sees to it. His sister and mother live there, too. They're town big shots like Mister Señor Lawrence Murphy to us. The old barracks make a U shape, and they have everything — gambling, baths, butchering, livery. You'll see." When he spoke, little soft hairs above his lip and on his chin moved with his words. That growth had thickened without my notice.

"*¿Y La Jewels?* Is there a parlor house?" I veered my horse down a slight arroyo after Yginio. He did not answer, so we left that question there in the dirt ditch.

The terrain turned drier, flatter, and rosier. The pink soil softened our hoof pounding. Thank God the wind was not blowing or the loose powder would be up in our faces. A rock with little white chips caught my eye, so I stopped and picked it for Garita. I looked beyond the flat basin, and the world stretched forever.

Walk, walk, and more walking put me into a daze. It was sleepy travel until Esperanza snorted and shook her head. Following her eye view, up the trail on a bluff, a mangy coyote roamed below the shade of nearby mesquites. I patted her neck. We pushed to

411

a faster trot. When we came out of the basin, the blue Sacramentos and Sierra Blanca had disappeared. Hondo Valley and Capitan Mountain, my world, were a long way behind us.

The horses slowed down but never showed any need to stop, so we kept on that dry, dusty trail. To my good surprise, my brother found a dirt tank. Don't know how he did it. But, no matter, my butt begged for a chance to stand off my horse. The water sat in a wide sunken mud bowl with scattered tracks of hoofing animals all around. An open, donkey jawbone stuck out of the bank.

"Poor ass must've come when no water was here," Yginio said. "We're lucky for this little July pond. Winter snowmelt and spring rains fill it. There won't be much in a few weeks."

We watered our horses and ate cold burritos. Tired brains of our horses would drink themselves waterlogged, so we yanked them away. Rest was short, and too soon we got back on our trail.

In the distance, a man in quick trot movements came toward us. My mind played me a dirty trick, and I saw Beely. I imagined we hugged and turned back home. It wasn't him. Instead, an old man on a mule going west, toward the tank we just left, banged jerk-beats on his saddle like his mule knew the way and was thirsty. His large sombrero moved only to look up at us. Yginio tipped his hat, but the Mexican traveler didn't give us any sign back. To ease my mind, I found my sock of piñons and cracked a trail of shells behind me. The sweet bits, a comfortable reminder of San Patricio, gave me more than food. Life on horseback, familiar to Beely and many others, for me, mixed excited freedom with a strange fear of what was around the next corner.

Mesquite, cactus, and green-gray sage lined our trail. All low to the ground, no good shade broke the hot beams. Sun warmed our backs, and I was sorry I did not bring Mamá's old hooded sun bonnet. The heat blazed a stove fire over us and cut short glorious independence with boiled-up doubts. If Beely was not in Fort Sumner, our long ride was as useless as a mule with no legs. If we warned Beely and saved him, another lawman on another day would find him. His $500 bounty would always tempt someone. What future waited for me? Mamá's life? Sinforosa's sorrow? Each had a hell life, opposite of the other. Only Virgin Mary knew. One died of loose pleasure, the other of hard labor. Where was my destiny?

413

Between Ramon and a shadow man, I began to doubt our escape to Mexico.

"Look, a runner hen." Yginio distracted my contrition.

Up the distance, a roadrunner took a fast run across the way. Ornery bird teased us, raced over and back again for many miles. His fun gave us a distraction in this dry parched terrain. Heat waves hung over our trail ahead, and I had nothing else to do except put my spare blouse over my head for shade. I wanted to stop, but Yginio said we needed to push to a cooler place, so we kept Noche and Esperanza hoofing. Sundown finally came, and the horses picked up their steps. None too soon, we dipped into a cooler cradle. But still we didn't stop.

I missed Garita and Apá. Doubt set my tired mind into repentance. Father Martinez had warned me of my wayward, sinful desires. Apá said Beely was fool's gold. Yet, to pass an opportunity to save the man I loved would haunt me forever. Regret added to bitterness would scald the life I faced in the Hondo Valley.

I smoothed the hanging sweat off Esperanza's neck. She was a patient animal and rode this long unfamiliar trail like she had done it a hundred times. *Al fin,* like a miracle, green cottonwoods sprouted up in the

414

distance around a large, wet, stone pool. We stopped, hobbled the horses for the night, and Yginio built a campfire. Crickets sounded sweet in the night.

Flames spit hot sparks and held my eyes on their licking flames. A cold sunk in and the fire felt good against my sore, aching body. Without a complaint, my brother ate dried burritos and drank canteen water. Also without complaints, the horses chewed on Bermuda to last them until we reached Pecos River grass tomorrow. Food did not interest me. I wanted to rest my bones from the long horse ride. Nothing else mattered until I saw Yginio pull something from his pocket and thumb it.

"Where did you get money? I never remember you doing any paid work," I said.

He flashed a smile as good as his hero, Beely. "*No importa,* besides he wouldn't want me to tell."

"Who, Apá?" My eyes fixed on the green bills. Maybe my father dipped into the money Sinforosa gave him for our foolish cause.

"No." He stood and dug out a handful of oats from his saddlebag and fed our black stallion.

"Who then? Don't tell me Father Martinez sacrificed charity basket offerings?"

The pause was long enough to force me to ask again. "Who?"

He gave Esperanza her oats, lingering in the moment as if he were deciding on his answer. Her floppy lips picked up the morsels like two thick flesh traps chomping down. "Ramon," he finally said.

"Ramon? I thought he didn't know where we were going."

"He didn't, not exactly. He just knew it was far away and important. *Tu sabes*. He's not dumb. When I told him you were going with me, I swear, he made me take it. We can use it when we get to Sumner."

I laid out my bedroll and spread out on a flat rock.

"Better on the dirt, Brocia, that rock will feel like ice tonight. Right there by that mesquite. Ground will be softer for your tired back. Just make sure no rattlesnakes are around it."

Soft earth yielded to my aching body. I leaned back and rested my head in the palms of my hands. So Ramon *did* know. The early stars shined like blue dots poking the darkening sky to another world. The full moon-lamp lit the heavens. Sleep at last came and wouldn't have been any deeper if I had found my rest on ice needles with a rattler. Sacred rest held my lids shut until early morning light hit them.

Soon I heard Yginio saddle the horses. Necessity called me into the bushes before the long day's travel, so I took my quick leave close by. A rustling and stomp of horse hooves hastened my business, and when I finished, I heard voices.

"No, don't got one to lend." Yginio spoke.

I peeked through the brush to see a bulky man, standing beside my brother.

"Well then, I reckon I'll need it straight out anyway." Ragged hair sprung like a mesquite bush off his head. He spit dark tobacco juice into his hand and wiped it on his shirt, brown from overuse in this manner. His clothes, torn and dirty, held days of wear and trail dust. I wondered if Yginio knew him and hadn't told me we were meeting someone.

"No, Mister, not my horse to lend. Headed Fort Sumner way and don't expect to walk," Yginio said.

I wished my brother had a beard instead of little hair fuzz.

"See another one yonder there in the trees you can ride." His black thick beard partly hid a bumpy face, suffering embedded pebbles from a severe New Mexico sandstorm. Sunken eyes, flat and cold, shifted from Noche to Yginio. We had come so far without incident and now faced the likes of this ugly *hombre.*

Yginio spoke again. "Yes, the other horse. My brother will be back —"

Before Yginio finished his sentence, the man yanked the reins from my brother and jumped on Noche.

"Holy *demonio,*" I screamed. "Stop him."

Yginio leaped onto the thief and brought him down, a weasel on top of a black bear. I ran closer to see twisted, turning bodies. The bear had Yginio's neck in a choke hold and thrusted his knee into my brother's ribs. He was getting bear-kicked.

A stick, a rock, I needed to find a rock to . . . I had Garita's sling tied to my waist. I ripped my blouse and loaded the sling. As the men wrestled, I twirled the lance around my head, wishing Garita were here to help me. I flung my wrist like I had watched my sister do so many times and let the rock fly straight to the man's head.

Yginio saw the rock coming and sank behind the target. Got him. The *bruto* rolled over, rubbing his socket and setting his legs to stand again. He was clear of Yginio. In that second, my aim swirled full thrust at the stranger's temple. The heaved stone landed its mark broadside and knocked him back down. Yginio grabbed a long stick and waved it at him like David to Goliath. He slashed his hand and threatened to poke his good eye. "More, you want more, *Cabrón,*" Yginio screamed. "Come on." Blood oozed down his hairy cheek and over his palm, holding the gash. No mercy. Next reload hit his chest. He fell rolling in the dirt. That gave Yginio time to jump Noche and for me to mount Esperanza. We galloped full speed until nothing was behind us but a cloud of dust.

"Better we slow these hooves down, so we don't leave a powder trail," Yginio said. "*Chihuahua,* Ambrosia, you stopped that thieving no-count. Got him good, real good. He thought he was going to catch us off guard, but you showed him."

"Who was he and where did he come from? Why'd he want your horse?" I felt lightheaded and didn't want to slow down any for fear he was on our trail.

"Must have just come on us this morning or late last night and thought we were half-asleep. Caught him trying to rustle Noche. He'd have sold him either in Lincoln or Fort Sumner, whichever way he was headed. But no more questions, eh?" His eyes skittered and went down. "We safe now, Brocia. Put your blouse back on."

True, one blouse sleeve limped empty and

the other covered my arm. My bosom bounced bare with each horse trot. Half-draped, the sling dangled over my naked shoulder. "Me *mala* — bad, as Garita would say. *Perdon,* Yginio, what a wild woman I've become." The buttons dangled on strings, but I managed to wind the thread around each so they loosely sealed me back in.

"No, Brosia, you will never be without my respect. That, I know about my sister. Needed to get to the weapon fast is all. Don't let that thing go. We may need it again."

Respect? Yginio said, *respect.* Something I didn't deserve. I used to have self-respect. Was as hard as a rock lodged in the mud along the river's edge. I thought I was perfect, but truth be told, I was ill-shaped, jutted-out and rough-edged. By chance, the Ambrosia rock fell in the river. The gray granite rolled on the bottom, hit other rocks, beat itself up, knocking into floating logs. Rocks and people like me have to take their licks. Wears down high-mindedness. Beely would agree.

We chewed a few strips of mutton jerky and rode our horses more north than north-east now that we hit the Pecos River Valley. In the cooler air, we shorted our stops. As the river's edge curved out, we led the horses to its bank, stopped, and let them drink and nibble sprigs. *Río* Pecos water rattled a soft welcome. *Your kingdom come.* My prayer was cut short as Yginio readied his leave sooner than I wanted. Noche mustered up without a pull, but queenie Esperanza had to be jerked away from her food, water, and rest. Her tired legs had to be forced into a fast trot.

The lazy river turned away from our trail, but we held our line north.

"Don't worry, it will curve out again, and we'll see its waters many more times before we get there," Yginio said.

He was right, but the next time we reached the edge, a deep bank kept us from the water. From the upper level we looked down onto a brown, liquid snake cut into soft limestone. We gave the horses water from the wet bag and kept moving. When I thought we had lost the Pecos, it curved around to us again and again. Then the ground sloped a little, bringing us to dribbles on shallow rock, which led into a deeper, rushing canal of three or four feet. Alamo trees, floating white cottonwood balls, lined the riverbank like summer snowflakes. Yginio whisked the airy tufts aside and said those thick cottonwoods in the distance were Fort Sumner.

CHAPTER TWENTY-EIGHT

Our horses sensed moisture and rushed their footfalls. I loosened reins and gave Esperanza a nod with slight kicks. As we neared the tall Alamo fluff trees, little adobes sprung up every mile or two, and we could see early lanterns streaming out open windows. We had reached Fort Sumner. Soon, along with the greenery, wood buildings formed rows. Set close, they made straight lines as if a giant had set them in that tight fortress. A group of them opened into an orchard. What hung from the branches in the dim light looked like some kind of fruit. Too early for apples, they must have been peaches. Discomfort came over me, that feeling when all of what you know has been left behind. Unknown, scary but thrilling — Fort Sumner was like a bejeweled box with a caution sign carved on top.

Accordion and fiddle notes overtook loud chatter, humming with break-outs of yelpy laughter from one long building. We walked our horses closer. Two swinging doors from that same place opened and closed to men and ladies, drinking, hugging, and dancing. Those lively, ache-less people caused me to rub the saddle burns on my back end. What were they celebrating? The roar of dust, smoke, music, and that question reminded me that it was a weeknight, not Saturday. This spirit gathering, this bar round-up, feisty *fiesta,* or whatever this was, would never do in San Patricio, not like this, during the week.

Early evening was darkening to night, and we didn't yet have a place to rest.

"Head over there, close to the river. We can wash. All these wood buildings used to be military. That's why they're grouped like this. See that big one, in the corner? Pedro, son to the old *haciendero* Maxwell, who I told you about, lives there."

"How you know so much, Yginio? From one day here?"

"It's not much to know. You don't want to see what's going on in that big building. The saloon, I mean. Maybe you want to wait for me by the river."

"What? No, Brother. I didn't get saddle sores to wait by the river, *solita.* I want to see everything."

One bean burrito sat at the bottom of our bag for us to share, but I gave it to Yginio when we got to the waterside. We found a good spot and hobbled the horses to graze on thick green grass. *Al fin,* Esperanza was having her fill of water and rest. After a few gulps, her wet nostrils touched me, and I stroked her ears and snout. Gave her a head hug. She was better off than me, for even though my stomach needed food, I could not eat. "Relax, *calma,* girl. We all going to be alright." Message was more for myself than for her.

Two days of dirt came off my face. I dusted my skirt, put on my untorn blouse, and tried to rinse my hair. The cold water shocked my sunburned skin. How I wished I had a cleaner face and dress for Beely — if by chance he was here.

Yginio moved faster than me readying himself. But I didn't lag although my legs hardly moved. Dirty and sunburned, he was not going to leave me.

"Maybe we should wait until *mañana,*" Yginio said. "After we have at least one night's rest."

"No, *Hermano,* we promised Apá we would not waste time, look and go back on the turn-around. Beely's probably not anywhere around a place like this, anyway."

My own words didn't convince me. They churned a sour, hot upset — like burning chili in my empty, raw stomach. Didn't want to go any further, but my need to know and save Beely pushed me through all my aches and fears. Had to go. Wanted to find him. Then again, I hoped we wouldn't see him. If he was in this very strange, sleepless, and workless world, he was not the man I thought he was. Here, taking his share of happiness without any care for others.

We began our walk back toward the loud building. "We can start in that dance hall. But I don't want you to go in, Ambrosia. Hear me. Apá don't want you in such a place without him."

I nodded. "*Bueno* okay, but if he's there bring him out *pronto,* and we can both tell him what Tehde told you. Promise, Yginio, or I will go in by myself. I swear. You know I will."

"*Caramba,* Ambrosia, settle down. We're here to do good not anything else. You have the sling, right?" He took off his hat and whacked it hard against his leg. Trail dust flew up around us.

I moved my wet hair braid clear of him. "Yes, good. And in that good, we don't want to get hurt — at least not by gunshots or someone's knife." Light reflected from a different sun than the one I knew in the Hondo Valley. It wasn't full dusk, and yet it casted a dirty yellow over Yginio as if he stood in a dingy shadow. "Can you recognize *ese* Sheriff Garrett if you see him? Maybe he's been here already and has Beely locked up."

"He's tall as a ponderosa pine. We could see him and his handlebar 'stash over all the others from the front door. If he's here and Billy ain't, it could be good. Maybe Billy got word, and he's holding up in the hills or gone off to Mexico." Yginio quick-footed his march — as anxious as me to redeem the payoff for our long hard journey. "I'll find out."

Closer to the large square building, the high fiddle plucked my ribs with its squeaky notes. Then a grumble of voices and boots onto the wooden floor sounded into the street. The sign read Big Break Saloon.

"What are they breaking?" I said.

"What?" Yginio didn't know how to read and didn't pay any mind to signs.

"*Un* Break. That sign says, *Big Break.* What big thing do they chew up in there?"

Yginio didn't answer and went to look in the batwing doors. From the opening, we saw bottles of every shape on a shelf behind a long bar. A man poured copper, red, and

426

corn-colored drinks just like La Jewel Parlor. In a corner, a skinny fiddler with a thin *V*-rolled cowboy hat joined a straight-up piano player with swaying, stringy blond hair. Those two and a short, fat accordionist, so bald his head gleamed, filled the air with a happy *Ranchera* tune. Those not standing at the bar were up dancing a shuffle-up of a Mexican polka. A few sat at gaming tables with their attention on cards. When that song ended, another began.

"Listen, 'Turkey in the Straw.' " Yginio acted like I'd never heard English music before.

"What?" I leaned into the door opening toward him and heard the kicking tune. "What is it?"

"*En Inglés,* 'Turkey in the Straw.' Funny, no? Where else would the turkey be?"

"In the stew?" I said, but he didn't hear me. People bounced and flipped one shoe aside, like chickens scratching for a meal — very different. "Guess that's how they do it up here. Must be what they're big breaking — the floor. Do you think Beely's there? Can you see the sheriff?"

"No, don't see him or the sheriff. And if Billy ain't in here, he's not anywhere in town. That Chivato loves music and dance more than eating." His voice grew louder and raised my worried excitement.

"How do you know all this, Yginio?" I couldn't take my eyes off the hullabaloo.

"He told me when we worked for Apá and other times, too. Said he'd like to see how well you moved your feet on the floor."

"Oh, *sí*, Yginio, stop talking and go in." I pushed him closer into the large room. "I'll be here waiting. Don't stay long. If he's there, get him and bring him out. If he's not there, see if he's around and where. If no one has seen him, let's sleep by the *río* and go home before sunup."

He set his foot in and let the batwing doors close behind him.

My stomach belched a stink, worse than the smell from the saloon. I cleared a thickness lodged in my throat and rubbed bitter off my tongue with my blouse sleeve. More people went in without a glance at me. After the band finished the "Turkey in the Straw," people chattered a low rumble, not one separate from the others. To calm my shaking, I walked to the horse railing, stood a spell, and went back around to the door to have another look.

The room was bigger than our little *casita*. The walls and ceiling above the bar hung small oil lanterns with hazy glows, shedding a buttery glint on those standing around. Painted them a dirty burn, and I wondered what color of skin they had. What looked to be *gringo* faces took on a *Hispano* color in that strange light. Maybe they were neither, maybe they were a race I hadn't yet seen. A joy trance kept them moving and laughing. More brushed against me and went in. Liquor must give the drinker a free float, and I wondered what their looseness felt like. A short woman rambled from table to table serving drinks and thoughts of Sinforosa came to me. This must have been one of the things my sister did at the Jewel Parlor.

Yginio caught my eye. A straight-up *chivo* goat in a flock of bleating sheep. Anyone could see he didn't belong.

The band struck another song, and I walked back to the railing post. I stood for many minutes until I heard a familiar voice at my back.

"Ambrosia, Ambrosia — *milagro,* a miracle angel."

I turned. He was here, really here — resurrected from the dead. His bones carried more weight than when I saw him last. His light brownish hair touched his shoulders, and he sported a bright red scarf. His ever-present gun hung on his leg, knotted tighter than a horse halter. This was the *ole* Beely I remember. So long — I had waited so long for this, but my stone arms would not move, and my face froze.

"Saw Yginio here and couldn't believe my eyes. Jo-fired me up. Holy moly, done gave me a hallelujah enough for a year and then some. More than a wretched man deserves."

"Beely, *milagro sí,* how very good to see you." My lips cracked open. "Yes, yes, good."

He stood by Yginio, a fox in the henhouse. "Left my winning Monte hand to someone else. Had the players in a cold meat wagon, but this is too much, much too much to miss. Howdy do, I'll be a monkey's uncle. I see it, but it's too much for my eyes to believe." He shuffled a quickstep from side to side and *al fin,* there was that slant-tooth smile. He hugged me hard and long, and I, into him, felt his strong tight body against mine.

When we unlocked our arms, I said, "We are here for something important."

"All of it, all important, never mind that now. We got plenty of time." Beely hugged me again, enough to trap my mouth shut.

A group of mismatched people came to the door and fixed on us. They stood as if an invisible gate corralled them in the saloon. One woman stared at us straight and narrow. She was an Indian, not Apache like Tehde, but of a fuller face and taller body. She folded into the round of a Navajo blanket. Her braids plaited crosswise with black on white, skunk-colored ribbons. A silver turquoise ring weighted her finger down, and she made sure we saw her twirl it. Her frozen stare on Beely reminded me of Garita's worship of him.

She stood beside another lady, skirted in big, white flower material surrounded by blue-green leaves. When she moved, the petals looked to be floating in water. Her black, glimmering corn-silk bun made her face stand out. Round, night eyes with horsey, long lashes graced those near her. A dark beauty — one who could match Sinforosa's draw. Her wide eyes horned onto Beely, but when they landed on me, they became cat, pressed and slitted. I nodded, and she blinked. Our eyes said each of us knew the value of the other.

She was of polished silk and I of brown cotton. I brushed the dust off my homemade dress and could feel her unspoken questions about my hereabouts. I had some notions of my own about her. She and her Indian friend's willingness to rattle about in a *cantina* led me to believe they were without a father — one who would keep them latched in a safe coop. They had a joined purpose, yet, very different than me and Tehde. Looked to me, it was more than a friendship. They weren't sportin' women, not that kind of looseness. They were of another kind, but of what breed, I couldn't tell. Their eyes, underneath the Big Break Saloon sign, did not break away from us. Others gathered with them, one gringo and two *Hispanos.* They were men like so many others. All of the door huddlers met our eyes, one on one, rotating about, like a dueling eyeball shootout.

My arms wanted to wrap around Beely, to hold him as if he belonged to me, but no. I could not, so I stiffened my stance and hogtied my urges. Suddenly, a strange loneliness engulfed me. I was sure he did not want me anymore. I searched for that secret, hidden connection, but instead his eyes danced a fast jig around me.

"Beely, we came with . . . with . . . some good reason," I said.

"Yeah, Billy." Yginio shook his agreement.

"Come along, I have hoot tales to catch you up on." His old friendly flash raptured us like always. "Don't that beat all? Can't imagine you two riding from San Patricio." He turned his head. "Whee dogs, sight of you, I'll say, is bigger than tremendous."

He flipped his attention back to the others who would not move from their door gawk. Caught between us and those he left behind forced him to glance back and pause. He shuffled to the *cantina* door and scratched his head. *"Pronto"* and "soon," then "later" was all I could hear.

La India, standing by the beauty, asked in good plain English, better than mine, if she could come. She was not like Tehde and must be one raised by high-up English speaking *ricos* — must be a *genizara,* taken from her birth parents and raised or used by others. *Pobre,* but maybe she was one of the lucky ones. The other Indians we saw around here had no such charm.

I heard Billy say *no* to *La India* and mentioned something about tomorrow.

In a quick lean into Yginio, I whispered, "Look, he's here. *Dios mio,* he's not hiding. Maybe Tehde didn't hear right. You told him, for sure, Yginio, right, about Pat Garrett?"

"No, you said we'd both tell him, remember? Besides, others were around. We'll do it, Ambrosia. We just got here. Have some patience. You don't see any posses, do you? No guns drawn around here searching for him." My brother rolled his fingers over his closed eyes. He looked tired.

"No badges, okay, but who are these people? They follow like he can't be left alone. Maybe he's already arrested. The Indian lady talks like one of us, no, better English than us, and the other one looks at me like I'm here to kill him. Why don't they have some place to be?" The weight of it all came over me. I lost my balance as if I were the liquored-up one. I grabbed Yginio to steady myself.

"Don't fall and don't be making something that ain't there. *Amigas,* just friends, Ambrosia. You know Billy. Everyone wants to be around him." My brother spoke like it was me who needed the warning.

Before Beely came toward us, the ladies gave him a little lost wave with eyes pinned on us. Their stare stuck like hard clay onto the bottom of shoes. Less beholden were the men in the group who turned into the saloon. Hands in his pockets, Beely scraped the bottom of his boots on the wood porch back to us. Beely's world, *cantinas,* free time, monte, *bailes,* ho-downing, English Indians, words, words, words.

"Tell him *ya,* Yginio. *Pronto,* so we can go home." Empty stomach, sore butt, thirsty, confused, enraged, I wanted to go back home.

434

"Tell him what?" Beely quickened his steps and motioned for us to follow him. "*¿Que pasa?* You two got something that can't wait for a sunny day? I don't want no bad news. No sir, *hombre,* sure of it. Whatever's hanging out there in the storm can wait if it's not sunny. Always there for *mañana* or maybe never, bad news is better left unsaid."

We walked on each side of him, and the music began to fade behind us. He put his arm around Yginio. "Come on, *primo,* no one's died. Salamon's doing okay, ain't he? And precious Garita, too, right? And you're here — here with me. Beats all. Don't give me that look like you've had your last meal. In the way of chomping, are you hungry? I know where we can get some prime veal, just brung down today. What do you think? *Fiesta* time. A celebration by the river." He finally gave me that *a-time-ago* look of longing.

My eyes fell to the ground. "No, Beely, this can't wait. You have to listen," I said.

"No, no, no, don't tell me. Let me guess. Yginio has the new deputy post in Lincoln and is fixin' a full-speed fetch-up of me. Going to line his pockets with the silver reward."

"No, Beely," Yginio and I both shook our heads.

"*Locuras,* Beely. That's not funny," I said. "We're here to . . . *para* . . . to hel—"

"Hell? Hell, Ambrosia, I never known you to air your lungs like that." His arm pulled me so close to him, my shoulder rested in the curve of his armpit.

"Help, Beely, *alluda,* not what you change it to say." I didn't have the strength to push him away.

"Help — didn't think I needed any, but help you are. Seeing you two has taken the blue devils from me."

"*Pronto,* we have to talk." I raised my voice enough, others walking toward the Big Break stopped and looked.

Yginio silenced me with a slight shake of his head.

Beely, too, waved his hands in a motion that shook the air quiet between us. He gave a go-ahead to those who stopped.

Beyond the saloon, around the buildings sitting in a *U,* through a grove, we walked down a bank toward the Pecos. Surrounded by tall salt cedars before the river's edge, the ground opened onto a sandy flat that rested a lean-to. Poles shacked up a rickety, closed-in homestead. The dun horse Billy rode the day of his escape grazed off to the side. A circle of rocks, blackened from past fires, sat in the center.

Beely rounded up and snapped kindling into the circular rock pit already set with logs. "How long are you here for?" He took a match from his pocket and flicked it with his thumb nail. It didn't take, and he flung it away. He tried another, failed, and tossed it into the rock pit.

"Not long, Billy. Short time, maybe just this night. We here to give you a very important hearsay," my brother said.

I nodded and breathed in a deep relief. The trunk of a nearby tree served as my support.

"Dang, musta got soggy from my body dew." He took another match and struck it against his pants. The thing lit, and he dropped it onto the kindling. The small flame took to a thin twig, but Beely blew too hard and too early. The flicker went out.

"Yginio, you remember those *hombres* we saw at the water house? The bearded, ugly ones. Can you run back up there and get another supply of fire starters, so we can have a light here? Take your time. We ain't in any rush."

Yginio was digging his shoes into the riverbank before my tired brain reasoned what the backside of his shirt meant.

Beely's dusk-lit face turned and smiled. "I see you're not making your way over here. *¿Por qué?* Not scared, are you?"

"Yes, I'm scared."

He stood by the fireless pit.

I clung to the tree, sucked by an invisible force. He was close enough to cause me flusterations. Like a moth to a light, I ached for his heat, but I held my distance. Crickets lulled their presence around us.

He unstrapped his holster and hung his gun on a stub of a nearby tree. "See here." He held up his palms. "No gun so that won't scare you."

Minutes passed. An owl hooted a mournful call. Wished it had been a nightingale, but that lively bird was not the one singing. The owl was a death caller. Would I die before I reached home? Or bury something else — virtue, love, faith, hope, future dreams?

"Is it something I said?" He took a step toward me. "Didn't say? Should say? Tell me. Why you scared?"

"They are coming to kill you, Beely." My arms — coiled around the base of my bosom — did nothing to soothe growing trembles. "Tehde heard the new tall sheriff say his wife's brother, some Saval Gutierrez lives here with his wife, Celsa. She, this

Celsa, is supposed to have some kind of thing with you. Anyway, Saval must not be your friend and told his sister of your stay here, and she told her husband. The sheriff aims to come get you." My voice pitched like that of a small child, high and shaky over the river babble.

"Dime a dozen, Ambrosia, no, more like a penny a dozen, cheap, cheap, cheap and flying in the wind. Is that it? Is that what's got you clinging to that trunk, 'stead of me?" He took a half step in my direction. "Can I come closer?"

"How do you know it's gossip? When will you know the real one? The one who's there to do the killing. *Por Dios,* Yginio and I care more for your life than you." I turned and leaned my head against the tree. Who's more crazy? The one who puts the fly in the soup, or the one who knows it's there and eats it anyway? My foolish efforts were no better or maybe worse than Beely's *locuras.*

He pressed me from behind so tight it rendered me breathless. I could say Beely sensed his power and took his pleasure from a weak woman. Or I could say the long ride sapped me defenseless. Or an evil *Oowee* curse bewitched me. Those would be lies.

Truth would tell it another way. Wet lips against my neck brought a long forgotten touch of calm. Two Ambrosias fought inside me. The one who would lose if she gave in, and the one who would lose if she didn't. My lifted skirt and his slow rub made wrong all right, made my defeated sin a glorious victory. He moved me under him and smothered my words with his lips. He un-bloused me. Garita's leather sling didn't slow him one fiddle minute. Our thighs met, mixing heated moisture. Water rustled in the background. His skin on mine heated my sunburned face hotter. I tried to reach back from where I had come, from where this was wrong, but here, this strange, let-go place, so far from home, opened my insides, invited the animal in me out.

"Beely," my voice quivered.

"No, no stop. I ain't going to halt, Ambrosia. I want you and you want me."

My weak white flag surrendered. Beely's flesh dance was not a *solo.* Beside the Pecos ribbon of water, resting on wet earth, inhaling fresh night air and harnessing one another's warmth, we savaged each other.

The evening darkness, salt cedars, and the dip of the low river basin hid us. Where he was touching, how, and what to do in return, happened. I helped wrestle him there. His draw, a flesh pistol firing, filled me, soothed me, brought me peaked pleasures.

From the bottom of my muddy mind water, a hairy image broke the surface, gasping for air. One shiny green and one dull eye, drenched wet, came at me. The wretched cat's hollow eyes of death, guarding Sinforosa's decaying soul, cut my senses, shook me just as Beely wailed his release. Overtaken, I slapped him. Meant it for the cat, meant it for me.

"What in tarnation?" He was as shocked as the one who struck him.

"I'm sorry. I mean, didn't come here for this, Beely. Two long days on a horse — and now you . . . you ride me like some *burra*. You, with your lady friends." I looked for my unders, for Garita's sling, and began to button my blouse.

"I thought you wanted me, and I know I want you." He brushed hair away from my eyes and rubbed his fingers gently down my red face. "I'd do anything to understand you, *hermosa* Ambrosia. Rhymes, don't it? Beautiful Ambrosia." He smiled. "God, you're a hot cat. I liked it, the slap — added an extra punch — deserved it. Do think about fetching you, more than you can imagine."

"No, don't say it, *mentiras*. Lies, lies, lies.

441

Never a ring. Did you give that Indian the turquoise ring she wears?"

"What? A ring? Never happened, a ring for Deluvina. God Almighty, if I'd known it was easy as that? Get you one tomorrow. And, if I say I think you're beautiful, it's not a lie. It's the truth. All I have are my words." He played with hair tangles around the nape of my neck.

I pushed him away and buried my face in my hands. "Because . . . because, you just say and don't ever do." I stood and pulled up half-lost clothing. Garita's sling came to rest over my shoulders above my blouse.

He kissed me.

I backed away. Didn't have the strength the first go-round, but I would not be had twice.

"*Bueno,* okay. I see. You're tired and hungry. Yginio will be back soon with the matches. Tell him to start the fire. I'll fetch us a slab of beef for a hardy fix-up." He went to a wood box, pulled out a long knife, and wiped it on his pants. "And before you leave . . ." He pointed the blade at me. "I'll make it better. Trust me." He winked and smiled as if we had just done nothing, less than nothing at all. With no shoes and the top of his britches unbuttoned, he left.

Puros locos in Fort Sumner. Black is

442

white. Dancing and drinking don't stop. Nobody works, and the dirty deed is a handshake.

Rustling of leaves proved to be Yginio with the fire starters.

"I want to go home, right now, Yginio. Let's eat and pack up. Apá was right, crazy to come here. Beely don't listen. No good for nothing. If you think we can save him, you're as crazy as him."

He snapped the match and began the fire. Flames blazed, twigs vanished to ash like my will against Beely, like what was never to be. Withered, my stare fixed on the firelight. I sat, wishing the earth would open and swallow me.

The bang was distant, like someone dropping a rock from the heavens onto a tin roof. Another came.

"Hear that?" Yginio dropped the wood poker.

"Sounded like a *pistola,* over there." From some deep holding, I found panic.

"Which way did Billy go?" Yginio asked.

"*Alla,* that same way." I pulled off the leather sling and shook my hands like we needed to do something fast. "Beely had nothing on him."

My shoes inched along in deep mud. We ran up the riverbank, through the orchard, toward the large building in the corner where the Maxwell man lived. I held on to the back of my brother's shirt. We reached the wrap-around portal of the first buildings. A small calf, skinned and gutted, hung upside down. In the twilight, a stream of light glinted off red meat encased in white sheathing as blood dripped below. Two men sprang out of bushes nearby. We pushed passed them on our way to the last door before the corner turn.

At the entrance to a large bedroom, a group hunched in a circle. Like a Garita, I did not let go of Yginio's shirt. I saw the Indian woman and the beautiful lady. They stood hugging, crying. Two others stood in the room, one, the tallest man I had ever seen and the other with his hand over his eyes.

There he was. My Beely, a fallen, barefoot messiah, too late for any savior, sprawled out alone on the floor. His end did not appear real. His touch was still on me. I wanted to shake him awake. Say, it's not too late, get up. We can go back to San Patricio, to Mexico, away to live forever. A forever I knew would never come. His eyes opened to nothing; his hand, still with the knife, lay on his open palm; his dirty, jagged toenails, naked for all to see, pointed up-

444

ward; lips, with my breath still on them, gaped open. His blood soaked into his apricot hair. I grabbed my throat and half-choked myself.

One of the men, who had jumped out of the bushes, stooped and hung his lantern over Beely. Numb, Yginio and I stood in the doorway, and people began to move around us from the porch.

The room was at first silent. Shock, sorrow, and anger drew skin lines on people's faces. Demons of this place had sucked every soul in this room speechless. They saw, but like me, they didn't want to believe. The muffled spirit deadened me.

Deluvina was the first to break the quiet with a rattling yelp.

"Lowdown, God-damn bushwhacker, you shot him. *Ay,* you devil snake, look what you done? Shot our Billy. No weapon on him — he was unarmed." She unleashed her fury and jumped a-pounding on the tall man. Her fist beat his low-hanging badge.

The same instance, the beauty felled onto Beely's dead body. Kissed his dead lips. "No, no, no," she moaned. "*Mi amor,* no, can't be." Blood from his chest painted her white flowers red until they looked like they floated in blood. She began to unbutton his shirt and caress his wound. I wanted to shut my eyes and run away, but the scene nailed me like the others. No one knew which woman to watch.

"Paulita, stop," someone behind me whispered. "Get up."

She smeared his redness on to her face. "No, it can't be. Not true, *ay* my God *Diosito* say it's not true." Her whole body snaked over him with smothering despair like some *Cucuy* possessed her.

Deluvina, a mad she-devil of her own, kicked the sheriff, bit his arm holding her away, and with an open hand, thrust stiff fingers into him until her turquoise ring disappeared between his legs. Garrett yelped until the man, who carried a likeness to Paulita, jumped up from the bed and pulled Deluvina away.

Garrett grabbed the Indian's wrists, but she twisted his hold off and, in a springing force, went at him again. In her struggle, she stepped on Beely's blood and slipped. Nearly landed over Paulita and dead Beely. The lawman leaned over to catch Deluvina. She steadied her legs, spit, and scratched Garrett's face. Two red gashes ran down his right cheek, covered with wet hate. Four other men gave a hand and only then could they pull the unharnessed *India* away.

A woman, looked to be Paulita's mother,

showed up out of nowhere and lifted her daughter, who was covered with Beely's blood.

There lay the cause of it all. A sly smile from his other world told us, *you fools weep for nothing.* He lay in a glory no other had ever reached.

Paulita let out banshee screams as her mother and brother dragged her out.

I wished I could have wept, but a dry ache dug a stop in me. I inhaled ice. An invisible, strong-handed fist reached in and squeezed my heart so tight it strained to pump. Two fingers drew beadless, heart prayers on both my thumbs, and I mouthed Hail Marys. I felt faint. Yginio noticed, held me, and led me out.

CHAPTER TWENTY-NINE

The sooner Esperanza could carry me away from this place was not soon enough. I yearned for my quiet home, but Yginio said Apá would want us to bid our last *adios* to Beely. So on that July night, we moved our horses to Beely's river shack. I heard Yginio snore, but my mind could not rest and sleep did not come until daybreak. At first light, Yginio took off and put the burden of making a fire on me. I gathered more wood and tendered a flame. A throb seared me when I realized just hours ago, just right here beside the river, Beely had mustered his usual talk, fumbling with the matches, trapping, loving me.

The owl had warned us, and we didn't listen. I told Beely, and he didn't listen. I should have kept him here. I slapped love out of him. Spoiled his potboiler. Maybe one more romp would have spared him another day. Maybe if Yginio wouldn't have left us. If I'd loved him longer, harder. If I'd gone with him, I could have seen the slug coming. If this, if that. If I would have stayed home like Apá said. If I had not made such a fuss about his gun toting, he would have had his defense.

Soon Yginio came with eggs and bacon.

"Ramon's money?" I asked. "For the food, did you use Ramon's money?"

"No, I took Billy's dun horse to Pete Maxwell. He said he'd give it to the sheriff to take back to Lincoln. He gave me this food and little *dinero,* two dollars."

"Oh, sí, so little from Maxwell's $500 reward, *pendejo,* fool. Him and you. When we get back, give Ramon his money." My cussing turned his head. I stirred the eggs.

We ate in silence. The scrambled egg mess tasted of white limestone and the bacon of dry wood chips.

"Wrap up what you don't eat. This is all we got for our trail home," Yginio said. "You're right. We're all a bunch of *pendejos.*"

His joke, bad as the food, drifted downriver. I laid my weary bones on a dry rock for a few minutes of sleep, but it didn't come.

Midmorning, tears finally streamed out, and I washed off what little smell of Beely was left on me.

A parade of people walked toward Big Break, and we followed in that direction. Today, the saloon made into a chapel. That would have pleased him. The place where he played his winning hand of Monte last night now served as his viewing stage. He had been suited up in someone else's best because I had never seen him wear that kind of coat before. His hands, at his side, ready to shoot — some *loco* joked. Candles circled his body. Light came off a looking glass behind him and with one on the wall, it stacked reflections of many bodies posed side by side into eternity, his passageway. Someone whispered, "July 14, 1881, won't be forgotten." Beely, *al fin,* resting on a bar table, had found his peace.

The saloon, the largest place in Fort Sumner, didn't have enough room for all the mourners. A line of sad weepers wrapped around the building, making their way inside. Some filed past, many took seats, but other restless people, stood outside without gandering. Two musicians, a fiddler and a young boy with a concertina, struck songs in slow time believed to be his favorites. Many tough men, with heavy spurs and calloused hands, cried.

Ladies did not weep silent tears. Bawling

shouts filled the building like those I'd hear in my nightmares. Paulita appeared boneless. Her sorrow took the form of fierce wails like none I'd ever heard. Deluvina and Paulita's mother held her up as she howled her way to a seat.

Many inquiries about the killing whispered in and around the crowd. Was it on the porch or in the bedroom? His last words *¿Quien es?* Were they for someone he didn't recognize? Did Sheriff Garrett or Pete Maxwell answer or was a bullet the answer? Was Pete surprised or did he design the trap? Seems everyone knew Pete Maxwell didn't cotton to sister Paulita's yearn for Billy, but yet others said Pete was his friend. Why didn't they take him alive? Among many questions, I had reckonings for three. The questions about his shoeless feet and his undone pants. And why he was unarmed.

No Catholic priest gave murderers a funeral mass, so people gathered and prayed on their own. Yginio and I left when some drunk *gringo* stumbled onto Beely's body and cried mumblings no one understood.

As we walked outside to take our leave, I heard someone say Paulita was with child, and I had nothing in me to be angry, useless to resent my own sin. It was over. I traded worry for deep sorrow, a different kind of pain, new shuffling, bruises in different places. The happy dream Beely promised me was gone.

CHAPTER THIRTY

We began the long trip back to San Patricio at dusk, about the same time we came the day before. The horses sensed home and stepped it up. Yginio unreined Noche and Esperanza met his steps. When we stopped and watered our horses at the same stock tank, neither of us spoke of camping overnight. The ground was flat, so we continued in the full moon, which saved the horses and us from the heat.

The silver moon guided us, and stars, like campfires of fallen souls, brightened our journey. Two of those stars huddled together, Mamá and Sinforosa — my mother with her favorite daughter, I thought. In the distance, coyotes sounded frantic, nervous yelps. Esperanza jittered, so I leaned over and patted a comfort onto her. I limped along in endless, dark travel as my loose body swayed with Esperanza's motion. When Yginio thought we had made up the late start, we flat-landed on a low mesa. He burned some tumbleweeds and fed the fire with dried mesquite. We took in some water, then dropped our bodies next to the campfire — saying nothing and cooking nothing. I cracked a few piñons.

In the dotted sky, a star streaked a tail of light in its fall, and I imagined Beely blazing his way to his place in the afterlife. He faced death often and wanted a glorious parting, one with both guns firing. I wondered if he would have liked this finish. He, without a weapon, taken down in a bedroom, of all places, surprised and powerless. The dishonorable trap might have been a betrayal — this was not what my Beely stood for. He would not have liked a weak parting, but at least his end wasn't a lynching. What we had saved him from, back in Lincoln, would have been much worse.

We packed up early before dawn and went hard. Put Fort Sumner, *demonios y locos*, behind us. Gloomy place, people with nothing but aimless play, silly dancing, and forsaken joy. At least the *pobres* in the Hondo Valley gave a day's labor to get what little was owed them.

"We going to miss him. *El* Chivato, *loco*, we going to miss him a lot. He never wanted to hear the truth about Sheriff Garrett." I said it loud and clear, but my brother didn't have any voice. Nothing but horse hooves on hard rock sounded.

I wished I could have streamed my many tears into my dry throat. Everything ached as if my blood had been contaminated with lye. My spine lost its strength. I bent over Esperanza's neck and clung to her. I rode facedown for what seemed hours. Beely was really gone. Wet tears soaked Esperanza's mane. When I sensed her neck tired from my weight, I found the strength to sit up. "Are we going to pass through Lincoln?"

Yginio didn't answer.

My voice cut the air with sharp, hatchet words. "Give Ramon back his money and horse as soon as you can, hear me?"

"Can't." Yginio finally spoke. "Gave his money for Billy's box, the diggers, and the food afterward. We'll give him the horse when we pass by."

"You think they needed it more than Ramon? *Caramba*, Yginio, Ramon didn't even like Beely." Our eyes sealed that secret with all our others.

We left the Pecos Valley and followed the setting sun toward Hondo Valley. The west horizon filled with clouds flattened dark on the earth side and fluffed up bright blue against the heaven side. When desert greened up underneath us, we galloped some and saw Sacramentos in the distance about three that afternoon. Sierra Blanca welcomed us like a lost mother's calling. Sensing home, Esperanza quickened her legs.

"I need to go into Lincoln," I said. "It's not that far from Ramon's."

"That's added ground. Can't Tehde wait? *Carajo,* Ambrosia, what are you up to now?" Yginio stiffened his legs and lifted his sit bones off Noche's saddle. He rubbed his behind. "What's so important?"

"Do you believe when you die your sins go with you if you don't say *I'm sorry* while you're here, I mean?"

"I'm too tired and don't care either way. Talk to Father Martinez," my brother said.

"It's not Tehde, but I have to head into Lincoln. Father won't see us for another month."

I pressed in that direction while Yginio set his route straight to Ramon's.

The sleeping dead rested like stones in a graveyard garden. I dismounted and let Esperanza graze to the side. Mamá's rickety cross had fallen over. I straightened its grounding. The dirt, warm against my knees, cushioned me. I rubbed my back,

456

relieved to be off my saddle. "Thank you, *Diosito,* for bringing me here." Sinforosa's large marble tombstone faced me.

"I'm here, Sister, before you and God with my sin. *Virgin de Guadalupe* be my witness." I leaned over much like I had over Esperanza's neck. "Not right, Sinfo. I had no right to hate and judge you. Should have been at your side for your last breath. For I, like you with your Tunstall man, gave all. Beely took my heart, too. Something no man, even Ramon, had not done, and I gave a soul sacrifice like you." I waited for a sign, an answer, a breeze — nothing. A gray bunny skidded out from under a bush and ran back. A crow *nah nahed* from a pine top. *Chicharras* filled the air with their high, tinny buzz.

I moaned on. "Beely, like Señor Tunstall to you, showed me a way to view the world with an undeserved happiness." I stood and touched the lettering of her headstone. "*Al fin,* Beely's dead face gave me truth to give what you wanted." I shook my head and wiped tears. "I mean, what I should have given you is what I'm asking of myself now — forgiveness." I don't know how long I clung to what was left of her until I rose, gathered myself on Esperanza, and headed toward Ramon's.

Life paths are living rivers woven through unexpected woods. Never does one know where they will cut. A lost love, as great as Sinforosa felt in the killing of John Tunstall, curved the river for her with a most brutal force. Her heartache killed her. And I starved her of my blessings, didn't take her in my arms that day she could hardly breathe, didn't take her beautiful ring, didn't speak kindly of her at her funeral; now, my forgiveness sat rotting in me.

My loss steered me a side river — I, unlike Sinforosa, may have a second chance. Beely seeds streamed in me, and if so, this baby would be brave like her father. In me, though not certain, I carried more than just memories.

In my ride to Ramon's, another kind of emptiness filled me — black, broken glass. When I moved with Esperanza's lope, shards ripped my gut into loose bits of stringy flesh. I wasn't sure, life, as I knew it before, even the unfilled emptiness, would return. Maybe Sinfo was the winner, and I was the loser, for she had peace, and I had to face Ramon.

Yginio was waiting outside, alone.

"*¿Que pasa?* Where are the Salamancas?" I put my arm up to shield the sun and hide swollen, red eyes.

"*Chihuahua,* Ambrosia, what took you so long? I was about to take off, but I knew Apá would not like me getting there without you." He cut his reins around toward home and pulled Noche back.

"I had to give my sin up to Sinforosa." Saying the words released something from inside me. I wanted to say more.

"Never mind, I'm too tired to hear it. Who knows where Ramon is. He's not in his Smithy barn. Doña's not even here. Let's keep going. I can give him the horse tomorrow. My backside needs a bed." He turned and left me in a cloud of dust.

We rode hard and soon crossed the Ruidoso.

When she saw us, Garita was hanging wet clothes on the fence. She left her chore and ran toward us. Her unbraided hair flew in the wind, and she half-tripped on her untied boot strings. She looked beautiful.

Apá waved from the goat pen.

Ramon wasn't at his home and being Yginio took a leave from our place, I thought I'd see him here, giving a hand. I looked around the goat pen where Apá worked. Didn't see his big-rump bay. Looked around the barn, chicken coop, and house. No sign of him.

CHAPTER THIRTY-ONE

The sound struck constant, even beats like the seconds from July 1881 to 1883. A chain or machete or metal grate of some sort whacked a nearby surface. Reminded me of how quickly time was passing now. Each bang stole another second from me. I had not finished, and there was so much more to do. Not work and chores, those labors would always be there. I wanted to hold, laugh, play, and garnish those feeling moments — daughter to father, sister to sister, sister to brother, friend to neighbor, and, yes, most important of all, mother to son. I knew now those times were rare and precious as April snowflakes.

"Garita, that racket, what is it?" I sewed a patch on the elbow of Apá's worn shirt. The last stitch pulled through easily. I looped and tied it. He and Yginio rounded sheep as usual but would be back soon enough.

"No nothing," she said.

She and Guillermo sat beside me, twirling empty thread spools. Garita got the idea to run a knotted cloth-rope through the holes and string them together. A twirling chain of wooden wheels spun around the floor and became a *chooka chooka* train.

They laughed, and I smiled.

The outside noise clinked and clinked again. "Must be a tool Apá hung beside the stalls. The wind blows through the door and lifts whatever hangs in that spot," I said.

Garita hadn't said it was *Oowee El Cucuy.* Thank Father Martinez my sister had stopped blaming that prowling tormenter for every breezy noise. Maybe his lessons were catching hold, or maybe she, like me, didn't feel a cloud of doom anymore. I left them and walked outside. With Guillermo, she followed me out the door.

"*Pajo* — birdie." Guillermo fluttered his hands and pointed to the swallows flying by.

"Yes, birds, I see them," I said. "They are flying fast." *Just like my life.*

"*Pajarito* — birdie." Garita picked him up and kissed him.

There were times I feared Beely would leave me with child. I feared it would be an agonizing shame and upset, not only for me but also for Apá, Yginio, and Garita. My

461

sin, so visible growing inside me, would make me the leper of San Patricio. My mistake, popped out for everyone to gawk at with each passing month, would end me, worse than Sinforosa. Strange, I realized afterwards, those moments of dread were worse than the thing itself.

I didn't see it until what I anguished about happened.

Bigger than a horse, I tottered around. "See, there she is, just like her sister. *Pobre* Salamon, two daughters lost to naked romps with *gringo* men of another place who came, used our women, and got themselves killed." On Sundays, a time of prayer and salvation, I could see judging faces and hear whispers behind my back. I was lucky enough my apá and Yginio stood tall beside me, and Garita hummed and tried to feel any move from my growing belly. She, as usual, saw white when others saw black.

What I thought would be the end of my life became the new beginning. *Diosito* blessed me when despair could only be overcome by a joy greater than the best pleasure. I may have thought I knew love, but what I had tasted was one tiny morsel of a delicious cherry pie.

Guillermo brought me a love beyond words.

Tehde and Garita were by my side for his birth. Apá and Yginio stayed in the barn, but I'm sure they heard my cries.

"Up, no back," Tehde said. She had given me herbs and nailed a rope three times over from the ceiling.

"No, I want to lie down," I screamed. "Tehde, *por favor,* just let me lie down on the bed."

"Up like duck — better to drop new one," Tehde said. "Get rope. Hold Indian way." She looked at Garita, pointed to the rope, and then to me.

From behind, Garita looped her elbows around my armpits. In my ear, I could hear pants from my sister's open, breathy mouth. Mine joined hers as my hands took each end of the hanging rope. This was no time to begin doubting Tehde. Drops of fevered sweat hung over my whole body. Tehde rubbed a poultice over my back as I squatted and screamed, *"Dios mío Santisimo."*

The pain, like an act of contrition, did not overtake me. I braved its punishment. A part of me nodded its coming. Nothing could destroy me if I hadn't been defeated before this. If God was preparing me for this moment, he prepared me well.

Guillermo, William in English, came.

His spread of black hair sprung wild over

hazel eyes. Constantly chattering, he, like his Tía Garita, made up a language of motion. Fingers, hands, or head jerks moved with whatever came out of his mouth. His smile romanced the sky. His little hands harnessed the world, and his gleeful laugh reached in and shook our hearts with pure joy. Guillermo gave us uncommon delight none of us ever knew was possible.

My run away to Fort Sumner had brought back a most precious gift, wrapped with disgust from some people. Ramon Salamanca could accept Garita, and I think he would have accepted what was planted in me, but Doña Hurtencia could not. She bore undying shame as if she and I had been cursed with the same demon seed. By that time, I had learned jealousy and shame could decay a person like a poisonous weed. I had carried years of unforgiveness for Sinforosa like a dirty, unwashed stain. For Doña, the betrayal she felt was one I could never change. With the help of Father Martinez, not Doña Hurtencia, I found my own self-forgiveness and made my own life without any man.

With what suffering Billy caused me, he also taught me to stare down injustices and protect the helpless. Because of him, I had the strength to bare Doña's disgust. I wobbled, but I wobbled proud. I could not let Doña wield shame on an innocent child. Guillermo would not be tarnished for my wrongdoings. In the end, Ramon knew what he and I had to do.

The metal beat against the barn wall again and clanged me into the present moment. I continued out into the barn and took down the iron whip of time. It was a section of chain, caught in a draft.

"Mamá do," my *hijito* said. He pulled me toward him and Garita.

I sat and helped them tie a June bug's slippery, barbed leg with a thread. The shiny emerald beetle flew around as Guillermo held the string. I would not let this moment pass without enjoying it. I had grown that much.

AUTHOR'S NOTE

Based on actual events, *Rosary without Beads* follows the chronology (1877–1881) of the Lincoln County War and Billy the Kid's time in territorial New Mexico. A good friend of Billy's, Yginio Salazar, and the fighters mentioned in the war are actual; however, in real life it was Yginio who was wounded on Killing Day, not Billy. The fictitious cast, Ambrosia, Tehde, Sinforosa, Garita, Salamon, and Ramon, are alive on paper only.

In 1878 Lawrence Murphy retired to his luxurious ranch near Carrizozo, New Mexico. As *Rosary without Beads* notes, he died in October of that same month. He was forty-seven. Jimmy Dolan moved to White Oaks where he grubstaked. According to the local paper, *White Oaks Eagle,* he died in 1898 of "hemorrhage of the bowels" at the age of forty-nine. Before he left Lincoln County, he acquired all of Tunstall's land.

Susan McSween remarried in June 1880 and identified six of Tunstall's killers. She divorced her second husband and lived a long life in White Oaks. She was a survivor like fictitious Ambrosia.

Literary license, based on the era of the story, was exercised in the portrayal of La Jewel Parlor House and Big Break Saloon. The Torreon Tower, Wortley Hotel, the Lawrence Murphy House Mercantile, Tunstall's Mercantile, and the McSween home are accurate accountings of what once stood in Lincoln. The actual Wortley Hotel, the Torreon, and Lawrence Murphy House are still standing in Lincoln, New Mexico, and can be visited.

Fort Sumner and the Maxwell family, including Deluvina and Paulita, follow historical accuracy. Billy the Kid's death has always been a source of speculation. Knife in hand, shoeless, and unbuttoned pants have been reported by historians and provide a historical fiction writer inspiration. His famous last words were, *"¿Quien es?"* This rendition of his final day is within the realm of possibilities, given Billy's association with the locals. His grave can be found in Fort Sumner, New Mexico, although some believe William Bonney is not in it. Garrett was shot with unbuttoned pants (like Billy) along a side road, March 1908, close to what is now White Sands National Monument at the age of fifty-seven.

ABOUT THE AUTHOR

Diana Holguín-Balogh was born and raised in New Mexico. As a child, she spent many Fourth of Julys at Billy the Kid Days in Lincoln. After a cousin's funeral in Mescalero, her brother took her across the highway and showed her the graves of Shotgun Roberts and Dick Brewer. Two victims, one a Regulator, the other a House fighter, buried side by side near the old Blazer's Mill. She knew the Mexican señoritas loved the bilingual Kid and found the historical fiction possibilities fascinating — thus the catalyst for *Rosary without Beads.*

Shadowboxing Lupe's Ghost, her first manuscript, was named Top of the Mountain Book Award finalist for Northern Colorado Writers. The 2016 Rocky Mountain Fiction Writers' Anthology, *Found,* featured her story, "Telling Bones." She lives in Colorado with her husband, Nick, and Mia, a shy black cat. You can contact her at

Facebook, Diana Holguin-Balogh Author page, or visit her website: DianaHolguin -Balogh.com.